Stainless Steal Hearts

Stainless Steal Hearts

Harry Lee Kraus, Jr., M.D.

CROSSWAY BOOKS • WHEATON, ILLINOIS
A DIVISION OF GOOD NEWS PUBLISHERS

To Kris:
My wife and
my best friend

Stainless Steal Hearts

Copyright © 1994 by Harry Lee Kraus, Jr.

Published by Crossway Books
a division of Good News Publishers
1300 Crescent Street
Wheaton, Illinois 60187

Cover design: Bill Paetzold

First printing, 1994

Printed in the United States of America

Library of Congress Cataloging-in-Publication Data
Kraus, Harry Lee, 1960–
    Stainless steal hearts / Harry Lee Kraus, Jr.
      p.   cm.
     1. Heart—Transplantation—Moral and ethical aspects—Fiction.
2. Residents (Medicine)—United States—Fiction. I. Title.
PS3561.R2875S73 1994   813'.54—dc20   94-8019
ISBN 0-89107-810-X

02		01		00		99		98		97									
15	14	13	12	11	10	9	8	7	6	5	4	3	2

Note by the Author

THIS is a work of imagination. I have borrowed from reality only to make this fictional story believable. To imply that any of the characters found within these pages reflect a true image or the sinister intentions of any real person is ludicrous. My own experiences as a surgical resident at a university provided only the framework from which I could weave a story that, I hope, will seem real.

May God help us if the words printed here are in any way prophetic of reality. Perhaps the recognition of even the faintest possibility of truth in this scenario will prompt us to repent and to pray.

> *"If my people, who are called by my name, will humble themselves and pray and seek my face and turn from their wicked ways, then will I hear from heaven and will forgive their sin and will heal their land."*
> (2 Chronicles 7:14, NIV)

CHAPTER
1

MATTHEW Stone's sleep was fitful. It wasn't the climate or the noise. Certainly his noisy apartment near the railroad back in Fairfax, Kentucky, had prepared him for anything less than a quiet environment for sleeping. No, it was his anticipation of the events of the following day that crowded sleep into the far corner of his mind, a mind that seemed full of a thousand other thoughts. Dr. Stone rolled over again, dimly aware that someone had started the diesel generator that provided the electricity in the operating theatre. The low, regular rumble of the engine pushed him into a state somewhere between sleep and alertness. Slapping feet hurriedly approached the door to the small cinderblock apartment that had been his home for the previous two months. A sharp knock at the door followed, and the bleary-eyed surgical resident muttered to himself, wishing he wouldn't have been so willing to volunteer for one last night of call prior to his departure. A small plane was to meet him at the landing strip at 7 A.M., and as his mind was clearing, he read the small alarm clock by his bed. 3:30. *So much for joyful, willing missionary service.*

The pounding on the thin, wooden door pushed the last hope of sleep away. The shrill tone of the voice that followed told Stone that an emergency had developed. "Dr. Stone, an expectant mother is bleeding! Please come to the theatre right away!"

Matt pulled on a shirt and pants and forced on his already-tied

Nike running shoes. As he opened the door, he was greeted by the cool night air of the Kenyan highlands. The young African attendant began speaking rapidly in broken but clear English, speaking mainly about how far the woman had traveled for help, who her father was . . .

Matt was used to cutting through the superfluous information so often given in an emergency. "What is the patient's blood pressure?" Stone spoke firmly and slowly, but not with harshness.

"We were unable to hear it, Dr. Stone. She appears to have been in labor for a long time, and there is much blood on her clothing!"

As they drew closer to the hospital, Matt was aware that he still became winded at the climb up from his small apartment. The altitude was over six thousand feet here, and the effect on his endurance was noticeable.

The makeshift theatre was lit by a dim, overhead fluorescent tube, the overlying shield long since broken or vanished. The overall atmosphere was spooky, with the dim, yellow light casting long shadows through the screened windows that were always open to the outside air.

A young girl was lying on her side on the operating table and groaning quietly with active labor. She appeared to be approximately sixteen, and this would be her third child, Matt would learn later. He felt her left wrist. A pulse was present, but it was weak and rapid—approximately one hundred and fifty times a minute. Her arms were bloody from multiple futile attempts at establishing an intravenous line.

A second attendant placed an oxygen mask on the patient at Dr. Stone's request. He looked at the surgeon and trembled as he stuttered, "We were unable to g-get the IV. Her v-veins are f-flat."

"Hand me a cut down tray and some iodine prep." Stone's voice cracked as he spoke. *Slow down, Stone! You've done this a hundred times!* He was still breathing hard from his run up the hill.

He made a small transverse incision just above the ankle in search of the patient's greater saphenous vein. The patient moaned, and Stone realized that in his haste he hadn't injected any local anesthetic. He quickly administered 1 percent lidocaine into the open wound. *One centimeter cephalad and anterior to the medial malle-*

olus. Just where it should be. His actions were smooth and mechanical. He had harvested nearly fifty saphenous veins in a month's time during his last rotation on the cardiothoracic surgery service back in Fairfax, Kentucky. Of course, then the vein was used for coronary artery bypass grafting. Now he only wanted to find the vein in order to put in IV fluids. Using a knife, followed by a vein introducer, an opening was made in the vein, followed by a #14 gauge IV catheter. Within minutes, two liters of fluid were in, and the soon-to-be mother's blood pressure was up to a measurable range.

"Blood pressure one hundred ten." The attendant was noticeably calmer than during his trip up the hill.

The patient was repositioned on her back and her abdomen painted with an iodine preparation. Stone washed his hands at the single scrub sink. The water was piped in straight, unfiltered, from the nearby river, and its brown color made Stone wonder if it did any good to scrub at all.

Hurriedly, Dr. Stone and his assistant donned sterile gowns and gloves. Stone then placed sterile drapes around the patient's swollen abdomen.

This time Stone did not forget the local anesthetic.

"Lidocaine!" The drug was introduced along a straight line from navel to pubis. A scalpel quietly parted the flesh along the same line.

"More local." The fascia was infiltrated with more anesthetic.

The fascia and peritoneum overlying the uterus were then divided, and the uterus bulged into the operating field.

"Please give the ketamine now . . . in the IV." Stone worked quickly to open the uterus and deliver the baby before the drug could affect the small newborn. Skillfully he guided the infant's head through the freshly divided uterine muscle. The mouth and nose of the infant were suctioned, the body of the infant soon removed, and the umbilical cord clamped.

"It's a boy!" Stone was sweating despite the temperature, a cool 55 degrees Fahrenheit because of the altitude.

He neatly repaired the uterus, then closed the fascia and the skin. In the U.S. he would have stapled the skin, but here in this small missionary compound nearly everything was done by hand.

The mother named her child according to her tribal tradition.

In the Kipsigis tribe, each boy is Kip and each girl is Chep, followed by the time of day the infant was born. Kip Rotich is a male infant born when the cows are going out in the morning; Chep Koech is a female infant born in the afternoon when the cows are coming in. This child became Kip Chirchir, which meant, "the time when everyone ran around in a hurry."

Stone laughed when he heard the name, remembering how quickly he had run up the hill and how tired he had become. He silently promised himself that he would start jogging again when he returned to the U.S. to continue surgical residency.

The sun was beginning to rise as the young doctor headed back down to his small apartment. Although his accommodations were meager—containing only a single bed, one cupboard, a sink, and a gas stove—he lived in luxury compared to the tribal people whom he served. After visiting several of the local mud huts, all of which had thatched roofs and a raised, open fireplace for cooking, he remembered thinking the scene was comparable to camping for your entire life. Much of the Kenyans' time was spent gathering wood for cooking fires and tending their small plots of corn, which they prepared as gimyet. Stone had found no acceptable U.S. equivalent to this dish, except maybe cornmeal mush, which represented a thin version of the African staple. Even with his Appalachian Kentucky upbringing, Stone had to force himself to eat this thick, white substance in hopes of appearing grateful to his generous native hosts.

The time on his alarm clock now read 5:30. *Just enough time to sleep for another forty-five minutes.* This time his sleep was sound. Even with all the excitement of the day to come, a herd of elephants couldn't have disturbed him.

◆ ◆ ◆

To say that Michael Simons, M.D. was arrogant was an understatement. Arrogance, he felt, was an appropriate quality for someone of his stature. As the chief of the division of cardiothoracic surgery at Taft University Medical Center and vice-chairman of the whole surgery department, he prided himself on the accomplishments of his first thirty-nine years. His arrogance, however, didn't hinder him from his unending quest for knowledge. "Knowledge is power," he often exhorted his residents, "power that will propel you to do great things for your fellowman." Of course, most of his residents rolled their eyes behind his back, but they quietly and with almost complete sincerity acknowledged his words to his face.

Today Simons, a pediatric cardiothoracic surgeon, was continuing his search for better and innovative surgical therapies. His specialty, the surgical treatment of congenital heart disease, was often rewarding and heartbreaking. Never was Simons' search for increasing knowledge more apparent than in the time period just following a death on his service. Today was such a day, and the surgeon moved along the hospital corridor in contemplative silence.

When he reached the pathology lab, he opened the large, metal door. In the back room a pathologist was diligently performing an autopsy dissection. The subject, a two-week-old male, dead after a complex operation to correct an underdeveloped left ventricle, lay completely exposed on the metal exam table. Whenever an autopsy took place on one of his patients, Dr. Simons was present.

Simons listened quietly as the pathologist listed his findings. The pathologist spoke slowly and spelled many of the terms so that his inexperienced transcriptionist would get everything perfect. "The heart is enlarged due to dilation of the right atrium and ventricle. Period. The left ventricle is underdeveloped, and the aortic valve is atretic; that's a-t-r-e-t-i-c. Period. The ascending aorta is underdeveloped and measures only 0.5 cm. in diameter. Period. The ductus—that's d-u-c-t-u-s—arteriosus—that's a-r-t-e-r-i-o-s-u-s—has been surgically divided and ligated. Period. The right subclavian—that's s-u-b-c-l-a-v-i-a-n—artery has been surgically transected and anastomosed to the right pulmonary artery. Period . . ."

Simons sighed as the pathologist continued. *There do not seem to be any answers here. He can only tell me what I already know!* Simons seemed heavy with the knowledge that his field held only partial solutions, with many operations being performed for palliation only and not for cure. In a few minutes the pathologist finished his description, and Simons began to pace around the small laboratory.

In the corner, working diligently at the counter, a pathology resident, Dr. Scott Tanous, placed a small heart on the scales to obtain an accurate weight recording. Simons was immediately drawn to the small heart and began asking questions.

"Where did that come from?" Simons snapped without addressing the resident by name or introducing himself.

"Huh?" The startled resident looked up and, recognizing Dr. Simons, cleared his throat and straightened his posture. "Oh, it's the heart from a stillborn infant who was delivered only this morning. I'm just recording some of the data from the autopsy."

Simons took the small heart in his hands, holding it carefully as if it were a fragile object that would shatter if he held it too tightly. Tanous looked at Dr. Simons with curiosity.

Simons spoke again. "How old was the child?"

"Twenty-three weeks gestation," Tanous answered, staring at the inquisitive attending surgeon.

"Why was it stillborn?"

"Multiple congenital neural defects," Tanous replied. "The heart looks okay, though."

Simons stared at the small, perfect heart in his hands, slowly turning it back and forth. "This heart is only a few grams smaller than the one in the patient whom I just operated on," Simons stated with a remorseful monotone, nodding his head in the direction of the remains of his patient on the table in the center of the room.

Tanous could see that the surgeon was deep in contemplation, but he had difficulty discerning Simons' thoughts. Suddenly Simons straightened up and handed the small heart to the pathology resident.

"How many hearts like this do you deal with in a month's time?"

Tanous looked up into Simons' eyes, which seemed to be piercing right through his head. "I . . . I'm not sure . . . One, maybe two at the most," he stuttered. He paused, then added reflectively, "Fresh specimens of this age are fairly rare at the university hospital, sir."

It seemed as if a light had gone off within Simons' head. He turned and walked out of the lab without speaking.

As he passed, the pathology attending said, "I'll send you a full written report next week, Dr. Simons."

Again, Simons didn't acknowledge the communication.

Greetings and salutations were not part of the time-efficient world of chief pediatric cardiothoracic surgeon Dr. Michael Simons.

◆ ◆ ◆

The patient moaned softly as Dr. Adam Richards administered a local anesthetic medicine with a needle inserted under the skin of her swollen abdomen.

"Give her another milligram of Versed. I don't want her remembering this." Richards spoke mechanically to his nurse.

The nurse obeyed and slipped a needle into the IV line leading to the back of the patient's hand. Slowly she pushed another dose of the sedative medication.

"The Versed is in, doctor," the nurse replied, echoing the same monotone voice she had just heard.

Richards worked with the confidence that came with years of experience. No movements were wasted. Each one had been practiced hundreds of times before. Many patients came from West Virginia, Tennessee, and even Ohio just for the expertise that Dr. Richards offered. This patient, a thirty-four-year-old female, had sought treatment in Fairfax, Kentucky, by Dr. Richards simply because he was the best at what he did.

Richards removed the numbing needle and inserted a long needle through the abdominal wall and into the patient's uterus. He pulled back the plunger on the syringe he was using, then aspirated blood into the hub of the needle. Richards seemed irritated; he frowned and pulled the needle back one centimeter until clear fluid flowed into the syringe. *It really doesn't matter if the needle hits the fetus. It's only an abortion.*

"That's what we want." Richards spoke to his nurse and not to the patient, who snored loudly because of the sedative.

Richards drained the fluid from around the developing baby and replaced it with a concentrated salt solution.

The infant, now twenty-two weeks in gestation, would die a painful death over the next few hours. The mother would return to the Fairfax Family Planning Services Clinic in active labor the following day to deliver her stillborn male child.

◆ ◆ ◆

While Matthew Stone slept, three slugs slowly climbed the wall of his bedroom to replace the three he had removed the morning before. This had become part of his morning routine and was one ritual for which he held particular distaste. The slugs were often four or five inches in length, and Matt often grimaced as if he had just taken a bite of a rotten apple. He thought his reaction would be different by now, after all the bloody trauma victims he had worked with, but somehow the slugs still affected him. He supposed that if Indiana Jones could have an aversion to snakes, Dr. Matt Stone could have the same response to these slimy creatures and not risk injuring his manly pride.

Certainly pride and conceit were common components of the successful surgical resident, but these qualities were not prominent in Matt Stone. Confidence, yes; that quality seemed to be necessary to anyone who is trained to make quick decisions and follow through with them. Perhaps his deep belief that Christ was at the center of any good thing he had in his life prevented his head from swelling.

Stone was of medium build and height, falling several inches short of six feet. He had sandy blond hair and a frequent smile. He was naturally friendly, a trait that immediately endeared him to anxious new interns, and one that softened the calloused leadership role forced upon the senior surgical housestaff. He was now a fourth-year resident at Taft University Medical Center, having completed his medical school in Virginia. This rotation, a two-month elective at a mission hospital in western Kenya, was the result of hundreds of letters written to raise financial support, as well as months of schedule planning and hectic rotation swapping to be sure all of the university surgery teams were covered in his absence. When he returned, he would begin his fifth and final year of surgical residency, his chief residency year.

He had scheduled his trip as tightly as possible and planned to arrive back in Fairfax the evening before he was to be back on call at T.U. If all his connecting flights were on time, if the runway in Kericho was open, if the Landrover did not get caught in the mud, if he could get his money exchanged . . . he would be back in the U.S.

with enough time to have eight hours of sleep before his first trauma surgery call night. These were the thoughts that had interrupted his sleep as he retired the night before.

His alarm sounded. 6:15 A.M. Matt forced himself up and stood on the cool cement floor. The slugs were now at eye level, and although he saw them, he decided that this morning he would leave the ritual for someone else. He smiled. "Good morning, fellas." Matt washed his hair in the small sink with the same brown water he had used for the past two months. *It's a wonder my hair isn't completely brown by now.* He was dressed and packed within twenty minutes. He checked his tickets for the sixth time prior to walking up the path to meet a Landrover that would take him to the Kericho airstrip.

Despite the early hour, six of the "full-timers" had gathered for his send-off. Adverse circumstances or hardships such as these people faced every day welded friendships quickly. Matt knew he would never forget the time he had spent with these special friends. Dr. Bates, the first doctor this hospital had ever had, had toiled alone in his efforts for six years, beginning in 1959. He was a true medicine generalist as opposed to the hyper-subspecialists seen so frequently in today's medicine. He was just as comfortable setting a femur fracture as he was removing a bladder stone or treating the frequent cases of malaria. It was Dr. Ernie Bates who spoke first.

"Thanks so much for your time and efforts. You are welcome here anytime." He extended his right hand and then gave Matt a bear hug.

"Do come back. We'll miss you." The voice belonged to Melissa Schaeffer, a nurse who had been in western Kenya for five years with her husband, Ray, who was helping with local agriculture and cattle farming.

Other greetings were passed along with many handshakes and hugs. The staff here was used to many short-term missionaries coming and going. Matt would not forget their kindness. Matt hopped into the Landrover, but not before checking his tickets for the seventh time. He hadn't gotten this far without being compulsive.

A gentle rain began to fall, making the dirt road even more treacherous than before. They only got stuck once, but with the help of two strong Africans from a passing tea truck their delay only lasted several minutes. The driver was Paul Stevens, a quiet man who was working on a hydroelectric dam project that the mission hospital hoped would provide electricity full-time within the next five years. Paul's parents had been in Africa for thirty years, and he had returned after receiving his Master's degree at M.I.T.

The grass airstrip at Kericho was open, and a small Cessna 170 landed only minutes after their arrival. The Cessna was provided by African Inland Mission Air Service, and on this trip a couple was being brought from Nairobi to help with the work, just as Matt had done. As the couple exited the plane, they looked wide-eyed at the appearance of the muddy Landrover that would be their taxi for the next two or three hours. The man, Aaron Peal, was a pathologist who had spent several years in a surgical residency himself. He had hopes of setting up a more reliable blood banking system for the mission hospital.

The pilot seemed to be in a hurry to beat the upcoming storm system, so bags were quickly unpacked from and packed into the plane. After a short prayer, Matt checked the location of his tickets an eighth time, and the Cessna sped off down the grassy runway.

The flight was uneventful, and the views of the Rift Valley were not disappointing. The time from takeoff to landing was one hour, twenty minutes. That gave Matt four hours to get his money changed and find something to eat prior to leaving on KLM for Amsterdam. In typical fashion, however, the bank closed for thirty minutes to count the cash obtained in the morning's trading. This occurred just as Matt was nearing the front of the line. The young woman in front of him was visibly and verbally agitated, asking loudly if there was a drinking fountain in the building so she could take her necessary Valium. Matt suspected this must be her first experience at such a location and thought that after her stay she might be a bit more patient with the system. Matt smiled at the hopeful thought. The young lady did not return the smile and only marched off in search of a fountain.

Two hours and two more ticket checks later, Matt sat next to a window on a KLM Boeing 747 Jetliner. At last his anxiety over this trip was easing, and he was seeing the reality of his tight schedule falling into place. He wondered how much more he would have to endure before he really understood the reality of Philippians 4:6-7. *"Do not be anxious about anything."* Matt closed his eyes. *"In everything, by prayer and petition, with thanksgiving, present your requests to God."* Matt's head pressed gently into his headrest as the plane raced down the runway. His grip on the arm of his chair loosened as he drifted off to sleep, the first time he had ever done so during a takeoff.

CHAPTER
2

SUMMER 1960 had been wet in eastern Kentucky, and this September night was no exception. It was 7:30, and Sandra Stone groaned with active labor. She and her doctor, Sam Garret, thought she was going to have a large baby and expected its appearance sometime during this dark, humid night. The rain had been gentle at first, rising in caliber to a torrential downpour, turning the twisting, gravel road that led up to the Stones' red-brick flat into a river. The lightning started sporadically and later lit up the sky with the rhythmic regularity of a strobe light. Although it was usually light well up to 9 o'clock, tonight the darkness had crept in at around 6, along with the ominous, gray cloud cover.

A small group of men gathered on the porch of Jake's Hardware Store. Among them was Sam Garret, who was expecting a telephone call from the Stone house to tell him, "It's time." He had spoken to Henry Stone at noon that day and was advised that Mrs. Stone was beginning to have signs of early labor. The doctor told Mr. Stone to call when the contractions were close and regular and to reach him at Jake's store if he wasn't at home. By now Dr. Garret assumed the labor must have been false and began to mount hopes of a night of uninterrupted sleep.

Meanwhile, Henry Stone slammed the phone down in disgust. "Oh, just great!" Mr. Stone paced feverishly to the window and back again to his wife, who was lying quietly on their bed. Anxiety gripped him as he watched his wife moan with another contraction.

"You've got to get the doctor, Henry," Sandra gasped when the contraction ended.

"The phone lines are out. I can't get through."

"Take the car! Go to Phoebe's place. Maybe she can help me. She helped my mother."

"She doesn't know the modern ways! I'll try to find Dr. Garret," Henry protested.

"Just do something!" Sandra's face tensed, anticipating another contraction.

Henry grabbed his keys and ran out the door, not pausing for his raincoat. Once in the car, he raced towards Dr. Garret's. But the creek had overflowed the closest bridge, forcing Henry to resort to "Plan B." Reluctantly he drove to the home of Phoebe Slabaugh, the local midwife.

Frantically, Henry pounded on the wooden door. Inside, Phoebe dropped her crossword puzzle, frightened by the sudden knocking.

"Phoebe!" Henry yelled.

"I'm old, but I'm not deaf!" the white-haired woman replied, opening the door while holding a candle. The electricity had been off for two hours. "You nearly scared me to death!"

A breathless Henry Stone described his predicament. Phoebe quickly gathered her supplies and returned with Henry to find Sandra pacing between the kitchen and the bedroom, alternating between singing softly and loudly depending on the state of her uterus.

"Where does it hurt?" Phoebe was veritably all business.

"Ohh," was all Sandra could manage as she placed her hands over her lower back.

"You're in back labor. It won't be long now. Better get you into bed." Phoebe motioned for Henry's help, but he was already heading for the door.

"I'm going to get Dr. Garret. I bet the north road is open." To pacify Phoebe, who was obviously angered by this display of distrust, he said defensively, "The doc said it was going to be a large baby and to be sure to give him time to . . ." Henry's voice trailed off as he decided that this was no time to worry about anyone but his wife. What Phoebe Slabaugh thought about him didn't really matter right now. He grabbed his hat and sprinted for his Plymouth again.

Deep grooves etched in the gravel road by the rain hampered Henry's ability to keep the car from drifting. By the time he reached the turnoff for Doc Garret's house, the windshield wipers had quit working entirely, and Stone hung his head out of the window for a better view. Sam Garret was, of course, not home, but that was of no consequence by now, for he and Henry Stone were both too far from the Stones' house to be of any value to Sandra or Phoebe.

Stone headed on towards Jake's Hardware Store at the urging of Mrs. Garret, but soon his car became hopelessly trapped in mud up to both axles, his vehicle having independently followed several large ruts cut in the road. He tried unsuccessfully to free the car from its slippery position, causing only a settling of the car into a firmly established location in the surrounding silt. This was, of course, much to the dismay and florid language of Henry Stone. He wasn't sure whether to walk home or towards the store, but opted for the store in hopes of at least bringing Garret back to check out the new baby, if he or she was already born.

Twenty minutes later, as Henry Stone approached the hardware store, Matthew Ryan Stone was born. "He was quilled," the midwife would say proudly, referring to the technique that she had practiced for over forty years. Phoebe got Sandra to bed and waited until she saw the baby crowning. She then prepared a quill, a long goose feather that she filled with fine black pepper. As the next contraction began, Phoebe swiftly blew the contents of the quill into Sandra's nose. In the ensuing violent series of sneezes, Matthew Stone was delivered. But then a second unexpected child began to crown!

"You're havin' twins, dear!" Phoebe shouted. Another round of pepper wasn't needed. A second baby boy was out with the next contraction.

And so it was that Henry Stone missed the delivery or "quilling" of not one but *two* new sons at 9:35 P.M. on September 6th, 1960: Matthew Ryan and Mark Aaron Stone.

◆ ◆ ◆

Perhaps because the boys were always coming home with a new bruise or minor injury, no one took notice of the subtle changes in Mark that were only recognized in the 20/20 vision of hindsight. The boys were now ten years of age, and even the dropping fall temperatures could not keep them from their daily evening emulations of their favorite football heroes.

Mark and Matt had just finished dinner one night and were donning their coats when Mark had his first nosebleed. This was not just a few-drops-after-a-punch kind of nosebleed but a veritable hemorrhage. Matt screamed for help, while Mark grabbed a towel from the bathroom. Sandra managed to stop the bleeding with a full fifteen minutes of pressure held over the bridge of his nose. Of course she called Dr. Garret, and he assured Mrs. Stone that everything would be fine.

"There will be no football for you today!" Sandra spoke firmly to Mark after the bleeding stopped. She paused, noting the presence of several prominent bruises on his arms and legs. "You both have been playing too hard!" She gently ran her fingers over a bruise on Mark's arm. "Just look at you."

The boys reluctantly agreed and sulked towards their room.

Time passed, and the fall turned quickly to winter. The Stone boys' love for football grew as the Dallas Cowboys and Baltimore Colts prepared to face off in the 1971 Super Bowl. On a crisp Saturday in January, Matt and Mark practiced punting in the field next to Jake's Hardware Store. After an hour or so Mark leaned against a large oak tree, wanting to call it quits for the day. "Let's go." He headed in the direction of home, walking at an uncharacteristically slow pace.

"Mom said we didn't need to be there until 5 o'clock," Matt reminded him. "Go out for a long bomb."

Mark made no move to run the suggested pass pattern. "I'm beat. I just wanna go home."

"Don't be such a baby!" Matt scolded. Not wanting to stay behind by himself, he threw the football towards his brother and started after him.

The football struck Mark on the left ear. "Ow! Hey, I said I didn't want to play!"

Mark recovered the ball and heaved it into Matt's midsection. Matt picked up the football, and as Mark began to back away, he drilled it right at his brother's Cowboys sweatshirt. Just then Mark stumbled over an exposed pine root, and the ball caught him on the chin. He lost his balance and struck the ground with the full force of his body weight, hitting his head on the rocky path. He made a short gasping sound and then became quiet.

"Get up, you baby!" Matt taunted him the way they had razzed each other for most of their competitive lives.

Mark responded with a rhythmic jerking of his arms and legs. Thoroughly alarmed, Matt knelt over his brother's body. Mark's eyes were open, but his right pupil had already begun to widen.

Matt ran for help at Jake's Hardware, and his screams quickly drew a small crowd to the field where Mark was awkwardly sprawled beneath the tallest tree in the county. Dr. Garret soon arrived, and after a solemn exam of Mark's lifeless body, he turned his attention to the distressed twin. Matt would not be consoled and sobbed uncontrollably until he was finally medicated back at his home.

The days to follow were fogged with a scurry of activity that included a postmortem exam of Mark Stone's body. This was required by the county coroner because the death was unexpected and was associated with a "family dispute." The significant findings revealed the presence of acute lymphoblastic leukemia. An examination of his bone marrow showed massive proliferation of abnormal white blood cells to the exclusion of all other cell types.

Dr. Garret explained all of this to the Stones and said that the lack of platelets in Mark's blood made him a setup for easy bleeding, even from a trauma like a child's fall. When his head struck the ground, uncontrollable bleeding caused a fatal build-up of intracranial pressure. He simply didn't have enough platelets in his bloodstream to stop even minor bleeding.

Matt heard the doctor's words, but he did not comprehend or accept their meaning. He became fixated on the fact that he had killed his own brother, his lifelong friend, his only confidant.

Of course, his parents did not outwardly blame Matt for his

brother's death, but they were too absorbed in their own guilt to see Matt's suffering. They continually accused themselves for not picking up the warning signs of their son's leukemia. Gradually the Stone family pulled apart; each member had to handle the pain alone.

◆ ◆ ◆

As the months passed, Henry Stone poured himself into his trucking business. The threat of economic recession actually boosted coal sales, and his business flourished. His fleet of trucks doubled in twenty-two months. However, this success came at the expense of his family relationships. The reading time that used to be spent poring over stories with the boys was replaced by nightly paperwork from his business.

Sandra Stone began to seek help with a local psychiatrist and eventually found a pseudo-peace beneath a haze of tranquilizers and nightly sleeping medications. She had been tempted to drink, but she still had a strict religious conscience that was perhaps the only recognizable holdover from her Southern Baptist upbringing; she simply could not permit indulgence in such behavior. The pills became her escape and also her comfort as communication with Henry dwindled.

Matt pulled within himself to cope. He eventually made a few other friends, but he was afraid of becoming too involved. He was excited at hearing that Jim Plunkett won the Heisman Trophy that spring and again began to pick up his old football. It had taken him seven months to even talk about football again. In time he was able to suppress the continual thought that he was responsible for Mark's death.

During Matt's junior year in high school, his father was killed while away on a short business trip. Henry Stone was returning home in his Triumph TR-6 when a coal truck broadsided his sports car. He died instantly. The vehicle, which belonged to Henry's closest competitor in the trucking business, and its driver were unscathed. As Matt faced this new tragedy, the flood of guilty emotions over his brother's death returned in full force.

The funeral was the first time Matt had been to a church building in eight months. His mother attended regularly, but her visits had become shallow and social, lacking in any real commitment. The people at the funeral were polite, and the crowd seemed genuinely sorry. Too many of them reminded Matt of the loss of his brother.

"You've been through so much for a young man . . . If we can do anything, just let us know." The words were voiced with good intentions, but they served only to give fire to Matt's guilt feelings that he had successfully repressed.

At the funeral he learned about his mother's intentions of returning to Virginia where one of her sisters, Katherine "Kate" Downs, lived. "The change will do us both good." His mother smiled encouragingly at Matt.

Matt replied only with a shoulder shrug. He was unsure of any feelings of preference. In fact, he felt exactly *nothing*; he felt neither good nor bad; he felt neither pain nor happiness at the suggestion that they move. He was numb, anesthetized from all emotion by the repeated injections of nerve-deadening tragedy and the guilt and self-pity that followed as undesirable tag-alongs.

They moved the following week to a small town on the eastern shore of Virginia, or simply "the Shore" as the natives called it. Henry had been heavily insured and left the family a hefty dividend in addition to his successful trucking business. With the insurance money, Sandra purchased a house one block from the Chesapeake Bay, a small New England-style cottage with white cedar siding.

Sandra's brother-in-law, Tom Downs, was the administrator for the Virginia shore's only hospital. He had promised her a job, and he was true to his word. Soon she was busily involved with her work as the administrative assistant to the hospital's nursing recruiter.

Matt predictably did not fare as well in the transition. He spent most of his days alone, as summer was at hand and he had no school responsibilities. He became fixated with the idea of his own responsibility for his brother's death. The Downs seemed to be the only ones sensing the trouble Matt was slipping into. They repeatedly asked him over, and his Uncle Tom took him fishing on the bay on several occasions.

The Downs were Mennonites. They were excited, active

Christians who believed in a compassionate, saving Christ. They attended a small local congregation where many of the outward disciplines of dress, women's head coverings, and a cappella singing had been replaced by inner attitudes of separation and a holy life in the midst of a corrupt world, modest "normal" dress, and piano and guitars supplementing the songs of praise. Repeatedly they invited Matt to attend services with them, but he always managed to sidestep the issue and kept his distance.

Sandra was too polite to decline their offers and found quickly that she enjoyed the informal style of their pastor. Although their church was different from the formality she remembered in the services she'd attended as a child, she enjoyed spending more time with her sister, and if attending her church brought them closer, she was willing to go along for the ride.

One Sunday after the evening service, Tom brought up his concern about Matt. Tom, his wife Katherine, and Sandra sat around a small oak table in the Downses' kitchen.

"Have you noticed how withdrawn Matt has become over the past few months?" His question had been addressed to Sandra, but Katherine spoke up first.

"Come on, Tom, he's just adjusting to a new place. He'll be okay as soon as school starts and he can make some new friends."

Sandra set down her coffee mug. "I just can't seem to get him to talk to me. I guess I thought he needed to work through losing his father on his own. I think he needs a little more time."

"I'm not so sure it's that simple." Tom stood up and walked to the window, looking thoughtfully towards the bay. "He's certainly old enough to be depressed and certainly has been through enough to warrant a pessimistic outlook. I just wish he'd come with us to church."

"Oh, so that's the answer to the world's problems, is it? I suspect Matt and I can work through this problem. He's pretty tough, you know!" Sandra's voice quivered slightly.

Tom returned to the table and poured another round of coffee. "I don't mean to interfere where I'm not welcome, Sandra. We are just concerned for his welfare. It's not that we think you are doing a bad job as a parent. Everyone needs a little help to get by." Tom straightened up and clenched his fist as if he had been suddenly gripped with a new thought. "No!" He raised his voice. "Everyone needs a *lot* of help to get by! Everyone needs a Savior! And yes, I do think—no, I *know* that the church holds the answers to the world's problems—and not just mine or yours or Matt's for that matter!"

"Preach it!" Kate teased him.

Tom blushed. "I didn't mean to shout."

"Nonsense! If you feel strongly, go ahead and preach if you want," retorted Sandra. "You know you can always speak your mind around family. I may not always agree with you, but I do thank you for caring about Matt. I suppose I'm a little too defensive about things now and then."

"Hear! Hear!" Kate added, then stopped as her gaze met her sister's stare. "Hey, you said it—I didn't!"

Sandra smiled weakly. "I do hope things work out here for Matt."

Tom sat down and stretched out his hand to the two sisters. "I think it's time we did more than just hope." There in the quiet of the kitchen Kate took her cue from Tom and bowed her head. Sandra was unaccustomed to such action but joined in, sensing for the first time a powerful, peace-giving Presence.

◆ ◆ ◆

On the beachfront, not two blocks away, a troubled youth stared out onto the bay. *O God! . . . If I could only be free!*

◆ ◆ ◆

In the circle of prayer around the Downses' kitchen table, Tom began to pray. "O Father, we come to you as your humble children . . ."

◆ ◆ ◆

Matt closed his eyes, trying to quiet the inner voices of condemnation that tortured him unceasingly. *I just want to be free! . . . I just want to be free.*

◆ ◆ ◆

In the coming weeks Sandra began to understand what Tom had been talking and praying about. She began to see that Christianity was more than a Sunday social club; it was a relationship with a powerful yet gentle Savior. Jesus Christ could meet the needs of the world; and more importantly, he could meet the needs of Sandra Stone. She realized that Matt was not the only one who needed help. Years of bitterness were lifted from her shoulders as she began to commit each aspect of her life to Christ. And once she came to the realization that she was a sinner in need of a Savior, she began to pray that Matt too would begin to understand and seek.

Matt, however, slipped even farther down the path of self-pity and self-loathing. He began to sleep in, only rising after his mother went off to work. He even began contemplating a way out of his self-torture and fantasizing about being with his brother again.

At 9:30 A.M. one morning Matt struggled out of bed, his stomach cramped in a knot of anxiety. He had almost gotten used to the feeling that now seemed nearly continuous. He heard the door close as his mom hurried off to the hospital. Matt walked to the bathroom and stared at his face in the mirror. Even he couldn't ignore the thinness of his face. His appetite had not been good for several weeks. He reached into the medicine cabinet for some shaving cream. He had heard that if you shaved every day, your beard would come in quicker. A small prescription bottle caught his eye: Diazepam 10 mg. *Mom's Valium prescription!* He read the warning: "Do not drive or operate heavy machinery while using this medication." His heart raced with the thought that perhaps this could be his escape. *Certainly Mom will be better off without me. Mark, I miss you. Mark, I miss you. Maybe I can come and make it up to you. If only I could make it up to you* . . . Matt's thoughts raced. He felt somehow as if he were being prodded by an outside source. He didn't care where the thoughts were coming from. He was just so tired; he wanted to escape.

Matt shoved the half-empty bottle into his jeans pocket and quickly scrawled a note to his mother. "Things will be better without me. I killed my innocent brother. I want to make it up to him. I am going to be with Mark." He signed it only "Matt," then inserted, "Love, your son" above his name, for his mother's benefit, even though he wasn't sure he really loved anyone.

◆ ◆ ◆

Four hundred miles from the Chesapeake Bay, Dr. Adam Richards studied the patient's chart in front of him. Richards, a second-year house officer at a prominent southern university, prided himself on the independence he had earned while working in the obstetric service. He smiled to himself, remembering the "Intern of the Year" award his peers had presented him just two weeks earlier. *I knew my hard work would pay off someday.* He looked again at the chart in front of him and sighed. *Another abortion to do! It's the only task on this service I'm not really crazy about.*

On the pages before him he read the history recorded by the admitting resident the night before. The patient was a nineteen-year-old Mexican female who presented with spot bleeding during the second trimester of her pregnancy, a pregnancy she sought to end with an abortion. Richards read the notation at the top of the history-and-physical form that stated the patient spoke no English. *Great! Another case for a veterinarian! No use talking to this one.* He finished scanning the chart, noting specifically that the Informed Consent form had been completed and signed by the patient.

Unfortunately, what the resident had recorded in the chart and what the patient had attempted to communicate in broken, hesitant English were actually two different matters entirely. She tried to express her fear that she was having a spontaneous abortion—a miscarriage. The resident wrote down that a hysterical young mother *sought* an abortion! But of course Dr. Richards knew none of that.

Since everything seemed to be in order, Richards gathered the supplies for the saline abortion. He had already helped do so many of these that he didn't even need upper-resident supervision. *I guess I'll get the worst job done early before I head down to labor and delivery.* He carried the instruments down the hall to the patient's room and introduced himself. With the insight that the patient could not speak English, Richards decided to dispense with his own history and physical and proceed with the saline injection to induce abortion.

Richards managed to calm the patient down a bit and began prepping her swollen abdomen with betadine. The patient thought that surely this doctor had come to the aid of her and her baby. Slowly Richards introduced a small needle to anesthetize the skin and underlying subcutaneous tissue of the patient's lower abdomen. He then introduced a longer needle straight through the abdominal wall and uterus until he aspirated amniotic fluid, confirming the proper needle position. He did not use precise care for this step as he did when performing diagnostic amniocentesis, for a needle stick to the fetus contributed little to the final outcome in the situation at hand. Richards then drained a small amount of amniotic fluid off from around the fetus and replaced it with hypertonic saline. Normally labor started at least twelve hours after saline injection, assuring delivery of a dead fetus. This expected time-sequence was altered, of course, if the patient was already in early labor, a fact that the young O.B. resident in this case had unfortunately missed.

The saline had an immediate effect on the young, male fetus. His small body went into spasms as fluid was drawn from his cells to counter the harsh effects of the hyperosmolar fluid. His epidermis began to blister, much like the skin of a severe burn victim. His electrolytes slowly changed as he swallowed the searing liquid. The delicate air sacs lining his lungs burst as he "breathed" in his newly changed environment. His gentle kicks, previously so adored by his mother, became painful reactions that were very obvious to the already frightened young woman.

Richards completed the procedure with business-like coolness. The woman began to cry again as he readied his instrument tray for his exit. He needed to check with the chief resident to see what else he should be doing. *I'll let the nurses deal with this woman's obvious emotional instability. If I had wanted to deal with this, I would have become a psychiatrist!* He thus dismissed her groaning and walked quickly out into the hall. He wrote his perfunctory procedure note in the chart and headed off to find the chief resident.

◆ ◆ ◆

Sandra sped north down the main Eastern Shore highway. She suddenly felt very hot, although the outside morning temperature had only been 62 degrees. *Perhaps it's the "change of life."* She frowned a little at that thought.

She rolled down the driver's side window. *Pray!* The thought almost exploded from her mind. She was trembling now, unsure why she was feeling the way she was. Beads of sweat formed on her forehead. She was almost sure she hadn't made up the thought herself. She had never had such a strong impression that an outside source was encouraging her—no, *urging* her—to pray. Obediently she pulled to the side of the road and bowed her head.

◆ ◆ ◆

Matt wanted to spend a little time on the beach before he died. He planned to take the pills and then swim out as far as he could. He began by walking north towards a barren stretch of beachfront, empty except for a few old, abandoned rowboats. He had been here with his Uncle Tom once several weeks before, looking for sand dollars. It was then that Tom had told him of Christ's willingness to be his friend and his brother. Matt's only response was a polite nod. Now, however, the knot of anxiety within him seemed to melt, as he felt that soon his conflicts would be resolved. He wanted to look around and enjoy the beach one last time, but something outside of him seemed to urge him to hurry. He sat down on the bow of a rowboat half-buried in sand. He gripped the small bottle of pills and began to sob with relief. *Soon my suffering will be over.*

◆ ◆ ◆

Just as Richards returned from an early lunch—submarine sandwiches provided by a local pharmaceutical representative touting the newest in symptom relief for menstrual cramps, a frantic nurse greeted him, running from Room 324, where he had performed the saline injection. The nurse shouted to the ward clerk to signal an infant code emergency call for the pediatric resuscitation team STAT.

"W-wait a minute!" Richards stammered with confusion and then anger over this apparent independent action of the nurse. "That patient was given an injection to induce abortion not two hours ago! Don't call a resuscitation team! This is an abortion, not a delivery!"

"That's not what the patient says, doctor!" the nurse yelled forcefully. She turned to the ward clerk and screamed, "Now get me an infant code team down here STAT!" The ward clerk obeyed as Richards and the nurse ran back into the patient's room.

Richards gasped at what he saw next. The patient cried repeatedly in broken but almost unbearably understandable English, "My baby! Save my baby! My baby! MY BABY! MY BABY! MY BABY!" Lying between the young woman's legs, umbilical cord intact, a small male infant made obvious attempts to get a first weak breath. The baby rapidly moved his arms and legs almost as if it were still swimming in the amniotic fluid that had surrounded it just minutes before.

Richards moved on impulse, understanding for the first time, very clearly, the mother's wishes for the child to live. He rapidly cleared the oral and nasal passageways of the small boy with a bulb syringe. He then clamped and cut the cord and lifted the infant by the feet in hopes to empty the lungs of excess fluid. Overhead, the infant code 500 was sounding, announcing the patient's room number for the infant resuscitation team. The team members responded immediately and arrived in the room within three minutes. Just as Richards lifted the infant by his feet, Jan Sullivan, a neonatologist, entered the room.

"What's going on here, Adam?" Dr. Sullivan had worked with Dr. Richards before when the neonatologists went to the O.R. to resuscitate c-section infants.

"Saline abortion—approximately twenty-three weeks gestation. Now the mother is wanting us to save the baby." Richards started losing his professional poise. His lip quivered slightly. "I'm not sure what went wrong . . . I only did the injection several hours ago . . . She isn't supposed to deliver until at least tomorrow."

Jan Sullivan slipped a small-caliber tube into the windpipe of the tiny infant and quickly gave the infant a few breaths through the tube. She then attached a cardiac monitor, which revealed a heart rate of eighty, much too slow for a newborn. "Give atropine down the endotracheal tube!" Several other pediatric residents had gathered by now to help with the infant. Another O.B. resident had come to attend to the mother and to assure proper delivery of the placenta. Richards slipped from the room and headed down the hall, wanting to be anywhere but close to Room 324.

The infant lived only a few short, painful hours. The combination of the young age and the saline injection had their predicted and planned effect on the young fetus. But in this case the process proceeded under the watchful eye of the neonatologists.

◆ ◆ ◆

In the car, Sandra looked up after a short prayer. All this seemed quite new to her. *What am I to pray?* She was unsure. *Is someone in trouble?* Yes; she felt that she needed to intercede for someone in trouble. "Dear God . . ." Sandra spoke softly and with some insecurity. "Help whoever is in trouble. Send help for whoever is in trouble." She suddenly felt self-conscious and wanted to get back on the road. *I wonder what Tom would say about this? Certainly he would know what all this is about. Or maybe I'm just losing my marbles . . . All of this pressure must be getting to me.* She restarted the car and began to pull back onto the highway when she became aware that she hadn't brought the list of visiting nursing recruits who were to be arriving the following day. She said, "Darn it!" out loud, then did a one-eighty and returned south towards home. The traffic was never crowded on the Shore, but at this time in the morning it was particularly sparse. In only five minutes Sandra pulled back into her concrete driveway. *I wonder if Matt is up yet. It sure would be nice if he'd take some initiative and mow the lawn.*

Sandra left the car running and hurried up the front steps. The front door wasn't locked. *Funny—I always lock the door.* She glanced at the kitchen table and saw the file containing the information on the new recruits. *Perhaps Matt would mow the yard if I'd ask . . . Oh well, he seems so preoccupied lately.* She turned and started for the door with the new file under her arm. Hesitating at the doorway, she again sighted the uncut grass, turned, and headed for the stairs. *It can't hurt just to ask him. Besides, maybe the work will help him get his mind off his problems.*

"Matt."

No answer.

"Matt!"

Silence.

Sandra Stone had never been firm with Matt since his brother died. She had rarely even raised her voice to correct him, as if treating him gently would somehow protect him from further sorrow. Now, however, she was getting impatient; she needed to get back on the road to work. When she reached the top of the stairs, she could see that Matt's door was open slightly.

"Matt, I would like you to mow the lawn today. Can you manage that?"

No answer. Not even the expected grunt of an unwilling, sleepy teenager.

Sandra sighed and walked to the door to Matt's room.

"Matt?"

She entered the room. The bed was unmade, with yesterday's clothes hanging from the bedposts. She spotted a neatly-folded paper on his pillow. She scanned the brief note. Its meaning sunk in immediately.

"No, no—O God, no! Don't let this happen. O God, please ... !" She ran from room to room, looking for her son around each corner. "Matt! My son, my son, my son!"

Now sobbing, she flew out onto the driveway and peered into the garage-door windows. No Matt. She ran back into the house, stumbling on the top step and sprawling flat onto the hardwood floor. Her left ankle screamed with pain. Quickly she boosted herself up and hobbled over to the telephone, bearing her weight on her right foot and on the kitchen chairs that served as substitute crutches. Her nervous fingers dialed the Downses' home number. *Please be home!* She waited for four rings, each of which she was sure was much longer than usual. At the fifth ring, a warm, familiar voice answered.

"Tom!"

"Sandra?"

"You've got to help me! Matt is gone. He left a note. He says he is going to be with Mark."

"Sandra, slow down! Do you know where he is?"

"No! Tom, you've got to help me. You've got to find him!"

"I'm on my way. I'll tell Kate to start the prayer chain."

◆ ◆ ◆

Matt sat still, looking out over the blue water. Somehow he'd never expected things to end this way. Actually, he felt somewhat better just having come to an inner resolve to end his problems. He looked at the small pill container in his hand. He thought briefly of returning to get some water to help him swallow but decided to take them dry. He poured out the contents of the small, plastic container. Exactly eleven pills. He wasn't sure if they were enough but thought that, combined with a swim, he surely wouldn't have a chance of survival. This was one thing he wouldn't screw up, he assured himself. He lifted his hand to his mouth. As he did, he caught a glimpse of a dolphin school swimming not thirty feet from the shoreline. He paused for a moment to watch. His hand eased downward. He became aware again of an outward sense of urgency, as if he were being prodded to hurry.

A large dolphin shot from the water's surface and arched gracefully into the bay. The fish was very large, and rather unusual to be spotted this far north in the bay. Matt seemed to be satisfied to spend a moment watching the dolphins, turning his attention from his planned action one last time.

◆ ◆ ◆

Kate initiated the prayer chain by calling Emily Randolf. The prayer chain ran by unspoken rules; primarily, the prayer chain was designed only to relay requests, and other items of news were taken care of on separate calls. The chain did not exist for gossip and rarely gave details of personal needs; the people merely gave enough information for effectual prayer.

"My sister Sandra's son Matt is in some trouble with depression. We have reason to believe he is in a real life battle right now and needs the prayers of the church. Please pray and pass this request along the prayer chain."

Mrs. Randolf whispered a short prayer, then called pastor Jim Yoder. Kate called Robert Smith who called Lena Jantzi and the Grabers. Within just a few minutes, the entire Mennonite community on the Eastern Shore had been notified and were beginning to unite in prayer. Some felt an urgency in their request that they had not known in months. Ella Porter felt such conviction to pray that she knelt by her bed and began to weep. She felt strange not knowing the exact nature of this burden but felt compelled to stay put and listen. It was not until the burden lifted and she again sensed a quieting peace that she rose to her feet. She glanced at her watch. Eleven o'clock. She had been on her knees weeping and praying for two hours.

Meanwhile, Tom Downs raced south to the Stones' place, praying for guidance to help him find Matt.

Not ten minutes later, he was standing in the kitchen with Sandra Stone. He stared at the note written by Matt earlier that morning.

"Why does he say he killed his brother?"

Sandra explained the events of her son's death between sobs. "I had no idea he really thought he was responsible for Mark's dying. I thought we all understood that Mark died because of his leukemia, and only indirectly from his fall. I never dreamed Matt didn't understand. Perhaps he was too young."

"Where do you think he is?"

"Maybe down at the water. He's been spending some time there lately."

"That sounds like good thinking to me. Just the other night he and I took a walk there."

Tom gave the orders. He would go down to the beach; Sandra would stay by the phone. Kate would come over soon to be with Sandra.

Tom headed down the street on foot. The closest access to the beach was only one hundred yards from the front steps of the Stones' white house. Tom entered the beach and turned south. His shoes sunk into the dry sand, which spilled into his penny loafers.

Again he began praying. Actually, there was no real beginning or end to many of Tom's prayers. He often just said a "thank you" or asked for guidance throughout his day. His prayer at this time was a prayer with eyes open, spoken without slowing down, without fancy names or platitudes. He waited after asking the question, trying to sense what message God was sending to him. He paused, then turned around and headed north towards a barren stretch of beach he'd visited with Matt just a few nights before. It was not spooky or mystical to him that he should receive direction from his Father in this way. He just felt impressed that he was to turn around. He had learned to trust his inward impressions, particularly when in conjunction with prayers for guidance. In this case Tom also felt an urgency about the task at hand, as if an outward force compelled him to move faster across the warming sand.

Tom picked up his pace, charging along while his eyes feverishly scanned the horizon.

A few minutes later he spotted Matt sitting on the bow of a half-buried abandoned rowboat. He saw Matt's hand go to his mouth, then return to his side again. Tom was still several hundred yards down the beach from Matt, who seemed entranced, staring into the bay. Tom slowed to quiet his labored breathing as he approached Matt, who remained almost statue-like. He then saw what Matt was staring at: a school of at least thirty dolphins were in a fury of activity just a few feet from shore.

"Hello, Matt." Tom spoke in a way he hoped wouldn't startle his nephew.

Matt continued to look forward but broke his frozen state by pushing a small object that was in his right hand into his pocket. Tom caught a glimpse of the familiar pharmaceutical labeling before the object disappeared.

Tom joined Matt on the small rowboat's bow. Together they watched the activity at the water's edge. Several large dolphins leaped out of the water, executing near-complete flips prior to their entry back into the water. It almost seemed as if they were purpose-fully entertaining their audience. A few minutes later, the entire dol-phin school swam straight out to deep water. They were visible for several minutes as they traveled on a course towards the first island of the Chesapeake Bay bridge tunnel. It was as if they were acting on some cue; each dolphin turned towards deeper water at the same moment. When the dolphins were no longer in sight, Tom spoke again.

"I read the note you wrote to your mother."

"How? Mom's not due home until this evening."

"She forgot something and had to return home. She found the note and called me. She's very worried about you."

"Why should she care? I've caused her enough trouble already."

"She does care. She loves you, Matt." Tom paused. "This move, along with losing your father, has not been easy on her either. I know for a fact that she wishes she could communicate with you better."

Matt was suddenly very disturbed and again felt an urge to run. He knew he must not lose his chance to free himself from his self-torment.

"Can't you just leave me alone for a while? I'd like to be by myself to think."

Tom was aware that this was a real spiritual battle. He knew that forces of darkness were fighting for his nephew's life. He silently rebuked those powers of darkness in the name of Jesus Christ. As he did, Matt relaxed somewhat and sighed.

"I know you want to be free. I know that you feel guilty for what happened to Mark." Tom chose his words carefully, sensing the prayers of the saints at work. Tears began to form and run down Tom's face, and his voice quivered as he continued. "I would give anything to take your pain away." Again he paused, this time taking his eyes off the bay and resting them on Matt. "Do you remember when Mark died?"

"I was the one who was there. I caused him to fall. I wanted him to stay out with me."

"The doctors say that he had leukemia. Any minor fall could have ended his life anytime."

Matt snapped at this as one who had argued the point in his

mind a thousand times. "But I was the one who made him fall! I threw the football at him during a fight! I made him die! If I hadn't, he could have gotten medicine to give him a chance!" Matt stood now, physically shaking, trembling at the baring of his hidden emotions.

Tom folded his hands across his chest and looked at the sand on his shoes, praying silently. Then he brightened. "Okay, let's just say that all that is true. You caused your own brother's death. You did it. You're guilty. What shall we issue as your penalty?"

This line of reasoning took Matt off-guard somewhat, but he accepted the question at face value. "I deserve to die." Matt's voice was quiet but steady.

"Penalty accepted. That's good biblical judgment. An eye for an eye."

Matt seemed puzzled. Tom went on.

"The only catch is, you don't have to die!" Tom's voice was choked with emotion. "Whether you did anything wrong concerning your brother's death or not, you know that you have disobeyed God in one way or another. We all have! But someone already paid the penalty for you. Don't you see? That someone is Jesus. He paid the price to cancel the penalty of your sins and mine. You can be free, Matt! You can be released from the guilt because the price has already been paid."

Matt's trembling increased. He began to sob. Not just quiet, controlled tears, but large, inconsolable tears, spilling over his cheeks and onto his shirt. Matt fell into his uncle's outstretched arms.

"Everything's going to be okay now. You're gonna make it."

Matt continued to tremble for several minutes. Tom broke the silence first. "Come on back to the house. Your mom is waiting for you. She'll want to see that you're all right."

The two walked slowly up the hard-packed sand at the water's edge. Neither said a word until they arrived at the house. Tom was saying a silent "thank you" to God, and Matt was beginning to enjoy a new feeling—his uncle's unconditional acceptance despite his imperfections.

◆ ◆ ◆

Two weeks later, Dr. Richards sighed with frustration as he contemplated his recent past. He had nearly lost his job over the botched abortion incident. Fortunately, the patient did not sue. Richards wasn't even sure if she had been told the truth about the events that took place before the birth of her son. He did know that she had been assured that the doctors had done everything possible to save her little son *after* the early delivery.

He threw the medical journal he held across the small on-call quarters and sat on the edge of a single portable cot. *Abortions require technical expertise and the knowledge as to when and how to perform the deed to achieve the desired end neatly and swiftly . . . without the flailing I witnessed two weeks ago!*

I'll show them! I've seen the results of a sub-standard procedure. But instead of running away from this, I'll meet it head-on, with the same determination that resulted in my "Intern of the Year" award. I can perfect this technique just like any other. I can use my experience here to help me provide these necessary services in the future. Instead of running from my dislikes and fears, I'll face them head-on . . . I'll bring the abortion industry to a "new standard of excellence"!

Adam Richards, M.D. stretched out on the lumpy cot. His mind made up, he determined to make the past work in his favor. With that resolution, he closed his eyes and slept.

◆ ◆ ◆

Tom's acceptance provided Matt a model of God's forgiveness that he so desperately needed. Matt eventually forgave himself, and just two weeks after their talk on the beach Matt accepted the Lord's forgiveness at the altar of the local church. He experienced a true lifting of his burdens that day, but more importantly, he established a relationship with God that would grow to see him through future hard times.

The events of the next few years were ones of growth both emotionally and spiritually for Matt. He graduated from high school and attended the University of Virginia where he studied biology as a pre-med. A spark of interest in the health professions had blossomed during his last year of high school when he spent many hours as a volunteer at the hospital where his mother and his uncle were employed. He attended medical school at the Medical College of Virginia. His choice of medical specialties was not difficult; he would pursue a career in general surgery. For this, he decided to return to his home state of Kentucky and the Taft University Medical Center in Fairfax.

◆ ◆ ◆

Sandra Stone looked out over the Chesapeake Bay. Her son was flying back from a short-term medical mission trip in Kenya today. She prayed for him now, as she often had over the years since their move to the Eastern Shore. As she looked out over the bay, she saw a dolphin break the glistening water's surface. It was the first sighting of a dolphin in that area since Matt was seventeen.

CHAPTER
3

CAROL Jennings sighed at the familiarity of the routine here at the Taft University reproductive services clinic. Not that she felt completely at home in these surroundings, but she took a certain comfort in the fact that she had been through these very procedures numerous times. She had risen quite early, but not without first taking and recording her temperature on her bedside notepad. Today she was again undergoing a pelvic ultrasound to determine "follicle size and development." She was uneasy with how close she had come to the terminology that had become a big part of her life over the past ten months. She glanced around the busy room. Her physician, Dr. James Harrison, was reviewing the ultrasound pictures that had just been developed. This was to be her third and last try at IVF (invitro fertilization). She had wearied of explaining it all to her family. "It's a technique where my eggs are joined with Tony's sperm outside of our bodies, and then the embryos are placed back in my womb after they have been fertilized." Her mother insisted that all that is necessary to conceive a child is a "little relaxation."

Carol shook her head as if erasing the undesirable thoughts. She was aware that the room was too cool for the patient gowns to which she had grown accustomed. The only other thought in her head was that the ultrasound jelly on her lower abdomen felt rather gross, almost slimy, and she was anxious to have it wiped off again.

"These look very good, Carol. It appears that we have several follicles that will be ready for harvesting tomorrow. Of course, we will have to check your estradiol level and make sure the level is adequate prior to making a final decision to proceed." Dr. Harrison always appeared very businesslike with his patients. Standing at just over six feet tall, and having maintained his college athletic build, he typified the quiet, handsome doctor role that made him a frequent topic of local hospital speculative gossip. Carol found herself wondering what this man was really like. She had seen pictures of his family on his office desk and took some comfort in the fact that this man, to whom she had revealed her most distressing personal problems, was apparently concerned about his own family.

"Let's hope it's all systems go." Carol managed a quick smile. She was quite adept at covering her inner pain. "Should I just stop at the lab counter on my way out?"

Susan, a nurse manager, smiled. "It sounds as if you've gotten the routine down." She reached for Carol's arm as she began to collect her clothes and walk towards the small curtain to change. "We are all rooting for you."

Carol smiled again weakly. "Thanks. I'll have to call and tell Tony that it looks like we can try again tomorrow." She turned and slipped behind the curtain. After putting on her clothes, she quickly walked back out to the general lab area to have her blood drawn. Somehow it always seemed important for her to get away from the reproduction clinic area as soon as possible after her visits. Although she was facing her problem of infertility head-on, she still felt an uneasiness about spending a lot of time in the clinic's waiting room, as if she was advertising her problem for all to see.

In less than ten minutes, Carol sat in her silver Mazda, heading for Interstate 64, which she would take east to her hometown of Easton, Kentucky. It seemed that these daily drives had become a time of thoughtful review, particularly since this nightmare of infertility began.

As a thirty-six-year-old, she was all too aware of her own biological clock. She was a professional, having received her Master's degree in psychiatric nursing. She had worked full-time until recently, when the time constraints of her own clinic visits started to interfere. Of course, being a nurse did have some advantages for her in her present state. She was able to give herself the daily injections of Perganol (the hormones responsible for stimulating the development of mature ovarian follicles that would be harvested for the in-vitro fertilization) and thus avoid the one-hour drive to Fairfax. There was also the advantage of at least having a basic understanding of the physiology involved with the techniques. Her husband, Tony, had become predictable in his response pattern. He had no science or medical background at all, but he was too proud to admit his poor understanding of their current situation to their physician. He would, therefore, reply that he had "No questions" to Dr. Harrison's routine "Any questions?" and then have Carol interpret everything the doctor had said as soon as they were alone in their car.

Carol was a strong-willed woman with a clearly defined set of life goals. College, her Master's degree, community psychiatric clinic programs, activities for the local church youth group, as well as a rigorous daily fitness program—each had a neatly organized and set place in the plans she had outlined in her mind a thousand times. Perhaps her desire for structure and control made her own problems with infertility all the harder to face. She had made definite plans for two children, the first to be born after she finished her Master's degree and the second after establishing a local psychiatric clinic for troubled adolescents. Everything was moving along right on schedule. That is, until they met this unexpected roadblock.

Her husband, Tony, fit very much the type B personality profile. He had been an aggressive student and had graduated *cum laude* with a degree in business management. He then settled down in a comfortable routine as the manager of a local hardware store. The store had been run and owned by his father, and now that his father had retired, Tony had taken his place. Of course, there were certain business pressures, but he never seemed to worry about events that were out of his control. He adopted this same attitude with their current problem of infertility.

The long infertility workup had not been entirely to Tony's liking, but after some initial hesitancy he submitted to his wife's urging to come along. Once the workup was complete, the doctors had said that the reasons for their infertility were not understood—"idiopathic infertility." His wife explained that just meant there was no clear reason for their problem. It did not mean there was nothing wrong, only that the doctors could not identify the problem's source. The "idiopathic infertility" diagnosis could not be settled upon until all other known causes could be ruled out.

Tony had gone along with all of the tests quite readily, even the "postcoital" test in which the doctors had examined his sperm after it was collected from his wife's birth canal by pelvic exam. This all seemed quite natural to him. It was only when they started requesting semen specimens collected fresh in the clinic's restroom that he objected. It took him a full three weeks to be convinced of the necessity of the test, and then he cooperated only after the completion of an assortment of other tests, including a laparoscopic exam of Carol's pelvis and a biopsy of the inner lining of her uterus. It was only mildly comforting to him to know that the rest of his samples could be collected at home, as long as he agreed to use their containers and to proceed directly to the clinic after collection of the specimen.

The last ten months were now an unexpected blur. This problem was not supposed to happen to them. They were both from large, fertile families and had undergone countless ribbings when with their families for the holidays. The teasing had stopped, of course, when it became apparent that they really were trying to start a family.

Carol and Tony had met while undergraduates at Taft U. Their infatuation with each other and with life itself was overshadowed only by what can only be described as a true sense of purpose. They both felt that even in everyday routine activities they were somehow supposed to make others' lives better. Together they complemented each other. Tony was thoughtful and yet peaceful, without an overbearing worry in his body. Carol was assertive and yet gifted with a dry humor that kept those around her laughing at themselves.

Their romance had taken only eight months to move from the first date to the altar. Because of "The Plan" as they jokingly called it, they carefully used birth control until after Carol's Master's degree was in the bag. Then, after three years of marriage, they stopped protecting themselves from children. At first they only thought they were not hitting on the right times by chance. When Carol read an article on infertility in *Reader's Digest*, she realized she and Tony fit the bill exactly: over one year of unprotected sex without a pregnancy. She had been a bit reluctant to make an appointment at the reproductive clinic at first, but she finally went at the encouragement of her sister. "Only when you know that nothing is wrong with you will you relax and stop worrying about this." Her sister did not realize there would be a ring of truth to her statement. It was not until after a four-month intensive investigation by the clinic that Carol would hear, "We can find nothing wrong."

The diagnosis of "idiopathic infertility" haunted her. Why couldn't they put their finger on a specific cause for the infertility? This did not fit well into her planned life. It did not fit well at all. And explaining the diagnosis to her own mother proved even more frustrating. Her mother, the bearer of seven children, thought that the high cost of arriving at that diagnosis must surely mean that pregnancy would happen anytime, "as soon as the time is right." That phrase seemed to torture Carol now as she drove towards her modest apartment. *We'll give it one more chance—just one more chance to show everyone that it's all been worth it.*

The cost had not been cheap, both in terms of the financial burden and of the emotional price of rising hopes with each new technique and the crashing of their expectations with each new failure. The clinic bills had eliminated their savings, and the added cost of cutting back her work hours to half-time had made it impossible for them to meet their house payment. They had moved after the first in-vitro fertilization attempt and now were renting a one-bedroom apartment in a building occupied mostly by Easton State University students.

The emotional cost had indeed taken its toll. They had begun with medication only and later combined the medications with timing techniques guided by her morning temperature record. This was followed by changing the medication routines, more investigational studies, and artificial insemination with her husband's sperm. Nothing had worked. They agreed to proceed with IVF after having had their hopes rise and fall again, month after month. They had prayed that this would be the answer, and actually a pregnancy had occurred after the last IVF. Unfortunately, the success had been short-lived. In spite of the daily hormone injections to support the pregnancy, Carol miscarried after only three weeks. The loss of the pregnancy seemed to be the final blow for Carol, but at the encouragement of her husband and Dr. Harrison, she was willing to try one more time. *One more time.* Carol exited I-64 and turned on the radio. She needed something to take her mind off tomorrow. Tomorrow would come and go soon enough, but for now it just seemed like the distant future that would never arrive. *One more time.*

◆ ◆ ◆

Michael Simons, M.D. sat at his desk staring attentively at the multi-colored Macintosh computer screen in front of him. The fact that it was 2 A.M. did not concern him. The light from the computer screen made his face appear almost plastic, and because of his stillness, an observer could have believed he was looking at a mannequin if it were not for Simons' rhythmic breathing, which provided the room's only noise. The only other light in Dr. Simons' study came from a small green-shaded modern lamp on the teak table next to his desk.

Many would have described this man as a brilliant innovator, making life-saving contributions to his specialty of pediatric cardiothoracic surgery. He was only thirty-nine years of age. He had just been named chief of the T.U. Department of Cardiothoracic Surgery. His name appeared as author of well over one hundred articles, and he served as editor for the most prestigious journal in his field. At this very computer terminal he had written numerous book chapters and critiqued the work of countless others. He could be defined by his dedication to his profession. He was driven by the knowledge that he was somehow gifted above what he saw as "the common man." His drive for perfection was easily apparent to his fellow attendings and all too apparent to the residents who were at his disposal.

His wife had left him ten months ago. His job had become the other woman that his wife had feared would attract the young surgeon away. Instead, the tables had been turned, and his wife, Suzanne, ran off with her sculpture teacher who gave her lessons through a local community college continuing-education class. Dr. Simons had ceased caring about her anyway and could not help but think that her leaving was a positive move that freed him for further commitments to research.

He had become religious in his thoughts about himself. He truly felt as if he was fulfilling his destiny in providing innovations in his specialty. Far from a Christian man, he outwardly laughed at individuals who required such a crutch to survive. He had grown increasingly paranoid toward his colleagues, suspicious of anyone whom he regarded as a challenge to his authority. In actuality, he did not fully understand his own feelings about himself. He did know that he felt an increasing outward—perhaps even inward—pressure to perform and to cast a cautious eye towards others. He had come to understand that he carried a special mission, perhaps what some would say was a "call" to solve some of the life-threatening problems in his field. This had progressed from a normal desire to help his fellowman to a deep-seated belief that he was to be a central figure in his field. Just what his accomplishment would involve, he was uncertain. But he felt it had something to do with the project he was now formulating.

Dr. Simons had shared his grandiose feelings about himself to someone else only once, and then had instantly regretted it. He had explained his "destiny" with Lenore Roberts, a former operating room nurse with whom he had enjoyed a brief affair six months ago. He blamed his loose tongue on too much alcohol shared over a late dinner. Lenore had been drinking heavily and laughed heartily after hearing Michael talk about his eventual, unstoppable climb to international prestige and influence. He ended the evening abruptly and nearly as quickly had her removed from the operating room staff, citing multiple examples of work inefficiency documented in a letter to the O.R. supervisor. He had seen her only once since that time and made a personal vow not to involve himself in another relationship unless it would help in the fulfillment of his dream.

Paralleling the growth of his self-love was an underlying interest in several new-age writings. He read, and came to believe, that he had the power to control his own future. He had always been somewhat of a skeptic when it came to writings of this sort, but he became increasingly receptive after observing the link between positive attitudes in his patients and better outcomes and quicker recovery times. At first he began with some meditation techniques that he learned at a local university seminar. Occasionally during a time of meditation, or when he was envisioning himself in a position of great influence, he would gain the impression of an idea or thought that seemed to originate outside his body. Later he began having a strong sense of guidance in some of his research. He supposed that these ideas and impressions were evidence of the special power within him. He would surely rise above the masses simply by tapping the unused potential that was present within him. This power, available to many, but virtually unknown and unused, would carry him to the coveted position upon which he had become fixated.

Fortunately for Dr. Simons, his traits of superiority were not only tolerated but sometimes encouraged in his business. The other factor that let his egotistic quests go unchecked was the fact that he had already climbed high enough in the Department of Surgery that there were few people looking over his shoulder in objective evaluation of his performance.

His most recent brainchild was an idea that he was sure would revolutionize the entire treatment of most complex congenital heart problems. He confidently expected that once his colleagues saw the data he was gathering, most of the current surgical procedures, along with their high complication and death rates, would become obsolete, of historical interest only.

Dr. Simons sighed deeply, not from fatigue, but out of frustration that he could not move at a faster pace in his data collection. His idea had come to him only two weeks before, when he was reviewing the autopsy results of a patient who'd died with hypoplastic left heart syndrome, a condition where the main pumping chamber of the heart was underdeveloped. The condition was almost uniformly fatal.

The project, it seemed, would cost thousands, and grant application and funding of new projects were painfully slow processes. It was easy enough, however, to shift around funding from several of his other research grants, covering his tracks with carefully constructed paperwork. Each item he needed for his present project was covered by a fabricated need for the item in another funded project. He did not need to pay more than one person as a lab assistant for this new project. He wanted to do most of the work himself; he felt there were some things that were better handled personally.

Since the idea had come to him, he had reviewed every autopsy done on stillborn infants over the last ten years, paying close attention to the weight of each heart in relation to the child's gestational age. He charted his findings carefully during his nightly vigils on his home computer. He then returned to his own notes on cardiac embryology for review, and then finally to the results of autopsies done on full-term infants who had died within the first few weeks of life and who had their demise for reasons other than cardiac problems, and therefore had presumably normal cardiac function and weight. The development of the heart in-utero was rapid and amazingly complete within a few weeks of fertilization. Most of the pregnancy was devoted to growth of the heart and other organs whose basic structure developed early in the pregnancy. The growth of the heart was very rapid early on, with almost exponential weight gain.

Later in pregnancy, the growth was steady but much slower. Premature infants were dying not because their hearts were not strong enough to circulate their blood, but because their lungs were not mature enough to oxygenate the blood that was being circulated. Could the hearts of premature infants, whose other organs were too immature to support life, be used to support life in an infant whose only problem was a complex congenital heart defect? Perhaps so, but the availability of hearts from braindead infants was in extremely short supply when compared to the many children who needed cardiac transplantation. *Could he use the hearts of normal fetuses who had been purposefully aborted late in the second trimester of pregnancy?*

Dr. Simons' data seemed to support his hypothesis. All that was needed now was exposure to freshly aborted babies so he could test his theory. He would call Adam Richards from Fairfax Family Planning Services in the morning. Dr. Richards, he recalled, was still providing services to women wanting abortions through the second trimester. He had known Dr. Richards for a long time . . . And Adam owed him a favor. Dr. Simons smiled, his face somewhat sweaty from perspiration although the room was a cool 68 degrees. The moisture on his forehead reflected the flickering light from the Macintosh computer screen. *Yes, Dr. Richards, it is time we talked about this matter. Perhaps you will also be carried to greatness on the coattails of my rising fame. Tomorrow we will talk and arrange the start-up of my promising new therapy.*

He sat back up straight, moving quickly as if he had just received new energy. He clicked the *Save* button, then rapidly completed the sequence of moves to exit the program and shut down his machine for the night. Tomorrow would be a good day. He would conduct a light clinic of mostly post-op patients with their parents. There he would receive many expected thank-yous from concerned parents and would proudly observe the outcome of his work. Then he would call Adam Richards and get on with his current research interest. The time was right.

◆ ◆ ◆

Matt Stone aroused from sleep with the 5 A.M. news broadcast blaring from his clock radio. He had arrived home last night at 10, and after collecting his bags and catching a taxi home, he had sunk into his bed and slept the sleep of a hibernating animal. He rubbed his eyes and legs, which felt as if they had not moved since he retired the night before. He glanced around the small apartment. It was basically three rooms. A "kitchen" and "living room" were separated only by the arrangement of the furniture, with the couch marking the border between the two. Other than that, he had a small adjoining bedroom and bathroom. His apartment was actually the upstairs of an old house belonging to Lucy Pritchard. The house stood only two blocks from the university hospital and was therefore most accessible to Matt. In return for the cheap rent, Matt's only responsibility was to look after the elderly widow. As Matt looked around the apartment, he noticed the freshly neatened and dusted appearance and mused to himself about who was looking after whom. Obviously Lucy had been here the day before, preparing for his return.

Besides himself and Lucy, the only other occupant of the house was his Great Dane, Mike. Sure, it was an unusual name for a dog;

but to Matt, Mike was not an ordinary dog and thus was not suited for an ordinary dog's name such as Spot or Ruff. Matt often talked to Mike as if he understood what he was talking about, and he had in fact conditioned him to bark in response to the question, "Isn't that right, Mike?" This had become a routine with Matt, who would follow any exaggerated story told to a friend with that phrase. Matt would follow up the barked response with a "See, I told you that's how it was!"

Matt had left his dog at a friend's local farm and would not have a chance to pick him up until the next day after staying in the hospital for "call" tonight.

Matt put a cup of water in the microwave to make a cup of coffee, his first since leaving for Kenya. He prepared his small on-call bag and took a quick shower. He dressed, poured his coffee into a styrofoam cup, and headed out the door. Trauma surgery rounds began sharply at 6 A.M., and he wanted a few extra minutes to check the surgery schedule and pick up a patient census.

The trauma team at T.U. was essentially two teams in one, with each team covering a twenty-four-hour shift rotation. Actually each team would end up spending about thirty hours on in the hospital and sixteen off prior to returning for rounds the next morning. Both teams rounded together in the morning, so the team coming on could be updated on the events of the night before. Barb Stevens, another chief resident, would run the rounds this morning, as she had been on call the night before. Tomorrow Matt would be responsible to lead the team around to see the usual patient load of forty to fifty people.

"Any N.O.G.s last night, Barb?" The question had come from a third-year resident named Randy Brown. Trauma, it seemed, had a vocabulary all to itself, and each resident added to the expanding terminology. A N.O.G. was a patient whose workup took forever but had no indication for any surgery; hence the term Non-Operative Grief.

"Only one, and one more that came in dead and stayed dead." Barb appeared to have gotten at least an hour's sleep, as her scrub top was wrinkled. "Where's the rest of the nogladites?" (Nogladites were trauma team members.)

"They should be here soon. I left a message with the rest of the team that we were rounding at 6," Randy responded.

"Good. Let's turn in an X-ray list at the file room and get started on the eighth floor."

Rounds were completed by 6:45 A.M., in time for the weekly general surgery teaching conference. As the discussion of benign esophageal problems proceeded around him, Matt felt as if he'd never been away.

After the conference Barb handed off the trauma alert pager to Matt. The beeper went off only in anticipation of an incoming critically ill trauma patient. Usually these were brought in courtesy of the T.U. C.A.T.S. (Critical Air Transport Service) helicopter. "Have fun with this," Barb snickered.

"Yeah, sure. It's back to the old grindstone, I guess."

"I'm outa here!" Barb wasted no extra time asking about Matt's trip.

"Hey! Get a life!" Matt laughed as she walked towards the elevator. Barb tripped the almost-closed elevator door with a quick move of her left hand. "What are you doing, surgeon?" Matt called as she got onto the elevator. "You might need that hand someday!"

"Bye, Matt." Barb emphasized the "Bye." She looked happy to be getting out for the day.

Matt walked to the O.R.s on the second floor. There he helped the third-year resident with a cholecystectomy and an intern with a hernia repair. The remainder of his day was quiet except for a couple of I.C.U. (Intensive Care Unit) disasters, both of which involved patients who had been in the unit for many days.

It was now 6 P.M., and the trauma alert pager had been quiet all day. Matt headed for the call room to catch a quick nap, knowing that a trauma surgeon was always busiest after dark. "Always sleep and eat prophylactically." This was a rule espoused by most trauma residents—a rule not easily followed but frequently attempted. Matt closed the door to the trauma chief's call room, wondering how his first night back in the States would compare with his last one in Kenya.

CHAPTER
4

CAROL dressed while Tony fixed pancakes in the kitchen. The aroma of frying bacon easily filled the small apartment. Carol sighed after inhaling the delicious odor because she had been instructed not to eat anything before her IVF ovum harvest later that morning. Tony, on the other hand, whistled cheerfully, thanks to a reason not to go to work early and for the opportunity to "create" a suitable breakfast. This was his own term, which he coined to describe his culinary skills. Actually he was not a bad cook—he was quite good in fact, and he regularly "created" breakfasts for the two of them on weekends and other special occasions.

"Did you really have to make my favorite breakfast today when I can't eat any of it?" Though Carol was joking, she sounded rather hurt, calling from the bedroom at a volume the neighbors might not appreciate.

"Sorry, hon." Tony sounded rather sheepish. "Perhaps we could grab a nice brunch after the IVF?"

"Are you forgetting about the six-hour observation time after the procedure?" Carol walked into the kitchen, then quickly exited with a sigh as she saw the stack of pancakes, bacon, fresh coffee, and orange juice Tony had placed on the table.

"Sorry, hon," Tony mumbled, his voice muffled by a large bite of syrupy pancakes.

Carol shook her head and began to pack an overnight bag for the trip. *Just in case I have to stay over*. All in all, she was in a rather good mood this morning, her initial anxieties of the unknown having been erased by her previous IVFs. She looked around for some adequate reading material to take for her time in the hospital, put in her long nightgown, and gathered her hair-dryer plus other needed items. She paused and looked at their wedding photograph on the old cherry dresser. In spite of all their differences, she relied on her husband more than she would readily admit. He had not wavered throughout the whole ordeal once the decision to proceed with IVF had been made. Carol looked at her watch. They still had two hours before they were due in Fairfax. She again gazed at the photograph and then quietly changed her clothes for a second time.

"Have you finished everything you need to do before leaving?" Carol had crept up behind her husband where he stood washing the breakfast dishes. "I thought maybe I could help out a little."

"All I need to do is finish these dishes." Tony had not turned around to see his wife, who was now clad in his favorite nightgown.

"Aren't you forgetting just one little detail?"

Tony turned around to see Carol smiling. She could see him blush.

"I can't get this IVF without you, you know, Tony."

Carol nudged him towards their small bedroom. Tony put his arms around his wife's waist. "I love you."

Those were the last words they spoke until they were in the Mazda heading for Fairfax.

◆ ◆ ◆

Adam Richards sat alone at his favorite Italian restaurant, Georgio's. He was waiting for Dr. Michael Simons, who had called earlier that day and requested a meeting. Dr. Richards had suggested the place after Simons requested some privacy for a matter of "extreme importance to both of our futures." Simons had declined to give further details, so Adam agreed, looking forward to an excuse to sample a large portion of linguini and clam sauce that would be served with piping-hot Italian bread and red wine, which he always let Georgio choose himself.

Adam Richards would not have been so quick to recommend a dinner meeting in the past, but his own circumstances had changed recently, as a result of which he, like Dr. Simons, often found himself home alone preparing frozen dinners. His wife had left the previous May, citing their lack of communication and his long hours as the final breaking blow to a marriage that others had thought indestructible. It had come as no surprise to Adam, however, and his greatest regret was the impact this would have on his only son, Adam, Jr.

His son had been, from the beginning, the pride of his heart. It was somewhat of a miracle that he was alive at all, and some of that was due to Michael Simons. Adam, Jr. was born with a condition known as "coarctation of the aorta"; in other words, his aorta had a tight narrowing that compromised the blood supply to his lower body. Dr. Simons had performed the delicate operation to correct the problem. The surgery had gone well, and Adam's post-op recovery was uncomplicated until he had a near-fatal cardiac dysrhythmia on the second day. The doctors felt it was secondary to a low potassium level or perhaps to the manipulation of a small venous catheter that had been positioned just above the small boy's heart to monitor his blood volume. Regardless of the cause, Dr. Simons had been at the bedside and administered the necessary shock that broke the rhythm before Adam, Jr. suffered any brain damage from anoxia (lack of oxygen). Adam, Sr. and his wife, Doris, had been most appreciative, perhaps because they had the basis for understanding just what had transpired during the rapid seconds of their son's resuscitation.

Since that time, Richards and Simons had kept in touch, mostly in passing, but always with a large citrus box each Christmas sent from Richards to Simons. Because of this, Adam mused over the nature of this meeting and its urgency, but he knew he would find out soon enough, as long as Simons had not been delayed by an emergency. He ordered some breadsticks and a light beer to pass what he hoped to be a short wait and to stave off his hunger—he had not eaten since breakfast, due to a fairly large patient load of his own.

◆　◆　◆

Matt Stone endured a steady but tolerable night. His team had admitted only two patients—one a twenty-four-year-old with a basilar skull fracture, and a second patient with a lacerated spleen. The latter condition did not always require surgery, but did require close observation to assess for bleeding and so required an I.C.U. bed admission. The finding of such unit beds in a hospital overrun with patients provided a hassle requiring many phone calls to decide which patient was most suitable for transfer to a floor bed. After the bed had been secured, Matt managed two short hours of sleep prior to being called to see the other patient they had admitted. He had, it seemed, decided to act like many other disinhibited head injury patients and was yelling obscenities loudly enough to be heard on the adjacent wing.

The patient's parents wanted their son to be sedated. "He's never acted this way before," sobbed the distraught mother. "It's so unlike him!" Her husband stood silently beside her, glaring at the now fully awake Dr. Matthew Stone. After dabbing her eyes with a tissue she pleaded, "Isn't there anything you can do?" Matt offered a gentle explanation. "Unfortunately, sedative medications can alter his mental responsiveness, and we need to assess his mental status on an hourly basis. The medications would interfere with our assessment of his mental function." Matt paused, searching the faces of the concerned parents for signs of comprehension. He then added, "I know his behavior is very disturbing to you, but it is an expected part of this type of skull fracture."

The parents thanked Matt and walked slowly to the waiting room at the end of the hallway, holding each other as they passed their son's room and wincing as he shrieked another obscenity at the nurse in his room. Matt disliked the terminology but mused to himself that this patient would probably fall into the category entitled "N.O.G.s." Matt headed for the nearest coffee machine, inhaled a cup of coffee, and headed for the I.C.U. for rounds.

Rounds went smoothly but were slowed down somewhat by an attending trauma surgeon who came along and continually asked the team to wait while he dictated "short notes" on each patient. These would be transcribed and placed on the patient's chart as a part of the legal record.

After rounds, Matt had one thing on his mind: to pick up his Great Dane, Mike. He wondered how Mike would respond to him, having not been separated from him for more than a few days at a time prior to Matt's African excursion. There were no scheduled surgical cases or clinic visits until the following day, leaving Matt free to go after completing rounds. So after a quick change out of his scrubs into his street clothes, he nearly ran out of the front entrance, heading for his small apartment. He passed off the trauma alert pager to Barb before leaving but still had his individual pager clipped to his belt. He turned it off with an exaggerated flip of his thumb, jumping up and landing just as he switched it to the *off* position. He had repeated this little ritual ceremony over and over since his internship, his way of celebrating the freedom of being truly off, beyond the reach of any patient care demands. In short order, Matt swept in and out of his apartment. He wanted to pack a lunch but still had not been to the store since his return from Kenya. *Oh, well, I can pick up something for myself and Mike on the way.* He jumped into his small Isuzu truck and headed towards a small farm twenty minutes south of Fairfax.

◆ ◆ ◆

Linda Baldwin looked quite pretty, despite having paint on her left cheek, her hair in a bandanna, and having on her old, holey coveralls. She was only slightly happy that she had said yes to this most recent of projects, that of making ten additional posters for a pro-life rally to be held in Fairfax later that fall. She didn't need another activity to occupy her time. In addition to being a full-time graduate student at the Appalachia Christian University, where she pursued her Master's degree in education, she advised the staff of the small university weekly newspaper, *The Weathervane*, and also worked in a local attorney's office doing research in order to keep her financial head above water. She stood five feet, four inches high but carried herself as if somehow she were taller than that. Her fellow students knew her for her quick wit but saw that she did not carry the sarcasm that some who are considered "witty" possess. She spoke compassionately about many things but mostly about situations that displayed unjust oppression. She encouraged many *Weathervane* articles on topics of this nature and exhibited a well-grounded understanding of the biblical arguments touching the many fiery issues she debated on campus.

Linda adopted her views from both her parents' teaching and from the not-so-easy halls of experience. Since the death of her father from an unexpected myocardial infarction when she was thirteen years of age, she had thought of herself as self-sufficient, in need of no one but herself to survive. Her mother provided Linda with a role model of success as a small-town newspaper editor.

Linda modified her views somewhat when she met and accepted the teaching of the campus minister at A.C.U. She had always considered herself a "good person" and saw no great need of personal change. Her attitudes, however, were in for a great reorganization as she slowly yielded the center of her life to the Lord Jesus Christ and trusted in him to forgive her and to run her life. She realized that no matter how many causes she undertook, all of her best efforts were of no value in gaining the best gift of all: a personal relationship with a loving, caring God. Since her conversion, she'd seen her efforts in a new light and felt a new "correctness" in her motivation.

"There!" Linda stood back, admired the last poster, and leaned it up against the side of the house to dry. She was alone but felt no hesitation at her vocalization. "Perhaps I should have made the words red instead of black."

At that moment her large tabby cat raced around the front of her apartment with a large, tan, galloping Great Dane in pursuit. Attached to the dog by a short leash was a rather surprised and breathless man who appeared to be in limited control of the situation.

"Mike, stop!" The young man planted his heels into the grass at the corner of the brick house. Linda jumped out of the way of the animals, knocking her posters to the ground in a disorganized heap. The dog came to a stop, more from the clatter of the falling posters than from his owner's command.

"Oh, just fine! Now I've got grass on all these freshly painted signs."

"I'm terribly sorry, ma'am." Matt Stone paused to catch his

breath. Mike, on the other hand, wasn't even panting. The cat slipped off unscathed, and the dog lost interest in keeping up the chase. Apparently sensing that Matt was postponing his walk for the time being, and no longer seeing the cat, Mike laid down in the grass at his owner's feet. "Stay, boy!" Matt spoke the words but doubted that this woman in front of him would put much stock in his ability to control the large animal, considering what she had seen so far.

"Oh, I guess it will be okay. These first few were almost dry anyway." Linda saw the man staring at her posters, reading each one as she replaced them against the wall to finish drying. "Are you interested in the message?"

"Huh? . . . Oh, uh . . . yeah." Matt blushed as if he had been caught looking at something he shouldn't have. He slowed his breathing and hoped he didn't appear too winded from his run down the road. For the first time since his return from Africa, he remembered his promise to get into better shape. "Say, I'm sorry about my dog. It's just that we haven't seen each other for a few months and he's a little overexcited. Do you know the Tanners who live on the corner? They've been keeping him for me," Matt added, looking at the large animal resting at his feet.

"The Tanners? Sure, they seem like very nice people. Mr. Tanner helped pull my car out of a ditch last winter with his tractor. He wouldn't take anything for it either."

"That sounds like Mr. Tanner. I met them at church up in Fairfax."

"You said they were keeping your dog for you. Were you out of town?" Linda hoped this unexpected intruder wouldn't think her questioning too forward.

"I was out of the country for a few months." Matt declined to elaborate, hoping not to sound boastful.

His answer stimulated Linda's curiosity, but she was hesitant to ask any more questions. Instead, Matt changed the subject and began to ask her about the posters.

"Are you planning a protest?"

"Well, not me exactly. I agreed to make these to help out some friends who are planning a rally up in Fairfax."

"That's pretty bold . . . Aren't you afraid of being arrested?" Matt thought the question sounded pretty stupid and was aware that he felt very much like a schoolboy trying to talk to a girl for the first time. He relaxed a little when she laughed.

"No, I'm not afraid of being arrested. But then again, I'm pretty new at this sort of protest, and so far all I've done is make a few signs." Linda was also aware of some school-days feelings and found herself wishing she was not half-covered with paint.

Mike yawned and closed his eyes. Obviously his walk had been terminated for the time being.

"What's the matter, Mike? Did you get out of shape without me?" Matt stroked the back of the young, golden dog whose weight had last tipped the scales at 127 pounds.

"That's an unusual name for a dog." Linda knelt down and patted the dog's muscular shoulders.

"Mike's an unusual dog." Matt watched for a reaction but observed none. "What's your name?" Matt's eyes briefly locked with Linda's before returning his gaze to the apparently sleeping dog.

"Linda Baldwin." She held out her hand after a quick inspection to assure herself that her palm was paint-free.

"Matt Stone." Linda noticed that his hands were smooth but strong. "Are you a student?"

"Yes. I'm getting my graduate degree in education at A.C.U. What about you?"

"I'm finishing up a general surgery residency at T.U." Matt wasn't always comfortable telling people what he did; he was afraid people would immediately expect him to fit a typical surgeon stereotype.

Mike began to stir, interested in moving on. Matt hoped that the large animal would decide he wanted to stay a bit longer, but the dog began to stand and stretch his legs.

"I'd like to hear how the rally goes . . ."

"It's not until November. I just like working ahead to get everything taken care of early, so it doesn't pile up."

Matt held tightly to Mike's leash as the dog stood up to announce the restart of his walk. Matt wanted to continue talking to this attractive young woman, but he couldn't think of anything that didn't have the ring of a come-on to it; so he just slapped Mike's back fondly and kept quiet. He didn't understand how he could feel so confident in life-and-death emergencies but so self-conscious in other areas.

"Nice meeting you."

Linda smiled. "Nice to meet you too . . . and you too, Mike!" She knelt down and stroked the dog's ears.

Mike began walking towards the Tanner farm, Matt slowing him down and talking over his shoulder. "I guess Mike means to remind me that I did come out to walk with *him*."

Linda watched the pair walk to the corner. She didn't return her eyes to her work until Matt had disappeared behind a row of birch trees a good three minutes later.

◆ ◆ ◆

Tony passed the time in the clinic's waiting room reading *Sports Illustrated*. He was not allowed in for the "harvesting" procedure but would be included later when the fertilized embryos would be introduced into his wife's uterus. He did not mind the former and in fact freely admitted that the thought of introducing a long needle into his wife's ovaries made him a little queasy. And so he sat comfortably in his present role as supportive husband and seemed quite satisfied with the large, padded lounge chair and the magazine he had procured.

Down the hall from the waiting area, a nurse started an IV in the back of Carol's right hand. The ultrasound had confirmed that she had several ovarian follicles ready for aspiration. Also, her estradiol level had checked out okay. Everything was a "go."

"You'll be getting a little woozy now." The dark-skinned nurse introduced a needle into the IV line and injected a small dose of fentanyl (a narcotic painkiller) and Versed (a quick acting anti-anxiety drug that would make Carol forget these moments). In a few minutes Carol dozed off, only partially aware of her surroundings.

The nurse positioned Carol with her legs up in stirrups, as if on a delivery table. Carol cooperated passively. Dr. Harrison inserted a sterile lubricated speculum and washed the birth canal with an antiseptic and then with saline. He used a long needle to introduce lidocaine into the area adjacent to Carol's cervix. She remained aware of some pain and pressure but could not localize it well and drifted back to sleep after the doctor completed the injection. The doctor then placed an ultrasound probe in Carol's vaginal vault and positioned it to give a clear picture of her right ovary, then gently repositioned it to "see" or image the left.

"There . . ." Dr. Harrison spoke instructively to a resident physician standing to his right. "See, the left ovary has several maturing follicles that we can aspirate."

Dr. Harrison passed a long needle through the left vaginal fornix and into the left ovary at the location of a bulging cyst. He gently pulled back on the syringe after confirming proper position of the needle on the ultrasound screen. He repeated this technique four times over, each time withdrawing the cyst fluid along with the necessary immature egg cell that would be used for fertilization. The entire procedure took only fourteen minutes.

The collected oocytes were then carefully taken across the hall to an incubation lab, where their maturation could be assessed and where they could be incubated prior to combining them with Tony's sperm sample that had been collected that morning.

Just thirty-five minutes later, a nurse came and led Tony to a hospital room where Carol would be observed. Tony gave her a soft kiss on her forehead. "How are you feeling?"

"Mmmm . . . I'm tired . . . It wasn't so bad . . . I'm an old pro at this by now." Carol's voice trailed off. The limited amount of sleep she had gotten the night before plus the effects of the narcotic kept her asleep for the next four hours.

By 3 P.M., the Jennings were making the familiar trip back to Easton. In two days they would make the trip back for the implantation procedure. Neither Tony nor Carol felt much like talking. Both were in fact praying that this last hope for them to have children would be a success.

◆ ◆ ◆

Michael Simons entered Georgio's restaurant exactly one hour after Richards had been seated. In that time Richards had consumed two orders of breadsticks and two light beers and had started on a bottle of red wine. He obviously had not minded the wait; in fact, the small amount of anxiety he had about this meeting had slowly dissolved in his wine.

"Dr. Simons . . ." Richards stood up and extended his hand.

"Adam . . . hello." The two men shook hands and took their seats. "Sorry about the time . . . I had an add-on urgent case after clinic and then needed to stop at home to pick up these papers . . . Call me Michael. There's no reason for us to be so formal."

"Of course . . . I've taken the liberty to order some wine." Richards slowly poured Simons his first glass.

Simons purposefully evaded questions about the meeting's purpose, saying they would have plenty of time after they had been served. Richards, who was sufficiently relaxed at this point, had lost his strong need to know anyway.

The two men ate, drank, talked, and then ate and drank some more. The restaurant population thinned to only one other couple besides the two physicians. Georgio came and served the after-dinner coffee himself and greeted Adam Richards by his first name.

When the dishes were cleared, Simons opened the leather briefcase that had been at his side ever since he took his place opposite Richards. From that time until Georgio asked them to leave at 1 A.M., Simons presented his case. He began slowly with each example of fetal tissue research that had taken place in the past few years, including the use of aborted fetal tissue for experimental treatment of Parkinson's disease, diabetes, and other metabolic disorders, research that had met the approval of the Council on Ethical and Judicial Affairs of the American Medical Association. He answered all of Richards' questions in an orderly, sequential, and planned fashion. He prided himself on his own compulsive completeness and smiled, knowing he was captivating Richards with his presentation. Simons carefully detailed his own review of fetal heart anatomy and physiology and finally introduced the idea of using the hearts of aborted fetuses for use in transplantation.

Simons had prepared well. When asked about the legal implications of the work, he explained that no federal restrictions regulating the use of fetal tissue for transplantation or experimentation existed, and also that federal laws were in existence only for the protection of the recipient, not for the donor of such tissue. Some states had laws, Simons expounded, restricting the use of fetal tissue research—for example, Arizona, which forbade the use of fetal tissue for experimentation if the fetus was the product of an induced abortion. Other states, such as Michigan, forbade the actual abortion if it was contingent upon obtaining the fetus for experimentation.

"These conditions do not apply to us here in Kentucky. There are no current laws forbidding the use of fetal tissue obtained from abortion in medical research. The current administration in Washington has come a long way in lifting the previous restrictions on the use of fetal tissue from induced elective abortions." Simons' personality was vibrant, and his ideas were coming across as if what he proposed constituted a most natural and beneficial course of action that could salvage an untapped resource and perhaps provide help for hundreds of pediatric congenital heart patients at the same time.

Simons spoke with a steady, unwavering voice. He paused several times for effect, and also to allow questions when he could detect that Richards was about to interrupt. He kept his speaking volume low, so he could not be heard from the next table. Although he would not have doubted the respectability of his proposed project, he did understand that this was an area with explosive emotional implications; so he ceased speaking altogether or changed the subject whenever their waiter approached.

Richards felt somehow spiritually moved at the suggestions that Simons made. Perhaps it was because of the volume of Simons' voice, but for whatever reason, Adam Richards found himself leaning forward to catch every word. He felt as if he would be listening intently even if Simons were speaking at a normal volume. A subtle yet gripping sense of power began insinuating itself into Richards' mind. It seemed as if the virus that had snared Simons was now breaking down the initial defense mechanisms in its new host, Adam Richards. And Simons could see the transformation taking place. At first Richards questioned; later he would accept. Eventually he too would be throttled with a self-love and would add his own embellishment to the research plans Simons had initiated.

Both of these men were straying close to the edge of accountability. Each one possessed positions of leadership and had ceased to be watched by senior members of their professions at a level that otherwise would perhaps be likely to call such a project into question before it was underway.

Asked to help with the project, Adam Richards replied without hesitation, "Yes." He felt manipulated but also felt strangely like he was boldly progressing into an area of great need. His answer came at the end of a long evening, and yet somehow he felt very awake and alert, as if the plans they had discussed had left him more alive and rejuvenated than before. At first he had doubts, but he could not help being convinced that this surgeon before him was interested in the common good of his patients. *After all, this is the man who helped my son.*

Richards sealed his reply with a handshake. The two men knew they still had plenty of groundwork to do in designing their study. They made plans for their next meeting, at which time specifics as to the actual abortions could be discussed. Simons deliberately did not want to talk about the specifics at their first meeting. Although he was not an obstetrician, he knew some modifications were going to have to be made in the manner in which abortions were done. Currently, Simons knew, late second trimester abortions were done by hypertonic saline intra-uterine injection, a process that resulted in a burned, dead fetus. He knew alterations would have to be made if the hearts were to be of value to anyone else. He also knew that any suggested changes in a doctor's normal pattern, especially coming from an outsider, were not likely to be received out of hand. For this reason Simons carefully skirted controversial issues during his first meeting with Richards and suggested that they work out the details later, at whatever time he could sense a favorable response.

Adam Richards drove home alone. Had he been stopped and tested, he would have been found to be legally intoxicated. He felt as if he was in total control, however, and for the first time in months he was happy to have something other than his normal work to take his mind off his current social problems. After arriving home, he poured himself a small glass of his favorite brandy. Even with his mind full of new thoughts, he could not stave off the effects of the food and alcohol he had consumed. In fifteen minutes he lay asleep on his still-made bed, fully dressed except for his tie, which he had removed in the car.

CHAPTER
5

KENTUCKY politics had been as colorful as the surrounding countryside for as long as the state had been a state. Colorful, however, not in the sense of a beautiful landscape. The politics in and about the Bluegrass State were balanced by many contrasting shades. Poor coal mining communities were scattered throughout the eastern part of the state. It was here that industry met with rich traditional Appalachian mountain lore. To the middle and western parts of the state, tobacco was king. The pro-tobacco lobby was real and alive, and its economic rise and fall affected the majority of farming households. The rich also came to live and play in Kentucky. Nowhere else were the horse-related businesses and monies so loudly touted and dreamed. It was in this setting that a unique breed of Kentucky politicians emerged—friends of the poor and friends of the rich, supporters of tobacco and horsemen with an interest in the preservation of rich tradition.

Upon this palette of contrasting color were introduced the problems of education, as Kentucky politicians tried to improve the future for its youth in a state with one of the highest dropout rates in the U.S.A. Politicians also balanced the battleground of women's rights, animal rights, gay rights, and the ever-present issue of abortion.

None of these issues were particularly bothersome for Layton Redman. As a young man with a naturally rough exterior, he stood a full six feet, two inches tall and had been touted as a possible Heisman Trophy candidate as a fullback during his final year at Taft University. A candidate only, it turned out, because a knee injury plucked him from the lineup for a full eight weeks after his strong start. He had viewed politics with a watchful eye ever since his high school years. He had connections with the common man, as he successfully ran a tobacco farm prior to obtaining his law degree. He had gained statewide notoriety as a non-bending prosecuting attorney in the city of Louisville over the past three years. He was tough on crime, a promoter of pro-tobacco legislation, a supporter of the preservation of the horse industry, and also had helped argue several cases that had placed him on favorable terms with the large coal-workers' unions. Less well-known were his positions on abortion issues (he was firmly pro-choice) and his absence of any traditional church affiliation, an affiliation that had always been a plus for any successful candidate in Kentucky politics.

Redman now stood as the early favorite in a three-man race for the governor's office. He had become an official candidate during the hot month of August and had made his first official speech as a candidate at a tobacco festival held just outside Fairfax. He ran as an independent, and as such he depended on a large volunteer staff to coordinate his fight against established party politics. People of both parties liked him, and his public image was certainly not harmed by his engagement to the daughter of a former Senator.

Financing his campaign was a twenty-four-hours-a-day job. To his credit, he had courted the rich industries of the state early, and he had courted them knowledgeably. A remarkable but little-known fact was that a very generous contributor was the Fairfax Family Planning Services, Inc. Many simply called it the F.F.P. Obviously someone in that corporation was concerned about the return of decision-making power over abortions to the state. That person was Dr. Adam Richards, who had definitely done his political homework.

Redman worked heavily on first-time voters and had organized volunteer support on almost every college and university campus in the state. On one such visit to Appalachian Christian University, he met a particularly diligent young woman who eventually became the chairman of the Redman for Governor Committee on that campus. It was at A.C.U. that he did not expect to get support. In fact, he had come very close to writing off the campus entirely, except for a letter he received from this particular young woman, expressing interest in staging a political rally on his behalf. The woman's name was Samantha Stelling.

Samantha Stelling was, in fact, responsible for organizing two significant events on behalf of the Redman candidacy. She organized a very successful voter registration drive, and also a political rally to launch his outreach to the university and the areas south of Fairfax.

Despite her unquestionable help in the early stages of his campaign, Layton Redman had come to regret his association with this pretty, young political enthusiast. His pre-candidate commitment to himself had been to limit his social involvement with anyone who could not be seen as a strength to his campaign. He had definitely not planned on outside romantic interests beyond the highly public relationship he had with Janice Sizemore, his fiancée. Even that relationship had taken a back burner to his current aspirations for office.

And so, as with many in the public eye, Redman began to take steps to see that the brief affair he'd had with Samantha would not reach the platform of public debate. It truly was brief in its pleasure, but like many "small" mistakes he feared its destructive potential. He had never intended upon falling into a relationship of this sort, and certainly it was of no design of Samantha's, at least not from the beginning. A first planning session had turned into a second, and then a third, where the remaining other three members of Redman's volunteer A.C.U. campus staff were coincidentally absent. Samantha had innocently expressed physical hunger, and Redman had generously offered dinner in return for all her diligence. Dinner was a pleasant experience that included a lot of laughter and talk about everything but the campaign. Following dinner they stopped by Stelling's apartment. Unfortunately, that stop was not the only visit to her apartment that Redman would make. In the next two weeks an observant neighbor could have counted Redman's B.M.W. in Stelling's parking spot seven times.

Redman had made promises to Samantha that perhaps he intended to keep, perhaps not; but at least they had allowed him a little freedom to go on with his work without fear of public scandal from her. He had come to his senses and was glad that a majority of his public association with Samantha was over, the political rally that she had organized having been a historical success.

A full ten weeks after the rally, Redman finally returned a phone message from a rather distressed Samantha. She was, to his dismay, pregnant. He had not even considered that she might not be protecting herself. She was hurt by his questioning about whether she was sure who the father was. She had been inexperienced, he knew, and that had created an even stronger attraction for him at first. Just how inexperienced she was shocked Redman even more. He understood from their conversations that she was from a conservative background, and he knew she attended a school with religious affiliation, but he had no idea that this young woman was a virgin.

He grew immediately angry, suspicious, and unwilling to accept responsibility for the situation. He did not believe her story of her previous innocence. He was sure he would have known about that. Regardless, his advice was predictable: she should have an abortion. He would make arrangements for it himself. He had a close supporter who could help her out. Surely, he thought, she would go along with that. His comments reflected his cut-and-dry political savvy. Anyone could see that this was the best alternative for everyone involved. She had put up a minor fight but obviously was interested in maintaining her chances for a relationship with this promising politician and desperately wanted help, both financially and emotionally.

At Layton's urging she agreed to see Dr. Adam Richards. Her appointment slip arrived in the mail in only two days; the appointment was not for two weeks. Apparently his office was a busy place, and the abortion services he provided were in demand not only in Fairfax, but his waiting list bulged with the names, some made up, of many women from the surrounding counties and other major cities—the names of women who wanted only to slip in and out of a town other than their own unnoticed.

Kentucky politics would continue to be colorful for a long time.

◆ ◆ ◆

Carol Jennings looked around the procedure room in the reproductive services clinic. This time it was for "conceptus transfer."

Tony waited anxiously with her for this last technical phase of the in-vitro fertilization attempt. Her mature oocytes and her husband's sperm had been incubated prior to their combination. This had resulted in four newly fertilized embryos that were in need of implantation.

Carol was again positioned on her back with appropriate exposure obtained by the now all too familiar stirrups. A sterile speculum was inserted to provide clear visualization of her cervix. Dr. Harrison inserted an IVF catheter into Carol's cervix. He then gently washed the "concepti" into her uterus with a small syringe. They kept Carol on her back while a nurse carried the IVF catheter to the next room for an embryologist to examine. This assured successful transfer of each embryo. All of the embryos were placed in Carol's uterus to give each one the optimal chance of implantation. Carol and Tony had requested the clinic to follow a protocol that mandated an attempt at the implantation of each fertilized embryo, so that no extra embryos would be left behind to be discarded. In only a few minutes the door to the minor operating suite opened, and the embryologist gave the okay to Dr. Harrison.

"James, everything looks good from my standpoint. No embryos were left in the IVF catheter." The embryologist spoke softly, with only his head leaning through the partially opened door.

"Thanks, Ivan. That's what I want to hear." James Harrison removed the speculum and, with the nurse's assistance, helped return Carol to a more comfortable position. "We're all done with this part, Carol. They have a room for you on the third floor. They will be giving you a progesterone injection every day for a while."

"Oh, yes. Empiric luteal support, doctor." Carol tilted her head back and spoke in an overexaggerated, pompous tone, with her mouth drawn into a stiff frown. She immediately broke into a grin following her parody on the medical terms she knew too well.

"I forget that I'm dealing with a patient with a superior medical education!" Harrison laughed.

Tony rolled his eyes and made a mental note to ask his wife the meaning of "luteal support" once he and Carol were alone.

"When will I be able to go home?" Carol was not thrilled at this change in the routine.

"The admission will only be for initiation of the injections and to keep you in bed for a few days. We don't need you up and about caring for your husband or worrying about your job and sneaking in for a few hours here and there, you know."

"You can't keep me from worrying." Carol's voice had changed from sarcastic to sober.

"I know . . . and I promise that we won't keep you long." Dr. Harrison's gentle touch on Carol's right shoulder signaled the end of the conversation.

Tony helped push Carol's stretcher towards her room and assisted her into her bed. He ceremoniously fluffed her pillow. "There." They had not spoken directly to each other since the transfer procedure had been completed. Each was thinking about the hopes that had been dashed so many times before. Tony looked out the window and onto the front lawn of the hospital, his memory full of the previous attempts and their previous failures at conception. After what must have been ten full minutes, he turned again to face his wife.

Carol looked at her husband, who had become her strength and encouragement over the past few months in the face of their present ordeal. She bit her lip in order to squelch a sob of emotion. Tony's eyes met hers, and he saw the tears welling up in her eyes through the tears in his own. He wanted to speak but did not want to cry. Eventually he did manage to talk without faltering.

"It will work this time . . . I know it will work."

◆ ◆ ◆

Linda Baldwin hung up the phone and put a red circle around the 16 on the calendar. In black felt-tip ink she wrote, "Tanners' church fellowship meal, 6 P.M." She wondered what had brought on the out-of-the-blue invitation, but she seemed satisfied at their explanation that a visitors' fellowship meal was given twice a year and all the members were asked to invite their neighbors and friends. She preferred to use her spare evenings hitting the books, but she had just finished two papers and couldn't honestly use that as an excuse to stay home alone. Besides, the Tanners seemed like sweet people, and she found it difficult to say no to any sincere request. This one really wasn't demanding at all, except for the time.

She put on a tape—*Mozart's Greatest Hits*—and turned the volume up just past midway. She thought the title belittled this master composer, but it did contain some of her favorites, so she refused to let the album's title stand in the way of her enjoying it.

She then began fixing dinner. The meal typified her concern for nutrition and calories: a green salad, four ounces of broiled turkey, half an acorn squash seasoned only with butter substitute and light salt, and a glass of mineral water. While she ate, she lazily leafed through her well-worn copy of *Food Values of Portions Commonly Used*, noting the protein, calorie, and mineral content of her present meal. On the rare occasion when she was tempted to stray from her healthy eating pattern with a jaunt to a local burger joint, she merely turned to the pages on fast-food meals where she had highlighted the saturated fat content of the forbidden items.

Her discipline carried over into the other areas of her life by necessity. Her schedule was always tight, and she posted a master schedule on her refrigerator next to her calendar. On this schedule she recorded her successes and failures in a variety of categories including nutrition, aerobic exercise, study time, and daily quiet times of prayer and Bible reading. About once every two months, as her tolerance for her own obsessive organization waned, a schedule would be torn down when, falling behind in one category or another, not wanting to be enslaved by this cardboard planner, she would proclaim her liberty in a glorious trashing of the schedule. Invariably she would realize that her life was too busy and complex to accomplish everything she desired without careful planning; so sooner or later the master schedule would again take shape and find its place on the refrigerator door.

Linda cleared the dishes and stacked them in the sink. She then edged up the volume of the Mozart tape and vigorously washed the dishes while intermittently directing the symphony with a sweeping fork or whatever utensil happened to be in her hand at the time.

She looked over at the stack of signs she had painted for the pro-life rally. Her thoughts drifted to the startling encounter she'd had with the Great Dane and his boyish owner. *Hadn't he mentioned that he attended the same church as the Tanners?* She looked out the window without noticing her own reflection staring back because the night had already fallen. *Surely this invitation to the Tanners' church has nothing to do with him?* She blushed at the thought that he might have put the Tanners up to the request, but then scolded herself with a visible shake of her head. She felt as if she were acting like a schoolgirl, but she couldn't help her initial, hopeful speculation. She rejected the idea and told herself it must have been too long since her last date. Not because of a lack of chances, of course, but because she had promised to make her schoolwork a priority at this point in her busy, scheduled life.

Nonetheless, Linda found herself thinking about Matt Stone just about every time she saw the red circle around September 16.

◆ ◆ ◆

Simons looked around the vacant room that was located in the rear of the Family Planning Services Clinic and smiled. The room had been vacated nine months before when a former associate of Richards dissolved his partnership and moved out. The partner had joined Richards fresh out of residency, and his main attraction to the clinic's work was a monetary one. Richards' offer was easily double any other offer he had received. Perhaps this was because so much of the work demanded a near-constant exposure to distasteful second trimester abortion techniques, but the explanation that Richards gave was a predictable one: "We are doing highly specialized work within our specialty, and our salary should reflect that subspecialization." His new partner worked for just over a year before informing Richards of his decision to move on. Richards felt sure that he was quitting because of the increasing activity of pro-life demonstrators who staged two disruptive sit-ins during the month his colleague called it quits. Nonetheless, his former partner had expressed his desire to resume a busier normal obstetrical practice and had left after his minimal two weeks notice the winter before. Because his contract had included the common "covenant not to compete," he had been required to move outside of Fairfax prior to setting up a new practice of his own.

Now, however, this office space would take on a different function. Located just down the hall from the minor operating/delivery suites, it was accessible from only one door and had no windows to the outside. The space was actually two rooms, and one had already been equipped with appropriate electrical and plumbing fixtures should the space be needed for additional lab or examining room functions. Simons seemed definitely pleased at Richards' suggestion that he consider doing the experimentation in his facility, as that solved several major obstacles he had foreseen. For one, the fetal hearts would need to be tested immediately after they had been obtained, as prolonged anoxia would damage the cardiac muscle and render his assessment of their capabilities far from accurate. The second obstacle that would be overcome with this new development was the problem of gaining appropriate unsupervised time in his cardiac lab at the university hospital. If he were to do the work in his lab at T.U., he would need to seek approval to conduct the experiments he desired from the institution's research review committee. Even though he was the vice-chairman of that committee, he was not confident he could slip by an uncritiqued approval of this work in the timeframe he desired. What he *was* confident of, however, was the certain praise and approval he would get to perform the transplants if his research would confirm his calculations. *That will be no problem, no problem at all.*

Michael Simons had not anticipated that things would run so smoothly. He made mental notes as he inspected the rooms that would house his future lab. He would need good quality overhead surgical lighting and a place to set up his cardiopulmonary bypass pump.

The pump had revolutionized cardiac surgery, making successful open heart surgery a reality. The pump was an expensive item, but fortunately one he possessed in his lab at T.U. The pump would be necessary to circulate and oxygenate the infant's blood in order to keep the heart alive during the testing period, as the fetal lungs were still too immature to do their job, even if the heart was able to perform on its own. This hypothesis remained central to Simons' theory that infants too young to survive may still have useful hearts that could function as long as they were used in a second infant with other more mature organs. He was not using his pump at present with any of his projects at the university, and he could easily explain its absence by its need for continual service upkeep.

The last two weeks had been busy ones for both Simons and Richards. They had met five times and discussed nearly every aspect of their planned coordinated research effort. It had not been so easy to convince Richards that a change in his technique would be necessary. Eventually, however, he agreed to modify his technique on a few of his patients in order to deliver a specimen with an actively contracting heart with a minimum of anoxic muscle damage. From Simons' autopsy studies, they could easily show that the older the fetus the better, and this limitation would make delaying some second trimester abortions desirable in order to obtain a closer to mature cardiac muscle capable of sustaining adequate blood flow in the recipient fetus. They agreed not to encourage delays in planned abortions, at least not in the beginning, until they had more data to support the need for an older cardiac specimen. Richards saw no problem with obtaining older specimens later if needed, as delays secondary to a busy schedule or encouraging a patient to undergo a required wait to "think over your decision" could easily cause a one- to two-week delay while the heart matured.

While Simons busily formulated a needs list for his new lab and juggled financing from his other projects to cover the expenses, Richards began reviewing the clinic's records for previous years on abortions for patients far enough along in their pregnancies to fit into the guidelines of Simons' protocol. So far he had reviewed just over eight months of work and found an average of one to two acceptable candidates per week. Most abortions in his facility were still done in the first trimester, when the growing fetuses were much too small to be acceptable for use in transplantation. But because it was well publicized as one of the few centers performing late abortions, patients were attracted from many other cities to Richards' facility. Many came from the north—most of these from Cincinnati or Cleveland, responding to the expensive ads in their local newspapers, beginning their encounter with the clinic with a simple phone call on Richards' 800 line. Many paid in cash, not even submitting a paper insurance trail, even though many of these women continued to justify their positions as completely aboveboard.

Now Richards opened the door to the future lab. Simons was inspecting the electrical fixtures on the far wall. "I'll have a new lock put on this door."

Simons didn't look up. "Huh? . . . Oh, good idea . . . Say, have you thought about bringing oxygen hookups into this room?"

"It's on my list. For now I thought you could use portable tanks."

"I suppose we could make that work for a while . . . We really shouldn't have to stay in this facility that long, anyway." Simons seemed distant, almost distracted from his present conversation.

"I've almost finished my review of the cases done here at the clinic."

Simons brightened. "And?" His voice had a sarcastic, superior air about it, a tone Richards disliked.

"We can anticipate about one acceptable pump run a week." "Pump run" referred to placing a patient on cardiopulmonary bypass during an open cardiac operation. While the heart was still, the cardiopulmonary bypass pump did the work of the patient's heart and lungs, oxygenating and pumping the blood to the rest of the body. For this experiment, he was stating simply that he thought they would have one "donated" heart per week that Simons could analyze while on the pump, to assess just how strong the pumping ability of the heart was.

Simons' mind wandered as he contemplated what Richards had just reported. The more he looked at his data, the stronger his feeling became that thousands of donor organs would be available from this nearly untapped resource. He was confident of one thing: with four thousand abortions performed each day in the United States alone, he was on the verge of opening up a whole new source of potential transplant organs. *Who can predict where this will lead? . . . Liver transplants, . . . Pancreas transplants, . . . There is a shortage of infant organs everywhere you look.* Simons stared at the far corner of the room, not really focusing on anything. *I am at the pinnacle of this breakthrough,* he mused quietly to himself.

"One every week?" Simons' own spoken reply brought him back

to the here and now. "That's better than I would have thought. You are doing more of this kind of work than just about anyone, from what I can see."

"It pays to have the right connections, I guess." Richards looked at his feet as he thought about that bit of notoriety. It was a fact that Richards was quietly proud of, but not one that he advertised except to the few referring physicians who needed his help for patients of their own. "I need to get a bite to eat. You want anything?"

"No thanks. I've really got to get back to T.U. I have a clinic that is starting in fifteen minutes."

"Okay. I'll walk out with you." The two men moved toward the rear exit. "Did you park out front?"

"No . . . in the back."

"Good. I was going to suggest that you use the staff lot anyway." Simons walked towards a black Porsche parked in the far corner of the lot by itself, as if he were uninterested in Richards' comments. But Richards persisted. "That your car?"

"No, it's my mother's." Simons' sarcasm was broken by a faint smile. In less than a minute Simons deactivated the alarm system, opened the door, and was quickly out of the lot and heading for the university hospital.

Richards smiled and shook his head as he listened to Simons throttling north away from the clinic.

◆ ◆ ◆

Carol Jennings packed her small suitcase again. She neatly folded her nightgown and collected her toiletries. Tony planned to be there to pick her up by 10 A.M. She always multiplied that by the "Tony factor" so she would not be too upset at his relaxed approach to time schedules.

The news had been good, outstanding even. The early ultrasound results had confirmed a successful implantation. "Preggers!" she had squealed to Tony over the phone the night before. Although it was hard to contain her excitement, she wanted to be realistic about her chances for carrying this pregnancy to completion. She had become pregnant the last time too, she cautioned herself, and she did not want to have too much false hope. Nonetheless, she was almost outwardly glowing with her joy over this new situation and felt that her chances were good. Even Dr. Harrison had responded with "cautious optimism" and had agreed that she could resume her normal schedule as long as she avoided strenuous exercise and continued the daily hormone injections.

Carol looked out over the front lawn of the hospital. The weather was nice, a "Chamber of Commerce day," as some would say, with a promise of clear skies until the weekend. The weather reflected but did not produce Carol's mood. Even a blizzard could not have chilled her present feelings. She looked back at her watch and then slipped it off and set it beside the clock in the room. 10:20. She was trying to be patient, but perhaps her desire to get out of the hospital was taxing her ambivalence about the wait. She supposed Tony would have to be extremely late, even for Tony, for her to get too upset today.

Just as she slipped her watch back on, Tony walked through the open door. He carried a large bouquet of flowers and a large silver balloon with the word "CONGRATULATIONS!" on the front.

"Tony! Don't you think you're just a little early for all this?" Carol was putting up a protest, but she would have missed this kind of treatment if Tony had come empty-handed. He was quite predictable in this area, as were Carol's perfunctory, required protests.

"Oh sure, but I just couldn't keep myself from doing it . . . A genetic mishap in my childhood, I suppose." He was smiling sheepishly.

"Since when did Mr. Business-brain start understanding genetics?" Carol was laughing now. "Come on, my discharge has been ready for two hours!"

"Okay! OOOOOkay!" Tony was talking in an exaggerated whiny, sing-song tone. "We're out of here!" He picked up the flowers again, kissed his wife matter-of-factly, balanced Carol's overnight bag in his other hand, and headed for the door. "Coming?"

"Right behind you."

The Jennings celebrated at their favorite restaurant that night. It had been a long time since they had been this happy.

Under the surface, both Tony and Carol were cautiously anxious.

On the surface, and to each other, they were strong and optimistically confident. Technology and normal success rates of IVF were in their favor, and that is the voice they allowed at their mind's forefront. Somewhere behind all that, however, a sense of prayer was fueled by the persistent memory of past failures.

◆ ◆ ◆

Samantha Stelling threw the folded newspaper across the room where it collided with the tin trash can in a violent clamor. She had glanced at the first page and had no desire to read further.

Independent Candidate Wins Support
From Within Established Political Parties

In an unprecedented move, the governor of Kentucky today threw his unofficial support to the independent candidate, Layton Redman. In a speech in which everyone expected the governor to support his party's candidate, the governor gave his full support to the political newcomer, Redman, stating, "He stands for all the right things that my party has classically stood for. His record of straight talk and unbiased . . ."

Samantha thought it unamusing that another wave of morning sickness would be brought on by reading the morning paper. *Or is this really morning sickness at all? Perhaps it's just my frustration with the whole situation.* She picked up the newspaper and deposited it in the trash can, which she had missed on the first shot. She then scurried to the bathroom with her hand over her mouth and emptied her breakfast into the cold American Standard commode—an action her father had always called "hugging the porcelain Buick." Nothing about this pregnancy pleased her to this point, and definitely not this.

Samantha had been brought up by a Baptist father and a Catholic mother. She'd felt she was ready for just about anything until she found herself trapped in this present situation. *Trapped* is exactly how she felt. She was proud of her conservative background. She grew up attending Mass with her mother and later, in high school, took a zealous interest in the activities of her father's Baptist church. She would have told anyone that she was, without a doubt, a Christian. She had, after all, responded to her fair share of the weekly altar calls during her high school years. But now, in her present pregnant state, she had difficulty seeing herself as anything but a despised sinner.

Sam had not gone without previous trials of her Christian belief. She had lost her mother in an automobile accident when she was only ten and had lost her father during her senior year of high school, after watching him battle stomach cancer for a short four months. In the aftermath of her father's death, she felt as if she really had true faith. But now, in the absence of any positive feelings, her doubts began to emerge. Perhaps feelings had played too big a role in her own personal faith inventory.

She had decided to attend Appalachian Christian University both because of the excellent financial aid she qualified for and because of the overall atmosphere and Christian emphasis she experienced during her visit. She had gotten involved with various campus organizations and causes and served on the student government as treasurer for her first two years. Perhaps it was student government that whetted her appetite to assist in the present state governor's race. For whatever reason, she now regretted ever getting involved with the campaign process at all. She had decided, partly out of an elevated sense of patriotic and Christian duty, that she had both the ability and responsibility to help the best candidate get elected. She had studied the choices carefully and then determined to see if she could make a difference in the outcome for the candidate she felt was most qualified. This had led to her involvement with Redman and indirectly to her pregnancy and present bitterness.

Layton's personality had been almost overwhelming to Sam. She had never laughed so much as the night they first went to dinner. She was a physically attractive girl, with long, blonde hair and a smile that could melt even a politician's heart. Layton Redman had begun discussing his own background and his desire to help the people of Kentucky. Sam had been taken in by his charm and had trusted his sincerity. She sympathized with him when he later told her about his communication problems with his fiancée.

In the beginning she was more than naive. She encouraged him with innocent hugs that were intended as friendly gestures. In the end she found within herself a passion that she had no desire to turn off. She had been overcome with guilt and had eventually been able to sever the relationship because Redman feared for his public image and did not want to break his engagement until after the election. She had hoped that things would later work out for them and had secretly fantasized about a marriage to a governor and the elaborate wedding that would surely precede it.

Now all she had was an unwanted pregnancy and the confusion that surrounded it. She had withdrawn from all of her classes in the tenth week of the semester. She couldn't keep her mind in one place long enough to effectively read the morning paper, much less a college textbook. She had a small income because of Social Security benefits from her parents and a modest savings account because of her father's life insurance. Unsure of what to do, she strayed farther and farther from her conservative roots. Her background gave her a sensitive conscience and the belief that abortion was not an option. Layton, who seemed to understand the situation clearly and claimed that she could not possibly be objective, encouraged her to exercise her right to abortion; he said he would take care of every detail. He seemed to see everything in black and white. To Sam, nothing was definite any more; everything was in question, including her faith. *Would a true follower of Christ end up like this?*

Sam stood to her feet in front of the bathroom sink. "Uuuurruuuck!" She spit repeatedly into the sink, trying to clear her mouth of the bitter taste. She rinsed her mouth and washed her face prior to edging into the next room and sprawling out on the couch. An appointment reminder card had arrived the day before and was lying on the table next to the couch. The card had Dr. Adam Richards' name and the address of the Fairfax Family Planning Clinic on the front. Her appointment time was 10 A.M. for the following day. A small note in the corner indicated that payment for the appointment had already been made. Sam lifted the small postcard and read it again: "Adam Richards, M.D., specializing in the practice of obstetrics and gynecology."

Perhaps it won't hurt to at least go and discuss my options . . . He is a doctor—so at least he can give me a good outside opinion.

◆ ◆ ◆

Matt looked down at his scrubs and shoe-covers. The shoe-covers, which previously had been blue, were now almost totally drenched with dark blood, which also stained his scrubs in large, generous splotches. He shed his sterile gown and gloves and walked to the scrub sink just outside the operating room to wash off the blood that had soaked through his gown and onto his arms. He had just finished an emergency laparotomy in a thirty-year-old male who had sustained a close-range shotgun wound to the abdomen. The pellets had injured the patient's right colon and right iliac artery and vein and had peppered the small bowel. The procedure had gone well, but the blood loss had been substantial, requiring a sixteen-unit packed red blood cell infusion just to maintain the patient's blood pressure. Matt had started the procedure alone but was joined a few minutes later by the trauma surgery attending. The attending, Dr. David Gant, was obviously "pumped" by the save they had just facilitated.

"Good work, Stone." Dr. Gant joined Matt at the scrub sink. "It's been several months since I've seen that combination of injuries."

"Oh, yeah? I guess it's been about thirty years since I scrubbed on a shotgun blast to the iliac artery." Matt laughed, partly from the relief of completing a stressful case and partly because of the hour, 3 A.M.

"Oh, so this was a RANDO, huh?" Gant jousted Matt in the ribs. *RANDO* referred to a case the resident hadn't scrubbed on before, trauma-ease for "Resident Ain't Never Done One."

"Yeah, I guess so. I've helped on injured colons and even an iliac vein injury, but not both together at one time."

"You've got to start somewhere. Anyway, fine job in there. You looked as if you had everything under control by the time I got here."

"Obviously you couldn't see my undershorts." Matt laughed again.

"You weren't *that* scared!" Gant was laughing now, too.

Matt only laughed and gave no reply to his attending's comment.

Gant spoke up again as Matt was heading back into the O.R. "Call me if you have any more problems. I'm going to get some sleep. You shouldn't need me anymore tonight anyway, unless something else comes in."

"Thanks for your help."

"No problem. Sure beats non-operative trauma." Gant stripped off his shoe-covers and mask, both of which were blood-spattered. "See you later in the morning."

Matt helped move the patient to the recovery room, where he relegated an intern to the job of writing the post-op orders. Matt dictated a quick operative note, gave further instructions to the intern, and then went down to the waiting room to talk to the family.

There were over a dozen people waiting for word about the patient, including the grandmother of both the injured patient and the assailant. (The assailant's grandmother and the patient's grandmother were one and the same.) As was typical of so many patients, this one had been shot by someone he knew, and not by a stranger. Their reaction to Matt's words was showered with many tears, to the point that Matt was unsure that they understood everything had gone okay and that they expected the patient to survive. Matt explained everything a second and then a third time, until he satisfied even the patriarch of the family, and then slipped out of the room and headed for some fresh air.

Matt stepped out of the main entrance to the hospital and looked at the full moon, which highlighted the scattered clouds overhead. Often he would come out at night after a case or a patient evaluation just to think or to remind himself of his own smallness within God's vast universe of creation. Sometimes he would contemplate. Sometimes he would pray. Always he would remind himself of his own dependency on a power outside himself, of his dependency upon God.

Matt took long, slow breaths of the still, cool Kentucky air, as if each breath brought new life, new motivation to continue to work long hours. Tonight he also wondered about a phone call he had received just the evening before. Mrs. Tanner had called to remind him about the upcoming church supper. She had sounded almost mischievous in telling him of her wishes that he should come. She undoubtedly had another prospective match for him to meet. Mrs. Tanner had a big heart to go along with her generous waist and was forever playing matchmaker for the youth in the church fellowship. She had fixed her eyes on Matt Stone for some time now, and she had hopes that he could find just a little time for something other than his job.

Mrs. Tanner had known the Stone family for some time, having previously lived in Appalachia just down the hollow from the Stones twenty odd years before. Of course, that was a long time ago, and two husbands ago for Beatrice Tanner. Her first two husbands had both passed away, the first to a mining accident and the second to a ruptured abdominal aortic aneurysm just eight years ago. At the time of her first husband's death, Sandra Stone had taken care of Beatrice's then eight-month-old baby, Steven, for an entire week. Beatrice could never say enough about the Stone family ever since.

Perhaps it was because of this that Mrs. Beatrice Tanner decided to assist young Matt in the pursuit of the perfect helpmeet, or perhaps she was only doing what she felt natural doing for anyone. She did feel qualified for this sort of work, as she had landed three— count 'em—prime catches for herself in a twenty-year time span. And so it was that she invited her attractive young Christian neighbor, Linda Baldwin, to her church's bi-annual guest fellowship meal, in hopes of sparking the imagination of one young available Christian bachelor, Matthew Stone. Little did she know that the first sparks had already ignited a smoldering interest during a previously "arranged" meeting of the two aforementioned parties.

CHAPTER
6

THOUGH some believe the night is for renewal, it is not always so for the surgical resident, who often spends the night in sleepless activity, often waging small battles where the oft-used phrase "life and death hanging in the balance" gets its true meaning. Sleep for others, who take for granted its regular occurrence, brings about new energy, as the events of the day are sorted out and smoothed over in preparation for the next day's events and problems. For many, this sorting occurs in the dreams, where past events are filtered and filed with our only memory being a confused consortium of our thoughts and experiences. For the surgical resident, sleep is a reward—sometimes rare, but always appreciated. For others, concrete memories of past events have formed vivid, haunting dreams that make sleep a despised event, leading to its avoidance. This avoidance is short-lived, as natural drives continually prod us to seek daily renewal in the arms of our dreams.

And so it was for Dr. Adam Richards, who found his sleep a springboard for recurrent haunting memories, even while Matthew Stone found his renewal with a short-lived break, enjoying the night air while sitting on the front steps of the hospital.

Richards had been sure that the dream was gone forever. But now, as he sat upright in bed, his forehead studded with fresh perspiration and his heart racing, his memory goaded him again with the past he'd tried so desperately to bury. He slipped from beneath the sheets of his king-size bed, walked to the bar in the corner of his adjacent study, and poured himself a drink.

Richards shook his head as he returned to the present and sipped quietly at the bourbon in his glass. He thought he had successfully buried any negative effects of his early misguided abortion. Buried successfully, that is, until the nightmare recalling the events of that day resurfaced the night after Simons began requesting alterations of Richards' perfected abortion techniques to fit in with his planned experimentation. Now, for the past four nights, the dream had recurred with disturbing regularity. It also grew more grotesque with each passing night. As he poured himself a drink, the resurrected dream replayed itself yet again. In this night's variety, a swollen infant covered with blisters spoke to Richards in spite of the endotracheal tube that would prevent his talking. The infant clutched the edge of Richards' white coat, crying, "Save me! Save me! SAVE ME!" The infant's voice was overcome by the liquid rising from his lungs, and the voice died out in gargling, choking gasps.

Richards poured a second shot of Kentucky bourbon and drained it without pausing. The dreams had occurred once before, just after the event that had jeopardized his job. They had gone away before. He assured himself that they would go away again. At least he hoped—desperately—that they would go away again.

◆ ◆ ◆

Tony Jennings also awoke with a recurring dream. The dream had a familiar beginning, but the ending varied.

"Frow me the ball, Daddy!" A sandy-haired preschooler ran excitedly around the backyard, proudly displaying his new baseball glove.

"Stand still, son . . . Here it comes!" Tony beamed proudly with each catch. It didn't matter if the small boy only caught the ones that landed perfectly in the glove's pocket.

"Here, Daddy . . . catch!" The throw was high and bounced over the fence into the next yard. Tony climbed the fence and searched for the ball in the uncut grass. His neighbors were renters and rarely cut their grass until it went to seed.

The dream was always the same at this point. Tony spent a long time looking for the ball, while his son cried out, "Frow me the ball, Daddy! Frow the ball!" Tony got preoccupied with his search, and his son's cries faded. Finally, when he located the ball, he returned to his own yard, only to find his little son missing. Occasionally in the dream he found the little boy's glove. Other times he saw only a swinging gate. On one occasion he thought he heard the little boy cry out again. In tonight's dream he returned to the yard only to find an empty cradle, identical to the one he and Carol had purchased during her last IVF pregnancy. In each of the dreams he ran out into the street, yelling frantically for his son. Each time he awoke without succeeding in his search.

Like Adam Richards, Tony grunted and sat up with a start, covered with perspiration. Unlike Richards, he did not attempt to drown his dream in alcohol.

"Did the dream come back?" Carol asked softly, putting her hand on her husband's shoulder, noting that his back was slick with sweat.

Tony sat quietly for a few moments, ran his fingers through his dark hair, and sighed. "Yeah, the same dream again. I guess this thing is really getting to me."

"You can't control your dreams, honey . . . At least I can't control mine."

"Have you been having them, too?" Tony reached over and turned on the lamp next to their bed.

"A few." Carol sighed. The alarm clock radio read 4:05. "Now what?"

"I say we handle this the way we would handle any big problem that faces us. There's no way a few dreams should get us down after all we've been through together." Tony slipped out of bed and onto his knees, kneeling on the small throw rug just as he had done nightly since his conversion. His wife took this cue and joined him, dragging their large quilt around their shoulders as she went. She slipped her hand into Tony's.

They both began to pray, silently at first, then audibly, each in turn expressing both their fears and finally their praises to the Lord.

"Lord God, we come as your children . . ." Tony spoke softly, his wife squeezing his hand as he began. As they prayed, the peace they sought surrounded them as they gave their anxieties to their Father and Lord.

In the bedroom's far corner, a street lamp illuminated an empty cradle whose shadow darkened the couple as they prayed.

◆ ◆ ◆

Layton Redman tossed in his sleep even as the vision in his head prompted him into a lighter sleep cycle, one step closer to awakening. As the youngest governor to be elected to office in over two decades, he received the national publicity he desired via multiple prime-time news interviews. In this present interview, the reporter favorably compared him to the late John F. Kennedy. The questions and urgings always came around to the same end point: Where would he go from here? Would he seek national office? The Senate? The White House?

Redman only laughed and replied that anything was possible. The interviewer then closed the session, and Redman walked off the set.

Tonight his dreams were interrupted by a new face. This time as he walked off the studio set, he was greeted both by his current fiancée, Janice Sizemore, and by Samantha Stelling, each beckoning for his attention.

"Layton! You were tremendous, honey!" Samantha appeared to be late in her pregnancy and struggled with an awkward hug and a kiss, which took both Redman and his soon-to-be bride by surprise.

"Whoa!" Redman was physically and emotionally unbalanced by the greeting.

"Layton!" Janice Sizemore looked as if she were ready for a fight. "What's going on here?" She turned to Samantha, who was still hanging on to the governor's arm. "And who are *you*?"

"Ladies, please!" The governor tried to regain some semblance of composure.

Just as he was about to embark on an explanation, he became aware of the film crew who had refocused their cameras and their attention to the new excitement that had presented itself.

"Hey, the interview's over!" Layton Redman squinted at the unexpected camera lights.

"Governor, you're on the air!"

Hideous laughter began erupting from behind the camera and spread throughout the studio audience. The laughter swelled to a deafening roar as Redman struggled to free himself from the two clutching women.

Redman sat up suddenly in bed, the third person to do so in a drenching sweat on the same dream-filled night. He calmed his rapid breathing with slow deliberate breaths, exhaled through pursed lips. His heart rate would not return to its normal 72 for a full ten minutes.

He walked to the bathroom and washed his face. The facility was typical for a hotel room of high quality. He glanced back at the hotel room's king-size bed and then pressed his face into a soft, white, luxurious handtowel. "It was only a dream, Layton," he whispered to himself, "only a dream."

In the soft light coming from the bathroom a second figure was outlined on the far side of the bed. Janice Sizemore could sleep through just about anything.

CHAPTER
7

MATT arrived home by 2 P.M. on the 16th. The night before had brought a typical patient load: a G.I. bleeder, an MVA (motor vehicle accident) victim with bilateral femur fractures and a ruptured spleen, and an elderly patient with a sigmoid vovulus (a condition where the lower colon twists, causing bowel obstruction). None of the patients required surgery; however, each one required some of Matt's attention. The routine, spaced arrivals of the new patients again robbed the residents of any acquaintance with a call room, much less allowing adequate sleep. In the case of the patient with vovulus, Matt assisted the intern with a rigid sigmoidoscopy to untwist the lower bowel.

As the intern slowly advanced the lubricated scope into the patient's lower bowel, he experienced for the first time the explosive power of an obstructed colon that had just been relieved of its obstruction—in this case the apex of the twist. Fortunately, Matt had been quick on his feet; however, the intern had not been so lucky. As the point of obstruction was reached, the colon quickly untwisted, spraying its contents into the face of the unsuspecting first-year resident. Matt had just begun to speak up with a warning about the possible upcoming geyser when the obstruction was passed. The good-natured intern joined Matt in a healthy, side-splitting laugh prior to cleaning up. All combined, the patient felt immediate relief, and the simple act of untwisting the vovulus saved the patient an emergency trip to the operating room.

After rounds, Matt helped with one elective inguinal hernia repair and did a literature search for an upcoming conference he was planning. He then slipped home to enjoy his alternate "off" day on the trauma service.

Upon entering the backyard behind his apartment, he fended off a slobbery greeting from his Great Dane, who had never been very good at gentle hellos. The large dog nearly knocked the unsuspecting Matt to the ground with his excited, wet salutation. After a brief recuperation and resumption of his balance, Matt skipped up the stairs, hung his coat on the bedpost, and within a matter of seconds stretched horizontal on his bed. The sleep-deprived never make good company, and Matt planned to avoid falling asleep at the fellowship meal that evening. He had taken enough grief over his last Sunday morning church visit during which he'd dropped his Bible as he dozed off to sleep during the sermon. The "grief" had been in fun, of course, but it embarrassed Matt enough to make him not to want to repeat the performance tonight.

The shrill voice of Matt's bargain telephone startled him from sleep at exactly 5:30. At first he was unsure of the actual time. *Is it 5:30* A.M. *or* P.M.? It wouldn't have been the first time he'd slept through a social engagement. The electronic chirping of the phone forced him to focus. *It's still light outside . . . must be* P.M. He reached for the phone, practicing saying "hello" three times prior to picking up the receiver so as to hopefully disguise the fact that he had been sleeping.

"Hello . . . uughuuuUUGH . . . .hello, hello . . . hello." Matt spoke only the last "hello" into the receiver.

"Hello . . . Matt?"

"This is Matt," he replied, searching his mind to identify the feminine voice.

"I was just calling to remind you of the church's fellowship meal . . . You are coming, aren't you?"

Mrs. Tanner . . . Of course. What other female would be calling to make sure I'm coming?

"Yes, Mrs. Tanner, I'm planning on attending."

"Oh good! I know how busy your schedule must be, so I thought I would just call and check—"

"Thanks, Mrs. Tanner."

"Now don't worry about bringing anything. You just let those of us without so much on our minds worry 'bout that."

"It wouldn't be much trouble to pick up something on the way. That's what I usually do—"

"Not necessary, Matt. We always have plenty of leftovers. Well, I've got to run now. I'll see you in a bit." *Click.*

Matt looked curiously into the receiver. Every phone conversation with Beatrice Tanner ended that way. When she finished talking, she just hung up.

Matt scanned his small apartment. One good thing about being a resident was that he didn't spend enough time at home to make his apartment dirty. When he did, however, it was usually a full week before he cleaned it up again. He spent a few minutes straightening up his bed and desk. He showered, shaved, and dressed, selecting the sweater his mom had sent him for his last birthday. He then scoured his small kitchen for something that could take the edge off his appetite. He hated eating too much in front of others. A Twinkies twin-pack was the best he could do on short notice. At least he wouldn't look like a pig that night.

Forty-five minutes later Matt walked into the crowded fellowship hall at Dayspring Presbyterian Church. Matt hadn't been raised Presbyterian, but the people he'd met there were warm and had a sincere desire to learn what the Bible said to them personally. Besides, Matt felt at home because they accepted him with "no strings attached." He began looking for a place to sit when Mrs. Tanner caught his eye with a mildly frantic wave. "Matt! We've got a seat for you over here."

At that point Matt saw Linda Baldwin seated next to Mr. Tanner. It slowly registered with him that this beautiful young woman was the same one he had seen with paint-smeared coveralls. Matt took his seat opposite Linda, as indicated by Mrs. Tanner's directions. Matt stared without speaking until he saw the young woman blush. Mrs. Tanner spoke up, unaware that either had any idea who the other was. "Dr. Stone, I'd like you to meet our neighbor, Linda Baldwin." She turned to Linda and stated with a volume that embarrassed Matt, "He's a surgeon at the university and—"

"I'm a surgery *resident* . . . and I believe we've met."

"Yes." Linda smiled, noticing Matt's embarrassment and not the talkative Mrs. Tanner.

"You two know each other?" Mrs. Tanner looked as if someone had taken the surprise out of her little matchmaking scheme.

"We've met before . . . The day I came to pick up Mike at your farm. Mike and I met Linda and her cat while we were out for a walk."

"See, Beatrice, I told you the boy could take care of himself." Jim Tanner chuckled.

"Now, Jim, there's nothin' wrong with introducin' nice people to one another."

Fortunately, the Tanners were interrupted by the pastor, who stood to offer a prayer of thanks. He then instructed the people on filling their plates and the location of the drink lines. Linda and Matt got in line with the Tanners but were soon involved with talking together, leaving the Tanners to their own conversation, during which Beatrice pointed out at least six other couples whom she had helped set up in that very room alone.

The mealtime went quickly and gave Matt and Linda a chance to cover a variety of current topics and each other's basic life background. Despite Beatrice's earlier prediction, they did run short on desserts, which gave Matt an excuse to invite Linda out for some ice cream. Linda was careful with her food selections but, after some minor persuasion, agreed to go out as long as she could choose a fat-free yogurt alternative. She laughed to cover the seriousness of her request, hoping Matt would go along with her suggestion. Linda offered a quiet thank you to Mr. Tanner and informed him that she would not be needing a ride home. Mr. Tanner winked and chuckled, "Be home early . . . School night, you know."

"Gee, thanks, Dad!" Linda said, drawing out her words sarcastically. "Bye!" She turned and walked out the door with a smile.

The remainder of the evening included a combination of laughter, low-fat frozen yogurt (even Matt selected this and confessed, "It isn't bad"), and conversation, both lighthearted and serious. Their topics ranged from Matt's love of sports to abortion to each other's basic Christian commitments. By the end of the evening (which ended early by many people's standards, due to Matt's daily A.M. rounds that began at 6 o'clock sharp), Linda easily said "yes" to Matt's request that they get together again in the future.

If a relationship ever had a natural chemistry to it, this one did. Neither he nor she had any intentions beyond pursuing a friendship at this point, but both could not help but feel accepted and comfortable with the other. They understood that their ability to love others came only from the unconditional love with which God had loved them. Perhaps Matt was a bit more cautious than Linda about opening up his feelings to his new friend. Several weeks and many phone conversations later, he eventually spoke freely about his own conversion, the loss of his brother, and his own battle with self-acceptance. Linda listened and cried along with him as he shared the story that only a few others had heard.

A full two weeks later, Linda Baldwin noticed the red circle around the 16th on her calender as she diligently reorganized another master priority planner. When she saw the little note, she chuckled and remembered the efforts of Beatrice Tanner. Even if Beatrice's husband did think she was a bit forward, Linda knew two other people who appreciated Beatrice's matchmaking efforts. Linda paused from her work on her schedule long enough to write Mrs. Tanner a thank-you note. As she wrote it, she remembered how Beatrice had numbered off the couples she'd introduced. She smiled and couldn't help wondering if she and Matt might end up on that list. She chuckled to herself, imagining Beatrice carving another notch in the back of her large-print King James Bible.

"Enough of this! Get some work done!" Linda interrupted her own thoughts with a spoken command, as if this would force her to stop daydreaming. She quickly addressed the little note and sealed and stamped the envelope. She then returned to organizing her plan of the week. Periodically she drifted off the track again, however, and when she did, she smiled. She couldn't keep from thinking about this new relationship in her life, wondering just what the future held.

"Focus, girl, focus!" She spoke aloud again to snap herself back to the work at hand. Unfortunately, she had little motivation to obey her own firm instructions and found her thoughts continually and regularly returning to her new friend, Matt Stone.

◆ ◆ ◆

Michael Simons sat at his desk at home, busily reviewing the final draft of his first planned experiment that would follow later in the week. He had managed to finish the work in his new "lab" at the Fairfax Family Planning Clinic the day before. Now all he needed was his first subject. He went over each step carefully in his own mind and on the papers scattered before him. First their small subject would be rushed from the procedure room to his lab, where the infant would then be placed on the operating table where the chest would be opened and the subject quickly placed on cardiopulmonary bypass. Simons would allow the heart to beat normally and mainly wanted the bypass machine or pump to oxygenate the baby's blood to keep it "functional" throughout the experiment. He underscored the word "functional" in his mind, as he knew he needed to avoid terms like "living" or "alive" in his descriptions of his subjects. As much as possible, he had used and would use the terms "nonviable products of conception" and "nonliving conceptus" in the formal writing he would do in recording his data. He would do this to avoid legal ramifications, as his lawyer had informed him that Kentucky law specifically forbade experimentation on "live" aborted fetuses. Just what constituted a "live" abortion remained up for debate. Simons' lawyer did not know the details of Simons' planned experiments, and he did not want to. He was well-paid and just did what he was asked to by Simons, whom he respected as the foremost authority on pediatric cardiac surgery in the Midwest. He had merely done what was requested and had reported his findings back to Simons.

The phone rang, breaking Simons' train of thought. He glanced at the antique grandfather clock that stood in the corner. Its face recorded the time as 11:30. It was early evening by Simons' standards. He picked up the receiver. As he did, he checked the calendar on his desk to make sure he wasn't on call.

It's probably one of the residents telling me of a failed emergency angio-

plasty, which means I'll have to go in . . . No . . . I'm not on call for emergencies tonight . . . Who is bothering me at this hour? "Hello."

"Simons? It's me, Adam Richards."

"Oh, hey, Adam. For a second there I was afraid that this phone call would mean I'd be operating tonight."

"No, no, nothing of the sort. I just wanted to see if everything is ready for your first 'run' on Thursday. I've got a patient scheduled for 10 A.M. who should fit your criteria exactly. Twenty-two weeks pregnant. The girl is from out of town. I should be about ready for you by 11, give or take a few minutes."

"Sounds good. I haven't scheduled anything for the mornings when you are doing abortions on patients who might fit our criteria for donor mothers."

"Say, I saw another young girl in the office today whom I've scheduled for later in the month. Her name's Stelling. Seemed a bit unsure of herself and wanted to put the procedure off for a few weeks. I didn't try to dissuade her, knowing she will still easily fall into the appropriate age limits. Pretty girl, too . . . a friend of our new candidate for governor and—"

"Save me the details, would you!" Simons' interruption caught Richards blind. "I don't want to know anything about these girls. Not where they're from! Not who they're friends with! Nothing! Nothing at all! I only want the patient's name, so I have a way to keep my data straight. Name only, along with the date I collect the data." There was an uncomfortable pause in the conversation. It was only ten or twenty seconds, but it seemed much longer.

Richards spoke first to end the silence. "Hey, I'm sorry I ran on. I just thought you'd be glad to hear about another data provider."

"Okay, er, yeah, uh . . . yes, I am." Simons was slightly embarrassed by his own harsh tone, but he was not apologetic. He normally delighted in intimidating others, residents and other attendings in particular.

"So everything's set for Thursday, then?" Richards was aware that he'd repeated himself but couldn't think of anything new.

"Yes, everything's a go from my end."

"Okay, that's all I wanted to hear. See you then."

"Okay, bye now."

"Bye."

Simons continued to sort through the data he'd collected. He then straightened his desk, forming a neat stack of the papers he would file in his briefcase for the morning. On top sat a list of upcoming second trimester abortions to be done in the clinic as listed by Richards. Each had a last name and a date. This list would have to be continually updated, as most procedures of this nature were scheduled for shortly after the patient's first visit.

With a pencil, Simons added a name to the bottom of the list. "Stelling." He then filed the papers in his briefcase, spun the case's rolling combination lock, turned out the small lamp, and left his study. The time was midnight. Simons smiled, glad to have most of the plans for his study completed. Now all he needed to do was get on with his data collection.

◆ ◆ ◆

Tony tapped Carol's "champagne" glass with his. "To our baby and our future life together." Carol smiled. Even though it was only sparkling cider, and even though their baby's due date was still seven months away, they felt like celebrating.

"Two months old. Happy birthday, little one." Carol gently patted her lower abdomen, which had not yet begun to swell.

Tony drained his glass with several gulps. "Mmmmm—hey, not bad stuff here."

"Better watch yourself. You aren't used to the hard stuff, you know."

"Yes, but you're the designated driver, right?" Tony smiled, then laughed aloud. "How about another glass?"

Carol poured another glass for her husband. "Now try and show a little culture. Drink this slow enough to give your taste buds a fighting chance."

Tony obeyed sheepishly by taking a small sip after swirling the golden liquid beneath his nostrils. He looked around their small apartment. The ambiance was not exactly conducive to romantic dinners. One of the things he missed most since moving out of their house was the fireplace. Tony sighed and looked across at his wife, whose green eyes met his. "Someday I'll take you and our baby out of this place."

"I know you will . . . This place is just fine. All I need is right here." She reached for Tony's hand as she spoke, squeezing it softly as she reemphasized, "All I need."

Tony broke the gaze and looked around again. Carol had done a good job of decorating with what she had available. "I know. It's just that I think you deserve better."

"I'm fine. We're so much better off than most people, you know." She was stating a fact, not asking a question.

"You're right." Tony paused and then stood up and took on the exaggerated air of a pompous, high-priced waiter. "Are you ready to be served yet, madam?"

"Oh yes, quite ready, thank you," Carol replied with the same exaggerated tone. "What year did you say that cider was from?"

Tony rotated the bottle and read the imaginary small print at the bottom. "1990. Excellent choice, ma'am."

"Of course."

Tony had "created" a special meal for their little celebration. They could hardly believe that two months had already passed since the successful IVF. They remained cautious about being overly optimistic and made regular attempts to talk about other things. The upcoming baby was the center of their thoughts, however, whether they allowed those thoughts to be verbalized or not. They successfully warded off the temptation to completely stock up on baby supplies, partly because of their own unspoken fears and partly because their one-bedroom apartment was just not large enough to tolerate much more. They had shared the good news with only their own parents and knew that once the word got out to their friends, they would have their hands full trying to suppress their friends' desire to help with providing necessary furnishings. Their "church family" would be the next to find out, and they did not want to tell them for another two months. This dinner was the first formal celebration they had yielded to since coming home from the hospital with Tony's flowers.

The simple dinner elegantly fit the occasion. Caesar salad, garlic-laden sirloin grilled out on their small patio in spite of the 35-

degree temperature, baked potatoes, hot rolls, coffee (decaffeinated, as Carol now abstained from caffeine), and "Polar bars" (a favorite ice cream treat, taken out of the wrapper and eaten with a fork, to simulate a "high society" dessert) made up the fare. The evening was a total delight.

After dinner Tony stacked the dishes in the sink and promised to himself and his onlooking wife that he would complete the task in the A.M. Carol propped up her feet and opened a *Good Housekeeping* magazine. Soon she was comfortably submerged in the depths of a short story, while Tony read a Tom Clancy novel. Forty-five minutes later Tony began to yawn. Carol stood up with one hand on her lower abdomen, her expression one of subtle discomfort.

Tony yawned largely. "Oooh me! What a meal! . . . Say, are you feeling okay?"

Carol stood to her feet and took inventory of her own feelings. She felt some slight crampy lower abdominal pain. "It's just the amount I ate, I'm sure. I'm gonna get some antacid." She walked to the kitchen. Her Maalox bottle, which had been on the counter before Tony's "creation," was now absent. "Where's the Maalox?"

"I put it away."

"I realize that. Where?"

"Spice counter. In alphabetical order beside the Mexican chile powder."

Carol shook her head. She thought she would never understand her husband's organizational skills. She had given up arguing about where to put things and would just ask him where something was. He usually remembered and had some reason for the placement of the item in question. "Thanks."

She took a healthy swig of the thick, white liquid. Her pain eased somewhat, reinforcing her hopes that her discomfort was due to the meal. She remembered a girlfriend who had had a lot of heartburn during her pregnancy. *Surely that must be what this is*, she thought.

Carol returned to the den to find Tony's eyes closed and his breathing deep and regular. "Come on . . ." She coaxed him with a gentle jab to the rib cage. "Let's get some sleep." She walked down the short hallway to the bedroom, pausing briefly at the doorway to touch her stomach again. A few minutes later they were both in bed. "Remind me not to enjoy your cooking so much the next time."

"It is difficult to restrain yourself, I know." Tony smiled.

Carol did not share in his happy sarcasm. She only rolled onto her side in an attempt to lessen the nagging crampiness in the pit of her stomach.

◆ ◆ ◆

Physically speaking, Samantha Stelling felt a lot better. Better, but not good. Better is, of course, a relative term, but at least her daily bouts of nausea had been curtailed. She hadn't done anything except modify her eating habits a little. Perhaps she just needed to let her baby get a little older. At any rate, and for whatever reason, she felt better. Mentally, however, she was approaching her limit; she had seen Richards and initially agreed to proceed with an abortion. He told her the procedure carried very little risk, could be done as an outpatient, and was part of her legal right as a citizen of the U.S. He had been careful not to push her to make a quick decision, however, and had promised her that a wait of several weeks or even a month would not hamper her chances at proceeding.

She felt very confused. Several years ago she would have never considered abortion an option. Now, finding herself in this situation, wanting to please Layton and appease her own conscience at the same time, she found herself in a quicksand of worry and doubt. No matter what decision she made, she expected some retribution. If she could just get away with proceeding with the abortion without a lifetime's worth of guilt, she thought she would be okay. Layton had never told her plainly there was no chance for their relationship if she kept the baby, but it was obvious that he felt it would be an interference. She made tentative plans to proceed but wanted to wait a few days to talk to Layton about the cost. He had made an inference that everything would be taken care of from a financial standpoint.

It seemed that all she could think about was Layton and their future together. After all, hadn't he implied that things would work out after the election? Sam thought back over their conversations again and again and found herself beaming at the remembrance of his statements of comfort in her presence, his ability to talk to her, her ability to understand him, and his desires to spend more time with her, if only his schedule would allow it. She seemed to selectively forget that he wanted to hide his relationship with her from everyone and that he had even once accused her of sleeping around.

Sam's rose-colored vision hindered her from seeing the truth and from hearing the soft promptings of the Holy Spirit that she had once sought. Guilt-laden fear slowly pushed aside her once-faithful prayer life. The more she contemplated her next step, the more she doubted her own faith and considered the possibility of life as Layton Redman saw it: if a problem arises that prevents you from reaching your goal, deal with it, remove it, or change it to work for you, if the problem can be changed. The issue seemed black and white to him. Sam hoped to please him and had decided to take on his attitude in an attempt to avoid her misgivings and fears. Sam was running. The battle lines were drawn, but she no longer prayed for help. The Holy Spirit kept pushing for recognition, but a thickening callus of disobedience muffled his gentle promptings.

The small baby within her was a boy. If given a chance to develop, he would have the same hair color as his mother, and eventually the handsome, rough exterior of his father. His inherited intelligence would surpass both of his parents' above-average intelligence. To this point, as far as his growth had been concerned, everything had proceeded as normally and miraculously as ever. His heart was strong and beating. With every organ system established, the young fetus matured according to plan. He had a functioning central nervous system and would soon be able to sense pain and other sensations. He did not have any say, however, in the outcome of his mother's decision, a decision that would affect not only him but the lives of those whom he would touch if only given a chance.

CHAPTER
8

MATT'S apartment sat beneath a direct east-west fly-over approach for C.A.T.S., the T.U. hospital helicopter. Fortunately, he had learned to sleep through just about anything, so the bird, a semi-quiet Sikorsky S-76, did not disturb Matt during his nights at home. This time, however, the drowsy surgical resident wasn't quite asleep anyway and planned to rise when the helicopter made its approach to the top of the critical care wing at the T.U. hospital, just two blocks from his house.

Matt sat up and shook his head. 4:30 P.M. He had slept for two hours. *Linda said she would be over by 5.* Matt leaned on his single porcelain kitchen sink and looked out the window, searching the sky for the helicopter that he could hear but not yet see. The blue and white lettering and the bright orange E.K.G. stripe on the side of the Sikorsky would be visible if the chopper took its normal approach. He had grown to both love and hate the helicopter service. He loved it for all its power and grace in flight. He hated it for keeping him up on countless nights. His love for the bird led to his frequent stops while on call to visit the "booth boys," the men who worked in the small, booth-like hospital flight dispatch office and directed the chopper from place to place.

The Sikorsky S-76 was indeed a beautiful machine. It was the baby brother to the Army's Sikorsky "black hawk" and was powered by two Allison C-30x engines, each generating around 850 horsepower and boosting the chopper to speeds of greater than 200 mph in cool weather. The helicopter service for the university was provided by P.H.I. (Petroleum Helicopter, Incorporated), the largest helicopter service in the world.

Matt cringed whenever he heard it lift off while he was on call, hoping it was only on a cardiology run. The cardiology fellows, likewise, wished for trauma and a break from working up acute cardiac patients who were flown in from all over the eastern Kentucky foothills. When "in house," the residents called the Sikorsky the "Death Star" or other not so complimentary names, reflecting their disdain for its effects on their sleep. When Matt relaxed at home, he took the time to admire the bird and quietly held a respect for the flight team and the job they did.

Matt watched the chopper pass over and then turned his attention to straightening up his apartment. He cleared his desk, sorted the mail, and "filed away" a six-inch stack of "throw-aways" (free medical magazines) in the waste can beneath the kitchen sink. He had already washed the dishes, which had sat in the sink for three days, prior to sleeping. He had come home after helping on only one operative case that morning—a sigmoid colon resection on the elderly patient who had come in with vovulus a few days before. Because the trauma team did most of their surgery on an emergency basis, the residents could often expect to escape at a reasonable hour on their off days, as Matt experienced today.

He had called Linda two days before and asked if she could come up and play racquetball. She had required little encouragement and had promptly accepted his invitation. They had decided on 5 P.M., hoping the YMCA courts would have an opening. Linda had suggested that they make dinner after that and volunteered to bring the necessary ingredients.

Matt changed into his sweatpants and an "Air-Jordan" T-shirt. He sat down to read his latest copy of *The American Journal of Surgery* and was busily scanning the abstracts when he heard his dog barking, heralding the arrival of his guest. Matt went out onto the back steps and called off the Great Dane. "Hey, Mike! Enough already! . . . Linda?" Matt looked down between the slats on the steep back steps. Linda stood cowering as Mike slobbered his wet greeting. She escaped from behind the stairway when the dog looked up in response to his master's voice.

Linda stumbled up the stairs, clutching a brown grocery bag in one hand and wiping her face with the back of the other. "Yeeeuuucckk!" Obviously she hadn't yet acquired an appreciation for Great Dane saliva.

"Sorry about that. I think he likes you." Matt laughed but tried to restrain himself until he could determine Linda's true reaction.

"What gives you that idea?"

"He doesn't lick people he doesn't like, you know." Matt ushered Linda into his little apartment. Just then the 5 o'clock southbound train blew its whistle, warning the approaching cars a block to the west. Linda trembled slightly at the apparent closeness of the coming train.

"You have a nice place." Linda hoped her words sounded more convincing than she thought they did.

"Thanks. I call it home," Matt replied, not doubting her sincerity. Matt directed her to the small set of cupboards next to the small gas stove and half-sized refrigerator. He was aware that she was inspecting his grocery supply as she unpacked the ingredients for their dinner later that evening. They made small talk, and Matt teased her about her facial expression when she was cowering behind the stairs to get away from a lovable hound like Mike. Linda seemed distracted by what she was seeing: sugar-coated cereal, Twinkies, Pop-Tarts, hot dogs, corn chips, and several liters of soda in the refrigerator.

"Do you really eat this stuff?" Linda had an obvious scowl on her face.

Matt looked at Linda's expression. It didn't take a rocket scientist to detect her seriousness. "Sure," Matt replied a bit sheepishly.

"Who shops for you, a ten-year-old? Just look at this stuff! A surgeon eats Lucky Charms?" Linda stood with her mouth hanging open in disbelief.

"Yeah, I eat this stuff. At least it's fortified with vitamins, right? Besides, it's quick, and all this stuff has carbohydrates for fast energy."

"At least you're aware of the existence of vitamins and carbohydrates!" Linda began looking through the small freezer.

"Hey! Did you come over to critique my groceries or play racquetball, huh?" Matt raised his hands in a teasing boxer's stance.

Linda got off a quick jab to Matt's midsection just below his ribs. The unsuspecting Matt opened his mouth to protest but came up only with, "Ooooff."

"Racquetball," Linda retorted, smiling. "I shouldn't have any trouble keeping up with you if your energy comes from all these!" She emphasized the last word by throwing a Twinkie at Matt's forehead. He caught the small cake in mid-flight.

"Thanks," Matt replied, grabbing his sweatjacket and heading for the door. "Don't mind if I do!" He unwrapped the Twinkie and downed it in two bites.

"That's disgusting!"

"Good, though," Matt replied in a muffled voice.

"Does your mom know you eat this way?"

"I'm a big boy now. I eat what I want." Matt stuck out his chest to exaggerate his point.

"Looks to me like you still need someone to care about you."

Matt looked back from his position in the doorway.

Linda blushed.

"Coming?" he inquired.

"On my way." The two scurried onto the back stairs. Matt threw a chewbone into the yard to distract Mike long enough for them to make a clear, slobber-free escape.

In ten minutes they were encased in a competitive racquetball challenge. Matt may have had poor eating habits, but he had not told Linda that he had also been his college dorm's racquetball champion for two years running. He had had little time for anything besides his biology and chemistry studies, but he had always made time for a weekly court workout.

But Linda held her own and beaned Matt several times with solid hits when she felt she couldn't hit the front wall. With that tactic, they replayed the ball instead of giving the point to Matt. Matt took the ball-wounds with a smile to hide the brief sting; inwardly he appreciated Linda's competitive approach. After a full hour, Matt thanked the next players for the knock on the door that signaled the end of their playing time. So far Matt had paid only an occasional jog to his mostly lip-service promise to himself to get into better shape.

A few minutes later they were again in Matt's pickup for the short ride back to Matt's apartment. "I hope you're not sore about my comments about your diet." Linda spoke softly and glanced cautiously at Matt.

"Kind of caught me off-guard, I guess . . . I know I should eat better. It's just one of those things that I keep putting off till I get a little older . . . Pretty easy to do, you know?"

"Well, anyway, I'm sorry I jumped on it so fast. It's just something that I think about a lot, and I just assumed that you being a doctor and all would—"

"We're probably guiltier than most, what with our schedules and all. We've all received good nutrition education, unlike the doctors a generation ago, and we all worry about our patients' eating patterns. But education doesn't guarantee compliance, does it? I've seen thoracic surgeons remove a lung for cancer, and the first thing they do after finishing the surgery is reach for a cigarette . . . Pretty stupid, I guess." Matt glanced over at Linda, who sat quietly looking out of her window. He didn't want her to feel like she had made him too uncomfortable. "I tell you what—I'll try to eat better if you promise to limit my cupboard inspections to every other visit." Matt chuckled as he looked at Linda and then back at the road. When he got to the hospital he turned up the one-way street where he lived.

"Deal!" Linda was relieved to see that he was unscathed by her previous comments. She knew you can never be sure how someone will take criticism. After all, for all she knew from watching "St. Elsewhere," all surgeons grew into uncaring, snapping bulldogs. But from what she could see of Matthew Stone, he didn't fit the Hollywood stereotype.

Back home at Matt's apartment, Matt turned off his lights and engine a hundred feet from the house, allowing the truck to coast quietly to a stop in front of the house. He then stealthily approached the back of the home, gently raised the gate latch, and tiptoed up the stairway. He pointed to the sleeping dog in the corner of the yard. Linda nodded and tiptoed up the stairs behind him. "He goes to sleep with the sun," Matt whispered.

Inside, they prepared a meatless, vegetable lasagna and salad, along with sourdough rolls. When the meal was ready, they sat down to eat at the small card table in the "greatroom" (the dining room/living room). Matt reached out, took Linda's hand, bowed his head, and prayed. He paused briefly after the prayer, still holding Linda's hand. He looked up, aware that he was blushing. A squeeze signaled the end of their hand-holding, and they turned their attention to the food before them. Matt could not help but smile at the reaction his surgery buddies would have if they saw him with his date. If their exaggerated stories of "date conquest" were anything close to true, they would think he was closer to having a meal with his sister than enjoying a romantic evening with a date. But he felt sure he would eventually be appropriately rewarded if he stuck to his standards, no matter how old-fashioned they seemed or how hard his so-called friends would laugh.

They had both worked up good appetites, and in no time at all Matt cleaned out the corners of the 13 x 9 casserole dish. Linda enjoyed seeing Matt appreciate nutritious food, but she also marveled at the speed with which he ate.

Matt looked up to see the expression on Linda's face as he scraped out the last of the lasagna, then glanced at her half-full plate of "firsts." "I'm sorry . . . I learned to eat fast at the hospital. I eat at least two or three meals there a day. I guess I forgot to shift gears and slow down. Most of the residents eat twice as many meals with their fellow house-officers as with their families. It's a bad place to learn to eat slow—"

"Don't worry about it. I understand," Linda interjected. She began to see just one of the small, nagging side effects of surgical residency training.

The remainder of their time together seemed to pass quickly, as most off times did for the surgeon in training. It seemed that once time for sleeping and eating had been taken, little time existed for the other mandatory items such as bill-paying and laundry, and even less time for outside relationships. As they cleared the table and washed and dried the dishes, Linda asked about Matt's future plans.

"How much longer will you be a resident? You said that you've been doing this for nearly five years, since you finished medical school?" The question had a familiar, incredulous tone to it, as Matt had heard it over and over from relatives and friends who were continually confused by the stages of his training. It seemed that each family gathering he had attended since medical school had been punctuated by at least one comment like, "When are you going to be a real doctor?" or "Are you a doctor yet?"

"I'll be finished in July." Matt smiled at the thought.

"What happens after July? Do you have plans?"

"I'm not really sure. I have plenty of options. The one I'm considering the strongest is to return to the Eastern Shore of Virginia to help a busy general surgeon there." Matt looked for a reaction but couldn't discern Linda's thoughts. "I really don't have to decide right away. I've still got a lot of praying to do."

Linda finished drying the now empty casserole pan. "I'll put that item on my prayer list. It sounds like a big decision to me. Maybe you could also keep me in mind, as I'll be finishing up at the end of this year and will have similar plans to make."

Matt eagerly agreed. Before Linda left, they took the opportunity to pray together.

◆ ◆ ◆

The patient moaned softly, awake but sedated. Richards used a higher dose of short-acting Versed to quiet the woman's fears and to increase the chance that she would remember little of the morning's events. He exhaled nervously, desiring that this first experiment go off without a hitch. In an attempt to ensure that, he did most of the work himself, finding first one excuse and then another for sending his nurse out of the room.

He had seen the patient four hours earlier, started an IV, and inserted an additional prostaglandin vaginal suppository to soften the cervix in preparation for delivery. A pitocin drip had been started and titrated to maintain steady labor. He examined the woman again and decided to mechanically dilate the cervix to help the labor along and facilitate breaking her water. By ultrasound, he had estimated this baby right at twenty-two weeks. *Perfect for our protocol*, he mused to himself.

Richards knew that Simons had arrived to prepare the "operating suite" for his first data collection. Simons brought along a lab assistant, John Gentry, who had been working for Simons for a year and a half. John, a quiet man who had had research experience in Louisville, transferred to Fairfax specifically for the privilege of working with Simons. He knew Simons' reputation and trusted him explicitly. In addition, he understood how to operate the cardiopulmonary bypass machine and would provide the necessary extra hands Simons needed to carry out his work.

In forty minutes, as the team stood anxiously by, the baby crowned, and delivery was imminent. Richards injected a dose of intravenous ketamine, an anesthetic that did not interfere with the patient's respirations and would not affect the baby's cardiac status. If he gave too much narcotic or angiolytic medication (like Versed) to the mother close to delivery, the baby might be affected, and the experimental data would be altered.

The mother did not realize that the treatment she received differed from the ordinary. This was her first abortion. She had made up her mind, heard the explanation of the procedure, and had even signed a paper approving "appropriate use and disposal of the fetal tissue as may benefit medical science." She, like many thousands of other mothers seeking abortion, did not want to think about the baby in any concrete terms. The sooner she completed the procedure, the better. The only additional side effects she would have, besides those normally associated with abortion, were several "flashback-type" experiences related to the use of the ketamine.

With the cervix now fully prepared, Richards quickly pulled the child from the birth canal with forceps because the anesthetized mother could no longer cooperate and push. In a motion that Richards had used thousands of times before, he clamped and cut the cord and handed the small female fetus to Simons, who had appeared just after the nurse injected the ketamine. In a normal delivery, immediate attention would have been given to getting the infant to breathe and to clearing the upper respiratory tract. In this case, however, because the lungs were underdeveloped, they would waste no time trying conventional methods of oxygenation, such as suctioning out the baby's upper airway or the placement of endotracheal tubes into the infant's trachea to inflate the lungs. The heart would go on beating without problems for a very limited time before arrhythmias would intervene.

For this reason, Simons rushed the infant straight to the research suite, where the baby could be quickly placed on cardiopulmonary bypass to be oxygenated. Simons entered the new research lab through the open door. John Gentry closed and locked the door behind him. He had been told of the sensitive nature of these experiments and knew about every move he was to make, having been instructed by a calm and almost emotionless Simons the week before. The infant moved her arms and legs and made some respiratory effort with a grotesque, distorted expression apparent on her minute face. Simons quickly placed the infant on the procedure table, equipped with a warming blanket, and fastened two Velcro straps over the infant to immobilize her. Since sterile technique was unnecessary and would have only caused needless time delays, no skin prep or draping was used. Simons had previously laid out each instrument in the order in which he would need them. He reached for the first item on the table, a glistening number 15 blade on a new scalpel handle.

With a practiced motion, he guided the knife over the infant's sternum. The breastbone, which is bone in an adult and must be divided by a saw, is only cartilage in the infant and was thus swiftly and smoothly divided by Simons' scissors, the second instrument on his tray. The child had only been out of the protection of her mother's uterus for a mere minute and thirty seconds. Simons then lifted the pericardium, the lining around the heart, with a pick-ups and divided it longitudinally, exposing the small heart. It was beating rapidly but was beginning to slow, indicating that time was running out and that oxygen levels were low. Small cannulas were then inserted into the infant's right atrium and into the root of the aorta, the first to draw out the venous blood returning to the heart, and the latter to return the blood, now oxygenated from the pump, into the aorta to travel to the rest of the body. The cannulas were secured with purse-string sutures and hooked up to the cardiopulmonary bypass machine, which pumped the blood through an oxygenator and returned it to the patient. The heart rate immediately improved, as it was now being exposed to a new supply of oxygen. The baby's age was still under five minutes. Simons looked at the clock on the far wall and spouted off time intervals for Gentry to record. He was proud of the speed at which the procedure had been performed. He could now slow down and work on applying the appropriate monitors to the fetus so he would have a record of each parameter.

Simons looked momentarily at the small infant's face. The contorted expression and open mouth with groping lips distracted him for several seconds. He excused the quivering of the infant's lips as a normal reflex and quickly covered the baby's face with a towel. Likewise, he covered the infant's small abdomen and extremities, noting for a brief instant that it appeared as if the baby were straining its arms and legs against the tight Velcro straps. Simons shook his head, refocusing his thoughts. *Nonviable donor preparation, sacrificed by the mother and salvaged for the overall good of mankind.*

Simons made a mental note and placed a second drape over the small infant's face. *From now on I will not handle the infants until they are on the procedure table and covered with surgical drapes, so I will not have to see these nearly human reflexes. Gentry will take the child from the "delivery room" into the lab, where I will be waiting with scalpel in hand.*

The work was also slightly distasteful to Gentry, but he countered his dislike for the procedure by concentrating on Simons' arguments that the aborted products of conception were nonviable at this age and had been donated willfully by their mothers and otherwise would serve no purpose at all. He also enjoyed a healthy doubling of his university salary, the increase being received in cash each week directly from Simons' hand. In turn, Gentry agreed to be quiet about the work and to avoid mentioning it at the university hospital, where he maintained his 9-to-5 job. Simons did not want any word to go out until after they had presented their data to the institution's research review board, in search of permission to do the first real "transplants."

In this first experiment, Simons carefully recorded baseline heart rate, blood pressure, and cardiac output. He measured the cardiac output (the amount of blood the heart pumps in each minute) with a color-probe doppler that he held against the tiny aorta. Simons then slowly increased the heart-rate with an external pacemaker, applied to the right atrium. At each new heart-rate, Gentry recorded the cardiac output. Simons then turned the pacemaker off, and the infant was given small volumes of intravenous fluid while they measured the pressures in the left atrium with a third small catheter. At each recorded left atrial pressure measurement, the cardiac output and other parameters were collected and recorded. As the intravenous volume expanded, the cardiac output increased, until the small heart was finally overcome with too much fluid.

Simons carefully looked over his preliminary data. It appeared as if his original predictions would pan out. *This little heart is capable of producing adequate cardiac outputs for an infant twice its size!*

With his data collection complete, the experiment could be terminated. Simons instructed Gentry to turn off the pump, and Simons then removed the small venous and aortic cannulas, the pressure lines, and other monitoring equipment. By the time he had removed all of the lines, the infant ceased all respiratory attempts. Simons carefully reapproximated the sternum and the skin of the infant's chest. He closed the incision carefully with a suture from the inside, so that there were no external sutures to show that any work had been done.

He placed the small female infant body in a plastic container of hypertonic saline. In several hours the body would be almost identical to those of other aborted babies who had been exposed to hypertonic saline injection in-utero. The incision was a fine line that would be easily missed by anyone inspecting the fetus because of the surrounding skin changes caused by the hypertonic saline. The specimens would be seen only briefly by a pathologist to determine that the products of conception were actually obtained. Rarely did the pathologist have reason for a close exam of the late second trimester aborted fetuses, as a quick glance confirmed all the pathologist needed to know.

After the cleanup, Simons collected his papers and hurried back to the university. Despite having arrived late to his clinic and dealing with several aggravated parents, Simons' mood was one of elation. He was finally gathering the necessary data and was confirming his theory. That fact fed his ego for the remainder of the afternoon.

◆ ◆ ◆

Samantha looked out the rain-streaked window. The weather outside matched her feelings, and she almost enjoyed, in a strange sort of way, the dark sky because it mirrored her inner turmoil and would certainly dampen the moods of others. She had begun to despise sunshine and clear skies; they seemed to only heighten the contrast with her own emotional darkness. She felt so alone. She had shared her personal plight with only one person other than Layton, from whom she certainly felt limited emotional support. She had called her first-year roommate, Kathy Adkins, with whom she had once been almost inseparable. Now, however, it seemed as if no friendship had ever existed, at least to Sam. Kathy had been both surprised and slightly perturbed by Sam's story. Kathy saw things as black and white as Layton did, only with the completely opposite view. Abortion was wrong. Period. End of discussion. Sam believed she had an obligation to follow through with the right course, regardless of how painful the consequence. According to Kathy, the Bible could not be clearer on the subject.

Unfortunately, along with the end of her righteous proclamation of the right course came the end of the support Kathy gave to Sam in her darkening corner of despondency. "The ball's in her court now," Kathy had told her boyfriend. "I've presented the truth. Now it's up to her to act on that truth." Unfortunately, her attitude was not thought to be an uncommon one by Sam, and the resulting feeling of aloneness and condemnation for even considering abortion as an option drove Sam further and further from seeking other outside help.

Had she sought help, even in a local church, there was a chance she would have met the same uncompassionate, hard-line reasoning. But of course there was also the chance that she would find practical, compassionate brothers and sisters who were ready to bear the load with her, both emotionally and financially.

And so, slowly but surely Sam withdrew—first from school, and then from her friends. Several years before, she would have been automatically expelled from school. A.C.U.'s policy had been changed just two years before, and a "more supportive, more forgiving" policy had been adopted that allowed expectant mothers to continue classes and to even take special class extensions when necessary to complete classes that were interrupted by delivery. Sam had taken advantage of none of the available university solutions and had not even talked to a student counselor before withdrawing. Now she found herself supported only by what dwindling inner energy she had left and an occasional phone conversation with Layton Redman.

She had seen Redman only three times since the last night he had spent in her apartment. As time would have it, that was a full twelve weeks ago, and each time they talked, his message was the same: get the "problem" taken care of as soon as possible. He acted as if he were still interested in her and talked about a possible split with his fiancée as soon as the election was over. For now, he did not want to appear to be indecisive. She must understand that a break-up now would jeopardize his standings in the polls. At their last good-bye, Redman had left her with a drawn-out, tantalizing kiss that further sealed the confusion in Sam's mind. The last thing she wanted right now was to rid herself of the only support she felt she still had, even if what he wanted did run cross-grain to the doctrines she had been taught as a child.

It occurred to her only once that Layton might actually be afraid of her. She had sensed it in the way he treated her at their last contact. He had changed his original accusatory suspicions to the support of a still-interested, potential lover. The message that had not changed was that now was not the right time for them to have children. Perhaps, she thought, he feared her bringing the truth to the public in order to force him to acknowledge her. She enjoyed the change in him, regardless of what motivated it.

As she watched the rain, she placed her hand gently over her lower abdomen. She noticed that her once enviably flat waist was beginning to swell. It would still be several weeks until she felt the small male child move within her, a feeling she would both love and hate.

She had delayed making the appointment with Richards for several reasons. For one, Richards had not encouraged her to hurry. He informed her that there was still plenty of time before a decision needed to be made. This contrasted, of course, with the pressure from Redman, who had suggested that she see Richards in the first place. The second reason for delay was the small hope that Layton Redman would completely change his tune and sweep both her and her baby off into wedded bliss. Now she was beginning to understand that this was as likely as a blizzard in Miami; but she still had some hope, though small and tarnished. The third reason for the delay was her doubt about the abortion itself and whether her former roommate, however insensitive, could actually be right. With these thoughts, the emotions built up and again flowed down the cheeks of Sam Stelling.

She sat there in silence for a long time, staring out at the cold, November rain. Since quitting school, she'd had too much time on her hands, time she spent ruminating over her present situation. Large tears formed and dropped onto the small African violet on the window ledge in front of her. She did not bother to wipe her cheeks but only continued looking through the windows, which were now becoming fogged as she leaned forward, touching her forehead on the icy windowpane.

Tears often precipitate prayers, and vice versa, of course. It was no different for Sam that wet, November day as she began, for the first time in several months, to pray.

CHAPTER
9

THE cool wetness of November quickly turned into the cold wetness of December. Fairfax did not typically get much snow, but the forecast often entailed precipitation of some sort. At least that seemed to be the case for *this* winter, as records for rainfall and flash flood warnings became commonplace.

Regardless of the season, life for the surgical resident was much the same. The same pale-faced resident crew that stood out so much in contrast with the summer population of those with "normal" jobs in September blended in more easily when the weather forced everyone to stay inside. Matt Stone rotated off the trauma service and onto the general surgery team at the local V.A. hospital. Fortunately for the residents at the T.U. medical center, the V.A. sat adjacent to the university hospital, attached by an indoor tunnel that was not-so-affectionately called "the fistula" by the resident staff. As with many of the best university training programs, the Taft University sugical residency incorporated several hospitals other than the university medical center, including the V. A. hospital. This gave the residents a broader surgical experience. For Matt, the change meant more independence as a chief resident, as attending surgeon input had become more of an "as needed" basis at the V.A. as compared to the university.

In Fairfax, Dr. Adam Richards would have a lonely holiday, finding himself more and more in a state of quiet depression that hid beneath the surface. He turned once again to the solace of alcohol, feeling the temporary peace to be a partially satisfactory relief.

Simons continued to work feverishly both in his university practice and in Richards' office "lab." Four additional school-age children came into the hospital for cardiac operations during their Christmas vacation, adding to the stress of the residents rotating on Simons' cardiothoracic surgery service. Simons had never been much for holiday cheer, and he quietly delighted in turning up the heat for those working for him during those times. His residents, along with those working on the other surgical services, would continue to work regardless of the holiday. Fortunately, the O.R. staff closed the operating rooms for Christmas or certainly someone would have wanted to schedule an elective case or two. Of course, the O.R. and the residents would always be available for emergencies.

The extent of Simons' involvement in Christmas activities was his perfunctory appearance at the annual surgery Christmas party. He did this for political reasons more than to enjoy the holiday with his coworkers. He was second in line only to the department chairman, and as the head of his particular division, his appearance was necessary. Simons often sensed that people were talking about him. Lately he felt that many of those around him were envious of his accomplishments. Certainly he must not disappoint them by his absence from the party.

On the political front, the winter was anything but cold. Several debates had been held, and with each public appearance Layton Redman captured more and more of the public and media support. The campaign had not mirrored the goodwill of the season, and the mud-slinging began early. The Redman camp had overturned enough dirt in the background of his opponents to cause attention to be directed away from him. His camp had needed only to leak the information to the other opposing parties and allow them to throw the mud at each other in public. Although his scouts were busy searching out the private and financial lives of his opponents, he rarely brought any of this to light directly, lest the public be dissatisfied with a contaminated campaign.

Perhaps the most meaningful change of the season could be seen in Samantha Stelling. For Sam, the Christmas holiday symbolized a fresh start. She had finally made up her mind about her unwanted pregnancy and went to Richards' clinic for an abortion. The parking lot was filled with the cars of pro-life advocates, and there was no room left for the clinic workers, much less any patients who desired services. For this reason she parked in an adjacent parking lot and walked to the clinic's front entrance.

As she approached the clinic, sidewalk counselors greeted her. They carried signs, some of which had been fashioned by Linda Baldwin just a few weeks before. Their positive messages weakened her mental resolve. Instead of ugly, condemning protests, the marchers challenged her with powerful proclamations of truth:

JESUS FORGIVES

JESUS LOVES THE LITTLE ONES

WHAT DOES ABORTION COST? ONE LIFE

The familiar message she had heard as a youth struck her. The prayers she'd expressed along with her November tears were not going unheard. She eventually left the clinic that day without ever stepping through the front door. After a tearful conversation with one of the counselors, she stumbled back to her car with her head bursting with emotion, her decision to abort her baby delayed, at least for the moment. Finally alone, she gripped the steering wheel and sobbed. *Dr. Richards said I still had some time. It will be okay if I wait another few days. Maybe Layton will even come around and see this through my eyes. We could be a family . . . If only he could see things like I see them.*

In Easton, Carol and Tony planned for a quiet family Christmas. Both were in hopeful moods. They felt that because of Carol's pregnancy travel was inadvisable. They welcomed the excuse to stay at home, however, and planned their own family celebration together.

The Christmas season excited Linda Baldwin as much as it did any small child. Her relationship with Matt Stone had grown in spite of his schedule. She communicated by mail with Matt's mother, Sandra, who sounded warm and supportive of this new development in her son's life. Sandra invited her to accompany Matt on his next trip east, information that neither woman shared with Matt. Linda also planned to be at the surgery Christmas party, as Matt had issued an invitation to attend along with him, just after the Thanksgiving holiday. She was more excited about attending this function than was Matt, who merely viewed his attendance as fulfilling his resident obligations. Linda, however, anxiously anticipated meeting all the colorful people Matt talked about so often.

Linda missed the pro-life rally entirely, spending the entire day in bed with the flu. She had sent her brightly colored signs along with a friend but could not physically bring herself to leave her own bed. She had been convicted about her complacency in the matter, but she reasoned that she would attend a second follow-up rally her church was sponsoring in another month.

◆ ◆ ◆

The atmosphere dripped with holiday festivity. Several hundred people filled the convention hall at the Oasis Hotel in the northwest corner of Fairfax for the annual surgery Christmas party. They gathered around tables in small groups, their heads leaning close when they attempted conversation, as the music provided by The Earthlings was loud enough to feel. Many of the residents looked around as if they were having trouble recognizing anyone other than their immediate fellow staff members. They were amazed at how different people looked in their street clothes. The bar was open, and it was apparent that health professionals and their staff had quite a thirst for the so-called golden beverages. The dance floor was empty the first hour, speckled the second, and crowded the third. As people continued to arrive and the dance floor became more crowded, the lines at the restrooms also lengthened.

When Matt Stone arrived, the party had already been in full swing for at least an hour. He despised arriving early and could be counted on to appear fashionably late for most social functions. When he arrived, quite a few heads turned—not to see the chief surgical resident, but to catch a glimpse of the elegant young beauty whom he escorted. His date stood dressed in a silky, green, sleeveless party dress that could be seen to almost perfectly match her eyes if you saw them in the light, which was bright in the hotel's lobby but dim in this room except for the stage where the band performed. She wore her thick, shoulder-length, brown hair in large, loose curls that were carried gently away from her face with a stylish ornamental hairpin.

Linda Baldwin felt more comfortable in her blue jeans and an A.C.U. sweatshirt, but she had looked forward to coming to this event, even if Matt had downplayed its importance a thousand times. She, in turn, had asked him a thousand questions about what to wear, who would be there, and what they would say. Matt had never really been much help in all of this and would always reply that she could get by with any of the Sunday outfits he had seen on her. She had resorted to planning her attire on her own, and Matt's honest appraisal had been an affirmatory "Wow!" when he saw first her earlier that evening. Matt now held his head high and enjoyed introducing his new friend to his resident cohorts.

As the music played, Matt and Linda sampled the fruit, roast beef, and other hors d'oeuvres that were present on long tables bordering the dance floor. In between band numbers they drifted from group to group talking about the music, the rigors of residency life, sports, or any number of current events. Most of the time was spent in introductions and brief identifying comments such as "We worked together on the trauma service" or "He's the only resident to sleep through every Grand Rounds (the surgery department's Saturday morning conference) in his entire training," etc.

One person who stood out in Linda's mind was Michael Simons. She had read an article in the *Fairfax Daily* about him not two weeks before. The article had been about several of his high-risk patients whom had not only survived but were now in accelerated learning programs at their local elementary schools. The party was not a black-tie event. However, Simons wore the same tux he wore to this party every year. The introductions came when Matt and Linda found themselves in line at the punch bowl directly behind Simons, who seemed almost distant to the party going on around him.

"Dr. Simons, I would like you to meet a friend of mine, Linda Baldwin." Simons and Stone shook hands professionally. Linda extended her hand to the professor, and he took it gently in his. Simons held on to her hand and gazed into her green eyes. Linda was uncomfortable with the intensity of his stare.

"I read the recent newspaper article about the two children whom you helped." Linda forced herself to keep from pulling her hand away from his. She could tell that this man pampered his hands carefully, as they were as smooth and soft as any woman could desire for herself.

"Yes, we were very pleased about the outcome in those cases. It's nice for the university to get some positive press for a change." Simons looked at the attractive woman as if preparing for a holiday meal. Her dress was not provocative, but she felt embarrassed at the careful attention he was giving her. Fortunately, the band was between numbers, so at least they did not have to lean close to each other to communicate.

"Nice to have met you." Linda withdrew her hand, fighting the urge to wipe her palm on the side of her dress.

"The pleasure's mine." Simons turned away suddenly and began a conversation with another resident, a male accompanied by a short attractive blonde who appeared to be in her early twenties. Linda stole a glance Simons' way and observed him holding the hand of the young woman the same way he had held hers just a moment before.

"Is he always that intense?" Linda whispered into Matt's left ear.

"He's worse at the hospital. He is a perfectionist right down to the last detail. He expects us to know everything about everyone on his service . . . every bowel movement, every chloride level . . . everything." Now Matt also looked in Simons' direction. He shook his head, as if rejecting a thought. "I don't remember him treating women like this, though. Maybe he's just lonely . . . I heard that his wife left him this year."

"Eeeeuuuuhh!" Linda shivered and shrugged her shoulders quietly. "He gives me the creeps!" She wiped her right hand on her napkin as if it had been contaminated by some unseen impurity.

For the remainder of the evening, until just after 11:30, Matt and Linda met and chatted with more of Matt's fellow-workers and friends. It relieved Linda to see that not all of the surgery attendings were as arrogant or overbearing as Simons. When they finally excused themselves to the department chairman and stepped into the cold night air, the previous light rain had turned into gentle snow flurries.

Once in Matt's small truck, they talked over the events of the evening. Both of them agreed that they had an uncomfortable feeling when they were talking to Simons earlier. *Was it his manner . . . his stare? Or was it something more? Perhaps something even spiritual?*

As they neared Linda's house, she changed the subject. "When will you be traveling back to your home again?"

"You mean in Virginia?"

"Yes." Linda edged closer to him on the bench seat.

"Next month I'm going to return to talk about getting a job." Matt looked over at Linda to see if he could tell what she was getting at. He couldn't.

"Your mom has invited me to come along." Linda spoke at a low volume, with just a hint of hesitancy.

"She did?" Linda wasn't ready for the surprise in his voice.

"I'd only come if it would be what you'd want, of course . . . if I wouldn't be in the way."

Matt started imitating her timid response, then stopped when he realized she may really have some insecurity about meeting his mother. "Of course I want you to come." Matt paused and shook his head disbelievingly. "Man! A guy can never be too careful when his mother and his girlfriend start plotting against him!" He laughed and slid his arm around the shoulders of his now very close companion. "Of course I want you along. It will be great."

Linda rested her head against Matt's shoulder. She couldn't imagine it to be any other way.

◆ ◆ ◆

It wasn't exactly the quiet at-home Christmas day celebration Carol had planned. Instead, she found herself back in her small Mazda heading for the Taft University hospital. Tony was at the wheel, squinting slightly and driving well under the 65 mph speed limit because of the light snow. The horse farms visible along I-64 were almost picture-perfect, with a light blanket of snow covering the gently rolling hills of Kentucky bluegrass. There was very little traffic on the road at this hour: 9 A.M., Christmas day. Around them everything seemed to be at peace. Inside them, their fears pushed the peace away.

Since her successful IVF nearly three and a half months earlier, everything had gone according to plan . . . Carol's and Tony's plan, that is. Now Carol was experiencing renewed memories of her last spontaneous abortion. Remembering the miscarriage made it difficult for her to think anything but anxious, fear-stimulated doubts.

She had gone to bed last night after a quiet celebration with Tony. They had exchanged gifts under the Christmas tree. She had given Tony a new rag sweater and an outdoor thermometer with colorful Canadian geese painted on the metal background. He had given her a new winter coat that was large enough to be worn during her pregnancy. She had not felt that good in a long time. She was tired, however, and had begun to have some mild indigestion, which she attributed to too much Kroger eggnog.

When she got up this morning, she felt no better, with a small case of what felt like menstrual cramps. When she went to the bathroom in the morning, she noticed a small amount of blood on her underpants. Immediately she called Dr. Harrison. He had sounded happy to hear from her, but she knew it was Christmas and that he would want to be with his family. He told her not to worry but to come down for a blood test. "Oh, by the way, you had better pack a few items in an overnight bag . . . just in case."

Not worry? . . . *Just in case?* He might as well have spoken to the wind.

They drove along in silence for much of the trip. Tony began to sing Christmas hymns about halfway to Fairfax. He had a rich baritone voice, but it did not carry well in the environment of the small car. He had sung many of these hymns as part of their local church choir and had even landed a short solo part in this year's Christmas cantata, performed just three nights before. Carol was thankful for the distraction from her own thoughts and rested comfortably, listening to her husband's voice singing the familiar Christmas melodies.

Carol looked out at the passing white countryside. *Music seems to have a power of its own to soothe the troubled waters of our hearts.* She knew she needed to rest and to trust in her Lord. Knowing in her mind and knowing in the depths of her heart were two different things, however, as anyone who has had their faith tested in the furnace of everyday life will testify. Carol spent the last few minutes of their trip reminding herself just who controlled her present situation. It certainly, and comfortingly, wasn't her.

As they pulled into the familiar parking deck and headed for the emergency room, she found herself reassured by the memory of Romans 8:28, a verse she must have turned to a thousand times since the beginning of her infertility ordeal. She quoted the verse to herself and then again aloud, to share her thoughts with Tony, who took her hand as they approached the automatic entrance to the E.R.: "And we know that in all things God works for the good of those who love him, who have been called according to his purpose."

With that, they entered the noisy and often chaotic environment of the T.U. emergency department and exited the snow-laden early quiet of Christmas morning in Fairfax, Kentucky.

◆　◆　◆

Dr. Adam Richards had planned to spend Christmas day with his son, Adam, Jr. The boy remained the delight of his father's heart and at his present age of thirteen had just begun to mature to the point where Adam, Sr. thought they could begin to relate more on a man to man basis, something he had been looking forward to for a long time. It wasn't that he hadn't enjoyed all of the stages up until this point; but now that his wife had left, he was anxious for another blood relative to relate with on a more mature level. In all the chaos of his separation from his wife, being away from Adam, Jr. caused him the greatest pain, as he felt that young manhood was a critical time for his son to have a father figure around. "You were never with him anyway," his wife had truthfully argued. But the doctor had been looking forward to a closer relationship with his son as he reached the teen years just the same, even if he hadn't done the necessary groundwork over the years. Somehow he had always thought that when his son reached a more mature stage, they would naturally hit it off. But things hadn't moved rapidly into the close relationship he had foreseen; and worse, just as his son reached his teenage years Dr. Richards and his wife separated.

Regardless of how the past had gone, Adam, Sr. was determined to make a new start with his son, and he had hoped that being with him on Christmas day would be a catalytic start. So much for his Christmas plans! Adam, Jr. had called just two nights before and told his dad he had an opportunity to go on a ski trip with some neighbors over Christmas. Could he go? Adam, Jr.'s excitement had been hard to contain. What else could his father say but "Yes"?

Richards stood in front of the ten-foot Christmas tree in the den of his Fairfax home in Forest Point. He had bought the tree just two nights ago, before his son had called, hoping to decorate it with Adam on Christmas day. Now it stood adjacent to the fireplace, elegant in its size and fullness, but without any ornaments to grace its boughs. The time was 6 A.M., December 25. He had not been able to sleep in for several weeks now, perhaps even longer, ever since the recurrence of the nightmares. He stroked his hand across the gleaming chrome handlebars of two new Trek mountain bikes he had purchased for himself and his son. As he did so, he noticed that the fine tremor to his hands was returning. He walked to the kitchen and poured himself a second small glass of bourbon.

He was changing. He had never been more aware of what other people were thinking about him. When he was around Simons, he could not help but feel somehow more alive, perhaps just because Simons talked so enthusiastically about their project. For a while, in the beginning, he was sold on the idea that what they were involved in was for the common good of mankind. Lately his thoughts had become slowly clouded, and he found himself more and more facing self-doubt. The love that Simons carried for himself had also infected Richards, but it wore thin the longer they continued their association. At first Richards would go back in the lab and observe and even make a few suggestions about the work to Simons. Simons would nod perfunctorily but would never implement any of Richards' suggestions. Now Richards confined his activities to finding the appropriate subjects for Simons and letting him take care of the data collection. But parallel to his disinvolvement with the project was the waning of his newly stimulated feelings of self-importance that Simons had emphasized as a part of this potentially lifesaving work.

The dreams had not been so quick to go away this time either. Perhaps that was one reason he found himself retreating from the "lab research" room in his clinic while Simons and his cohort, Gentry, were working. In the dream that had startled him from sleep at 4:30 that very morning, the small, wrinkled, aborted infant who grabbed at his white lab coat also had a new feature, different from past dreams—a fine scar from an incision just over the sternum. The scar was well-hidden at first, but just as Richards was leaning closer to inspect the fine handiwork, the scar widened, first allowing only a single drop of red blood to ooze from the top of the incision. Slowly the incision widened and deepened, until the very heart itself was exposed. As Richards looked closer, he could see small tubes entering the baby's right atrium and aorta. The small cannulas flopped back and forth rhythmically with every heartbeat, spraying first small and then massive amounts of blood onto Richards and anything else close by. It was as if the cannulas were connected to a red river with a volume much greater than the blood from a small infant such as the one in his dream.

As before, Richards awoke drenched in sweat, adding realism to his nightmare of being sprayed with blood. He had wiped at his face rapidly after turning on the light; he looked at his wet hands in anxious wonder. Relieved, he rose from his bed, poured himself a drink, and took his place in the lounge chair opposite the tall Christmas tree he had purchased just a few days before.

Perhaps he should decorate the tree anyway, he mused. He felt his confidence return somewhat as the alcohol found its way quickly into his circulatory system. *Maybe I should call on a friend or two. After all, that's what the holiday season is all about, isn't it? Maybe I'll just try out this new mountain bike by myself or invite someone else over for a ride if it isn't too cold.*

First, he decided, a little breakfast and another Christmas bourbon would make the morning a little warmer.

CHAPTER
10

For Layton Redman, the holidays had become a blur of public appearances and travel. He had been in six different cities in the last week and had participated in several highly publicized Christmas volunteer activities. In one, Layton donned a white apron and helped serve the homeless people of Louisville a Christmas turkey dinner. As he dished out large helpings of turkey and dressing, he talked to the people about their concerns and appeared to be genuinely interested. Shortly after the local news crew left, Redman scrambled to get to another interview on a local radio talk-show.

His views had been impacted by the opinions of the majority of Kentuckians as determined by extensive polling by his ever-increasing volunteer staff. He began with his own private views and slowly modeled himself into the "candidate of the people" by slipping into the mainstream and speaking out on those issues. On issues where he departed from the popular views, he remained cautiously silent. On the issues where he found himself in the majority, he spoke out plainly as the only true representative of the people. On controversial issues he was careful to say just the right thing or nothing at all. For example, regarding abortion he remained solidly pro-choice when speaking to audiences who agreed with him and avoided the issue altogether when speaking to other groups. He needed time before introducing this issue into one of his main public speeches, waiting for his pollsters to get a handle on the feelings of "middle Kentucky."

The schedule exacted its toll on Redman. He rarely ate regular meals and kept extremely irregular hours. As a result of his time on the road, he saw less and less of Janice, his fiancée, a fact he blamed for his brief venture into the arms of Samantha Stelling. He wasn't about to take personal responsibility for his actions. His busy schedule and the stress would be his scapegoats if they were later needed to help provide an explanation to Janice. For now, he prided himself on his ability to keep Sam quiet and Janice unsuspecting.

When he had visited Janice recently, their time together had been less than ideal. She did not suspect him to be unfaithful, for she knew nothing of his "outside" interests. The thing that stressed their relationship more than anything was his commitment to the campaign to the exclusion of other matters. Christmas had been one big emotional blowout. Janice was upset at his missing her parents' Christmas dinner just so he could serve in the soup kitchen. Her biting remarks about his sudden burden for the homeless had capped an evening of sulking by Janice and sullen defensiveness by Layton. In the end, he left and spent the night in a motel alone, and Janice cried herself to sleep in the frilly double bed she had grown up with in her parents' home. If he had been governor at that time, the tabloids would have had a heyday. Instead, the increasingly pro-Redman press only reported his humanitarian Christmas spirit. If the media had a bias, it was, so far, solidly behind the seemingly golden Mr. Redman, Mr. Middle Kentucky, friend of the oppressed.

The following morning, Layton found an open florist shop (after calling at least twelve florists) and showed up on Janice's doorstep repentant and with roses in hand. He may have had twisted intentions, but Janice had melted and received him warmly . . . too warmly for the unwed. When he left for another engagement in a short four hours, they were again on speaking terms and he had made promises to do better by their relationship.

When he walked into his office on January 4, he was greeted by a stack of phone messages to return: confirming the dates for upcoming debates, a speech at the opening of a new addition on the

Shriner's Hospital for Crippled Children, and . . . the last item caught his eye: "Please call Sam."

He hadn't spoken to Sam in almost a month. He'd assumed her "problem" had been disposed of, or at least should have been, over two weeks ago. He had written a check for the full amount for Richards' services when he'd first made her appointment months ago. Now as he sat fingering through his mail, his eyes were drawn to a second interesting item: a "missed appointment" slip that had been mailed to him from one of Richards' secretaries. His address had been listed on the check he included when he made the appointment for Sam in the first place. The slip was simply a polite reminder asking the patient to check the appropriate boxes and to drop the card in the return mail. Redman looked at the small card.

> Would you like us to schedule a new appointment? Please call the above number for a convenient time. Our records reveal that your account balance is $480.00. Since you missed your appointment, would you like us to continue to apply the balance to your account or refund your pre-payment?

She missed her appointment! Just what is she up to now? Layton Redman sighed, pressed his forehead against his hands, and stared out the window of his sixth-floor office suite in downtown Louisville. He had been avoiding answering any calls from Sam. He felt sure she had assumed he was away campaigning and couldn't be reached. *Now perhaps it is time to call. Or should I risk a surprise visit?* He sighed heavily and placed the small card from Richards' office in his sport-coat pocket. He was unsure of the best approach. One thing he knew for sure: this needed to be taken care of quietly and expediently.

He spun suddenly in his desk chair, having made a quick decision. He would make a new appointment for Sam. And this time he would make sure she kept it. He was sure he could influence her to make the "right" choice. *After all, she is still fond of me, isn't she? Most women would do anything for an opportunity like the one you have, Samantha Stelling.* He was confident he could make her see it in that light. Redman smiled, admiring his own skill in coming to an answer so quickly for such a potentially explosive problem. Problems like this were Redman's specialty. Redman's smile broadened as a plan solidified in his mind. *Sam will certainly see things differently in a few days.*

He pressed the button on the small intercom. "Jean? Get Dr. Adam Richards on the phone."

◆ ◆ ◆

A red-faced Linda Baldwin raised her voice above the murmuring in the room. "I want to know who wrote this article!" She had the attention of everyone present in the small *Weathervane* office, where the weekly campus newspaper was being laid out in preparation for printing. She slapped a copy of an article whose author was only listed as "Staff" onto the corner of the chief editor's desk. She was nearly always in a great mood, especially in recent months, and had never ever raised her voice in discussing possible articles for the school paper before. As the advisor to the editorial staff, she did not have veto power, but her advice was generally appreciated and heeded. Now in her hand was a copy of an editorial that centered around the policy regarding pregnant but unwed students. The main premise was that pregnant students still felt pressured to quit school regardless of "official policy," and many of them were still failing to seek available resources. That much Linda had no argument with. What bothered her was the listing of several recent pregnant dropouts by name, and an example in the second paragraph stating "... the chairman of the Redman for Governor Committee, who was known to have become quite friendly with the young candidate, became pregnant and quit school just eight weeks later, despite good standing in all her classes ..."

"This sounds like tabloid gossip to me. There is no place in *The Weathervane* for such uncaring conjecture!" Linda looked around the room. She enjoyed working with these young, talented students. All of them worked as volunteers, and most had full school workloads as well. There were four staff members present, and all had their eyes on the floor in front of them. From their reaction Linda could not tell if it was one of them or one of their absent compadres. The room was silent. Finally she added, "I don't really want to know where this came from. If you want to edit this and turn it into an objective look at how these unfortunate students are being discriminated against, that's fine. You might even try getting a few confidential interviews if you promise not to print names. You all know that I like to get on the bandwagon for anyone I think is being treated unjustly. If these young women are still feeling unaccepted and rejected despite a change in policy, document it! But for goodness sake, *do not* print what is only conjecture or hearsay!"

Dean Franklin and Anne Caudill stood together. Dean spoke up. "We wrote the editorial, Linda. We didn't realize how much like gossip it sounded."

"We'll change it. It does sound a lot worse once we heard you read it aloud. We weren't thinking about their feelings, I guess," Anne chimed in, still looking at the floor.

A moment of silence followed. "Kind of proves your point, doesn't it? I mean, who *is* thinking about how these girls *feel*? Perhaps we even share in the attitudes that are making them feel rejected." Linda glanced around the room. Each of her young friends met her gaze and nodded their heads in agreement. She was proud of this group. She knew they would meet her little "challenge" and come up with something much better.

From that point until the last worker left at 1 A.M., the small office was a flurry of activity. It always seemed to be that way when a publishing deadline was near and all of the writers were busy with other classwork for the majority of the week. As for Linda, her input was over, and she knew when to step out and leave it in the hands of her editors. As it was, she had stayed longer than expected. She rushed out at 7:30 to finish an overdue paper of her own.

As she exited the front of the Administration Building (where the *Weathervane* office was located), the cold night air sent a shiver down her spine. Her breathing easily visible, she tightened her scarf and quickened her pace across the large, well-landscaped lawn in front of the building. As she walked, she mused about the extra time she had been spending with the newspaper staff and wondered where she could ever find time in her schedule to fit in everything she felt pressing for attention. As a graduate student in journalism, she was facing her last semester on her way to her Master's degree.

Certainly now was no time to slow down, as she was so close to being done. On top of all of her studies, she now found herself in the middle of an unexpected relationship with Matt Stone. She had no desire to cut back on seeing him, but she knew that something had to be done to ease the strain on her time schedule. She smiled as she thought about Matt but also found herself slightly anxious about the fact that he also was very busy and would be leaving in another six months anyway. *Perhaps*, she thought, *it is time to carefully reevaluate things a little bit here, before getting too committed, too fast.*

Her little red Volkswagen Superbeetle sputtered, then roared to life. Partly out of habit and partly out of the necessity to keep the aging bug running, Linda repetitively pumped the accelerator, sending out a small, smoky cloud bank that enveloped the car. *It's definitely time to look at the master planner. Something's got to give somewhere!*

◆ ◆ ◆

Carol threw down the small paperback novel she had been reading. She yawned, even though all she had been doing for over three weeks now was lying in bed. *"Strict bedrest" has to be the the doctor's idea of medieval punishment. But if it can help save my baby, I'm all for it.* Boredom provided the biggest mental battle . . . just plain old, every day the same, nothing to do but lie in bed boredom. She had been in the T.U. hospital since Christmas day. Hopefully she would be able to be discharged soon. She could lie in bed just as easily at home.

What had kept her there, in need of actual admission, was the fact that every time she stopped getting the tocolytic medications (medicine to stop labor), she began having contractions. She had now been off IV medication for nearly forty-eight hours without having contractions. If she made it the full forty-eight hours, she could be discharged.

So far, she'd read a host of paperback novels, wrote twenty-two letters, and watched at least ten movies on the V.C.R. Tony had rented for her room. Nonetheless, she discovered that everything got old after doing the same activity over and over. At one time when she was busy in graduate school, she would have longed for an extended time period with nothing to do. Now she would have gladly returned to work or even cleaned her apartment, just to get out of bed again. She looked down at her softening body. The trouble was, the longer she stayed in bed, the more her tiredness seemed to be accentuated. And so, even though it was just midafternoon, she closed her eyes to take a short nap.

When she awoke forty-five minutes later, Tony was sitting in the lounge chair next to her bed.

"How long have you been here?"

"Only about fifteen minutes. You were snoring pretty good there. Sure you're not related to any lumberjacks?"

"Pretty funny . . . What time is it anyway?"

Tony twisted around in his seat and looked at the clock on the far wall. His wife was without her glasses at the moment and squinted but still couldn't read the clockface. "Almost 4:30," Tony informed her.

"What's it like outside? Dr. Harrison says if I behave myself I might get to go home in the morning."

"Not too bad out right now. A lot warmer than yesterday . . . 47 degrees when I passed the bank on the way out of Easton." Tony folded up a *Field & Stream* magazine and asked, "Want anything special for dinner? How about something from Olivia's Steakhouse?" He had brought in take-out food from five different restaurants since Carol had become an "in-patient" in an attempt to satisfy his wife's palate. Of course, he knew that hospital cafeteria food could not possibly please all of its patrons, especially pregnant ones who have been pampered by the kitchens of such culinary greats as Tony Jennings.

"This is definitely an Olivia's kind of evening. I've only had red meat twice since I've gotten here. Besides, I'll probably be home tomorrow."

"Oh, oooohhh!" Tony grunted, patting his stomach.

"Enough from the peanut gallery! Let's show a little mercy on the bed-bound, would you!"

"Hey, I'm not saying anything!" Tony replied, standing up and leafing through his wallet. "What would you like?"

"The usual . . . a garlic-laden, eight-ounce sirloin, rolls, and a salad."

"Coming right up!" Tony began walking towards the door. He turned when he heard his wife's sheepish voice behind him.

"Tone? It's just because I've gotten used to your cooking. You've spoiled me."

"Right!" Tony turned and began to leave. He paused once in the hallway and stuck his smiling face through the doorway. "Be right back, lumberjack!" He slipped through the doorway before she could reply.

As she waited, she picked up a novel. A few minutes later she got up to use the bedside commode because she wanted to be entirely comfortable when her dinner arrived. Nothing like a half-full bladder to make a pregnant woman antsy.

Carol struggled with her flimsy hospital gown and sat on the portable, plastic potty-seat. Then she noticed, for the first time since Christmas day, some dark blood on her underwear. She finished quickly and got back into bed. Just getting up and around that minimal amount made her realize how tired she really was. *Just when I thought I was doing a little better!* Anger gripped her and then dissipated into gnawing fear. She pressed the *Call* button.

"Yes? How can I help you?" The voice was female, and almost too sweet.

Carol disliked explaining her problems over the call speaker to the ward clerk. "Could you have my nurse come in here please? I think I'm bleeding!"

"Your nurse will be right there, ma'am." The speaker clicked as the clerk hung up the phone. Carol heard her nurse being paged in only a few seconds. "Theresa, please check 326."

Carol wished Tony hadn't left so quickly. He always seemed to be able to keep a proper perspective on their problems. Now, alone for only a few minutes, Carol felt her emotions riding a frightening rollercoaster. Before the nurse could arrive only minutes later, tears filled Carol's eyes and began running down her paling cheeks.

Her nurse, a compassionate, graying woman of about fifty, entered the room. "Carol?" The nurse sat on the corner of the bed, sensing rightly that silence was the right medication for the present moment. There would be plenty of time in a few minutes for talk. After a few minutes Carol shared her concerns. The nurse checked the bedside commode, which now contained some blood-spotted tissues in addition to Carol's urine. After taking her patient's vital signs, Theresa left the room, quickened her step down the hall, and paged Dr. Harrison.

◆ ◆ ◆

Matt looked down at the January call schedule and sighed. Just when he thought he'd done enough trauma call and had started his V.A. rotation, the trauma chief resident was going on vacation for a week, and the other three general surgery chiefs, including himself, would have to take some extra calls. He was between cases at the V.A. He had only one case left to do, a "staging lap" on a patient with Hodgkin's disease. He had hoped to get out at a decent hour tonight so he could prepare for some time off of his own next week. Besides, he'd just been reminded by his look at the schedule, tomorrow night was a trauma call night, so he wouldn't be home at all then. He checked at the front O.R. desk and saw that his next patient was still not in the room, so he scurried down the hall to the elevators. If he hurried, he would have just enough time to eat a bite before starting the next case. Once in the cafeteria line, he saw one of the junior residents who was currently on the trauma service, Jack Turner.

"Hey, how's the trauma service?" Matt wanted to get a feel for how busy they had been during the winter. Doing trauma during the summer and fall, when Matt had done it, was definitely not the right time if you wanted any sleep.

"Oh, same old stuff, I guess." Jack wore spotted scrubs and appeared in need of a shave. In general, all the residents were required to wear street clothes and ties and white coats outside of the O.R. The trauma service, however, was the exception, as it just wasn't practical to see bloody trauma victims in good clothes. There were also unwritten guidelines that made the surgery residents and the medicine residents easy to tell apart. The medicine residents rarely wore white coats beyond the internship year, the year in which they needed the extra pocket space for all of their books and instruments. The surgical housestaff always wore their white coats. Also, the medicine residents carried their stethoscopes around their necks. The surgical residents carried theirs folded in their lab coat pockets.

Matt studied the menu selection, then requested turkey on wheat bread, thinking to himself that even Linda Baldwin would approve that selection. Matt asked for the "to-go" styrofoam container, thinking of his need to get back to the O.R. He turned to Jack, who was paying for his lunch. "At least you guys are getting a little time to eat. No business today, huh?"

"We had one F.O.O.T. injury, but he had mostly orthopedic problems, and little for the general surgeons to get involved with."

Matt laughed, shaking his head at yet another example of "trauma-ese." F.O.O.T. injuries were those sustained by Falling Out Of Truck, a not so uncommon occurrence in a state richly populated by pickups.

As Matt again passed the front O.R. desk, he stopped to check his beeper for messages. The residents all left their pagers at the desk when they were operating, as they obviously couldn't return calls during cases. His beeper only contained one message: "Call Linda at her home." *I hope everything is okay! It's not like her to call me during the day. She probably has a question about our trip to the Eastern Shore next week. It's about time we get to spend some time together.* Between their two busy schedules, he had only seen her twice since the surgery Christmas party. Matt finished off the turkey sandwich he had carried up from the cafeteria, reached for the phone, and then stopped when he heard his name over the local O.R. intercom. "They're ready for you in room 3, Dr. Stone."

Oh well, I'll have to return her call later. This case shouldn't take too long anyway, he thought optimistically. Matt donned a new O.R. hat, mask, and shoe-covers, and entered the central O.R. corridor to scrub his hands.

◆ ◆ ◆

Tony had only been gone for forty-five minutes. In that short time, his wife's IV had been restarted and medications resumed to suppress labor. Dr. Harrison had arrived and was just finishing an exam when Tony made his entrance, balancing two styrofoam dinner containers and two iced lemonades. He could tell by the atmosphere that things were not like he'd left them. He quickly put the containers of food on the mobile serving tray beside the bed and went over to Carol, who was tightly holding the sheet in front of her in a twisted knot. Tony looked around. Dr. Harrison was folding up a pair of bloodied examination gloves in a large blue, absorbent pad.

Dr. Harrison looked up at Tony, who had not spoken since his arrival. When their eyes met, Dr. Harrison spoke. "We've had a little unexpected trouble here, Tony. Carol has bled again and had a few sharp, cramping pains."

"Labor?"

"I'm afraid so." Dr. Harrison wanted to sound optimistic but did not want to give false hope. "Carol's cervix has already started to dilate. So we've restarted her medications." Dr. Harrison looked at the silent, stunned couple who had placed all of their hopes on this one last try. Tony sat next to his wife with his hand on her shoulder. Carol would not let go of the sheet she was twisting in both hands. "We can only wait and observe now. I'll get new hormone levels to see if the pregnancy is still intact. I'm also going to bring down the ultrasound machine to document the health of the baby and will apply a uterine and fetal monitor to follow the course."

Tony looked at Carol without speaking. After a minute, he spoke softly to Dr. Harrison, while keeping his eyes fixed on his wife's fearful expression. "Do whatever you need to do, doc."

"We sure will." Dr. Harrison turned and walked briskly towards the door.

Carol slowly released her grip on the sheet and touched her lower abdomen. She was aware of her uterus becoming very firm. She was not having a great deal of physical pain but appeared to be in grave distress, with both her mouth and eyes closed tightly as if trying to stop her contractions by mere concentration. In truth, she was trying not to cry, but closing her eyes could not suppress the flow of tears.

Subcutaneous injections of terbutiline were followed quickly with a magnesium sulfate IV drip. For monitoring and for the mag drip, Carol was moved to the labor hall. The continuous magnesium infusion made it difficult for her to focus properly. Time passed in a literal blur.

Dr. Harrison ultrasounded the baby, who still seemed to be alive. But after two hours it was apparent that a spontaneous abortion was imminent. Carol did not respond to the medications and continued to pass some blood and fluid. On examining her again with his gloved hand, Dr. Harrison discovered the newly aborted fetus right at the vaginal introitis. He cleared the vagina of blood and tissue and carefully placed the stillborn fetus in a container for future pathologic examination.

A nurse administered a mild sedative to Carol, who had ceased crying and apparently understood, even in her clouded state, what the doctor's findings were. She felt betrayed, angry, and tired. After Harrison had checked her for the presence of any afterbirth, she was sent back to her room, and the magnesium drip was weaned to off.

Tony had fled from the room upon seeing his wife pass blood for the third time within the hour. This was just before Dr. Harrison's exam, when he discovered the loss of the small fetus. Dr. Harrison looked around the generous waiting room and spotted Tony standing against the windows along the far wall. He approached slowly and placed his hand on Tony's shoulder. He did not need to speak. His actions were message enough. Tony spoke first.

"It's over?"

"Yes."

Tony stared out the window, seeing only his own reflection due to the darkness of the night beyond.

"Can I see her?"

"In a moment." Dr. Harrison turned and gripped Tony's hand. "I'm terribly sorry."

Tony hesitated, then spoke haltingly, "Doc, did you see it? C-could you t-tell—"

"Yes, Tony, I saw it. It was a boy."

"O God!" Tony sobbed, sinking into the nearest chair. He wept for a long time as he released a deep well of emotions for the first time. He then sat quietly for a moment and blew his nose. Dr. Harrison touched Tony's shoulder. "You can see her."

"I want to . . . I need to see her now." Tony spoke in an unexpressive, devastated monotone.

Dr. Harrison stopped at the desk and wrote a note on Carol's chart, followed by several orders. The final order was a note to the secretary to give Carol a return appointment to the reproductive services clinic in two weeks. He was planning to discharge her the next day and wanted everything taken care of today, so she could leave early in the morning if she wanted to.

He wanted to discuss with the Jennings the possibility of trying again. He was not confident. They had been reluctant to try again before. Now it would be even more difficult . . . and even more of a risk.

CHAPTER
11

IN the V.A. O.R. doctor's lounge Matt took his feet off the coffee table in front of him, stood up, and began pacing. He held the phone in his left hand and rubbed his neck with the other. Intermittently, he shut his eyes and lowered his voice. He wasn't sure he liked the conversation he was having. He knew he hadn't anticipated it. He looked around. The only other resident in the lounge had just left, leaving Matt Stone alone with his phone conversation.

"I thought we both felt the Lord's leading in our relationship . . . I know I did. It isn't like we were striving very hard to establish something here." The slight exasperation in Matt's voice was beginning to show.

"Matt, I felt it, too. It's just that, . . . Well, maybe the Lord set this up so we could be friends." Linda struggled to put her feelings into words. "I guess I just don't want to commit myself so soon, Matt. We haven't even seen each other in over a week. It just seems that with our schedules like they are, maybe we shouldn't expect things to go much farther."

Matt didn't reply instantly. The silent periods on the phone always seemed longer than the silence experienced with a person face to face, perhaps because body language has no role to play when speaking over the phone. "What are you getting at, Linda? Are you coming with me to the Eastern Shore? It seems like this is the chance we've been waiting for—a chance to spend some extra time together."

Linda sighed. She wanted to go. She wanted to get closer to Matt. But she also knew that she did not want to be hurt by expectations that were never meant to be stimulated. Linda paused, then spoke softly. "I want to come, Matt. I just want to be careful. I don't want to fall in love if you're only going to move away. I don't even think we see enough of each other while you live in the same town to develop that kind of closeness."

Matt's heart raced. The word "love" was a powerful one. It excited him that she even mentioned it as a future possibility. He also knew that if he raced ahead or outside of God's plans for his life, the consequences would not be rosy. He formulated his reply carefully. "I hear what you're saying. You need to make the final call. The invitation's open. I want you to come. I know it seems like a step closer, what with visiting my mom and all, but just a visit doesn't mean we're entering a lifetime commitment, does it?"

"No."

"No, and—?"

"No, and I'll come, on one additional condition."

"What's that?"

"That you make me spend at least *some* quality time writing for my composition class. I have another paper due, and not enough time to finish if I put it off all weekend." Linda paused, then reflected, "Time, or lack of it, seems to be a central problem with me today, doesn't it?"

"Yes."

"Yes, and—?" Linda greatly exaggerated the "and" to imitate the way in which Matt had just finished questioning her.

"Yes, and I'll make sure you get some work done. I can even do most of the driving, if you can write while we travel."

Matt smiled, stopped pacing, and took his seat again.

◆　◆　◆

Samantha Stelling put down the history text she had been reading for her new political science class, distracted again by the gentle movements she perceived in her lower abdomen. After starting back at A.C.U., she had successfully arranged a lightened second semester of course work and had even been able to apply herself to the task of the timely completion of most of her assignments. Overall, she felt much better than she had only a few months ago when she dropped all of her classes. Her concentration was better now—better, not perfect, as she found herself continually drawn to the colorful atlases of prenatal photographs and away from her other college courses. Now, however, she at least tried to discipline herself to study for one hour prior to allowing herself any time for reading the myriad of books about pregnancy that she had checked out from the local library.

This time the sound of the mailman filling the mail slots in the hallway outside her apartment distracted her. She stood up and placed her ear close to the door. When she heard the postman leave, she slipped out and checked her box. Only one small card today. It was from the Fairfax Family Planning Services, Dr. Richards' clinic. She read the card, which simply reminded her of a new appointment that had been made to replace her last missed clinic visit. A small notation was handwritten in the corner: "Paid in full, check #34531." This puzzled her. She hadn't made the appointment. *Perhaps they automatically issue another appointment to the patients who miss visits? Who paid for this appointment?*

A light bulb snapped on in Sam's head. *Redman! . . . Didn't he say . . . ? Could he be responsible? But how would he know I needed another appointment when he doesn't even answer my phone calls? Now I know I need to talk to him!*

What Sam did not realize was that Redman planned more than a returned phone message for their next communication.

◆　◆　◆

Simons removed his sterile gloves and used a clean towel to wipe the sweat from his neck and forehead. He had just completed a right thoracotomy to close a patent ductus on a 1200-gram premature infant in the N.I.C.U., the Neonatal Intensive Care Unit. Dr. Simons spoke to the onlookers. "This is a rather routine operation, undertaken to close a connection between the pulmonary artery and the aorta, a condition that is normal before birth, but abnormal if the connection persists past birth. I perform this procedure in the N.I.C.U., because the highest risk for the infants involved is in transporting them out of the unit to the O.R. for their surgery." For this reason, and because Simons enjoyed playing to the crowd of nurses and other paraprofessionals gathering to watch, he preferred to do simple operations right in the unit. The cardiothoracic surgeon smiled. *These people would never have the good fortune to see me perform if I did all of my operating in the operating suites.*

Simons knew he was an unusually accomplished surgeon, and today was no exception. Simons had acted swiftly and skillfully and had completed the entire affair in less than twenty minutes. As he dissected, he gave the onlookers a blow by blow account. "I'm now encircling the patent ductus," he would explain, or "The stitch occluding the flow is now secure," etc. He removed his sterile gown and motioned several of the orienting nurses over to the side. He opened the small infant's chart and began to describe what he had just done, drawing with remarkable artistry the patient's arterial anatomy before and after the procedure. The three young nurses felt flattered by this prominent young surgeon's attention. The tallest of the three was particularly enthusiastic, asking questions about the physiology and anatomy involved. After a few minutes of talking, the other nurse recruits walked off, leaving Simons and his new admirer talking quietly, the noisy sounds of the N.I.C.U. drowning out their words to all but those within a few feet.

The tall, slender nurse leaned closer to the surgeon so she could look again at the drawing he'd detailed in the chart. Her beautiful, brunette hair attracted Simons in spite of the scrub outfit she wore. A small, prominent mole on her right cheek added to rather than detracted from her appearance.

Within minutes Simons concluded his charting, walked at a surgeon's pace to the waiting room, and talked to the young infant's family. His ego having been bolstered by the thankful parents, Simons walked away feeling no guilt for taking all of the credit for the efforts of his operating team.

After his post-op chat, he quickened his pace even more. He had promised Adam Richards he would be available in his lab by 3 P.M. *That gives me ten minutes*, Simons thought, looking at his watch. *Just enough time*. He put on his overcoat, not bothering to change out of his scrubs. *The work I need to do at the Family Planning Clinic is best done in scrubs anyway.*

◆ ◆ ◆

Tony entered the kitchen just as Carol threw the day's mail forcefully into the trash. She had received another invitation to a baby shower, this time for a girl she had known since high school and who now worked as a secretary at Carol's old workplace, the psychiatric floor at St. Michael's Medical Center. She had never really enjoyed baby showers before she and Tony were trying to have a child of their own. She definitely didn't relish them now.

"Baby shower?" Tony asked meekly.

"Yes," Carol answered curtly, obviously not wishing to elaborate.

Tony walked to the refrigerator and poured two diet sodas. Carol's abstinence from caffeine had ended when her pregnancy ended. At least now she could drink Diet Coke. He headed into their small living room next to the kitchen. "Coke?"

Carol slumped onto the soft blue couch. She reached out and took the cold glass. "Thanks." Tony flipped through a fishing magazine. After a few minutes had passed Carol added, "I'm sorry about my attitude towards the baby shower. I feel like I should be happy for my friends, but I just feel so envious. I don't want to feel this way, but I do! Sometimes I wish they wouldn't ask me to come. I suspect they want to include me because they feel sorry for me."

Tony didn't reply right away but just put down his magazine and gently squeezed his wife's shoulder. "Did you notice I took down all of the photographs we received in our Christmas cards?" The Jennings' refrigerator had become a collage of photographs mailed in from friends starting families of their own. "It just got to the point where I didn't want to think about children every time I went to the kitchen."

"I hadn't thought about it," Carol confessed. "I didn't realize that it affected you so deeply too. You always seem to have it together. I didn't think it was getting to you."

"Maybe I'm a better actor than you are." Carol's gaze met Tony's. "I know it's all going to work out. I know God's in control. I know it in my head. I'm just not sure that I know it in here." He motioned by bringing his open palm over his heart.

"I'm with you there. I've got all the answers in my head too." Carol took a long swallow of the Diet Coke.

"In time we will experience it in here, too . . . We will, by the grace of God." Tony spoke in a soft but very emphatic tone.

◆ ◆ ◆

Simons looked over at the digital clock beside his bed. 12:34 A.M. Wide awake, he felt compelled to use his energy reviewing the data he'd collected earlier that day. He slipped out of bed quietly, so as not to disturb the slender figure that lay beside him. He looked at the young woman carefully before moving. She appeared to be sleeping. Her breathing was deep and regular. Her lips were parted, and a mole on her right cheek was barely visible in the room's dim light.

Simons put on his robe and stepped silently into his study. Other than the soft illumination emitted by his personal computer, the full moon provided the room's only light. Within a few seconds, Simons accessed a review of the past experiments for display on the screen in front of him. He then entered the data from his pump run earlier that day. After twenty minutes he ran the data through a statistics program to determine its significance.

Simons stopped. He stared into the lit screen, his face reflecting its dancing light as the columns of numbers marched by. He was conscious of how powerful he really felt. Several times before when he worked alone like this, he had felt strange—almost as if he were on the verge of tapping an unseen power within himself. *My work will succeed. I have the power!* He closed his eyes momentarily and concentrated on releasing his own inner potential. He had used this method before and had been surprised at how quickly a new idea came to him, or a solution to a problem he had encountered.

His companion for the night, who had practically fallen over herself in worship of Simons, had not hindered his self-love. He always got along well with others who admired him as much as he admired himself.

He opened his eyes and examined the data in front of him. The data looked significant. What he needed was more numbers to lend credibility to his hypothesis. He had plenty of data on small, young fetuses who had strong enough hearts to support the circulatory demands of slightly larger fetuses, but what he needed were extremely late second trimester babies. The earlier ones had confirmed only that they had hearts capable of doing more work when called upon to do so, but they could never support a term or near-term "premie." *Perhaps Richards could delay abortions on some of his patients to provide even more time for their hearts to grow. Perhaps he could even falsify their fetal age on the clinic charts in order to justify delaying the abortions a few extra weeks. Ultrasounds aren't all that accurate in determining dates anyway, are they? A "mistake" in dating could easily result in underestimating the age by two or three weeks.*

A sound from the next room stopped his meditation. His "guest" turned on the bathroom light.

Simons quickly tapped out the series of commands to store the information he had just entered and exited the program. He didn't want anyone else inspecting his data. Not yet.

◆ ◆ ◆

Adam Richards dined alone . . . again. The one thing in his life that hadn't been affected by his present depression was his appetite. If anything, he ate more, and his bathroom scales, as well as his office coworkers, could have confirmed that. Richards had been extremely busy that week, and that in and of itself benefited him, in that it kept him from ruminating on the loss of his wife, the ever-distancing relationship with his son, and, of course, the dreams.

Being busy made him feel important. Working hard, he told himself, showed his dedication to provide a service to the community—a needed service to young girls in desperate trouble. He always pictured himself in this way. He felt good as an advocate for women's rights. Although he had talked himself into believing that he placed others' interests ahead of his own, he also desired to maintain his lucrative practice, and for this reason he had become a generous supporter of pro-choice candidates over the years.

Richards sat in his favorite corner booth at Georgio's. He had devoured his main course of linguini and clam sauce and had nearly finished a bottle of red wine. He had been there for over two hours. The darkened atmosphere matched his mood, which had mellowed considerably since his first glass of the spirited liquid.

Richards had never considered getting involved with politics. He had gone into medicine when many of his closest college friends were pursuing law and political science degrees. He had always desired to let others fight the legal battles; he didn't want to be involved. He had been, politically speaking, apathetic. His attitude changed when it became apparent that his wallet might be directly affected by new state legislation. Namely, it was now possible for state governments to place direct limitations on abortions . . . and abortions generated a full 85 percent of Richards' generous income. Now he was anything but apathetic. Once political fights jeopardized his income, he became instantly concerned for the rights of women to have safe, effective elimination of their pregnancies.

Currently he supported Layton Redman for governor. Richards, like many others with personal income at stake, had researched the positions of the candidates early and had made his decision based on personal conversations with each candidate. In Richards, Redman had found a faithful supporter. Neither person was outspoken about their relationship. Layton did not advertise the large, under-the-table contributions (which were in excess of $100,000) given by Richards for fear of loss of support from pro-life voters who were supporting him for a variety of other reasons. He saw no reason to offend any voters unnecessarily. And Richards kept his contributions silent so as not to be accused of selfish, conflict-of-interest motivation.

The doctor's very first contributions forged a solid bond between the two men. Redman and Richards knew that they had a great deal to gain from each other.

More recently, their relationship had taken on a more personal tone. Richards had agreed to provide services to a member of Redman's volunteer staff. Richards had admired the apparent support of Redman for his staff member and had noticed that Redman even sent a check along to pay for the "work" himself. He remembered the girl plainly. She had apparently been involved with Redman's campaign at A.C.U. Richards originally had no idea that the young girl's interest in Redman was anything but political.

Now, however, Richards was beginning to wonder about Redman's relationship with the girl. He had received a phone call a few days ago from Layton, who seemed very disturbed about the girl's missing her appointment. When Richards confirmed that she had indeed missed her appointment, he told Layton that missed appointments were not all that uncommon in his business. Layton's reaction gave him suspicion that Layton's interests fell beyond that of support for a faithful volunteer. He had insisted that Richards give her another appointment (which he was only glad to do) and explained that he would "see to it that she keeps this one." That kind of personal investment in the life of a volunteer supporter was almost nonexistent.

Richards did not voice his opinion, of course, and willingly complied with the candidate's wishes. He felt even better about the situation when he remembered that the girl would now be an almost perfect candidate for the study Michael Simons was conducting. With that in mind, Richards personally mailed a new appointment slip to the young woman, Samantha Stelling, on the very afternoon of his conversation with Redman.

Later he confirmed the appointment day with Simons, who said he would block off some time so he could be available for the "delivery of the goods." Richards had snapped at Simons for his use of the obstetrical term "delivery" and asked that he choose another word. He didn't want anyone, not even Michael Simons, to say he was doing deliveries in his clinic! The comment blindsided Simons, but he dismissed it as being due to Richards' inability to look at the work objectively, which in his mind would obviously ultimately serve the good of mankind.

Simons had in fact, much to Richards' liking, almost dealt him out of the experimentation totally, except for the screening and signing of potential "donor mothers." Richards still believed in Simons' research, but he found the work distasteful and preferred to leave the necessary "dirty work" to the surgeon. The fact that he found the work displeasing was, he assured himself, only due to his lack of familiarity with the cardiovascular physiology that Simons talked about so pompously. The fact that his haunting dreams had recurred since his involvement with the research began was a fact he would never leak to Simons. He knew Simons would not understand. It would make him seem weak in Simons' eyes . . . much as it made him feel in his own.

Richards asked for his check. His waiter eyed the generous tip that had been placed beside the wine bottle. After paying his bill, Richards walked slowly to the door. His waiter paused, almost ready to ask the physician if he should call him a cab. He stopped short of verbalizing his concern, not wanting to offend a regular customer, and such a generous one at that.

Adam Richards hit his head on some small, easily avoidable wind-chimes as he exited the front door. The waiter, still watching him, shook his head and then turned to the business of collecting his tip.

◆ ◆ ◆

Layton Redman looked at his watch impatiently. 10:39 P.M. *Why wasn't anyone home? Where could Sam be at this hour?* He knocked sharply on the door again, hoping no one in the neighboring apartments would be disturbed enough to look through their peepholes. He knocked a third time. No answer.

Redman put down the roses he carried, sighed heavily, and exited to look for Sam's orange V.W. After searching the parking lot, he circled the small apartment complex. There was no evidence of Sam's presence anywhere.

Redman had hoped to deliver a personal message to Sam. He needed to convince her of his interest in their relationship, and thus gain influence over her decision to abort or not abort her pregnancy.

This small roadblock in his plans more than slightly perturbed him. He had come out of his way to be here. Actually he did have a meeting in Fairfax the following afternoon, but he could have easily traveled to it in the morning. He returned to his car and waited. *Surely Sam will be back in a few minutes.*

By 11:15 P.M. the limit of Layton's patience had been reached. He felt pressured to accomplish something on this trip; his schedule would make it difficult to return to see Sam for at least two more weeks. That would be after the appointment he'd made for her at the F.F.P. Clinic. He scratched out a quick note to Sam on the back of one of his business cards.

> I wanted to see you tonight. I made you an appointment at
> F.F.P. Clinic. Sorry to have missed you.
> > Love,
> > Layton

I wish I could see her face when she sees these, he thought, placing his note with the flowers in front of her door. *Roses melt a woman's heart even quicker than my charm!* He sauntered back to his vehicle, confident that the present situation would work out to his advantage. His work accomplished, he sped from the lot in his new Ford Bronco.

Sam arrived two minutes after Layton exited the parking lot. She had been cramming for an upcoming exam at the library, where she found fewer distractions than in her apartment. As she approached the door, she saw the flowers. *Roses? For me?* She smiled, clutched the bouquet, and slowly read the attached message.

CHAPTER
12

MATT held Linda's gloved hand as they walked down a deserted stretch of beach along the western edge of the Eastern Shore. They walked slowly, each deep in thought about the events of the weekend. It had been an extremely full three days since they left Fairfax, and they anticipated another thirteen-hour drive back to Kentucky the following day.

The sky over the Chesapeake Bay began to color, first with orange and red, and then with deepening shades of violet and purple. The deep orange color of the sun seemed to intensify as the fiery ball prepared to plunge into the bay. The cold wind blew straight off the water at the quiet couple who had braved the freezing temperature to enjoy the sunset from the beach. The two silhouetted figures walked alone.

The drive down had been relatively uneventful. Matt drove while Linda studied. They had packed their own food so they would not need to stop as often. Linda had insisted on supplying the food, as she was not ready to subject her body to the eating habits of her young surgeon friend. Matt had, of course, concealed a bag of cheese puffs beneath his seat, but he was unsuccessful at quietly opening the bag before his studying guest heard the cellophane crinkle. The fact that he sheepishly tried this little trick behind Linda's back became enormously funny to them and resulted in side-splitting laughter. It was likely because they had been on the road for so many hours that the event seemed entertaining at all. Regardless, their final snickers did not subside for nearly twenty miles. Fortunately, Linda got enough work done during the drive that she didn't feel an undue amount of pressure from her schoolwork for the remainder of the weekend.

They had arrived at Sandra Stone's at just before 10 o'clock P.M. and had stayed up talking until the early morning. Linda was immensely relieved at how easy it was to communicate with Matt's mother. The natural chemistry that seemed to flow between Linda and Matt seemed also to facilitate her new relationship with Sandra. Matt, in fact, fell asleep on the couch in front of the fire while Linda and Sandra talked, and Linda excitedly soaked up story after story about Matt's childhood. Sandra asked many questions about Linda as well and listened carefully to the struggles Linda had endured with the loss of her father and her turn-about towards the faith of her youth. She took comfort in seeing the commitment this young woman carried, a commitment to Christ and his plans for her life. By the end of the evening, a second Baldwin-Stone relationship had forged, one that would add needed understanding and depth to the first.

The next morning, on Saturday, Matt visited Dr. William Sandford's general surgery practice, took a tour of the local hospital, and ate lunch with Dr. Sandford and his wife, Julie. They talked about Matt's future plans and the possibility of his coming to the Eastern Shore the following summer to help with the work there. Sandford was in his forties, had three school-age children, and was interested in recruiting a surgeon capable of performing the gamut of general and vascular surgery. Matt fit the bill but made no commitments. He had several other concerns that he needed to clear up first. In addition, Matt was seeking the green light of God's will, as closely as he could determine it. He still had some praying to do before moving ahead with such a monumental decision.

Saturday evening found Matt, Linda, and Sandra up at the Downses' house for dinner. Finally Linda would meet Tom Downs, Matt's uncle and, more importantly, spiritual father. Tom and his wife Kate lived in a two-story cottage by an inlet along the ocean side of the Shore. Positioned on stilts to guard against high water, the house had a large wrap-around porch that overlooked the Atlantic. The evening began with a feast of she-crab soup, oyster fritters, broiled blue fish, coleslaw, cornbread, baked potatoes, and a never-ending supply of Kate's iced sun-tea. When they thought they could eat no more, they retired to the glassed-in sun room with cups of steaming, fresh coffee. During the meal they all talked about the present and the future. They also spent another evening sharing their memories of the past with Linda. By 11 P.M. the yawning started, and they concluded their stories. They shared their good-byes for the night after Tom led the family in a prayer centered on concerns for God's guidance for Matt in the future.

Matt, Linda, Sandra, Tom, and Kate spent Sunday morning in the local church. In fact, they sat right up on the front row. They hadn't wanted to sit up front, but they filed in ten minutes late, and the front bench was the only one available. Their arrival pleased Pastor Yoder, and he stopped after the second hymn to welcome Matt back and to ask him to introduce his guest. Linda blushed lightly as the pastor thanked Matt for introducing his "girlfriend." She had the uncomfortable feeling that everyone was staring at her, checking out this new friend of "our Matt." She felt better when Matt casually placed his arm on the back of the bench behind her.

Pastor Jim Yoder's message centered on the importance of seeking daily spiritual nutrition from the Word of God, the Holy Bible. The message struck home with Matt. As a resident with little time for anything outside his job, he knew that his commitment to daily quiet times with God suffered from inconsistency. He understood that he could never spend as much time reading the Bible and praying as he did with the activities his job required, but he also realized the necessity of serving the Lord within his job, which meant doing the very best he could. Nonetheless, he realized that he needed more daily refreshment from time spent in isolation with God's Word, no matter how brief. The key word that stuck out to Matt was "daily." The idea was not a new one for him, but he stirred at its remembrance and left with an invigorated commitment to show more consistency in this area of his life.

That afternoon Matt napped, and Linda worked on writing yet another paper. The previous late nights were taking their toll on everyone, however, and Linda went from studying at the desk to studying on the guest bed to studying with her papers on the floor beside her to a full two-hour, mid-afternoon nap. When Matt called up the stairwell to her room at 4:30 P.M., her delayed, gravel-voiced response gave witness that she had accomplished little studying.

After a light supper, Linda and Matt had headed out to the bayside beach to get some exercise and to enjoy the cold, salty air. They walked over a mile at a brisk pace as the sky began to color, signaling the end of a great weekend. As they reached their preplanned turnaround spot, a set of abandoned rowboats, they slowed their pace and turned to look out over the water. Their breath was clearly visible as small clouds of white vapor. They could barely see the lights of the Chesapeake Bay bridge tunnel as they twinkled against the nearly cloudless sky. Down on the beach, away from the lights of the bordering cottages, the night sky would soon be decorated with thousands of stars.

Matt and Linda had not been alone together since the ride down several days before. In the absence of human noise, the wind blowing briskly off of the water and the waves rhythmically crashing on the nearby land's end provided a magnificent orchestra of sound. The two figures walked slowly down the sandy shore, neither needing to speak to communicate their present feelings.

Matt finally broke into the night sounds with a spoken word. He squeezed Linda's hand. "I want you to know how I feel," he said softly above the sounds of the bay.

Linda turned towards him and grasped Matt's other outstretched hand. She met his gaze without any doubt lingering in her own mind about the feelings she also had for him.

"I love you."

Linda continued to gaze into Matt's eyes. "I want you to know how I feel," she began. "I love you too."

They did not need to speak further during their walk. They returned slowly to Sandra's house, each filled with a thousand thoughts that could be verbalized later. For now they were content to let the roar of the wind and the lapping of the bay behind them secure their memory of the three powerful words they had spoken.

❖ ❖ ❖

Sam held the door open for the young reporter as she left. The sandy-haired girl had been pleasant, and the interview had gone much better than Sam had expected. The reporter, Anne Caudill, turned and gave Sam a hug. "Thanks again. See you later!"

"Thank you. I only hope this helps," Sam replied.

"Oh, it will. Expect a story later this month," Anne called back from the covered entrance outside Sam's apartment.

Sam closed the door softly. The two women had talked for nearly three hours. They had shared some of Sam's most intimate feelings about her pregnancy, the pressure she felt to quit school, and the outside pressure she felt to comply with her "boyfriend's" wish for her to have an abortion, etc. In all, even though she had known Anne only in passing before, she felt funny that now Anne knew things about Sam that no one else knew.

She had not been willing to share her story at first. Anne had called the week before and told her that she planned a story for *The Weathervane* about unwed pregnancy on campus—its pressures and problems, and information for others who might need help. The last phrase finally convinced Sam to give her a confidential interview. Perhaps if she shared her story, it might in some way help others in the same situation who were feeling so alone.

Now that the interview was over, she convinced herself she had done the right thing. Concerning the outcome of her pregnancy, she continued to waver. Sam sat on the well-worn couch, her mind spinning with an ever-present argument. *On one hand, I feel so guilty for considering abortion . . . But on the other, what if I have the baby? Layton will never come back to me then! Don't I have a right to be happy? God will forgive me . . . God understands . . . doesn't he? At least I still have a few days to decide.*

Sam had seemed so definite in her resolve to keep her baby just a few days before. She had finally realized there was no chance to spend her life with Layton if he wouldn't even answer her phone calls. But then, when she received his flowers, her heart melted, and her indecisiveness returned in full force.

Perhaps some of her secret hope for being with Layton was

brought out in her interview with Anne, when she referred to the father as her "boyfriend." She had mentioned him several times during the interview—once only in reference to how both she and her boyfriend had wanted to deny the possibility of pregnancy at first, and a second time when she talked about the pressure of his wishes that she proceed with an abortion.

Sam resisted understanding just how slim a chance there was for any future together with Layton. She had spoken to him several times since receiving the roses, each time at his initiative. His persistence in calling her "just to see how she was doing" had made Sam question his motives. He seemed so sincere, and yet each conversation always came around to her pregnancy and his near insistence that she have an abortion. He not only implied but now stated outright that if she had an abortion, they could certainly work things out between them in the future. "Surely you can see that having a baby is the wrong foundation for starting such a beautiful relationship," he had said during their last phone conversation.

Her only regret at this point was her inability to make clear to Layton in no uncertain terms where she stood on the issue. The problem was, every time he started talking softly and sweetly to her about their future together, she would bite her tongue in hopes that he would finally come around.

And so it was that even though she carried a firm commitment in her head, she wavered a bit when she was under Redman's influence. He seemed so concerned that she do the right thing *for her . . . for them!*

Her appointment was for the following afternoon. She had not entirely ruled out going just to talk to Richards, if for no other reason than to please Layton. He had paid for the entire visit anyway. Perhaps Richards could give her more information about keeping her pregnancy, if she so chose. *After all*, Sam thought, *he is an obstetrician, not just an abortionist—by training at least.*

Sam looked at her appointment slip. 2:30 P.M.

◆ ◆ ◆

Twenty miles to the north, Michael Simons sat at his personal computer. He gathered a series of data collection papers in preparation for the following day's experiment. At the top he wrote the name of the donor mother, as a way to identify and sort his data. Later, of course, in the publication of his findings, he would only label each cardiac preparation with a letter or number, but never a name. For now, the name was useful, as it corresponded to Richards' records, which he could then access to find out how well Richards had predicted the age and maturity of the babies before delivery.

"Stelling," Simons wrote with handwriting that was uncharacteristically legible for a surgeon. *Tomorrow will be a wonderful and busy day*.

Simons double-checked his calendar. "F.F.P.Clinic, 3:30 P.M." He was always on time.

◆ ◆ ◆

Anne Caudill had always wanted to be a reporter. But as assistant managing editor of the small university's only weekly newspaper, she had gotten away from her first interest—namely, the thrill of searching out an interesting story or the true facts behind an issue, and bringing the truth to the public arena. At the present, she was only too happy to be able to get out of the small campus office to help with the development of her most recent project. She had started with a short editorial, noting the trends she had observed among the few pregnant, unwed mothers on campus. Her original idea had been appropriately vetoed by her advisor, Linda Baldwin. At Linda's suggestion, she had taken on the project and developed it, hoping to delve into the inward and outward pressures that the pregnant students felt, and to find out what knowledge they had of the resources at hand. She hoped to create a piece that could assess why many students shied away from help, and also to provide a format for reiterating what help was available for these young women.

Many thoughts about her story fought their way to the forefront of Anne's mind as she crossed the campus towards her small office. She slowed her walk from the brisk pace she had begun and settled into contemplative, slow, even steps. She stopped altogether once she was at the front steps of the red-bricked Administration Building and, despite the cold, sat down on the lowest step and took out her small, brown notebook so she could collect her thoughts. She was glad for an excuse to be out on the trail of a story, and not just editing and supervising others for a change.

Anne exhaled sharply and watched her breath hang in front of her. She looked over the notes she had taken during her visit with Sam Stelling. She had enjoyed her visit. Sam had seemed fairly easy to get information from, and she had some similarities with two of the other girls Anne had interviewed. Nonetheless, Anne could not help thinking that Sam was hiding something from her, as if total honesty threatened her in some way. Granted, the subject matter did not lend itself well to easy expression to a stranger, but a lingering suspicion lurked in Anne's mind. She looked up and closed her notes. *Am I being overly suspicious . . . or is this the sixth sense that reporters envy? Is Sam intentionally hiding information from me, or just protecting herself from facts that may give away her identity in the article?*

Anne put down her notebook and rubbed her hands together. She tried to put a finger on why she was feeling the way she was about the interview. Sam had seemed hesitant to share only when talking about the baby's father. *Was that it? Was she purposefully trying to conceal his identity?* Granted, that was not to be the focus of Anne's article, and she was trying to get away from a gossip format. Nonetheless, Anne found her curiosity stimulated by her present train of thought.

Anne had noticed a campaign poster for Layton Redman on Sam's cluttered desk. Lying on the surface of the poster were several wilted, long-stemmed roses. She thought back to the rumors that had circulated about Sam and Redman during the time Sam was working on his campaign at the university. The rumors were not widespread and were unsubstantiated except for one report that they were seen by another member of *The Weathervane* staff having dinner together one evening. All Anne knew was that Sam had withdrawn from school shortly thereafter.

"It's none of your business, girl!" Anne spoke the rebuke to herself under her breath. "That's not the focus of the article!"

She smiled to herself following her own quiet outburst. She reminded herself of Linda Baldwin, her faculty advisor. She had heard Linda talking to herself on several occasions, mostly in a self-policing fashion, like a sideline basketball coach shouting encouragement or correction.

Anne had always liked working under Linda's eye. Like Linda, she shared a commitment to the maintenance of a high ethical standard in her reporting. In Anne's case that standard was evolving, of course; it was strengthened by a new but growing commitment to Christ. Anne had been encouraged by Linda along that score many times since their first meeting in *The Weathervane* staff office during Anne's first semester at A.C.U.

Anne stood to her feet, determined to refocus her thoughts on the purpose of her report. Her determination, however, was thwarted by two new distractions. Her rear-end was numb from sitting on the hard, cold, brick steps; and her empty stomach cried for attention. She stood up quickly and repetitively bounced from her toes to her heels, hoping to jar some new life into her tingling skin. At the same time she struck her pant's seat with her small, brown notebook. The action took only a few brief seconds, and Anne was unsuspecting that anyone was observing her amusing antics.

"Problems, Anne?" The male voice came from Carl Danson, a fellow classmate who was just exiting the "Ad" Building.

Anne swung around, startled by the unexpected voice. A weak "No" was all she could muster. Blushing, she watched as her handsome observer passed. Anne just shook her head and inwardly cringed. She turned and kicked the step where she had been sitting, then slowly climbed the stairs to the building's front entrance.

Now for distraction number two. She felt hungry, and she definitely didn't feel like facing another cafeteria meal. Perhaps she could talk her roommate into ordering a pizza. With that thought, she returned to her normally brisk pace. A *pizza with everything . . . except anchovies, of course.*

◆   ◆   ◆

To Sam, Redman sounded as if he were in a little box. Layton enjoyed calling from his car phone. She reclined on her twice-recovered couch thinking about how Redman had held her on that very spot.

"I've taken care of everything, honey. Dr. Richards is expecting you." Layton spoke quietly, although there was no one around. Sam liked it when he called her that. She smiled. It felt good to think that someone wanted to take care of her.

"I know, Layton. I got the appointment slip." She hesitated before continuing. "It's just that it's our baby, and I've been thinking—"

"Sam!" Layton wasn't speaking quietly anymore. The word "baby" infuriated him. He almost trembled from his lack of control over this situation. Sam stopped talking when he nearly shouted her name. Layton paused a few seconds, trying to calm himself, then continued, "It's just not the right time for us to start a family. The election's coming up. I've got a million loose ends in the law practice to tie up, and . . . well, you know I still have to clear up this Janice thing."

Sam felt her emotions were as solid as water at room temperature. She cringed at the mention of Janice's name as much as Layton did at the word "baby." She wanted so much to do the right thing. She also knew that no one before had held the place in her heart that she had opened for Layton. No one had given her those feelings before. She didn't know what to say. She felt the tears welling up in her eyes.

Layton grew quickly uncomfortable with the silence. "Look, Sam, you know what will happen if the media gets ahold of this. I'll be destroyed! You and I know it's not what it looks like to them . . . We have something special, a connection. Let's not blow our dream. It's not just my idea! You're fighting for this campaign, too!"

Sam wavered. Had he really said "our dream"? She bit her still-quivering lower lip until it hurt.

"Okay," was all Sam could manage to say. She didn't want Layton to know she was crying.

"Okay what?" Layton held his breath without realizing it.

Sam took a deep breath and exhaled through tightly pursed lips. *Perhaps I can go through with this after all. Maybe Layton is right. It would all be over tomorrow, and by next week it would all be history . . .*

ready to be forgotten . . . and forgiven. Perhaps we can start fresh again after the election. And if he wins, who can predict where our lives will end up? "Okay, I'll keep my appointment with Richards."

Layton sighed. "It's the right thing to do, babe. The right thing for you . . . and the right thing for us." Layton paused. He needed to end this conversation, which had already gone longer than he'd expected. He was nearing his destination. He balanced the car phone between his left shoulder and ear and downshifted his Ford Bronco. "Look, I'll call you tomorrow night to make sure you're okay."

"I'd like to see you."

"Next week . . . I promise. Let's just get through this week."

"Bye, Layton."

Redman was relieved that she was ending the conversation. "Bye, Sam."

Layton pulled into the driveway of the large three-story brick colonial residence. He lifted the bouquet of fresh-cut flowers gently from the leather seat beside him and started for the front steps of the house.

He shifted his mind away from his conversation with Sam and onto a closer anticipated pleasure. He hoped Janice would respond to him like the last time he'd brought her flowers.

◆ ◆ ◆

Matt drove into Mrs. Pritchard's driveway at 10:30 P.M. He quietly slipped around to the back stairs that ascended to his second-floor apartment. Quietly, that is, until Mike greeted him at the top of the stairs. Mike's enthusiasm at seeing his friend after the weekend away didn't surprise him, of course. The dog was definitely not the strong, silent type. Strong, yes . . . silent, no.

Matt let the Great Dane into the small apartment. Several dog-snacks later, Mike was suddenly over his enthusiasm and plopped to the floor beside the bed for a nap. Matt, however, washed up and dressed quickly, complete with shirt and tie, and donned a white lab coat and his winter overcoat. He needed to see his "pre-ops," the patients who would be operated on the following morning. He looked at the large dog, who was now snoring comfortably. He decided to forego the battle of ousting the dog as he figured he would only be gone for an hour or two at the most. He slipped through the doorway and down the flight of stairs without a sound.

The night was crisp, and the moon appeared to be nearly full. The cold temperature prompted Matt to enter the front of the university hospital rather than to walk around to the V.A. Hospital behind it. He quickly traversed the connecting walkway between the two buildings and took the elevator to the general surgery floor.

From the nurses' station, Matt paged the third-year resident who had been left in charge for the weekend. He dialed 55, followed by the beeper number 308. After the beeping sound, he began: "Steve, this is Matt. Give me a call at 6281 . . . 6281; that's VA6281. Thanks."

Matt waited impatiently for the phone to ring. One minute, then two passed. Time seemed to drag. The resident should have returned the call by now . . . unless he was in the O.R. and couldn't answer the page himself. *Rrringgg!*

Matt picked up the receiver. "Hello, this is Matt."

"Dr. Stone." The voice was female; this was not the resident he had just paged. "Dr. Edwards is in the O.R. Can I take a message?"

"What's going on in the O.R.?"

"Upper G.I. bleed." Matt could hear Steve Edwards in the background asking for him to come up.

"Who's up there with Steve?"

"Only a med student. The attending's on his way." The circulating nurse covered the phone mouthpiece to listen to Steve Edwards. She then relayed the message to Matt. "He would like you to come up if you are available."

"Okay, I'm on my way." Matt hung up the phone and sighed. So much for his intentions of being back home anytime soon. He walked up one flight of stairs to the sixth floor. In the men's changing room, he put on a clean pair of scrubs. Strangely, it seemed as if he had never been gone, as if his whole weekend away were somehow imagined. He quickly donned a disposable hat, mask, and shoecovers and entered the O.R.'s central corridor. The action was in suite number one. Matt walked though the swinging door.

He surveyed the room quickly. Obviously there had been a lot of hurried activity, as the normally neat surgical table holding the instruments was uncharacteristically chaotic for Denise Peterson, who was assisting Dr. Steve Edwards. She was known for her compulsive orderliness and would not let anyone touch her organized display of surgical instruments—at least, before they asked for the instrument by the proper name. If the surgeon asked her for the tissue forceps, she handed them quickly and accurately so that the surgeon never had to lift his or her eyes from the operative field. Denise was harmony in motion. She made the surgeon look very smooth. But have that same surgeon simply reach over and pick up a needed item off of the instrument stand without asking and Denise Peterson's reaction was as sharp as her surgical set-up was neat. No surgical resident would try that maneuver twice.

Tonight, however, the instruments were in disarray. Denise had abandoned her position as scrub tech and actively played a second assistant role to help suction the blood from the operative field so the surgeon and his assistant could see. She was as relieved as anyone to see Matt Stone push through the swinging door.

"What's going on, Steve?" Matt tried to hide his irritation at the obvious problems around him.

"Sixty-three-year-old alcoholic with hemorrhagic gastritis . . . Admitted yesterday. He seemed to stop bleeding last night after his fourth unit of packed cells. This evening he started again . . . Gave him two more units after he barfed up a large basin of blood. We moved him to the unit, but he dropped his pressure on me before I could get him scoped."

Matt stood on a stool looking over Steve's shoulder. From that vantage point, it appeared that everything was bleeding, even the cut skin edge, which should have stopped long before. "He looks like he's got a coagulopathy. Have you given any fresh frozen plasma or platelets?" Matt's last question was directed at the anesthesiologist at the head of the table. The FFP and platelets were needed to correct the patient's bleeding disorder.

"No." The anesthesia resident seemed preoccupied with just keeping up with the packed red cell transfusions and other fluid lines that were tangled in a hopeless mess above the operating table.

Matt directed his next statement to the circulating nurse. "Call down and get us four units of FFP and a ten-pack of platelets STAT!" He then looked back at Steve before exiting to wash his hands. "You've called the attending, haven't you?"

"Yeah, but it's Ewing, and he said he needed to check on a case at the university first."

Matt sighed and pushed his way quickly into the central corridor to scrub up. The door swung noisily behind him. He wondered just what Edwards had told Dr. Ewing when he called. He knew Steve had an annoying tendency to paint a stilted picture because of his own overconfidence. The attending surgeon was perhaps taking his time just because he was unaware of how critically ill the patient really was.

Matt finished the scrub and reentered the room. He dried his hands with a sterile towel and was gowned and gloved by Denise.

Steve Edwards tried with futility to stop the bleeding stomach by oversewing the bleeding sites with suture.

"It looks like we need to do a gastrectomy." Matt wasn't making a suggestion.

"I thought he wouldn't tolerate a resection," Steve countered.

"He won't tolerate *not* doing a resection. Now let's get this stomach out and get out of here before he exsanguinates on the table!"

Steve didn't argue back. Surgical training was militaristic enough that junior residents usually followed orders just the way the interns followed theirs—swiftly and with minimal questions.

"Kocher! . . . Debakey's . . . Vanderbuilt!" Steve Edwards called out the names of the instruments as he needed them. Denise was happy to be back passing instruments and reorganizing her surgical tray.

The stomach was out by the time Dr. Trent Ewing came through the door. "Matt! I didn't know you'd be helping us tonight." He spoke with a sing-song quality to his voice, giving Matt some friendly but expected grief for daring to take a few days off.

"Neither did I." Matt was not in the mood for taking any grief. He gave the details of the operation to Ewing. The patient was extremely unstable. Jointly, they decided it was best to put in a jejunostomy tube and get the patient off the table alive. They could always come back at a later time and connect the patient's esophagus to his small bowel. Always, that is, if the patient survived.

They finished the remainder of the case in thirty minutes. Matt headed for the door after they got the patient back to the I.C.U.

"Call me if you have any trouble. I'm back in town, so that means my beeper's on." Matt fastened his watch band as he talked. The hands of the watch told him he'd been gone longer than he'd thought . . . 2:30 A.M.

In ten minutes he arrived back at his small apartment. It didn't look as if the snoring dog had even budged.

"Sounds as if you could use a tonsillectomy, my friend."

In another seven minutes, Matt was adding his own sonorous noises to the guttural snorts of his dreaming Great Dane.

CHAPTER
13

Tony waited in the large, busy parking lot for Carol to pick him up. His small Mazda pickup had gone the way of their house . . . sold to help pay for their medical bills. Tony was happy to be getting off work. He was not happy to be waiting.

He had taken a second job as a clerk in the hardware section at Wal-Mart. With his experience at his own store, it had been easier than he thought to get the part-time position. He had mixed feelings at first, and he'd waited three full weeks before he told his father. He felt like he was working for the competition. His father understood, of course, as would anyone who looked at their medical expenses, which had piled up during the past months. When he first picked his insurance carrier, it seemed only natural to go for a basic medical coverage policy, which unfortunately omitted special treatment and diagnostic workups for infertility.

Dr. Harrison had been as lenient as the university hospital would let him. He referred the Jennings to the hospital's financial counselors, and they were making a good-faith effort to meet the required monthly payments.

In one way, Tony was thankful that they had access to the very best that modern medical technology had to offer, and for that privilege he was prepared to pay. On the other hand, he would have been more enthusiastic about the bill if he was now a father. He had worked on a horse stud farm one summer after high school. At least in that business the customer was guaranteed a successful pregnancy. *Oh well, this ain't horses, and we were never given a guarantee.* Tony sighed.

Tony looked at his watch for the third time. He'd been waiting for twenty minutes. Even with his usually relaxed demeanor, he had little tolerance for this kind of "down time." *Where is Carol?* He was just getting ready to head back inside to find a phone when he saw her silver hatchback pull into the far corner of the lot. As she approached, he could see that she was smiling. Just leave it to Carol to be in a good mood when the opposite feelings had overtaken her spouse. It seemed that the normal situation lately had been just the reverse, but not today.

"Hi, honey." Carol leaned over and greeted her husband with a kiss.

Tony could already tell that he was going to have a tough time staying mad at her for very long. "Hi," Tony sulked.

Carol continued to smile as if she had a proud little secret. She wasn't content to hold it in for very long. "Don't you want to know where I've been?"

"I want to know why you're late, yes."

"Is that why you're so quiet?" Carol took her eyes off the road long enough to study Tony's reaction. "Look, I'm sorry I'm late. I was in a very important meeting with one of the hospital's new social workers. She used to work for the state's adoption agency. She filled me in on all the details. She even gave the name of an attorney who helps coordinate private adoptions and could help us out in this—"

"In what? Who says we want to adopt a child?" Tony stared out the window at the passing tree line. "I said I wanted my own children. I never said anything about adoption. Besides, even if we were in agreement about this, perhaps we should start with the state agency, not a private adoption lawyer. I'll be working two jobs until I'm a grandfather!"

It didn't take much discernment to see that her timing at approaching this subject was poor. Carol curtailed her excitement and inwardly vowed to bring up the subject later, when Tony seemed to be in a more favorable frame of mind.

They drove into their apartment complex parking lot. Carol

jumped out and got the mail before Tony could get out of the car. She stood with her back to Tony and quickly stuffed three bills into her purse, then turned and handed her husband the remaining junk mail. Creating the proper frame of mind for continuing their conversation would have to include getting his mind off their financial straits. Carol again smiled as if she were hiding a proud little secret and entered their small apartment behind Tony.

◆ ◆ ◆

Richards stared at himself in the bathroom mirror. He wasn't sure that even an invigorating shower and some strong coffee would erase the dark circles from beneath his eyes. He reached up and touched his forehead on the right, just behind the hairline. A large bruise was barely visible beneath his thick, dark hair. His fingers explored the swelling as he strained to remember how it had gotten there. *I must have fallen.* He stepped back and put down the shot glass he held with the other hand. *Just a little eye-opener to start the day.* Richards stumbled towards the kitchen and flipped on his Mr. Coffee. He had prepared the machine the night before so he could save time in the morning. He had been meaning to get a new coffee maker with an automatic timer so he could wake up to his favorite brew, but he hadn't seemed to find the time or motivation to get much done lately.

He stepped back into the bathroom. He didn't remember getting undressed last night. He started the shower and began to shave as the steam rolled from beneath the shower curtain.

There was a half-empty bottle of Maker's Mark bourbon on the night table. A bottle of Halcion stood beside it, also half-empty. He had just gotten another prescription for it filled three days ago. He discovered that he could keep his dreams at bay as long as he took enough of the sleeping aid. They were good for his sleep but bad for his head. *Last night I used three . . . or was it four?* He was having a hard time remembering much about last night at all. The liquor, he told himself, was just for the present time. He would lay off once the dreams went away again. They always had in the past.

After a shower, Richards poured a large steaming mug of coffee.

The mug was a personal favorite of his. It wasn't that attractive, really. The red lettering on the side, "HEAL WITH STEEL," referred to the ability of the surgeon to cure by the knowledgeable application of the stainless steel knifeblade. As a gynecologist, he prided himself in the fact that he participated in both the medical and surgical aspects of modern practice. Richards had been given the mug as a part of his "Intern of the Year" award at the end of his first year of residency.

As he sipped his coffee, he rubbed his neck and checked his daily planner. It looked to be a full day up into the early afternoon. He had purposefully kept the afternoon light, as he knew Simons would be working. Simons had asked him to keep his patient load to a minimum so there would be little chance of distractions. Simons had nearly stroked when he saw a patient being treated in the exam room next to where the last donation/abortion had been done. One of the last donor preparations had actually made a feeble cry as Gentry carried it to the back room where they performed the experiments. After that, Simons had insisted that no one else be allowed in the adjacent rooms while he worked.

Richards sighed as he anticipated the afternoon with the cardiothoracic surgeon around. He disliked the disruptions the experiments caused in his schedule. He still believed in what they were doing, but he didn't like the idea of delaying the late abortions even more, just to get a stronger mature heart. *After all, restrictions still exist on third trimester abortions*. Simons pointed out the advantages of the older cardiac preparations and had even suggested to Richards that he alter his office records so the dates of conception would look as if the patients were not as far along in their pregnancy as they really were. Of course, Simons had added, he would carefully record the correct ages of the cardiac preparations so that his data would be meaningful.

Adam Richards also disliked the way Simons carefully avoided the term "fetus" or "baby." Not that he relished the terms either, but he preferred the term "P.O.C." or "products of conception" to Simons' more frequent use of the term "abortion donor" or "cardiac preparation."

He scanned down over his patient list. The day had the potential of being quite lucrative. His eyes fixated on the name of the patient with the oldest pregnancy, the chosen donor mother for this afternoon's pump run . . . Samantha Stelling. *Didn't Layton Redman call me about her just last night?* . . . "Just calling to let you know that everything is all set . . . I know she missed her last appointment and all, but, uh, everything is fine now . . . Uh . . . Say, . . . you won't mention my name, will you? . . . She was a volunteer in the campaign and . . . uh . . . well, this sort of thing needs to be kept quiet . . . You understand." Richards thought he remembered assuring Redman not to worry, that everything would be strictly confidential, but the details of his conversation were clouded with the bourbon that now caused a rhythmic, throbbing sensation in his temples.

Richards took four Ibuprofen caplets and drained the coffee from the old mug. *A prophylactic painkiller or two will certainly be needed for a day like I'm planning.*

He rushed out without eating breakfast and didn't take time to put on a tie either. He planned to put on scrubs as soon as he got to the office anyway. The activities he had planned today were not best performed in a coat and tie.

◆ ◆ ◆

Scott Tanous truly loved his job, a job that not just anyone could love. Scott, a fourth-year pathology resident, had come in early that morning to do the one thing he didn't like—examine and record pathology reports on the P.O.C.s from the Fairfax Family Planning Clinic. He had avoided doing it the night before, as he was too busy preparing a talk for the weekly Tumor Board conference. Since all the residents divided the worst jobs evenly, this distasteful responsibility only fell to his work roster once every few months. The pathology attendings rarely even looked at these specimens. The only thing that needed to be done was to locate the small embryo or fetus and confirm as well as possible that a complete abortion had been done. There were no microscopic slides to be made, so the work normally proceeded at a quick pace.

The older saline abortion fetuses were easy. The pathologist just weighed the specimens and recorded their sex if it could be determined. There was certainly no need to do an ultra-careful examination to make a diagnosis. Most of the residents did the work hurriedly, knowing that no one's health or prognosis hung in the balance, as could be the case with other diagnoses the pathologists rendered. The quicker the specimen was weighed and recorded, the quicker the resident could move on to something more challenging.

Dr. Tanous prided himself on being an extension of the arm of clinical medicine. He not only looked at the patient's tissue under the scrutiny of the microscope, but he often searched out the patient's clinical history to correlate with his pathologic analysis. He had spent his first two years after medical school as a surgical resident just so he would have a better knowledge of what happened to the specimens before the pathologist examined them. He viewed himself as a sort of Sherlock Holmes of medicine, searching for clues, never giving up until there was no doubt about the pathologic diagnosis. He was planning to do a forensic medicine fellowship after his pathology training just to get closer to the vision he so often imagined.

The pathology resident set down his large cup of Hardee's coffee on the corner of the lab counter. He crumpled the paper from his sausage biscuit and tossed it successfully into the large trash container in the room's corner. The walls of the lab were completely papered with "Far Side" comics, reflecting the unique humor of the pathologists who frequented the lab. Scott reached for the first of thirty-five containers, a full week's worth of specimens from the F.F.P. Clinic.

The containers were of various sizes, depending on the size and therefore the age of their contents. He started with the smaller ones to get the more time-consuming work over with quickly. As he worked, he dictated into a small dictaphone the mother's name and identification number and a brief description of the contents of the P.O.C. He operated the dictaphone with a foot pedal, leaving both hands free to examine and measure the specimens. All specimens were submitted for "gross only," indicating that the examination by the pathologist was to be with the naked eye only. Scott worked his way through the containers and necessary dictations with the speed and ease that came from doing the same job the same way hundreds of times before. As he worked his way up to the larger containers, he winced as he lifted each specimen from their plastic dwellings. *I went into pathology for this?*

As he lifted one small male fetus from the container, he noticed bloody fluid dripping off the infant's body. *Strange—I don't recall ever seeing the formaldehyde this color before.* Scott quickly scanned the infant, noting its sex and weight. Unsure of the significance of the bloody fluid, he did not dictate this detail into the pathology report. The fetus did not appear obviously traumatized other than the routine skin changes seen as a result of the hypertonic saline injection. *The needle injecting the saline must have pricked the baby, causing it to ooze blood after the abortionist extracted it.* Nonetheless, it made no difference to the mother or the specimen, and Scott declined to spend any more than the minimum required time with these specimens. He hurried on to the next one.

As he dropped the male fetus back into the container, an incision hidden in the middle of the sternum separated slightly at the top. A small amount of blood from around the heart area again darkened the already pink formaldehyde preservative. Dr. Tanous snapped on the lid, not recognizing the subtle evidence of what the fetus had recently experienced.

Scott finished up his job, then put the containers in a stack to be taken to the incinerator. There existed no reason to save these specimens. As far as he remembered, no one had ever doubted the pathologist's diagnosis for one of these cases. They would save their storage space for other cases with educational benefit.

Scott picked up his coffee cup and swirled the remaining liquid. He brought it close to his mouth but stopped short of taking a sip of the now obviously cold liquid. He trashed the cup and flipped off the light to the otherwise uninhabited lab. Glad to have the job behind him, he headed for the residents' lounge to study.

◆ ◆ ◆

Lucy Pritchard was all too willing to help out where Matt Stone was concerned. She thought of him as the son she'd never had. Even though she was old enough to be his grandmother, she could not envision herself as that, having never had any children of her own, much less grandchildren. Lucy never really liked formality. Her renters were usually residents, and most stayed for three or four years before moving on. She gathered pictures of the children of each of her former renters from yearly Christmas cards and covered her refrigerator with them. She had grown to love each one. She had tried not to interfere with any of her tenants. They all seemed so busy to her, always leaving early and many times arriving home after her bedtime.

Matt, however was different. It seemed she could never tire of his stories of the hospital and his life there. She often wondered if he embellished some of the better ones just for her. Because of Matt's friendly, open manner, their relationship had grown. He would look in on her as often as he could. She would collect his mail and put it on his card table, which served as not only his kitchen table but also as the repository of anything that hadn't seemed to find a more suitable location. That was as far as their agreement went—she would bring in the mail only. Matt could tell, however, that often she would do more, emptying the trash and filling his small refrigerator with food items she no longer wanted, things of course that he would eat without any problem, such as Lucy's homemade derby pie or other calorie-laden palate pleasers.

And so when a pretty brunette woman with a mischievous smile showed up at Lucy's door asking for a key to Matt's apartment, Lucy knew exactly who the visitor was. "You've just got to be Linda." Lucy extended her hand as she answered the shy request. "I've heard so much about you," she added, never once thinking of pausing for a reply. "I've never seen a young man so taken with a woman before in all my life."

Linda Baldwin smiled pleasantly. Lucy appeared just as Matt had described her. "That's nice to hear—" She stopped abruptly as Lucy took her hand and gently steered her through the crowded living room. Lucy hadn't really verbalized an invitation. It just seemed natural to her that she and this new young visitor needed to sit and talk for a spell. Lucy finally released her guest's hand when they were next to a large oak table.

"Please, have a seat. Would you drink some coffee? I always make too much for just me."

Linda indicated she would. She could not politely refuse the generosity. *There is little chance that I'm not going to spend the next hour right here listening to stories about Matt Stone from the perspective of his friend, Lucy Pritchard,* Linda mused to herself. At any rate, Linda wanted the keys to Matt's apartment, and this seemed the only way to get them.

Nearly two hours and a complete pot of coffee later, Lucy exclaimed, "My oh my! I've talked on and on . . . Now, what was it you came for in the first place? . . . Not just to talk to me . . . Certainly you didn't expect to find Matt at this hour of the morning?"

"I just wanted to put some things in his apartment." Linda stood and smiled. "I was hoping you'd let me in."

"Why, that's no problem at all," Lucy said with a smile. "Why didn't you say so in the first place?"

Linda couldn't think of a reply. Thankfully, it didn't appear necessary to Lucy, who added, "Just bring it back when you're through."

It amazed Linda that something as small as a house key could be found and retrieved so quickly from a black purse so large, but with one swift motion Lucy had the key and handed it to her open-mouthed observer. Linda couldn't help but wonder what all Mrs. Pritchard kept in her nearly luggage-sized purse.

With the key in hand, Linda headed up the wooden back stairs to Matt's apartment. If she could get around the sleeping dog on the landing, she just might finish the little job she'd set out to do.

"Nice, doggie, . . . niiiicccccce doggie," Linda whispered as she inserted the key and slipped past the sleeping canine. Her mischievous smile returned as she closed the door quietly behind her.

◆ ◆ ◆

Anne Caudill caught only a fleeting glimpse of the back of Sam's car as she sped out of the parking lot. She had called out after her with an urgency that Anne herself didn't understand. Sam certainly had not heard her because she was well over a hundred yards from where Anne stood in front of Sam's apartment building. Anne stayed there in the freezing temperature for what must have been two minutes, just staring off in the direction of Sam's car. She didn't understand her feelings. She just knew she had to visit Sam that morning. Anne sighed heavily, her breath a crisp column of moisture in front of her. She turned and headed back to her dorm room, on foot, just as she had come.

In her hand she held a stack of literature for expectant mothers, a magazine with an article by an unmarried woman who had decided to give up her baby for adoption, and two other articles on nutrition that Anne had promised to bring by for Sam to see. Anne rolled the literature up into a tight spiral wad and smacked it sharply against her gloved hand in frustration.

She hadn't really planned on coming by to see Sam that morning, but when she got up, Sam was on her mind. At first Anne thought it was only natural for her to think of Sam, as she was doing a story about unplanned pregnancy on campus. But the more she tried to get her other work done, the stronger the urge to visit Sam became. She had visited six other single girls who were either pregnant or had delivered babies during college. She had also interviewed two who had opted for abortion. She did not feel inclined to visit any of them . . . only Sam. Finally, more out of frustration than obedience to the Holy Spirit's prompting, Anne stood up and shouted, "What do you want from me?"

Anne wasn't even sure whom she was talking to. As a young Christian, she wasn't familiar with daily, regular communication with her Heavenly Father. She looked around the room and flung the notes she worked from onto the desk. Her mind strained to understand the urgency of the thoughts she experienced. Slowly, quietly, she began to understand. *Pray.* Anne turned her head as if she were beginning to hear. *Pray for Sam . . . Pray for Sam and her baby.*

Anne obeyed the prompting and began, somewhat hesitantly at first, to pray. "Lord God, I have been thinking about Sam all morning. I'm not sure what to pray, but perhaps the reason she is on my mind is because she needs some help right now. If there is trouble somewhere for Sam, please be with her and her baby, and help all things to turn out according to your plans."

Anne shook her head. She hoped she'd heard the right message. The whole experience had so far left her with more questions than answers.

At that point she grabbed her coat and headed for the door. *I'll just drop in for a visit. Perhaps then I can make sense of all this.* She stopped at the door and retrieved a small stack of articles and other papers on the corner of her desk. *At least if I have something to give her, I won't feel so stupid for just showing up like this, without even knowing why.*

Now, after missing Sam entirely, Anne strained to make sense of her unusual morning. Slowly she picked her way across the lawn in front of her dorm. The melting snow had left the grass dotted with small puddles. She started wondering if her whole morning would turn out to be a waste. So far she hadn't gotten a thing accomplished—at least nothing of which she was aware. She climbed the brick stairs to her dorm and resolved to give Sam a call later that day. She thought that Sam might tell her something to help her figure out the events of her strange morning.

◆ ◆ ◆

Tony looked at the columns of numbers in front of him. If nothing else, sorting out his financial miseries helped him to see concretely just what he could do. *Okay, ten dollars a month from our food budget, twenty dollars a month less for car expenses since we sold the pickup, packing my lunch should save a little, twenty dollars a month from our clothing budget . . .* Slowly, month by month, they would get back on solid ground. Fortunately, at least his hardware business was prospering. *Maybe, just maybe, we will be able to seriously consider an adoption.*

Tony never stayed angry for very long, particularly at Carol. It wasn't like he hadn't thought of adoption before, but his frustrations had stacked up and were nearly overwhelming, and he wasn't in the mood to admit it. Carol understood, of course, but she knew just how to reintroduce the subject at the proper moment.

For a change Carol prepared dinner. Tony did the dishes after they ate, and they made small talk about their day. After dinner they switched on Cable News Update. A basic cable TV package was still in their budget, though it had been debated during each of their monthly "budget talks" for the last four months. Tony watched the top stories, and Carol read a *Good Housekeeping* magazine.

Carol glanced at the TV during an ad segment. Colorfully clothed children from all races were running and playing as cheerful music played behind a voice-over. A soothing male voice explained how many were choosing to give life to their pregnancies even in the face of inconvenient circumstances. The concluding statement summarized the ad: "Life—what a beautiful choice." Carol glanced at Tony to see if he had been watching the children. She studied his response. She thought he'd even smiled as he watched a mud-covered little boy playing with a dog. She took her cue and moved to the love seat beside her husband. She cuddled up next to his shoulder and pretended to watch the news.

"Tony . . ." Carol spoke softly. "We can have our own children." She paused. "We can adopt our own children."

Tony listened, but his eyes remained on the TV.

Carol waited, then spoke again. "I know you'd make a great dad." Tony responded by putting his arm around her shoulders.

"I wouldn't have been so great today . . . I'm too impatient . . . I'm sorry."

"Forget it. It's been a tough couple of months."

Tony gave her a gentle squeeze. He felt better just admitting his impatience. By the next commercial, he started to feel playful. "So, what do we do first?"

"Do first, what?"

"I mean, like, do we just go to, like, Kroger's to pick one out?" Tony put on his best thick, valley-girl accent. Carol smiled, so he continued, "Oooh, look, these over here are, like, only 49 cents a pound!"

"You are hopeless."

"Not! You married me."

"Like, I couldn't help myself, dude!" Carol jabbed Tony in the right flank, interrupting his laughter only momentarily.

The conversation spiraled downhill from there, each one in turn drawing out their sentences more and more with generous portions of *Wayne's World* expressions.

Sadly, despite their many months of infertility struggles, neither

Tony or Carol knew much about the adoption process. As they searched, they would learn.

It would be an eye-opening process.

◆ ◆ ◆

Mr. Whithers had been a faithful employee of the university hospital for twelve years. He thought he'd seen just about everything. He was picking up all of the pathology specimens from the stack earmarked for the incinerator and had nearly completed the job. He put all of the trash of this type into red bags marked "Biological Hazardous Waste." The containers were an opaque white, so you couldn't tell what was inside. Sometimes Mr. Whithers opened the larger ones just to see what kind of specimen floated in the formaldehyde. Once he'd even seen a hemicorporectomy specimen from a radical surgery where the entire lower half of a person's body had been removed. It had shaken him up pretty badly, and he didn't sleep well for days after that. But somehow he hadn't quite been able to shake off his morbid curiosity and still found himself opening the mysterious containers when his urges got the best of him. He had been known to play a mental guessing game with himself to see if he could correctly name the contents of a given container. He had also been known to brag to a few friends, "I bet I could identify just about any body part there is by now. Next thing you know, they'll be asking me which parts to take out!"

Today he held the last container, one of the largest of the group bound for the incinerator. He slowly moved it up and down to judge the weight, closing his eyes as he did, as if he could make a better guess in that way. By the size of it he estimated it contained a uterus or a breast or maybe a portion of a colon. He looked around the room. The pathology staff were all off at a lunchtime conference, the weekly Tumor Board. He set the container on the edge of the nearby table and gently pried off the lid. The gray-haired man was not prepared for what he saw. He tried to quickly reseal the lid, but in his excitement he knocked the entire container onto the floor, spilling bloody formaldehyde and saline all over his blue pants. The specimen, which even a non-medical employee could identify as a tiny, male fetus, rolled under the table after a sickening splat on the floor.

Whithers scrambled to pick it up, and and as he did, his finger slid right into the open sternum. He gasped and turned pale. He thought sure the chest had just split open as a result of the fall, that perhaps somehow the fluid the baby was soaking in had made the skin stiff and likely to tear. But then, just as he was placing the fetus into the white tub again, he saw the evidence of the baby's recent "surgery." There were sutures carefully and evenly spaced along the edge of the sternal bone and skin that had torn as a result of the fall. He had never seen work like this from a pathologist. *This is somebody's dead baby, a baby who has obviously undergone some surgery but didn't make it!*

Whithers felt violently nauseated. He dropped the small specimen into the container and emptied his breakfast into the stainless steel sink next to the table. *This must be a mistake. This child should be going to the funeral home, not the incinerator!* He checked the tag on the container. It was clearly marked as "waste." *Someone has made a mistake—a terrible mistake! Someone has misplaced a body that some parents likely want!*

Slowly Myron Whithers lifted his head. He trembled violently, and beads of sweat glistened on his forehead. His shirt practically dripped with perspiration. He carefully set the container aside as if he had forgotten it. He felt he could not be responsible for incinerating the little male fetus, even if it meant appearing to do incomplete work.

Mr. Whithers quietly pushed the loaded cart filled with red bags of waste to the loader next to where the trash would be incinerated. He was not even aware of the fluid that stained the legs of his pants.

He turned and slowly walked back to the time clock in the maintenance office. While he walked, he analyzed his dilemma. Several months before, when his supervisor caught Myron bragging to his coworkers about some more unusual specimens he had seen, he had been stiffly warned to stop opening the containers. Now if he told, he would be turning himself in, and his job would be in jeopardy. But if he let the specimen go to the incinerator and someone really wanted it—Whithers' mind whirled far faster than he was capable of following.

Whithers felt nauseated again. He excused himself to his boss' secretary and headed home.

He determined to never open a pathology specimen container again.

◆ ◆ ◆

Simons rose early and was already staring at the data sheets in front of him. He had only slept for four hours, an amount that seemed sufficient for him in his nearly manic state. He felt vibrant, tuned, ready . . . almost unstoppable. From the cursory calculations he had just made, it looked like his original hypothesis would be correct: donor hearts from aborted fetal tissue could be transplanted successfully into newborns with complex cardiac malformations. The youngest hearts he had tested were strong, but not strong enough to produce the kind of cardiac output that was needed. What he seemed to require was a slightly older specimen to assure the success of a transplant. In most states there were restrictions on abortions in the third trimester. Some abortions were allowed, such as when the life of the mother was in jeopardy. *I wonder if such allowances could be made for the life of the cardiac recipient? After all, it would still be justifiable on the basis of "medical necessity."*

Simons knew he stood on very sensitive ground. If the public did not focus on the donor as a baby, his proposals would be accepted. The more he could convince the public that the abortion donor was just P.O.C. or immature fetal tissue and was clearly a non-viable entity on its own, the more likely his research would find the broad approval he needed to transform the treatment of congenital heart disease. By his calculations, literally thousands of infants could benefit. *Surely no one in their right mind could see my efforts as less than humanitarian, as less than producing a higher standard that will potentially raise the quality of life for all.*

Simons continued to analyze the data in front of him. He looked up momentarily beyond the screen of his personal computer, his eyes not focusing on anything. A second idea formed in his mind. If he was hindered from getting strong enough hearts from aborted tissue that was still within the legal pregnancy age restrictions, perhaps the small hearts could be challenged chemically in-utero to mature at a faster rate and thus be ready for transplant and still fall within legal abortion limitations. He already knew of some clinical applications of this sort. Steroids were sometimes used to stimulate fetal lung tissue so a baby could be delivered a week or two early if the mother's health was problematic. Could steroids also stimulate cardiac development?

He would have to be careful that he found a way to selectively speed the process of cardiac development without maturing the whole fetus. The thought of delivering live specimens was ironically distasteful even to Simons. He seemed blind to the fact that he was already doing exactly that. He simply refused to consider the "donor P.O.C. specimen" to be "living," as it could not survive without its mother. If Simons didn't salvage this tissue for something, it would be wasted. *After all, I'm not the one who decided these women should have abortions. The mothers alone determine that! I'm only salvaging a potential benefit from a situation that otherwise would benefit no one.* He refused to accept any responsibility for the abortion itself. He was merely utilizing what would otherwise be discarded.

He felt that the implications and applications of his latest brain-storm could be far-reaching. At any rate, he knew that any data he obtained hinged on knowing the exact age of the aborted specimen. Richards had not customarily used ultrasound on the pregnancies destined for abortion. There was really no justifiable reason for an expensive test to carefully date a pregnancy that fell clearly within legal abortion range as noted by dates and a physical exam.

He scanned his daily planner. His morning would be full with rounds and a clinic. His afternoon would be spent at the F.F.P. Clinic with his assistant, John Gentry. He had written the name of the donor mother on the line beside the 3:30 slot. "Stelling."

Simons would have his secretary call Richards as soon as he got to work. He wanted to be sure to have an ultrasound dating of this donor specimen before he got started. Richards might throw out some perfunctory objections, but Simons knew he would eventually comply. He always did.

◆ ◆ ◆

Sam received the call from the nurse at the Family Planning Clinic early on the morning of her appointment. The female voice sounded very cheerful, almost too happy, Sam thought. Any amount of cheerfulness would have seemed too much for her on that morning. The nurse had explained that a modification of the technique was being used. "Could you drop by the clinic this morning for a vaginal suppository to be placed?" She explained mechanically that this would shorten the amount of total time Sam would need to be at the clinic. *That part sounds great to me. I just want in and out. I just want to forget this day ever existed!* The prostaglandin suppository to be given in the morning would soften the cervix or lower uterine segment, making the extraction easier. She would be free to leave as soon as the doctor inserted the suppository. That afternoon she would return at her regular appointment time.

Sam secretly hoped that Layton would show up and go through this with her. *After all, isn't that what this is all about . . . so we can be together?* Personally, she was opposed to abortion. She would even go as far as to acknowledge that from a moral standpoint a life was being taken and that such an act should be avoided whenever possible. She also realized that war and the killing that takes place within it are not things to be relished, but that they were sometimes necessary for the overall good of mankind. At least that's what her father had taught her. *If only Daddy were here now! He'd know what to do; he would make it all work out.*

After her discussion with Layton the evening before, her previously made-up mind had definitely wavered again. It sounded as if he really loved her and intended on their being together as soon as they could get it worked out. She thought that perhaps if she sacrificed and compromised for him, it would put their relationship back on solid ground. She understood that sometimes one small evil needed to be allowed in order to accomplish a larger good. She felt as if she were back in philosophy class debating ethical issues. Only this time it was different. She inwardly debated her own pregnancy and her future. The future—that was what this was all about. *Don't*

I have a right to be happy, too? Layton had made her feel that way once. She thought only he could make her feel that way again.

Before she had a chance to leave her apartment, she received two other items that seemed to confirm that Layton wanted to be with her and that they would be together again soon. She thought he would have chosen for her little presents to be delivered after her clinic appointment, but nevertheless, first came a colorful rose bouquet and on its heels a small box, delivered by Express Mail. Both gifts were signed, "Love, Layton." The second gift was a six-month supply of birth control pills, prescribed by Adam Richards and paid for by Redman.

Evidently Layton really does plan on continuing this relationship! She blushed when she opened the package, then smiled. At least there were certain aspects of the relationship that Layton Redman wished to continue . . . and certain "mistakes" of the past that he intended on avoiding in the future.

Sam dressed quickly and headed out the door. She jumped in her small Volkswagen and hurriedly left the parking lot, heading for the clinic. Completely unaware of anyone calling out her name as she left, she was off, her mind a complex blur of hopes, guilt, and, she thought, love.

Anne Caudill stood in the parking lot, watching her leave, not sure why she had come for a visit in the first place.

CHAPTER
14

IT irritated Dr. Richards to hear of yet another necessary modification in his abortion routine. Now Simons insisted on an ultrasound on every one of the donor mothers on the day of the abortion in order to get the most accurate prediction of age possible. Richards had groaned but, as predicted by Simons, agreed to go along with the suggestion. He had used the ultrasound to guide the saline injection needles, but since they were not using that technique because they needed a "live" abortion, he had abandoned not only the needle but also the ultrasound. Reinstating the ultrasound bothered him only slightly, but the fact that Simons seemed to be running more and more of Richards' own practice really made him steam. *First a major modification of second trimester abortions to preserve the donor hearts, then a modification of my office schedule so the donations can be done without risk of interruption or discovery by other patients, and now this!* He silently predicted there would be more "suggestions" as his research relationship with Simons continued.

Perhaps what bothered him the most was that Simons himself had not even called. Rather, a secretary, who knew nothing about their research at all, delivered the perfunctory message. "Dr. Simons needs an ultrasound dating of each patient who is to be a cardiac preparation donor, on the day of the donation. Please begin with an ultrasound today on Stelling." There was no use in arguing with the secretary. She had no idea what her message was even about.

Richards realized the futility of opposing Simons. He imagined that he ought to feel privileged to be working with him. Opportunities to participate in major advances in clinical medicine were few and far between for the private practitioner. For that reason he had politely agreed, all the while shaking his head no and rolling his eyes.

As for Stelling, she had already come and gone from the clinic that morning. *Oh well*, he thought, *it won't be that hard to ultrasound her this afternoon just before the extraction.*

◆ ◆ ◆

Norman Driver had worked with Myron Whithers for six years. He liked Myron, even if the man had somewhat of a strange sense of humor. He usually didn't work directly on the same job with Whithers unless it required two people.

The news that Myron had left early surprised Norman. In twelve years of service, Myron had never taken a sick day, a fact he'd bragged about to just about all the other environmental service workers. Mabel, the secretary to their manager, had commented, "I've never seen someone look so pale. It was almost as though something frightened him!" Mabel chewed her gum audibly, then added, "He sure left in a hurry."

"Did he finish his morning work roster?" Norman thought he'd better check to see if Myron had left anything for him to do.

"Didn't say."

Norman walked over to Whithers' time card and picked up the work assignment list beside it. Norman checked his watch, then headed for the door. He called out over his shoulder as he left, "I'm heading over to pathology lab to see if he finished there. Tell the boss if he thinks I'm out taking a long lunch or something. Bye, Mabel!"

"Sure, Norm. See you."

A few minutes later he walked into the now busy surgical pathology lab. Tumor Board was over, and work had commenced as usual.

Norman spoke to Dr. Scott Tanous. He called all of the doctors, "doc." "Say, doc, did Mr. Whithers pick up the waste for the incinerator?"

Scott looked up from a microscope. "Huh?" He paused and looked around. "Looks like it. Why? Is there a problem?"

"Oh, no problem, doc. Whithers left early, so I was making sure the work was done, that's all."

Norm turned to leave. As he entered the hallway, he heard his name. "Hey, Norm!" He turned to see Dr. Tanous bringing one specimen container towards him.

"He must have missed this one. It's marked 'waste pickup' as well."

Norm took the container with both hands. *It must weigh close to eight pounds, what with the liquid formaldehyde and all,* he thought. Five minutes later he set the container down beside the other trash in the incinerator room.

By 2 P.M. the small male fetus had been reduced to minimal ash along with the remainder of the hazardous biological waste.

◆ ◆ ◆

Tony and Carol sat close together, holding hands during much of the conversation. It was their lunch hour, and they had scheduled a work-in meeting with Dot Henderson, a social worker who worked to facilitate both state and private adoption services.

"Once we've been accepted by the state adoption agency, how long should we expect an adoption to take?" It looked as if they had a lot to learn about the process, and Tony was anxious to get to the bottom line.

"Mr. Jennings, there is much ground to cover before being accepted by the agency. There are interviews, more interviews, home assessment visits, letters of reference, etc. All of these things take time and money." Dot was polite but firm, and somewhat cautious. She had fielded many serious and many not-so-serious inquiries before this visit with the Jennings.

"I'm beginning to understand some now. But after you spend all of the time with the interviews and all, and we are finally accepted, then how long does it usually take?"

Dot wanted to diffuse his question and put it in perspective. "There are many factors involved. For a baby of a certain sex preference, the time is longer. For a baby of a specific race, particularly Caucasian, it takes even longer. For a baby without special needs, it takes longer. If you will accept an older child, it doesn't take as long. If you have been providing foster care to a particular child you want to adopt, that may shorten the adoption process, or at least allow you to care for the child until the adoption takes place."

"Okay, okay. About how long for a Caucasian male or female infant?"

Dot could see he wouldn't be satisfied with generalities. "After the approval process, which usually takes a minimum of several months, the waiting period for a Caucasian infant can be measured in years, not just months."

Tony and Carol both stared straight ahead as the implications of the last statement registered. Their neatly planned and packaged life was not ready to accommodate such a waiting period.

Dot searched for something that might help diffuse the bomb she'd unloaded. "There are ways to shorten the process. Avoid the state agency, hire a private adoption lawyer, cooperate with a private organization that allows the mother who is giving up her baby to choose the parents. You never know—in that kind of setting you might be chosen right away."

Carol squeezed Tony's hand. Tony turned to his wife. "Honey, you know we can't afford that kind of private adoption."

Carol sighed. Dot went on to explain the whole process in detail and gave them a few names of other organizations, as well as an application inquiry form for the state's adoption agency. Carol picked up the stack of papers.

The remainder of the hour-long session passed without any further questions by Tony.

◆ ◆ ◆

Samantha Stelling hadn't made it all the way back to her small apartment near A.C.U. In fact, she hadn't even made it out past "Circle 6," Fairfaxians' name for Rt. 6, which formed a circle around Fairfax's perimeter. Instead, she found herself dry-heaving with her head over a small ditch in front of a shopping center on Centerville

Road. At the clinic they had warned her what the side effects of the vaginal suppository might be. She really didn't have anything in her stomach to lose, as she had been instructed to take a clear liquid breakfast only, in anticipation of the procedure. Her "breakfast" was four hours ago. She returned to the clinic, and they quickly put her in an examination room near the back of the building.

Sam looked around the dimly lit room. They had given her an injection for the nausea and turned down the lights so she could rest. Everything around her seemed surreal. She was having trouble focusing on anything. She squinted up at the bottle of clear liquid that was dripping through a tube inserted into her right hand. With her left hand she clutched a kidney-shaped emesis basin. She had used it twice in the first half-hour since her arrival. Instead of an exam table, she had been placed in a regular hospital bed with the armrails up to prevent her from falling or climbing out. She didn't feel like crawling anywhere. In fact, she thought that the sooner this was all over, the better. She supposed she would have to be moved to a different table for the "delivery."

She thought she had dozed off for a while. When she awoke, her head was clearer, but she still felt queasy. She heard a nurse in the entrance to her room ask about starting the pitocin. She couldn't hear the reply clearly but thought she heard Dr. Richards say something about an ultrasound first.

Richards stood in the hallway outside the room. He looked at his watch. 2 P.M. If Simons was predictable, he would be early. That quality irritated Richards even more as he would have rather had his clinic to himself until Simons was actually needed. He had nearly forgotten the ultrasound. Now time would be running short. He really needed to check Stelling to see if her cervix was soft enough to begin dilation and to start the pitocin. Richards picked up the chart in the rack outside the exam room and went in.

"Ms. Stelling?"

Sam didn't reply. She acknowledged Richards' statement only by looking in his direction. A nurse walked in behind Richards.

Richards was putting on a pair of sterile gloves. The nurse helped position Sam on her back so the doctor could check her cervix.

"Let's have a look to see how things are coming."

◆ ◆ ◆

It wasn't every day that John Gentry got to ride in a Porsche. Dr. Simons had offered the ride, and Gentry hadn't refused. He assumed Simons liked it when people complimented his car, and Gentry didn't disappoint him. He didn't make any intelligent comments, however—just enough boyish "Man, oh, man's" and "Wow's" to needlessly fuel the doctor's ego.

Gentry thought Simons was putting it on a bit for him, too. His starts were quick, forcing Gentry gently but very noticeably deeper into the plush, leather passenger seat. Every necessary stop was punctuated by a rhythmic punching of the throttle by Simons, rocking the machine ever so slightly, like a horse in the starting gate.

All in all, it made for a quick ride, and soon they were driving into the back parking lot of the F.F.P. Clinic.

◆ ◆ ◆

Linda's "work" was finished in a few minutes. She crept quietly out past the impressive but sleeping "guard" dog and down the stairs, clutching in her hand a now empty basket. She stopped at Lucy's door just long enough to return the key and to refuse Lucy's offer for lunch.

"I really can't stay. Thanks so much."

"Let me know how Matt reacts," Lucy called after Linda, who had already turned to go. She had a hunch she would hear about it from Matt soon enough, but she liked this new girl of Matt's and she wanted to stay in touch. Lucy smiled as if she were recalling fond memories. She shook her head in a gesture of wonder and guided the screen door closed, so it wouldn't slam. The mechanism built to slow the rate at which the door closed had broken years ago.

Linda hopped into her red Volkswagen bug and headed south. Behind her, in Matt's apartment, the dinner she had fixed was sitting prominently at the front of the highest shelf inside the refrigerator along with brief instructions taped to the old appliance's door. On the kitchen card table, Linda had cleared off enough space for a slender vase with a single long-stemmed red rose. Throughout the rest of the apartment she had put at least a dozen little notes—one taped to the bathroom mirror, one under his pillow, several taped to food items in the refrigerator, three more hidden in books on a stand beside the bed. The rest were less conspicuously placed, so Matt would find them over the next few weeks.

The last one wouldn't be found, in fact, until several months later when Matt was packing his things for a move.

◆ ◆ ◆

The effects of the anti-nausea medication had definitely worn off. Not only did Sam feel more alert, but she was also aware that she was again on the edge of the dry heaves. The lubrication gel that was placed over the swelling in her lower abdomen didn't help, either. She thought that any stimulus would make her feel nauseated at this point, but particularly the wet, slimy transducer lubricant.

Richards was doing the ultrasound himself, gently rubbing a mushroom-shaped probe over the lubricated area of Sam's lower abdomen and pelvis. He was quite good at this, having practiced this helpful skill literally thousands of times during his four residency years. Although he really only needed to date the pregnancy, he was compulsively checking the whole fetus. The snowy black-and-white images were visible to the nurse and to Sam, who was somewhat taken back that she could make out a few of the details in the pictures Richards was silently providing.

"It's a boy." The nurse was speaking quietly but was cut off quickly by a fiery stare from Richards. The nurse retreated physically from her position at Sam's side. But her comment had not gone unnoticed by Sam, whose eyes were now fixated on the screen. Richards had quickly moved the probe and was now trying to measure a head circumference.

The small male baby wasn't in the mood for cooperating with the process. He rolled from side to side, making Richards constantly readjust the probe angle and location to get a better look.

"It's about time for some sedation, isn't it, doctor?" the nurse remarked, hoping to deflect attention from her last statement.

"Versed, three milligrams, IV. STAT." Richards spoke quietly but was easily understood by the nurse . . . and by Samantha.

◆ ◆ ◆

Simons surveyed the room; everything appeared ready. An instrument tray was set beside the well-lit operating table. A stainless steel blade was fastened to a knife handle and was positioned on the far left corner of the tray; it was the first instrument he would need. In the corner, Simons had set up a new microscope and had laid out some glass slides. After this experiment, he wanted to remove the small heart to make slides of the cardiac muscle, so he could study its microscopic structure and compare it to slides made of mature cardiac muscle. He knew he could do this and never change the outward appearance of the specimen. So far he had conducted many pump runs, and the pathologists had performed their perfunctory documentation of the specimens without noticing a thing.

Simons had checked the pathology dictations after his first three experiments. There was no mention of a sternal scar on any of the reports. He doubted whether the pathologists even looked; he doubted whether they cared. He was tempted to just leave the incision open to see if they would even notice it. He would never do that, of course. He would carefully close the incisions with sutures meticulously hidden beneath the skin. He would reveal his work to the scientific community only at the right time. For now he was confident that no one would have reason to suspect his little "steal."

He was becoming impatient. Richards should be ready for Gentry to pick up the specimen anytime. Simons looked at his watch and then at Gentry. He was never much for small talk when he had his mind on his work. "If he hasn't signaled us in five minutes, I'm going in there myself."

◆ ◆ ◆

Sam bit her lower lip to try to keep from crying. The nurse was drawing up the medication to be given directly into the vein.

"Let's move up to the examination table first. If we give that now, she won't be able to help us move her." Richards was getting impatient himself.

Sam was helped from the hospital bed and onto the nearby examining table. Richards carefully opened a small tray containing uterine sounds—special instruments for exploring body cavities—and a series of dilators for opening the cervix. "Begin the pitocin."

Sam's mind was racing. All along she thought she would be able to go through this without breaking down. She felt like her mind was about to go out of control on a cliff's edge. The room felt oppressive and dark, although she could see that the room lights were on. Gently, firmly, and unseen, God's Spirit was pushing for recognition. Sam felt an urgency to quiet her screaming emotions.

The nurse slid a needle into an entry-port on the IV tubing leading to a vein in Sam's hand. As she began to inject the medication, Sam jerked her arm violently, just short of control, knocking the syringe and needle to the floor. "Wait!" She began to sob—deep, heavy, regular outcries, punctuated rhythmically with wheezing gasps.

The nurse left the syringe on the floor, leaned over, and gently gripped Sam by the shoulders. Sam was now sitting up on the exam table with her face hidden by her hands. "There, there, honey. It will all be over soon." The nurse was perturbed at the emotional outbreak but managed a weak smile.

Richards was more than perturbed by the display. "Give the Versed now! It will calm her down. Use five milligrams instead of the regular starting dose!"

"No!" Sam was trying to talk between sobs. "No! No! No! No! Noooo-oo-oooo!" Her words were broken by her rhythmic weeping.

The nurse continued to hold her gently but firmly. "It's okay, honey. Let's take some slow, deep breaths. We'll go on when you're ready."

Sam took a deep breath and, with as much control as she could muster, exhaled slowly through her mouth. "You said it was a boy?" Sam was looking at the nurse, who quickly looked towards Dr. Richards.

Richards was the one who provided the answer. "It's pretty much just undifferentiated pregnancy tissue at this point. We'd have to be prophets to be able to tell that," Richards lied.

"No!" Sam was gaining her composure.

"Listen, honey. No one here will force you to do this, you know." The nurse was speaking as Richards looked on with disdain. The assistant carefully avoided eye contact with the doctor as she continued speaking softly to Sam. "You can take a few more days to think it over if you like."

All Richards could think of was that Simons was definitely going to be upset. *If the arrogant so-and-so hadn't "recommended" the ultrasound, this would have never happened. I'm not taking the responsibility for his mistakes, that's for sure.*

"I want to wait . . . I just can't do this today." Sam was talking to the nurse as she too avoided eye contact with the obviously irritated physician.

Richards snapped out of his angry thought train. "If we're not doing an abortion here, we'd better stop this pitocin *now*." He rolled the flow regulator on the IV to the *off* position. He then turned to his assistant. "We need to do a vaginal lavage to see if we can remove any of the medication. I'm not sure any will be left by now. Help me get her up." He was referring to getting her legs up in the stirrups, so he could insert a speculum to lavage the birth canal and inspect the cervix.

Sam was positioned with her bottom facing the windowless door behind Richards. Richards inserted the speculum and started his examination. The cervix was still closed. He touched it with a long swab. It was softening, but not to the degree he would have wanted. "Hmmm . . . Seems like all the prostaglandin was doing was to make her sick."

◆ ◆ ◆

Simons was pacing. Gentry had slipped down the hallway to the exam room a few minutes before and cracked the door open just enough to see what was going on. He brought back a report that Richards was opening the dilators and sedation had begun. Simons was well aware of the effects of the Versed; he knew it was an effective sedative, as well as causing amnesia for the events taking place during the administration of the drug. That's one reason they had selected it. They didn't want the donor mothers remembering much about their visit to the clinic at all.

Simons headed down the hallway. "I'm going to check. With the Versed on board, the patient won't even know I'm around."

◆ ◆ ◆

Simons opened the door to the exam room unannounced. He didn't see any reason to knock. He could see as he opened the door that the patient was appropriately exposed and that Richards was working intently from his position on a small stool between the patient's legs. Undoubtedly the procedure was underway.

"Have you got my specimen yet, old boy?" Simons was being uncharacteristically casual, confident that the patient was well sedated, if not asleep entirely. He continued, undaunted by the forceful look of reprimand issuing from the eyes of Richards' assistant. Richards couldn't turn around fast enough to cut Simons short. "I've got work to do, experiments to run, breakthroughs to establish—"

Sam rocked up on one elbow and looked at Simons. Her eyes locked on his face, arresting his arrogant rambling with one glance. She memorized every detail of his face in a second's time. His white lab coat had his name embroidered in red thread, followed by the words, "Pediatric Cardiothoracic Surgery." Sam broke the awkward silence that followed Simons' grand entrance. "And just what do you want?"

Richards had managed to lock eyes with the speechless cardiothoracic surgeon. "This one's canceled, Michael! There is no abortion for her today."

Simons stumbled backwards into the hall. He was not used to being surprised. He was used to being on top. This would not happen again! He turned and stepped into the new research lab only long enough to grab his coat and briefcase. Gentry, who was sitting in the corner by the new microscope table, was taken off-guard by the doctor's entrance. Simons didn't speak. He just grabbed his things and disappeared quickly without an explanation.

Gentry's request fell uselessly on the door as it was swinging rapidly closed. "Hey! What about my ride?"

Simons hadn't seen Gentry, much less heard him. He wouldn't have cared even if he had.

◆ ◆ ◆

Richards lavaged the vagina out with saline, hoping to dilute out any prostaglandin medication that was still around. After he finished, he gently removed the speculum.

The doctor issued a few orders to the nurse, who was still shaking her head after Simons' remarkable "visit." "Keep her here for at least three hours, and monitor her for signs of labor." Richards then left, ignoring the question that Sam called out behind him.

"What's really going on here, anyway?" Sam addressed the nurse, who was helping her move back onto the hospital bed.

"I really don't know the details, dear. You'll have to get that from Dr. Richards. He is conducting some research with Dr. Simons from the university—that's all I know. The work they are doing will possibly benefit thousands of needy children." She was speaking from the memory of the brief explanation Richards had given her for the changes she'd noticed in their technique of doing late abortions.

"That man wanted my baby!"

Samantha Stelling was filled with more questions now than even before her clinic appointment. She needed to talk to Dr. Richards! She carefully formulated her questions, anticipating that he would check on her before she was released. She never had her opportunity. Richards left a full hour before the nurse removed Sam's IV and told her she was free to go. Sam refused a follow-up appointment.

Sam was guided back to the front entrance. There she turned and spoke with the girl behind the glass at the registration counter.

"I want to speak with Dr. Richards."

"I'm sorry, but he's already left for the day." The young receptionist was pleasant but only offered standard information. She had only worked in the front office for three weeks. "Let's see," the receptionist said casually, "he's checked out to Dr. Thompson. I can have *him* paged if you have a question that can't wait."

"No, thank you." Sam turned and opened the door. It was already dark.

By the time Sam left the clinic, Adam Richards had already had four drinks.

CHAPTER
15

DR. Matt Stone slowly climbed the stairs to his apartment. Like so many times before, he arrived home after Lucy had gone to bed. An outside light burned brightly beside the entrance to his door. *I don't remember turning that on. Lucy must be taking care of me again—* His thought stopped short when he saw a small yellow stick-up note on the windowpane behind the screen-door.

> Some guard dog you've got there! I'll bet you next time I could make off with the whole apartment. More inside. Welcome home!
> Love,
> Linda

Linda had drawn a small smiley face above her name. Matt forgot all about the light. He fished for his keys in the pocket beneath his heavy jacket, opened the door, and went in.

He quickly found a second note as he put his books on the kitchen card table. Fastened to a vase which held a long-stemmed rose, another stick-up note caught his eye.

> I hope you had a wonderful day. I wish I could be watching you now. I LOVE YOU!!!
> Linda

Again a smiley face decorated the card, though this card had an additional feature in the bottom corner: XXOO.

Now Matt's curiosity peaked as he looked around the room for other obvious notes. He spotted a third note stuck to his small refrigerator. He sniffed at the rose, smiled, and then walked over to the "kitchen" to collect the note.

The maid's out of town! Your supper is inside.
I'm yours,
Linda

P.S. If you eat all your veggies and the brown rice, you can have one of the Twinkies I found in your cupboard.

This time there were two smiley faces—one beside Linda's name and one beside the P.S. Matt opened the refrigerator door and took out a plate of honey-roasted chicken, brown rice, and mixed vegetables. He partially removed the cellophane wrap and slid the plate into the microwave.

While he waited for the microwave to heat his supper, he found an additional note hanging from the bathroom mirror.

You sure do look great!
Linda

The four beeps sounded from the microwave, indicating his meal was ready. Matt sat down to enjoy a much better dinner than he usually had. First, however, he paused to thank his Lord. He started his list of thank-yous with Linda Baldwin. She had brightened his day considerably.

◆ ◆ ◆

Richards came home after stopping at Sammy's Tavern for Happy Hour, a name with a twist of irony, Adam thought, as recently he only frequented those events when his mood was far from "happy." There he had slowly consumed enough alcohol to float most seasoned drinkers away. The bartender asked him to stop, an event that had only happened once before in his life. The other was only four nights ago, and he did not care to repeat the event. Heavier on his priority list stood a desire not to repeat today's events, which goaded him to seek solace in spirited liquids.

Richards made a vow never to be caught in the same situation again. Even with his head comfortably clouded, he recalled soberly his resolve to more carefully screen the abortion donor candidates. Never again would he rely on someone else's word that a particular patient wanted to proceed with pregnancy elimination.

Inwardly he cursed Layton Redman. *Hadn't he guaranteed that the patient was going to follow through?* He still didn't understand why Redman was so interested. *Oh, well, it doesn't matter anyway. I don't care if the President calls next time. I'm still going to screen the potential donor mothers myself. From now on, only those who have not missed previous appointments will be considered—only those who are stable-minded enough to stick to their decisions!*

He had been sitting in the driveway for five minutes. He seemed to have lost his garage-door opener, and in the dark car he couldn't find the switch to turn on the dome light. Finally, with an audible curse, the disoriented Richards exited his car through the passenger door, swinging it forcibly into a pine tree on the edge of his driveway. A loud stream of expletives followed. Richards slammed the door and stumbled towards his front door.

In the morning it would take him several minutes just to find his car, which was not in its usual resting-place in the garage. When he did find it, he wouldn't remember how the dent got in the passenger door. At least he didn't have any nightmares . . . none that he could remember anyway.

◆ ◆ ◆

At 10:30 P.M. a very upbeat Layton Redman returned to his law office to sign a few papers before heading home. He had reason to be jubilant. Tomorrow, if he had done his homework correctly, he would see himself in at least three news stories.

"You live or die by the photo-op, my friend," Layton had boasted to one of his law partners the week before. He was referring to the well-known political principle that an opportunity to be photographed, whether in a favorable or unfavorable light, could make or break a politician in the eyes of the voters. It wasn't necessary that the person really care about the situations that were photographed. A seasoned politician *seemed* to care and worked the media to prove it. His law partner had agreed with him and slapped him on the back. Janice Sizemore, who recognized the truth in the statement but didn't like the common practice of misleading the public, had been less gracious in her response when Layton made a similar comment in her presence a few weeks earlier.

Layton had forgotten all about his scuff with Janice now. He did know that today he had involved himself in three beautiful photo-ops. Each event had been less than an hour. One had been only ten minutes. The media had followed obediently like dogs on a leash. At the first event, a publicized Louisville prayer breakfast, Redman emphasized just how much his Christian upbringing meant to him. It didn't seem relevant to him that he hadn't been in any church building in over six years.

From that event, he had traveled into the rolling bluegrass southeast of the city to the site of an auction of a family farm, a casualty of hard economic times. He spoke for three minutes on economic reform and didn't fail to emphasize a second buzzword of the times: "family values." The media cooperated implicitly.

He had his last opportunity in Fairfax, where he addressed a crowd gathered to celebrate the opening of a new retirement village and nursing home. There he spoke of health care reform and his commitment to Social Security. Redman smiled compassionately for the strong representation of the *Fairfax Daily* who were present to faithfully record his statements.

Oddly enough, just when Samantha Stelling wished Layton could be with her that day, he was taking advantage of that third political opportunity less than a mile away from the clinic where she was being "treated."

After his speech, Layton dined at Sammy's Tavern. Although he had met Adam Richards once before in person and had spoken with him dozens of times and had received large contributions from him in the past, he did not recognize Richards when he entered the restaurant and passed Richards as he slouched at the bar. Richards would not have been in the mood to talk to him on that day, anyway. Redman, however, would have been very interested and disturbed by the words he would have heard if they had talked. But he would find out that information soon enough.

Redman, too, consumed several drinks that night. But his were in celebration of success, in contrast to the drinks imbibed by Richards that were used to haze out his anxieties. The candidate for governor smiled at the thoughts of his successful day and sipped the glass of Maker's Mark in his hand. He stopped after two drinks, devoured a large dinner, and left after coffee and two refills.

He considered a late-night surprise visit to Sam's place, but he figured he should give her some space after the day she must have had. He would let the flowers and the other gift he'd arranged to be waiting for her be communication enough between them today. Instead, Redman got onto I-64 and headed west. He set the cruise control on his B.M.W for 72.

Redman smiled. *After today my problems with Sam are over! Nothing can stop me now!* He adjusted the rear-view mirror so he could see his own reflection. Every few miles he looked at himself again and practiced his favorite media-pleasing grin. *There! . . . You really do knock 'em dead, don't you, governor?*

◆ ◆ ◆

Tony and Carol Jennings were getting a heavy dose of "reality therapy." They sat soberly on their love seat with an assortment of adoption information in front of them. They needed to somehow fit the intangibles of adoption into a neat framework so they could resume some feeling of control in their lives. They were beginning to see that this whole process would be an exercise in walking by faith. It also looked as though a commitment to a definite adoption would take a matching financial commitment.

Carol spoke first. "Remember 'The Plan'?"

Tony looked up from the pamphlet he held. "The plan?"

"You know, 'The Plan,' with a capital P. I would get my Master's degree—we'd have our first child—I'd help establish a clinic for troubled adolescents—we'd have our second child. That plan!"

"Oh, *that* plan. Sure." Tony remained uncharacteristically sober. "Why?"

"It's been blown apart, that's why! It's not even recognizable anymore." Carol did not want to end up crying again, but she felt the tears cresting in her green eyes. "I used to think I had such control over my life. Maybe I'm a slow learner, Tony. Maybe if I wouldn't have been so headstrong, we wouldn't be in this mess right now. Just look at us, Tony! Our friends all have houses, children, two cars . . . even savings accounts. All we have is a plan that didn't work, a plan that never got beyond my little me-centered world!"

Not knowing what to say, Tony responded by putting his arm around his wife and holding her as she began to sob. "I've got you," he said quietly. "That's more than I deserve."

"I—I just feel so out of control lately. One minute I'm fine, the next I'm on the edge of losing it entirely." Carol wiped her eyes with the back of her hand.

"There are a few things we can do, and without any dollar commitment. Perhaps if we formulate a 'plan,' you'll feel more secure. But at each step I think we've both learned that we need to trust God to do what's best."

Tony got out a pen, opened a small notepad in front of him, and began to write. At the top, he wrote "The Plan."

1. Tell our friends we want to adopt a baby. Ask them to spread the word.

2. Call Dr. Harrison. Perhaps he is in contact with pregnant females who are interested in adoption.

3. Make an application to the state adoption agency.

4. Make a list of references for the adoption agency.

"There—how's that?" Tony hoped Carol wouldn't mind spreading the word around.

"There's just one problem here," Carol stated with an authoritative air. She picked up the notepad and swiftly plucked the pen from between Tony's fingers.

"There," she stated as she completed her modification. She had scratched out "The Plan" and wrote, "His Plan." At the bottom she added numbers 5 and 6, which stated:

> 5. Pray daily for God's direction.
> 6. Trust God regardless of the outcome.

"I stand corrected, madam!" Tony spoke with a pompous, aristocratic, exaggerated accent.

"Apology accepted. You may kiss my hand," countered Carol as she extended her hand in an elegant manner. Tony obliged with an audible, squeaking smack.

"I forgot something." Tony smiled. "The list, please." Carol handed it back, and he in turn plucked the pen from her in a move mimicking hers just moments earlier.

He held the pad to his chest and shifted his body so she could not see what he wrote. Carol rolled her eyes but played along. Tony wrote below the last numbered entry:

> 7. Practice making our own "homemade" child on a regular basis.

Tony turned, smiling mischievously. He lifted the notepad for his wife to read and then held up his arms to guard against an expected friendly punch.

Carol didn't want to disappoint him. She shouted, "Men!" and raised her clenched fists for a playful attack. Seeing that he protected his head, she delivered her blows to his exposed rib cage instead.

◆　◆　◆

"Good night, Linda. I'll talk to you tomorrow." Matt hung up the phone and smiled. Their conversation had been short. Linda sounded as if she'd been asleep for several hours. She had been glad for the call, though, because with Matt's tight schedule phone conversations were about all the time they'd had since returning from the Eastern Shore.

Matt looked around the room. It sounded by his conversation with Linda that he hadn't found all of her notes yet. He was too tired to look for very long. He needed to see his hospital patients at 6 A.M. so he could be at the general surgery case conference by 6:45. Fortunately, he didn't need to look very hard. Just as he prepared to hang up his coat, he found another note stuck to the back of the closet door.

Hanging up your coat in the closet instead of on your bedposts? I'm truly impressed with you, doc!
Love,
Linda

Matt left the note, which contained a record three smiley faces, hanging in the closet. He hung up his coat and walked back to his bed. He hung his pants on one post and his shirt on the other. Old bachelor habits were hard to break.

Matt collapsed on the bed and pulled his comforter around his neck. It wouldn't take him long to fall asleep. Before that, however, he excitedly read a note he found sticking to his pillow.

Sweet dreams, Matt. I'm dreaming of *you!*

This one was unsigned except for the words "The Intruder," followed by XXX.

Matt switched off the light. It had turned out to be a pretty good day after all.

◆ ◆ ◆

Sam had been home for over an hour before she calmed down enough to drink some tea. She still had what seemed to be a million questions, but at least she was now able to sort them into categories. *What was Dr. Simons doing at the F.F.P. Clinic? Why did Dr. Richards deny what I heard so clearly . . . that my baby is a boy? How could I have ever consented to have an abortion in the first place? Can I ever tell anyone about Layton without ruining our relationship or his political career? Does he really care about me? Why would he put me through this? Can God still care about me after what I did? Will the medicine I received harm my baby? My baby . . . my boy! What am I ever going to do with my baby boy?*

The phone rang, startling Sam and arresting her thoughts. *It's Layton! I can't talk to him!* She let the phone ring eight times. *Whoever it is must really want to talk.* Sam sighed, then picked up the phone.

"Hello."

"Hello. Sam? It's me—Anne. I was worried about you today. I had the weirdest feeling I should come to see you." Anne wasn't sure how much to say, but every time she paused, only silence followed, so she went on. "Almost like you were in some sort of trouble or something." Another silent pause followed. "Are you all right, Sam?"

Sam breathed a sigh of relief. *It isn't Layton!* What she heard amazed her. *How could Anne have known I was in trouble?*

Sam started, halted, and then started to speak again, rapidly, as though if she said it fast enough, the words would be difficult to retrieve. "I went to Fairfax for an abortion today."

This time Anne left it up to Sam to dispel the silence.

Sam continued, "I couldn't go through with it. I almost freaked out. They said my baby was a boy. I didn't know what to do!" Sam began to weep. "I couldn't let them do it. I cried for them to stop." Sam's voice trailed off. Anne could hear her blowing her nose. "I'm sorry . . . I'm such a wreck! They told me to think it over and come back in a few days." Sam paused again. Anne still couldn't find a reply. "Anne, I'm never going back there again. *Never!*"

For the second time that day, Anne felt a gentle nudge from the Holy Spirit. This time she recognized him.

"Sam, I'm coming over."

Sam made a polite refusal.

Anne remained firm. "Sam, I'm on my way. You need someone right now! I'm your friend. I'll see you in a few minutes."

Sam heard a *click* in the receiver. Anne hadn't given her a chance to refuse again.

◆ ◆ ◆

After supper, Myron Whithers finally told his wife what was bothering him. She knew it had to be something. "You can't be married to the same man for thirty-two years without knowing when something's eating him," Eunice Whithers would say.

"There's got to be a logical explanation for what you saw." Eunice hadn't seen her husband this upset in a long time. "You said yourself that they didn't have one pediatric heart case in the O.R. last week or you'd have known about it. There's always a sight more waste to clean up from those cases. You've said so yourself!"

Myron sat at the small kitchen table, shaking his head. "I know, I know, it's just—"

Eunice interrupted, "—and I know that no one's lost a live baby recently. That kind of stuff is always in the obituaries." Eunice had missed the obituary column just once in four years, and only then because she had gone to Florida with Myron and stopped the paper for a week.

Myron mused silently. Eunice continued, "Whatever you do, don't tell your supervisor about it. You can't afford to get in any more trouble!" An observer would have thought she was talking to a child, had they not seen the gray-haired man holding his head over his unwashed plate on the table. Eunice had another thought. "If you have to ask someone, ask that pathology doctor, Dr. Tanous, about it." She paused. Myron continued to stare at the table in front of him. "But mostly I'd recommend you just forget about this. It's not your fault anyway. You didn't label that container. You were just doing your job."

Myron lifted his head. "I guess you're right."

"I know so!" Eunice looked over at her husband and shook her head. "Now get on out of here so I can clean up these dishes." Myron walked into the den obediently and turned on the news. Eunice smiled and shook her head again. She knew her husband would do as she "recommended." He always had before.

◆ ◆ ◆

John Gentry cursed under his breath. It had taken him a full hour to walk back to the university hospital where he had parked his car.

He didn't mind the walk except for the cold. After the sun set, the temperature had dipped to a mere 15 degrees. By the time he arrived back at his car, he couldn't even feel his car keys with his ungloved hands.

John was a quiet man. That fact alone endeared him to Simons. He had gotten his cardiopulmonary bypass pump technician certification in Louisville and had stayed on there and worked both as a pump tech in the O.R. and as a research assistant in the lab. His research interests led him to apply for a job with Michael Simons, undoubtedly one of the world's most prominent men in cardiothoracic surgery. Simons himself had called one day the previous fall. "Could you start tomorrow?" stuck out as the only thing John could recall from that momentous phone call. John ran the cardiopulmonary bypass pump flawlessly for three pump runs on his first day. He did his job and stayed quiet both in the O.R. and out. Simons loved him.

By the time he had been there a year, Simons approached him about extra work over at the F.F.P. Clinic. The work was secretive, but he would be paid well for his involvement. Simons had not specifically told him not to mention the work, but Gentry understood that implicitly.

Gentry fully supported the experimental goals in theory. The details of his personal involvement bothered him the most. The extra money, however, quieted his misgivings about the necessary unpleasant tasks associated with bringing about a revolution in the treatment of congenital heart disease. The younger nonviable cardiac donor preparations didn't seem to bother him. More recently, however, it seemed they were using older and older P.O.C.s as cardiac donor preps. Gentry had found himself wincing recently as he watched a twenty-two-week-old female cardiac preparation jerk her legs violently as Simons performed the sternal split. Simons never used anesthesia. "It could suppress the cardiac output and skew the data," Simons had replied curtly. Simons just threw a Velcro strap over the child's legs, covered the fetus with a towel, and kept operating.

Time was of the essence in the first few minutes post-abortion, in order to get a heart as close to "living" as possible. *That is the irony of it all*, thought Gentry. *Dr. Simons modified the abortion technique to assure that the P.O.C.s would be "born" with beating hearts, then turned around and defined the same P.O.C.s as "non-viable" to justify his use of their hearts for experimentation and eventual transplantation.*

Gentry told himself over and over that it was all for the best, but nagging doubts continued to surface, in spite of Simons' weekly encouragements: "We're on the cutting edge of transplantation research . . . This work has the potential of benefiting thousands each year . . . We will never be forgotten as true pioneers who revolutionized the treatment of complex congenital heart disease forever."

This afternoon's fiasco when Simons left him in the lurch without a ride was the final straw on top of his longer hours and underlying displeasure with the details of the experiments. That all prodded Gentry to consider looking into the private sector for another job. He heard that Fairfax General Hospital was looking for another cardiopulmonary bypass pump technician. *Perhaps it isn't such a bad time to look elsewhere for work. Let Simons run someone else's life for a change!* Gentry fumbled with his car keys with numb fingers. He wouldn't forget this for a long time.

◆ ◆ ◆

Simons' self-absorption kept him from realizing he had even left Gentry behind. It also kept him from accepting any responsibility for the events at the clinic that day. Others were responsible. Others would have to change. It wouldn't be Michael Simons.

The fact that he'd been seen at the Family Planning Clinic by Samantha Stelling did not bother him at first. He knew that someone seeking an abortion would likely never raise much public noise about what activities were present within the walls of the very place where she had sought treatment.

Simons would quickly put the embarrassment of the event behind him. That was an emotion for those who, unlike him, could not rise above their ineptitude. He would never speak of the incident to anyone, except Richards, and then only once, in reference to another change in protocol. His new plan was that now Simons would be summoned from his university office only after the donor mother was well into the procedure with pitocin dripping and an examination confirming the readiness of the cervix. Simons would then travel to the F.F.P. Clinic, notify Richards of his presence, and give him the okay to commence with dilation of the cervix and to perform the forceps extraction of the P.O.C. Never again would Simons waste his time waiting for a heart that would not be made available for study. He would send Gentry over early, however, to set up and be sure the pump was primed and ready. Gentry was reliable. Gentry was quiet. Simons loved that about Gentry.

Although the embarrassment would be quickly put away, lingering doubts would speak to Simons, quietly at first and then more loudly as they fed on his paranoia. The nagging voices would tell him of the need to be sure his research was first brought to the public in a controlled manner, and only through the information he alone would present. There would be no broad-sweeping public announcements to a general audience by an emotional, angry woman. Such an event could certainly spell a disastrous setback in reforming his surgical subspecialty. Making sure that the events of that morning would not be repeated in any fashion became Simons' first step towards assuring himself that the research would not be leaked until he was ready.

He had, in fact, called Richards promptly that very night to inform him of the changes. He thought Adam's speech had seemed a bit slurred and he therefore made a mental note to have his secretary call Richards with the modifications the next morning.

Adam Richards would never remember that night's call.

CHAPTER
16

SAM and Anne talked well into the morning. In fact, Anne ended up staying with Sam all night, catching what sleep she did get on the couch in Sam's apartment. Sam had been somewhat cautious at first, but just hearing Anne's account of her urge to pray and visit Sam seemed to uncap the whole ugly story. With the top off, all the bottled-up frustrations, all the dreams for Sam's future, and now all of her suspicions about the activities at the F.F.P. Clinic came rolling out, including the details of her relationship with Layton Redman. Both cried, first out of sorrow, and then for relief at Sam being able to get out of the clinic with her baby alive.

Sam's questions became Anne's questions. A second mind definitely helped by asking pointed questions from an uninvolved angle, a fresh perspective for Sam. Several things were becoming clear, at least to Anne. She hoped they would soon become as clear for Sam: Layton Redman was interested in only one thing! His own reputation took the highest priority over anything or anyone else. He would be governor even if it cost the life of an unborn baby. Anne felt that all ties with Redman should be cut before Sam could be hurt again. But she couldn't tell if Sam was ready for that move yet.

Additional questions remained unanswered: What was Simons doing at the clinic, and why would he apparently be waiting for an aborted fetus? Anne needed more information on this one before any judgment could be made.

A third relationship needed some clarification, although Anne formulated some early hypotheses of her own. Namely, the relationship of Layton Redman and Adam Richards. She knew from what Layton had both bragged about to and confided in Sam that Richards quietly sat as one of Redman's biggest financial supporters—to the tune of over one hundred thousand dollars. Evidently Richards had made donations in the names of hundreds of patients in order to stay within the legal and ethical codes of campaign contributions. She also knew Redman to be avidly pro-choice, and his choices in office could mean big bucks to an abortionist like Richards. Was that all Richards was after, or did he have political aspirations of his own, perhaps hoping for a state appointment? Did Richards only want to stay in favor with Redman in order to keep his lines of influence open and for that reason provided abortions and/or birth control pills to Redman's "friends" in addition to the campaign contributions?

Anne knew she was balancing on a political powder keg. Sam shared with her with the understanding that at least for now all the information she shared was in confidence. For reasons unknown to Anne, Sam seemed to still be protecting Redman. She knew Sam would keep her confidences tight as long as she possibly could.

"Expose him for what he is, Sam! He's a lying, unfaithful—"

"I can't," Sam interrupted. "Promise me you'll keep this under your hat until I get it all sorted out."

Anne couldn't know how hard that would be.

◆ ◆ ◆

It looked like a light morning. At least that's what Matt thought when he originally looked at the schedule. He arrived late, however, for the surgical oncology clinic for two reasons. First, an intern called asking him to help with a minor case—the placement of a long-term, indwelling intravenous port so a patient could receive chemotherapy without being stuck for IVs over and over and over. This kind of case involved no glory. If things went perfectly, the surgeon had done what was expected. If complications arose, the surgeon looked inept because everyone thought it was just a "little" procedure. In the normal case, the large vein beneath the clavicle, the subclavian vein, was found by placement of a needle through the skin, guided only by external landmarks; then a catheter was threaded via this vein down into the superior vena cava, the large vein just above the patient's heart. The case was done under local anesthetic with the patient awake.

In the case at hand, that fact had definitely worked against the young resident. One of the first rules of thumb when operating on an awake patient was not to express frustration in a way that may aggravate or worry the patient. Statements like "Oops!" or worse were strictly forbidden in a case with a comprehending patient. That's exactly where the case had begun a downward spiral. The resident had difficulty placing the line and expressed his frustration audibly. The patient became anxious and moved while the needle approached the vein, misdirecting the needle into the nearby lung tissue. This caused the lung to collapse. The resident then had to place a chest tube to correct this problem. By this time, the patient had been in the O.R. a full hour for a procedure that on a good day took only a few minutes. To make it worse, they were no closer to getting the line in than when they had started.

By the time Matt had been paged, the atmosphere in the O.R. was clearly tense. Just having his chief resident in the room helped the intern relax considerably. In fact, the young surgeon successfully placed the line in just one additional attempt after Matt walked in to help.

Matt hadn't minded the first delay. He knew what it was like to be on his own in the O.R. Sometimes when things were not flowing along smoothly, it just helped to have someone else in the room for moral support, if for nothing else.

The second delay irritated Matt a bit more. A group of very vocal animal rights activists physically blocked him from entering the clinic building. They were opposed to the use of animals for experimentation and were advocating the use of advanced technical models instead of innocent animals, whom they claimed were treated and housed "inhumanely." *They're not human, are they?* Matt had not voiced his thoughts. The protesters greatly outnumbered him, and he suspected he would get nowhere by arguing anyway.

An orthopedic resident nearby, trapped by the same throng, did not hold his tongue. "And what can be done when advanced technical models for a particular therapy are not good enough to predict results?"

A tall woman with braided hair spoke first. "You can always experiment on willing, informed human subjects. At least they can be warned of the risks." Her volume increased as she concluded, "Unlike these!" She shoved a large poster picturing two rabbits in a small metal cage into the face of her opponent. "Do you think anyone informed these patients, doctor?"

A second woman who, Matt noticed, wore leather shoes and eye shadow spoke up next, saying, "There is also human tissue culture and fetal tissue research. There's a lot of human tissue that surgeons remove and is wasted every day. After they make their diagnosis, let the researchers use the tissue."

Matt thought her arguments were shallow. The irony of advocating fetal tissue struck him. *You oppose the use of a lab rat to advance medical science and yet would advocate the use of an unborn human for the same purpose?* Matt shook his head in disbelief. Fortunately for him, the crowd had descended on the more verbal target, leaving Matt unattended. He slipped by as the orthopedic resident had a second poster pushed in his face.

Matt turned when he had the entry door open and was apparently free. Part of him wanted badly to yell, "Get a life!" but he suppressed the urge and managed to arrive forty-five minutes late for the surgical oncology clinic.

◆ ◆ ◆

Myron Whithers arrived at work early hoping to satisfy his curiosity and ease his conscience, if possible. He had told Eunice he needed to go in early to fill out forms explaining his sick-leave the previous afternoon. She certainly hadn't known any differently. Her husband had never missed work in all the years she had known him. Whithers wanted to check the O.R. schedule for the last few days. He hadn't mentioned the truth to his wife, as he understood clearly her advice on the subject: "Let sleeping dogs lie."

Whithers now thumbed through the O.R. schedule book for the last ten days. He was sure that would be enough. There wasn't one recorded pediatric open chest case listed. *Okay, maybe it wasn't an O.R. case . . . Or maybe it wasn't done here.*

He stopped in the pathology lab next, to see if the specimen was still around. Dr. Tanous sat at a table sorting Kodak slides for a talk to the medical students.

"Say, doc, were all the waste specimens cleared out yesterday?" Whithers nervously tried to look as though he had a valid reason for stopping in.

"Yes, sir," Scott replied. "The one container you forgot was picked up by your coworker. Don't sweat it. It didn't bother anyone."

Whithers turned to go, then added hesitantly, "Say, doc, you didn't notice anything strange about them specimens, did you?"

Scott looked at Whithers curiously. *What is he driving at?* Scott had known Mr. Whithers for a long time. *Something is obviously bugging him.* "Like what, Mr. Whithers?"

Myron rubbed the back of his neck with his hand. He couldn't admit that he'd opened the specimen container against his superior's orders. He didn't think so fast on his feet usually, but today he surprised even himself. He paused, his eyes fixated on the floor in front of him. "I let one of the containers fall . . . the one I left behind. The contents went everywhere. It was a mess. This . . . this baby rolled out onto the floor . . . It looked like it had been through some kind of operation, with a gash right down the middle of its chest." Myron gestured with his hand, drawing a line down his own sternum. "I was afraid it was someone's dead child. I didn't want to take it to the furnace."

The resident could see that the old man was visibly shaken even at the memory of what had happened. "Mr. Whithers, I wouldn't worry about it anymore. That child wasn't wanted by anyone." He studied Myron's furrowed brow to follow his reaction. Scott wasn't sure how much he should tell him. Whithers seemed to be mainly concerned that he might have been disposing of someone's naturally born child. "That child was an abortion."

The words seemed to hit Myron Whithers cold. He hadn't even considered that!

Scott continued, "It wasn't done here, Mr. Whithers." He assumed that his friend would be comforted by that fact. He was.

Whithers didn't say much after that. His mind was eased of its main concern that he'd allowed a specimen to be mishandled and had participated in someone else's error. He didn't know much about abortion, really. He'd never had much reason to think about it. He figured it was up to each person to decide personal matters like that for himself or herself. He hadn't much cared for what had been done to the small fetus, but he just figured it had something to do with the abortion process. His mind was relieved. He had done the right thing. For now, he would be content to do just what Eunice had told him: forget the whole thing.

Scott Tanous, on the other hand, made a mental note. He figured the fetus would have had to hit the floor pretty hard to split the chest open. He hadn't been told about the sutures. Neither had he any reason to ask. The fact that he'd seen blood around one of the aborted specimens was a connection that he wouldn't make for some time.

And so, like many others before, a "donor preparation" had passed through the routine pathologic examinations and had been destroyed without anyone suspecting what had actually occurred *before* its life had been stolen.

◆ ◆ ◆

Adam Richards walked down the hall at St. Christopher's Hospital. It was unusual for him to have more than just a few inpatients. Today he only needed to see three: a post-operative patient who had just had a hysterectomy for large uterine fibroids, a twenty-two-year-old woman with pelvic inflammatory disease who had failed outpatient antibiotic therapy, and a thirty-year-old with cervical cancer who received radiation implants. Richards had given up on a regular obstetrical practice. The only pregnant patients he saw anymore were seeking pregnancy termination. Richards rarely used the hospital O.R. He did so only when his own outpatient clinic facility was unsuitable. Ironically, the opposite was more frequently true: a Catholic O.R. was unsuitable for the majority of Richards' "work." It was also a bit odd that Richards maintained privileges to practice gynecology in only one hospital in Fairfax: St. Christopher's.

Richards had just stepped out of the room of his last patient when his beeper sounded. He had a digital electronic pager that stored messages up to fifty characters in length. This one was brief: "Call Dr. Simons 322-5000." Richards sighed. *That's all I need. Simons can wait. He's just ticked off about yesterday.*

Adam Richards went to the nurses' station and jotted a quick progress note. He knew he didn't have any office patients before 10 that morning, and he hoped to get some breakfast before facing his desk. He certainly hadn't felt like doing paperwork the evening before, after the day he'd had. Now he would have even more paperwork. He checked his watch. 8:30. *Plenty of time to eat first and still clean off my desk before the morning clinic heats up.*

Richards was halfway down the hall when he paused to touch the arm of a staff nurse. "Discontinue 231's foley catheter, will you, dear? I forgot to write for it."

"Sure, Dr. Richards."

Within two minutes he strode across the parking lot, approaching his Mercedes from the passenger's side. "What the @#*#!" Richards looked around to see if anyone was listening. He rubbed the football-sized dent in the passenger door with his hand. He had no recollection of his putting the dent in the car himself. *Someone must have done this while I was inside!*

He got in the car, a fine tremor noticeable as he placed his keys in the ignition. He reached in the glove box and pulled out a small flask. He took three deep swallows of the aromatic liquid before replacing it in the glove box. That's when he found his garage door opener. Richards just shook his head and exited the parking lot on his way to the clinic. He would stop at Hardee's on the way.

◆ ◆ ◆

Simons circled the name at the top of the incomplete data entry sheet: "Stelling." He then struck the paper repetitively with his pencil eraser as he thought. He did not like "What if?" situations. He didn't like intangibles. He liked to be able to strictly control every variable in an equation in order to predict one or two unknowns. He was having second thoughts about the advisability of leaving Stelling alone to start rumors that might reflect badly on his research. He needed to start with Richards. He would have to deviate from his disdain of knowing the personal details about a donor mother. He needed to know certain things so he could accurately predict whether a threat to his work even existed at all. His paranoia, which had in the past been an asset in his rise through the ranks, now precipitated a mountain of new questions. What had really gone on? Had the patient refused an abortion, or did Richards produce a complication that prevented it? Richards hadn't really shared any of this with him yet, and he certainly seemed incapable of doing so during his phone conversation with Simons the previous night. Did the patient even recognize Simons? Could she identify him at all?

Simons pounded his pencil harder. He didn't like being out of control.

You're overreacting, Michael. It occurred to him that even if Stelling could identify him, the thought that she had any idea what he was doing there was ludicrous. Or was it? Certainly Richards would know these details. *I need to talk to Adam about this. Perhaps no real threat exists at all. And if we find out she knows more and becomes a threat of public exposure later, she can be dealt with at that time.* Simons was experienced at getting what he wanted, especially from women.

"Iris?" Simons pushed the intercom linked to his secretary and continued, "Page Dr. Richards again for me please. This time use the word STAT."

"Right away, Dr. Simons."

◆ ◆ ◆

"Call him again," Anne urged. "It's your right to know about your own treatment and who's doing the treating." Anne looked at her watch. Her curiosity and "reporter's sense" prompted her own assertiveness in prodding Sam to call Richards' office. "It's been almost an hour since you called last. Call him again!"

Sam was curious too, but she doubted she would have been courageous enough to call the clinic without Anne's urging. She knew that if any information was to be given out, it would have to be given directly to the patient. Anne couldn't do the talking for her. Reluctantly, she dialed the number again.

◆ ◆ ◆

Adam Richards sat at his desk quickly sorting through a small mountain of paperwork. Most of it just required his initials and was rapidly filed in his *Out* box. He paused when he came to the ultrasound report of Samantha Stelling, which had already been typed for him to initial. By the head circumference and length, it appeared that the pregnancy was approximately twenty-two weeks along. He avoided any documentation of his age estimates in case she decided to change her mind again in a few weeks when they would be pushing the limit of abortion restrictions. *Better not to have documented the age at all than to seal my own fate if my records ever get reviewed.* Richards merely left a blank beside the term "E.D.C."—"estimated date of confinement," an old medical term meaning "the due date." He initialed the form and put it in his *Out* box to be filed in Stelling's chart.

Richards looked at the unusually large number of phone messages for him. Most were patients calling for results of tests. There were three phone messages from Stelling. Whenever the calls were from a patient, the messages were written on a stick-up note and placed on the patient's chart for him to review if needed. He picked up the ultrasound report he had just signed and slid it into the thin folder. He kept a financial statement of each patient's account in an envelope in the back of the chart. They stored advance payment checks there until he rendered the service. He leafed though the chart, noting Redman's uncashed check. He studied the brief phone messages. The first just said, "S. Stelling called. No message. Please call back." The second was somewhat more specific: "S. Stelling would like ultrasound results." The last one really caught his eye: "S. Stelling is asking questions regarding Simons' presence at the clinic. Can you call her? She sounds upset."

#$@&!! That's all I need . . . an emotional female questioning what goes on in my clinic!

Richards had no desire to talk to her at this time. He wrote on several stick-up notes and shoved the file into his *Out* box. He also quickly formulated a message for his front office: "Tell her the ultrasound dimensions of the fetus. Then tell her that Simons came merely to pick up specimens that are examined by the pathologists at the university. Tell her we send all our tissue specimens there because we have no pathologists here." He smiled. He knew that he had written the truth. *Perhaps not the whole truth, but enough of the truth to quiet her concerns.* Richards paused, then retrieved the file and added another stick-up note: "Dr. Simons apologizes for the intrusion during your exam. He was in the wrong room at the wrong time and didn't realize what was going on with you." Richards knew he was being a bit presumptive by apologizing for Simons, but after all, she was Richards' patient, and he needed to diffuse the situation before the story could be distorted any further.

Richards wanted nothing more than to put the case behind him entirely. He definitely didn't want the patient receiving a bill. He knew that would only inflame an already upset patient even more. He signaled the intercom for a secretary. "Mail back the check for Sam Stelling's procedure to Layton Redman. Send a brief note stating that the services paid for were never rendered." Richards was about to hang up the receiver when another thought came to him, so he buzzed the secretary again. "Better yet, void the check yourself, then fax him a copy along with a note. Do it this morning. I want to close this case and its account today."

"I'll get right on it, Dr. Richards."

Richards' pager sounded again. He looked at the display. *It looks like Simons really wants to talk to me.* He picked up the phone and pressed 1-8 to speed-dial Simons' office.

"Dr. Simons' office. May I help you?"

"Dr. Adam Richards. I'm returning a page."

"Dr. Simons will be right with you, Dr. Richards."

Richards steamed a little as he waited. *What? No message from the secretary today? I get to speak with the doctor himself?* His sarcasm reflected his dislike for the arrogance he saw in Simons.

"Adam, tell me what you know about Stelling," Simons barked without saying hello.

"Hello, Michael," Richards replied, placing heavy emphasis on the word "Hello." *He's really upset about this.* "She's a mixed-up kid, that's all. She's confused about what she really wants. It's not that uncommon in my business, you know." Richards was a bit surprised at how confident he sounded to himself. He continued, "I've taken care of everything. She won't be asking any more questions."

Simons had begun to feel a little more comfortable until Adam mentioned "questions." "Questions? What questions?"

Richards decided to let Simons stew in his own paranoia. *You're the one who barged in on my exam, creating this whole problem, aren't you?* "Oh, you know, the routine. 'What did my ultrasound show? How far along am I?' That kind of stuff."

"Is that all?" Simons was stewing alright.

"Yes . . . Well, she did ask what you were doing there."

"@@#$%$@"

Richards held the receiver back from his ear. He paused, then added, "Cool your jets, Michael. She doesn't know anything. I explained things and apologized for your intrusion. Everything's cool now. Don't have a stroke!"

"What did you tell her about me?"

"I told her we didn't have any pathologists at our clinic and that we send all the tissue to the university for testing. I told her you were there to pick up specimens to take to the pathology lab at T.U. For all she knows, she probably thinks you're a pathologist."

Simons seemed to calm down a little. "You know we can't have the public getting an idea of what we're doing before I can release it in a controlled, timely fashion . . . first to the scientific community, and later to the public, appropriately filtered by those of us who are capable of understanding these things."

"I understand, Michael. The public knows nothing about this."

"Let's keep it that way, Adam. But if this Stelling ever starts raising more questions, let me know. I'll see to it that she doesn't talk again."

Richards wondered exactly what Simons had in mind but

decided against asking. He wasn't sure he wanted to understand everything.

The rest of the conversation was one-sided, with Simons spelling out the modifications they would make in the future to prevent another foul-up like the one they'd just had. It all centered around maximal convenience and minimal waiting for the cardiothoracic surgeon. He didn't want to make another wasted trip to the clinic. As for Richards, he wasn't in the mood for an argument. As he listened, he occasionally grunted his approval. He then pulled a small flask from a locked desk drawer and took a drink. He placed the bottle back in safekeeping before his secretary came in to empty his *Out* file. After several minutes the conversation concluded.

"Good-bye, Michael."

Simons simply hung up without a farewell.

Richards tried not to think about the situation any further. He had work to do. It wasn't until that night, when his inhibitions had been significantly reduced by a bottle of 1978 Chablis, that he was unable to suppress his concerns anymore. He reclined in his favorite chair, staring blankly at the TV. Simons' paranoia seemed to feed upon his own. His concerns focused directly on the changes he had made in his techniques to accommodate Simons' need for a "living" abortion. *Maybe I should be more concerned. What if Stelling tells someone what happened? What if it gets out that I'm doing cervical dilations and extractions instead of saline injection abortions?* He knew that both the medical and legal community frowned upon any deviation from the "standard of care." Any physician who takes it on himself or herself to change acceptable medical practice had better have a good reason or be subject to stiff penalties, including the loss of his or her medical license.

Richards squinted his eyes tightly, as if that would drive away the unwanted protrusions into his thoughts. He reached over to a side table for a bottle he had been saving for a special occasion. *But I've got a good reason to change acceptable medical practice, right?* He took a long drag of the aging liquid. It seemed to help him believe his words were true.

◆ ◆ ◆

Layton Redman relished the praise of the media. His faithful statewide volunteer staff had faxed him today's newspaper stories, which had surfaced as a result of yesterday's photo-ops. It seemed every small paper in the state had at least one of the stories. Actually Redman thought it was better that way, because if one paper carried a report of all three photo-ops on the same day, people would soon get the idea that Redman just showed up to get photographed, and not out of genuine concern. He liked to schedule things in different parts of the state in the same day for that very reason. It made for tougher travel arrangements, but it reaped broader newspaper and TV coverage.

He had his feet on the desk. His secretarial staff had brought him seven separate newspaper clippings sent in by fax that morning. All the reports were good. He was the media's golden boy. His opponents hadn't always had the same favorable experience with the media. One had hired an illegal alien to work on his horse farm and knowingly did not pay appropriate Social Security tax for his wages. His other opponent dodged the draft during the Vietnam war. The media had been merciless with them. So far, however, no dirt had surfaced on Layton Redman.

Redman put down the small stack of clippings and smiled. He didn't have any appointments before 2 P.M. He pressed down the intercom button to talk to his paralegal staff. "Let's go to lunch. My treat! The media has done our job for us today."

Redman heard the fax machine start to chirp again. He hopped to his feet and went to the machine excitedly, anticipating another good news report. Instead, he received a one-page transmission from the Fairfax Family Planning Clinic . . . a copy of a voided check followed by a brief explanation: "No services were rendered."

"@#%#@*!!!" Layton looked around to see if any of his staff had heard. He turned back to the fax machine and ripped the paper from the receiving slot. He lowered his voice this time. "@#$%!"

He picked up his coat from the chair in his office and hurried out with the last fax in his hand. He forgot all about lunch.

CHAPTER
17

SAMANTHA Stelling slept the contented sleep of a child. Her day had been full. When she had finally retired for the night, she prayed an earnest prayer for forgiveness and guidance. She was peacefully aware of the former and confident that the latter would materialize in time. She felt sure that God had saved the child within her because of Anne's simple yet timely prayer.

She had, in response to Anne's encouragement, made small steps at distancing herself from Redman's influence. She had told Anne that she melted whenever he called and always ended up promising to do whatever he wanted just to please him. She also knew she had made up her mind to keep her baby, but she didn't know how to tell him and definitely didn't want to talk to him until she stood on surer ground emotionally. She had solved that problem by unplugging her phone. She would call or write to Redman when she felt ready.

She had also scheduled a work-in appointment with Dr. Ron Beitler, Anne Caudill's obstetrician. Anne nearly insisted that Sam be seen somewhere that day. He worked Sam in graciously when he heard about the situation. He carefully examined Sam and found no evidence of harm due to the prostaglandin suppository. Her story did not alarm him, because he had not kept current on modern abortion techniques, which he morally opposed. He gave her some prenatal vitamins and enrolled her in a class to teach her some breathing techniques to use during delivery.

As Sam rested, several dreams rippled through her contented sleep, disturbing her but not pushing her into an awake state. As her subconscious mind filtered the events of the last few days, a recurrent image stood out. In each dream she was alone with Adam Richards, who was performing the abortion. He would give her more and more sedative, but it seemed as if the pain was never dulled. Richards yelled, "Give her more Versed, STAT!" Then, as Richards completed the abortion, Simons would burst in.

"I've got work to do, experiments to run, breakthroughs to establish! Work to do! Experiments to run! Breakthroughs to establish!" Richards handed Simons the small male infant. Simons only brightened, holding the baby up to show Sam and the nurse, who now appeared on Sam's right. Simons continued, "*It's a boy!* Gotta go, old boy! Work to do! Experiments to run! Breakthroughs to establish!" Simons walked out with the baby.

Sam screamed, "That's my baby! My baby boy!"

The nurse held Sam by the shoulders and said calmly, "Sure, it's a boy. A baby boy. We could tell that by the ultrasound."

Sam said, "You could tell that by the ultrasound?"

Richards countered, "It's pretty much just undifferentiated pregnancy tissue at this point. We'd have to be prophets to be able to tell that."

In the end, the dream was always surrounded by a feeling of warmth and soft glowing lights, in contrast to the darkness that predominated the first part of the dream. Anne arrived carrying a small baby boy in her arms and handed it to Sam. Sam looked up as she heard Simons returning, always repeating the same phrases: "Where's the baby? I've got work to do! Experiments—" The noise was abruptly shut out as Anne closed and locked the door. With the disturbing dream over, Sam slept until 9 the next morning.

◆ ◆ ◆

Layton Redman had called Sam's apartment twenty-two times: five times before 2 o'clock, another ten times between appointments, and then hourly between 7 P.M. and 1 A.M. After that he finally gave up and went to bed. By 1 A.M., he really wasn't thinking that clearly anyhow. The beer he was drinking had even affected his ability to dial the phone. The last time he tried to get Sam, he speed-dialed Janice instead. Unfortunately, she recognized him right away when he called her by the wrong name. Fortunately, he hadn't said anything about the abortion by the time he too realized his mistake. Redman laughed it off and said it was a joke, that he'd just called because he missed her so much on this cold night. She was suspicious but satisfied.

Layton collapsed on his bed, still fully clothed, and fell asleep. He too would dream.

He stood proudly on stage at a political rally with a large number of TV and newspaper reporters. They were shouting, "Redman! Redman! Redman!" Eventually he would quiet the crowd and begin a speech, but enthusiastic reporters frequently interrupted him with their chants: "We love you! We love Redman!"

In the dream he was festive and jubilant, with Janice on his left arm supporting him as he spoke.

Then he would see that the crowd was beginning to murmur, and the chanting had subsided. He felt a tugging on his right arm. It was Sam! She was very large and obviously in a pregnant state! She began to pull him to the side, while Janice pulled Redman in the other direction. He spoke to Sam, but she remained silent, never replying to his questions. Eventually Redman awoke as the media throng turned angry, demanding information about the pregnant woman.

Layton wiped the sweat from his forehead. He thought about trying Sam's number again, then looked at the clock and decided against it. 2:30. He took off his clothes and laid them on the floor beside his bed. He got in and went to sleep.

Again the dream returned. The opening was the same. The speech, the loving crowd, and Janice supporting him on the stage were all the same. This time the crowd fell silent as Samantha Stelling placed a young boy on the stage.

Sam and her son appeared to be poorly dressed in T-shirts and faded jeans. "Go ahead, son! There's your father!"

The little boy ran towards Redman shouting, "Daddy! Daddy! Daddy!"

"Someone take this child away from here!" Redman shouted as the crowd fell silent.

Adam Richards appeared from within the crowd. "I tried to stop him. He's too old now! You'll have to support him. You should have enough money because I gave you your refund. The services were never rendered!"

Redman called to Samantha to take him away, but she would never reply.

The small boy continued to scream, "Daddy! Daddy! *Daddy!*" The reporters closed in and passed the boy back and forth among themselves.

"Look what we found! Look what we've got! It's a boy! Layton's boy! *It's a boy!*" The reporters howled. Redman began to run, with the throng of reporters carrying the boy right behind him.

Redman sat up with a start. "#@$% dreams!" He continued talking to himself in a whisper. "It's only a dream, Layton. Only a dream." He got up and washed his face. He needed to get a lid on this situation. First he needed to talk to Sam. He resolved to try again in the morning. *I'll find out more about this tomorrow . . . uhh, today.* He glanced again at the alarm clock, which indicated that "tomorrow" was indeed already here.

The sun was coming up before he slipped off to sleep again.

◆　◆　◆

Carol was on the phone to the adoption agency. Good news! They were getting a baby boy! In only seconds Dot was with her, carrying the small bundle with her hands outstretched. "Take care of him, Carol. I'm sorry it has taken so long." Dot smiled pleasantly.

As Carol reached for the baby, she saw that her hands were freckled with age, wrinkled and weak from the long wait. She looked at Tony, who was now stooped and bald. He walked towards her with one hand on his back and one hand on a brown, wooden cane. "We've got our baby, darling!"

Tony's voice was frail but unmistakably his. "Like, the wait was, like, only a century," he said, still capable of fabricating a sarcastic valley-girl imitation.

Carol then looked around at their surroundings. Their apartment had been replaced by a large cardboard refrigerator box. Dot looked at the box and then at Tony, who offered the explanation, "I've sold everything for this child. And I've just paid off the infertility bill and the adoption lawyers."

Dot began to shake her head firmly. She reached out to retrieve the child. "This will never do! The agency will never approve this!"

Carol turned around, gripping the child tightly to prevent the boy from being taken away. "No! He's our baby now!"

Dot grabbed the blanket that surrounded the child, then wrestled with Carol until she had the now-crying infant by the wrist. "Give him back!"

"I'll take another job! I'll take another job!" Tony's cries went unheeded.

"The agency will never approve!"

"He's our baby now!"

"I'll take another job!"

Carol forcefully pulled the blanket out of Dot's grasp.

Tony gently poked his sleeping wife in the ribs. "You're hogging the blanket, honey. How about sharing it with me?"

It was only a dream! Carol awoke and slowly released her white-knuckled grip on the blanket. She shared the blanket with Tony, who fell quickly back asleep, his breathing deep and regular. The blanket she would share tonight. The dream would be shared in the morning.

◆ ◆ ◆

Back in Fairfax, Myron Whithers got up to fix some coffee. The time was 5 A.M., an hour earlier than he normally fixed breakfast. This morning, however, he had already been awake since at least 4. He had been pushed from sleep by his dreams and eventually pushed from his warm bed by his wife, who was tired of his restless search for a position compatible with returning to sleep. "Why don't you just leave me alone so at least one of us gets some rest tonight?" Eunice had growled. He had learned not to try meaningful conversation with her in the morning until she had at least one cup of strong coffee. Myron had silently agreed, slipped out of bed, and headed for the kitchen. As the coffee began to drip, he strained to remember the dream that had interrupted his normally solid sleeping pattern.

A well-dressed couple could be seen arguing with Whithers' supervisor. As Myron walked up, the couple exploded, "That's the man! He's the one who stole our baby! He's the one who took away our child!"

"No! No! I left the baby in the pathology lab! I didn't take it!"

"How did you know what it was, Myron? Have you been looking at the specimens again? You know how I feel about that!" His supervisor's eyes were bulging.

Suddenly they were all in the incinerator room together. Norman Driver was throwing the biological waste into the incinerator. The red bags were full, and only one remained. As Norman picked it up, the bag split open, spilling the contents onto the floor. The small male fetus rolled out onto the cold, concrete surface. Slowly Norman picked up the spilled trash. He heaved each item into the fire individually in slow motion. As each specimen hit the flames, the fire sizzled, belching steam from the furnace's open mouth.

"Stop him! He's got our baby!"

Fear immobilized Whithers. He could have easily reached over to pick up the fetus and prevent Norman from adding it to the flames, but he seemed frozen, fixed in position by his own anxieties.

"Stop him! Stop him! He's got our baby!"

Slowly Norman picked up the small fetus. "Look at the little sutures, Myron. He's had surgery! No one operates on an aborted fetus, Myron!"

"Stop him! Stop him!"

"No one will ever know. No one else saw the sutures!" Norman hissed as he flung the child into the air above the fire. The child disappeared in a belch of smoke and steam.

The parents' agonizing cries accelerated. "You could have stopped him. You let him take our son away!"

Myron began to run. The parents' voices faded.

Myron had been unable to sleep after that. Now he stood over the coffee maker and tried to make some sense of his dream. He began to talk to himself as he poured his coffee. "Dreams don't mean nothin'. It was only a dream. Besides, it's all history now. Tanous said it was an abortion. Nobody wanted that child. It's none of your business, Myron! Don't go getting yourself in trouble. Eunice is right. Just forget the whole thing. It's none of your business!"

The volume of his quiet voice picked up slightly as he repeated the last phrase. He turned his ear towards the bedroom. He could hear Eunice snoring comfortably. *At least one of us was able to get some sleep tonight.*

◆ ◆ ◆

Simons rose from his king-size bed where tonight he had slept alone. He could not remember a specific dream, but he awoke with a feeling of dread, knowing only that his spirit was somehow darkly affected by the anticipation of an unexpected event. He slipped from his bed and sat on the floor facing a window that he had opened widely in spite of the coolness of the night air. He stared into the blackness beyond the open window. An overcast sky prevented even the reflected light of the moon from brightening the darkness. His home was set a full quarter of a mile from the road, and his nearest neighbor was easily twice that distance.

Simons closed his eyes, emptied his mind, and began to search for his "higher self," the untapped potential within him that would continue to propel him to greatness and give him understanding about his current uneasiness. After a few minutes he opened his eyes, but the images he saw were not those of the window before him. He sat motionless, not even blinking. After a few minutes his breathing quickened, and his eyes closed.

A threat to his work was at hand. Although unable to totally understand the nature of the threat, he understood that this had precipitated the dread he had felt just moments ago. That dread had been replaced by a pseudo-peace that Simons interpreted as his "answer." As he meditated on the success to which he was destined, the comfortable assurance grew stronger within him. *Soon the threat will be destroyed. The higher good of my work will never be stopped.*

Simons got up, closed the window, and slipped back into bed.

With his anxieties quelled, he slept soundly. His peace had returned again.

◆ ◆ ◆

John Gentry awoke by 5 A.M. His bladder, rather than his dreams, had nudged him gently into consciousness. After relieving himself, he had eased back into bed so as not to disturb Lori, his wife. Sleep, however, would not return for John, who found himself staring blankly at the ceiling's shadows cast by the street lamp near his window. Nighttime was often the best time for John to think, to plan, or to work through the problems of the day. For him, daylight meant work, deadlines, assisting Simons in his research, and running the cardiopulmonary bypass pump in the O.R. for open heart cases. After work he had family responsibilities. He had three daughters, ages two, four, and six.

He had come here simply to have the chance to work with Simons. Simons carried a worldwide reputation for getting work done. "A chance to work with him is a chance of a lifetime," Gentry recalled telling his wife before the move. Although he had specifically come to work as a pump technician, he also had his Master's degree in computer science and was therefore given more responsibility in Simons' lab projects.

Now, however, Gentry was seeing a slow decline of all his interests outside of Simons' research. Last week alone he had been required to spend an additional four nights split between the T.U. cardiothoracic research lab and the Fairfax Family Planning Clinic. His wife was growing jealous of his time. He had been home in time to see his daughters awake only once in the last four nights. Two weeks ago when his oldest daughter had been in a play, he had missed it to do a pump run at the F.F.P. Clinic. He had told Simons about the play, but Simons only grunted and then espoused "the necessity of personal sacrifice for the good of humankind."

Slowly his life was being absorbed into Simons'. He rarely thought about anything but the research, even when he had time off. Seriousness had overtaken his usual sense of humor. His normally reserved manner had lended itself well to Simons' liking. His timely dry wit had not been similarly rewarded, and Gentry had changed, unconsciously, in order to please the man he served. A subtle shortening of his temper also punctuated his relationships with his wife and daughters. He felt a not-so-subtle pressure from Simons not to speak of the work at the F.F.P. Clinic, and so he had become less communicative and silent, even with his wife, as his involvement with the project increased. A sullen darkness was deepening within him. An attentive observer would have noticed a change beginning with his involvement in Simons' latest research project.

Simons rewarded Gentry handsomely. Gentry's salary had almost tripled since moving to Fairfax. He had reaped professional benefits as well, with his name listed as the second author next to Simons' on six papers in his first year alone. The cost, however, had been high, taking its toll on his time, relationships, and emotional state.

Now the pressure pushed Gentry to again think of getting out— to dream of freedom from academia, freedom from the demands of Simons himself, whose self-worship and self-absorption led him to disregard the needs of those around him and now fed the growing anger and disrespect Gentry carried. A job possibility was opening up at Fairfax General Hospital. *It would mean a pay cut . . . certainly less prestige. But there would be more time for my family . . . and no more bowing down to please Simons' every whim.*

In the quietness, Gentry also began to give ear to the quiet doubts about their research that he had suppressed so successfully up to this moment. He had not been bothered as much when the pregnancies had not been far along, but lately Simons had been pushing for pregnancies at the very edge of the legal limit. *Simons always tells me it's for the good of all people, that we will change the treatment of congenital heart disease forever. I believe it, but I never feel quite right about the donor preps. I know they're non-viable on their own, but I've seen them move, seen them wince—even heard one gasp, almost cry.*

Somehow in the darkness John Gentry could sense the night within himself. He felt a quiet prompting in his spirit to distance himself from Simons and his work. Strangely, he knew that if he listened now, he still had a chance. He feared that if he waited, the quiet voice would fade, and his opportunity would be lost.

Gentry crept from his bedroom and into the hall. The doorway to his daughters' room was open. He could see that each girl slept peacefully. He was happy that his present job had allowed him to provide for them so well. He didn't want to return to the financial struggles they had endured before he had worked for Simons. And yet . . .

John Gentry again felt a strange urgency about needing a change. He shook his head as if trying to dislodge an unwanted thought. *Something's got to give! Something's got to give soon!*

◆ ◆ ◆

Not even the 1978 Chablis had been able to prevent Adam Richards from dreaming during the early hours of that winter morning.

Richards busily performed a late second trimester abortion according to his modified technique. He finished with the cervical dilation, but persistent bleeding from a small tear in the cervix prevented him from moving faster and added to his impatience. Simons stood behind him. "@#%$! Now I've torn the cervix with the dilator!"

"I've got work to do, old boy!" Simons paced rapidly.

"Look, I'm working as fast as I can. There's a small laceration here, so I've got to be careful. The bleeding is making it difficult to see. Just cool your jets!"

"I've got experiments to run!"

Richards tried to ignore his egocentric "partner." He reached for the forceps and slid them into the dilated cervix.

"I've got breakthroughs to establish!"

Richards manipulated the forceps into position, but in doing so he extended the cervical laceration well up into the uterus and the placenta. Torrential bleeding resulted. Richards quickly delivered a small fetus, about twenty-two weeks gestation. Blood literally poured onto the tiled floor.

"Increase the pitocin!" Richards yelled.

Just then two men burst into the room from the Kentucky State Medical Board. "What's going on here, gentlemen? A deviation from the standard of care?"

"Sir, this isn't a good time to—" Richards was cut short.

"This isn't a good time. I've got work to do! Experiments to run!" Simons shouted rhythmically. The small infant gasped, almost beginning to cry.

"Are live abortions the standard of care here, doctor?"

"We have good reasons to deviate from the standard medical practice! Tell them, Simons!" Richards then turned to the patient, who was now blue and lifeless. Her entire blood volume seemed to be on the examination room floor.

The man from the state board picked up the patient's limp wrist and let it fall. "Is this your standard of care?"

"Tell them our good reasons for doing it this way, Simons!"

Simons smugly turned to leave. "I can't. I've got work to do! Experiments to run—" His voice trailed as he took the kicking infant from the room and proceeded down the hall.

Richards awoke just as the board authorities grabbed him by the arms to lead him away. He wiped his eyes and moved his lounge chair to the upright position. "#@$%$@!!" He didn't remember falling asleep in the chair. He rubbed his neck and sighed. He wanted a way to silence the dreams, to escape the sullen depression that constantly dogged him. He wished for a permanent remedy. Instead, he reached for the bottle on the side table. He finished the half-empty bottle in one tilt and closed his eyes again.

CHAPTER
18

"CAROL?"

"Yes."

"This is Layton Redman calling. I hope I'm not disturbing you."

"Layton Redman! I can't believe you're calling me! I'd have thought you'd have forgotten all your old college friends by now."

"Oh no! I couldn't do that. How have you and . . . uh . . . Tony, is it? . . . How have you been?"

"We're fine. Why are you calling me?" Carol smiled and continued, "Especially since you've made the big time. Your schedule must be terrible."

"Oh, it's really not so bad. I've got a great staff." Layton paused. "Say, I've got a favor to ask of you. I was talking to Deb Raines the other day . . . You remember Deb, don't you? She dated my brother for a while—"

"Sure. Long, black hair. Glasses—"

"That's her. Listen . . . she recommended you to me. I thought maybe you could help me out."

"What have you got in mind, Layton?" Carol was definitely curious now.

"I really only want you to do this if you're comfortable, okay? I want that clear from the outset."

"Okay."

"Look, I'm putting together a grass-roots discussion group on

health care issues here in this state. I have very little experience on
this. We are hoping to put together some concrete plans for improving our present system. I know I don't know much about what you
and Tony have been through. It's not like I have a right to know. I
haven't even talked to you since college. But Deb had heard about
your money problems and the expensive medical workup . . . and . . .
Well, with your inside experience with the clinical world of medicine, I thought maybe your opinions would be of some value. You
have a perspective on things that I should hear." Redman paused,
trying to sense a reaction.

Carol felt both surprised and somewhat taken back at the knowledge that word of her infertility struggle had gotten as far as Debbie
Raines. She was also somewhat honored to be asked to participate
in the political process like this. "What would I have to do?"

"Just meet with me and one of my staff members, along with two
other families who have had other problems with our current health
care system. Your views would be kept anonymous. There will be no
media present." *This would be a great photo-op, but I did promise the
other participants that the media would not be invited.* "We will be releasing a statement to the press about the meetings and their intent, but
no names will be used." Layton paused and then asked, "Do you
think you and Tony can help me?"

"Well, I've never really studied the issues and—"

Layton interrupted. "That's why we're calling people like you . . .
people who have been abused by our system as it stands. We want
fresh ideas, not the same old stuff from the experts. We just want
plain people; we hope to get honest, unfiltered information."

"When is this meeting to take place?"

"My staff would have to get back with you on that. If you agree,
we will try to set up a session in Easton so you wouldn't have far to
go."

"Okay, I'll do it. I'll have to talk to Tony first though. I think he'll
go along with it. I'm really not sure we'll be of much value to you,
but if you really want us, we'll do it." Carol shook her head as if she
wondered if Redman really knew what he was doing by asking them.

"Great. Expect a call to work out the details within a day or two
at the most."

"Okay."

"Bye, Carol. Nice talking to you again. Thanks a lot."

"Sure. Bye, Layton."

Layton Redman hung up the phone, then punched his intercom. "Beth, count the Jennings in. Call them when you have a meeting worked out to be sure it will work with them. The Claybornes are from Easton as well, so try to work out a meeting there. I think there's a Holiday Inn right off 64."

"Gotcha, Boss. I'll give 'em a call this afternoon."

"Thanks, babe."

With that, Redman scratched another item off his "to do" list. Just beneath "Call Carol Jennings" was "Call Sam." Both items were handwritten by Redman to remind himself of his priorities. He wasn't surprised that he had made a note to himself about calling Sam. It was all he could do to think about anything else, particularly after his dreams the night before.

He dialed her number again. He had called the number so many times that he had contemplated programming it into the phone so he could speed-dial her number, but thought he'd rather not have anyone else in the office calling her by accident.

The phone rang! He had almost hung up the phone, anticipating not getting through again. After eight rings he finally heard a click but no answer. The phone had stopped ringing, but no one spoke.

"Sam?"

Click. Once his voice was recognized, the phone line went dead again.

◆ ◆ ◆

Sam was in the best mood she'd been in for weeks. Anne, who had become almost a fixture in Sam's apartment, sat at Sam's desk working on an English paper. "Just thought you might like some company," Anne had said when she appeared at the door earlier that day. Sam laughed. They had spent the day studying—when the two of them weren't talking, that is.

The phone rang, startling both of them. "I thought you had that thing unplugged," Anne said.

"I did, but I plugged it in to call the library. Just let it ring. I don't want to answer it. What if it's Layton?" The phone continued to ring.

"You've got to talk to him sometime, Sam."

Sam walked over to the phone. "If it rings one more time, I'll pick it up." The phone rang again, and Sam picked up the receiver but did not speak. She recognized Layton's voice.

"Sam?"

Sam quickly put the receiver back in its cradle. She looked at Anne sheepishly. "I . . . I can't talk to him yet. I'll let him know what's going on later." She paused and then continued with an air of certainty, "I'm in far too good a mood to talk to him right now."

Anne rolled her eyes but decided not to push.

Sam's mood had steadily improved for several reasons. First, she was relieved that her baby seemed all right; and two, it felt good not to be in the turmoil of indecision. She also enjoyed Anne's company and her nonjudgmental acceptance.

When they weren't studying, Anne questioned Sam about the events of the past few days, trying to make some sense of it all.

"You're acting like a private detective," Sam chided her new friend.

"Well, I do write for the school newspaper, and we do have some facts here that don't quite add up."

"Like what?"

"Like the fact that you said Richards' office told you Simons arrived to pick up pathology specimens because they didn't have a pathologist at his clinic, right?" Anne paused as Sam nodded her head. Anne continued, "But you told me that Simons' coat had his name embroidered on it, followed by the words 'Pediatric Cardiothoracic Surgery.'"

"Yes. I don't think I'll ever forget the image of him barging in like that. It's as if I have a photograph of him in my mind."

"Okay, so why would he be picking up aborted babies to take to the pathologists? He's a surgeon . . . a heart surgeon. I've even seen him in the news. He's really into research."

Sam brightened as she remembered the words of the nurse at Richards' clinic. "The nurse at the clinic told me! I asked her what Simons was doing there when Richards didn't answer. She said she didn't really know much, but that Richards was doing some research with Simons at the university. I called Richards' office three times. They won't let me talk straight to Richards. That's all the information they'll give me."

"So why don't we ask Simons' office?" Anne said with a slight smile.

"You've got to be kidding! What would we say?"

Anne thought for a moment while Sam tried to read the mind behind the mischievous smile. Finally Anne said, "I could just say I'm doing a story for the campus paper and would like to know what research projects are currently underway in Dr. Simons' lab. That's the truth, right? I *am* doing a story. I didn't say it was about him, did I?"

"Okay, Sherlock, let's see what you can find out." Sam threw a tattered phone book onto the desk in front of Anne.

Anne looked up the number, then carefully dialed it on Sam's digital phone.

"Dr. Simons' office."

"Yes, I was wondering if I could speak with Dr. Simons, please."

Iris Dunn answered quickly, "Dr. Simons is not in. May I take a message?"

"No message, but perhaps you could help me, ma'am." Anne proceeded before Iris had a chance to object. "I'm doing a news story for the campus newspaper at A.C.U. I wondered if you could tell me about Dr. Simons' current research topics?"

Iris laughed. She was used to taking calls from the media but knew little or nothing about the information she gave out. "Look, I'm not qualified to tell you any details. I suppose I could just tell you the subject that Dr. Simons is studying . . . no harm there." Simons had just given her the title of his current project in the T.U. lab, but had told her nothing about the work at the F.F.P. Clinic, so she could report the title to the alumni office of his alma mater. "Here goes—" Iris chuckled again. "Left ventricular myocardial oxygen consumption determinates before and after coronary artery revascularization."

Iris spoke slowly but with remarkable pronunciation, pausing to spell nearly every word."

"Got it. Thank you." Anne paused, looking curiously at the title she'd written in front of her, then added, "Does this have anything to do with babies?"

Iris assumed she was confused about the adult nature of the project, knowing that Simons was a pediatric cardiothoracic surgeon. "No, but Dr. Simons is involved with adult cardiothoracic surgery and research as well."

"I see." Anne paused once more. She decided that since she had a cooperative secretary on the line, she might as well go out on a limb. "Does the project have anything to do with Dr. Adam Richards?" Iris was silent. Anne added lamely, "I know he does some research, too."

Iris thought about the question. She recalled paging Richards for Simons several times, but she didn't know of any professional relationship between them. "Not that I know of, dear. He's a friend of Simons, but he isn't corroborating on any research with him."

"Oh." Anne was out of questions.

"I hope that's what you needed."

"Thank you."

"Good-bye."

"Good-bye." Anne hung up the phone. "Well, if I understand it right, Simons only has one project going right now. It doesn't sound as if it has anything to do with babies . . . and she says Richards is only a friend."

Sam threw up her hands. "Beats me."

"Me too." Anne got up and walked into the kitchen for a drink. She came back with two glasses of lemonade and handed one to Sam. "What we need is more information. Maybe it's nothing, but why would Richards' nurse say they were working together and Simons' secretary not know, or at least not admit to knowing, anything about it?"

"Anne, if it is something weird, maybe we shouldn't go stirring things up—"

"Sam! You said yourself that Simons barged in likely thinking an abortion was in progress and asked for the 'specimen.' And you hadn't been told anything about it! If they're really up to something, you can bet you weren't the first or the last. They were going to take advantage of you! You can't tell me Simons just picks up specimens for some pathologist, like they want you to think! They have flunkies for that sort of work. He's an attending surgeon. He wanted that fetus for experimentation, Sam! That's what he implied, didn't he?"

Sam avoided the question with one of her own. "What do you want to do about it?" Sam could see that Anne was serious about this and didn't want to give up easily. The situation had obviously stirred Anne's reporter's instinct.

"Listen, would you mind if I talked about this to someone else? I'd like to talk to Linda Baldwin. She's a grad student who serves as our advisor at the paper. Her boyfriend's a surgeon up at T.U. Maybe he could find out what's going on with Simons."

"Just keep my name out of this, will you?" Sam replied. Sam felt a bit queasy at the thought of anyone needing a fetus for research. She wanted to cooperate, but she wasn't sure if she really wanted to know what they wanted with her baby. She wasn't sure she wanted to think about that at all.

◆　◆　◆

"Tomorrow? Tomorrow's Saturday, honey! It's the first day I've had off in three weeks!" Tony wasn't exactly thrilled about a lunch discussion group on his day off. "Why so soon? His staff just called you today."

"You know Layton, honey. He does everything like this—an idea one minute, a project the next. Besides, I thought you might be honored to speak with him . . . and I told him we'd do it." Carol smiled sheepishly.

"Honored?" Tony smirked. "To talk to *him?*"

"To-o-ny . . ." Carol drew out his name, emphasizing each syllable.

"All I remember is that he seemed to have eyes for you . . . and every other female with two legs on campus."

"That was a long time ago. He's a successful attorney now—and the prosecuting attorney in Louisville. He's running for governor, for pete's sake! Besides, Tony, I hear he's engaged. I'm sure he's settled down. He was very sincere on the phone. He says he wants our opinions."

"I know. You explained all that," Tony sulked. He knew they were going to do it. He just wasn't planning on being too enthusiastic about it yet.

"Besides, Tony, it's at the Holiday Inn. They said they would be providing our lunch."

"Free lunch, huh?" Tony replied, patting his trim waist. He knew he was going to give in, but he wasn't sure Carol had "suffered" enough for giving up his day off. "I don't know—"

"Tony!" Carol nudged him in the ribs. "I should have asked you first. I'm sorry. I just assumed you'd want to participate."

"Oh, I'll go. I really didn't have big plans anyway. Maybe it will make a difference in some small way."

"Maybe it will make a difference at that," echoed Carol.

◆ ◆ ◆

It excited Linda Baldwin to see a package in her mailbox. She wasn't expecting anything. A *catalog perhaps?* Linda smiled as she looked to see what company it was from. There was no name—just a small heart and an address.

Linda skipped inside and retrieved a knife from the utensil drawer in the kitchen. She sat down at the table and carefully opened the brown package.

Inside she found a short letter.

> Dear Linda,
> Since you are unfortunate not to have a "Lucy" in your life, as I do in mine, I cannot "intrude" into your apartment without being accused of forced entry. So I will have to let you "intrude" for me. Please follow the instructions carefully.
> > Love,
> > Matt

Beside his name was a smiley face with one eye shut in a wink.

The package seemed to be filled with shredded newspaper. Linda reached through the packing and retrieved a Hostess Twinkie with a yellow note taped to the wrapper.

Dear Linda,
I couldn't send a whole dinner, but I could send over something for dessert. Please place this in your cupboard for future use.
Love,
Matt

P.S. I suppose you really ought to eat your vegetables before eating this.
P.P.S. Go ahead! Just one won't ruin a nutritionally balanced day.

Again, following the pattern that she had set, a smiley face punctuated Matt's signature. She reached into the paper again and found a small card. The envelope said, "Hang this on your coatrack." Inside Matt had printed:

Welcome home! May I take your coat? I hope that you had a nice day. I have been praying for you every day since our trip to the Shore. I can't seem to stop thinking about you and the way I feel about you. I meant what I said. I love you.
Matt

Linda held the small card for a few moments as if it were a piece of antique glass ready to crumble at any moment. Gently she laid it on the table. She didn't hang it on the coatrack. Instead, she excitedly returned to the package before her. She piled up the shredded packing paper beside the box, then withdrew another card. On the envelope it said, "Place me on the bathroom mirror." Again Linda was too excited to follow instructions. Inside, it said:

A mirror alone cannot reflect the beauty I have found in you.
Love,
Matt

Linda paused only briefly before continuing her search for any remaining notes. There were two. The first said, "Hang me on the radio in the kitchen." And inside,

> Tune in to what I want to say. Your name is music to my ears. I'm taking requests—I want to play your song.
> Matt

Matt had almost written, "Tune into WLOVE" but thought that sounded too corny.

Linda pulled out the last card, a red construction paper heart reminiscent of a child's valentine. On the front it said, "Place me on your pillow." On the other side Matt had written:

> When I dream, I dream of you. When I wake up, you're still on my mind. I hope we can see each other soon.
> I'm yours,
> Matt Stone

Linda slowly got up and gathered the notes together. She knew she would talk to Matt tonight by phone, and she knew he'd ask if she'd been a good "intruder" and followed his instructions. She obediently and cheerfully went from station to station, first to the cupboard and radio in the kitchen, then to the coatrack and the bathroom mirror. Finally she walked to the bedroom and gently placed the small heart on her pillow.

◆ ◆ ◆

"Hello."

She answered! Now just keep her on the phone!

"Hello, Sam—please don't hang up! We need to talk." Layton Redman spoke rapidly.

Silence followed.

"Sam?"

More silence.

"Yes, Layton, it's me."

"I've been trying to reach you. I—"

"I know we need to talk, Layton. It's just . . . Well . . . I haven't been ready . . . I guess you know I didn't go through with the abortion."

"Dr. Richards' office notified me. Honey, I thought we'd been through all this. It's not the right time for us. Why—"

Sam cut him off again. "I just couldn't do it, Layton. They did an ultrasound. I could see him move and everything."

"Him?"

"Our baby. The nurse told me it's a boy."

Redman winced. This wasn't going like he'd hoped. He decided to shift tactics. He needed to talk to her in person. "Look, Sam, I'm going to a meeting tomorrow in Easton. Can I come by and see you after that?"

I knew he would ask me that! Her apartment held too many intense feelings for her to see him there. It was here in her apartment that she'd given herself to him, thinking they would always be together. Sam responded, "It would be okay to see you, but not here. I just can't see you here, Layton."

"Well, how about Fairfax? I can meet you at the Springdale Mall. They have some nice restaurants there. We could talk, maybe eat some dinner. Do you know where that is?"

"Yes." She wasn't sure she was ready for this. She had always melted in his presence before. She added, "What time?"

"Is 6 o'clock alright?"

"That's fine with me. See you then. Bye, Layton."

She hung up before she heard him say, "Bye, love."

CHAPTER
19

TONY, Carol, and Layton were the last to leave. They stood under an awning at the Holiday Inn in Easton, Kentucky. The sun was shining, but the temperature had fallen to just above freezing. The early-morning precipitation had been a mixture of sleet and snow. Now, thanks to the shining sun, the snow had been chased away.

"I really want to thank you two for coming out and talking with me like this. I think I've at least got a fresh impression about what problems people are having with the system. Hopefully our team will be able to address each issue that you spoke about and come up with some workable options." Layton squinted up at the clearing skies. "Nice to see that the weather might cooperate for my trip home."

"Nice talking to you again, Layton," Tony replied. Much to his surprise, his statement truly represented his feelings. He wasn't just being polite like he had when the meeting began several hours before.

"Yes, it was very nice, Layton," Carol added. "Thanks for the dinner."

"No problem. You guys are really helping me, remember?" Layton paused and looked at his watch. He still had two hours before he needed to be in Fairfax to meet Sam. He continued, "Listen, I'm not sure what I could do after all you've been through, but if you ever need something I can help you with, don't hesitate to call."

"Nice of you to offer, but—"

"Do you do private adoption work?" Tony interrupted, quickly drawing a sharp look from Carol.

"No, I don't." Layton seemed taken back by the question. He looked at his watch again. Tony decided to let the subject drop.

Carol responded, thinking he must be in a hurry. "Do you have any more meetings today, Layton?"

Layton appeared distracted. "Huh? . . . Oh, no. No more meetings for me today. I just need to travel back to Louisville," he lied. "I hope the weather cooperates."

"I hope so too. I could stand to see a little sunshine," Carol added. "Thanks again." Carol extended her hand. Layton shook it gently and then turned to Tony.

Tony grasped Layton's outstretched hand and said, "Have a safe trip back. It's still a bit slick out there. I'm glad just to be staying in Easton today."

As they parted, Layton looked at the sky again. He got in his B.M.W. and started the engine. *I should have driven the Bronco today.*

◆ ◆ ◆

Sam looked around the apartment, wondering if she was forgetting something. She picked up the book on fetal development that she had checked out of the library. She wanted to show Layton what their son looked like at twenty-two weeks. *At least twenty-two and a half now, aren't you?* Sam patted her abdomen gently. She walked to the door, then turned and went into the bathroom. She picked up the supply of birth control pills. *If everything goes as planned, I won't be needing these. Maybe he can get his money back.*

Sam turned and checked the clock in the kitchen. She still had an hour before she was to meet Redman. She wanted to allow plenty of time for travel since the roads would become icy as the temperature dropped with the sun. She walked to the door and went out, the chill causing her to cough slightly as she crossed the parking lot to her car. She spent the first ten minutes scraping the ice from her windshield. As she did, a cloud of exhaust billowed from the back of the car, making the atmosphere almost eerie. The parking lot was empty and quiet except for the irregular throb of Sam's 1975

Volkswagen and the scraping noise of chipping the ice from her windows.

More than once a chill came over Sam. She knew it was cold, but she felt it was more than that, as if a dread were creeping coldly upon her. *Maybe it's just my anxiety over meeting with Layton.* Sam looked around anxiously. She wasn't used to this uncomfortable feeling. *Just a few more scrapes and I'm getting out of here!*

◆ ◆ ◆

Twenty miles to the north, Matt Stone, M.D. checked in with the "booth boys," the men who worked in the T.U. hospital flight dispatch office and directed the chopper's comings and goings. The chief resident who was on the trauma team was on vacation, and Matt was filling in for him. Matt talked to the men to see if they'd been notified of any flight requests to pick up trauma patients.

"Can you fly in this weather?" Matt asked. Often when the helicopter service was grounded by bad weather, the trauma residents had a lighter load.

"We're green all around." Steve Hampton smiled. "It may be slick for cars on the ground, but this cold air and these clearing skies are the best conditions for us."

"That's what I was afraid of." Matt laughed.

"Are you carrying the trauma alert pager tonight?"

"Absolutely."

"Where's Bicket?" Steve asked, referring to the current chief resident on trauma.

"Vacation. I think he went to see his parents in Florida." Matt turned to go.

"Sounds rough." Steve picked up the phone that had been blinking, then covered the mouthpiece and said, "I'll give you plenty of warning if I hear of anything coming your way."

"Thanks." Matt walked through the new E.R. trauma bays as he left. Everything was in place for a major emergency, if needed. *Maybe people will just stay home tonight and I can get some sleep.*

"Matt!" The voice was that of Charlie Edwards, the third-year resident on the trauma service who would be helping Matt out that night. "The team's gonna grab some dinner at our 'greasy spoon' right here in the hospital. You up for a burger?"

"Always. I can go without food, and I can go without sleep. But don't ask me to go without food *and* sleep." Matt clapped the younger resident on the shoulder, then asked, "Who's on the team tonight?"

"Sheila is the intern, I'm the third-year, and Clayton is on back-up from over at the V.A."

"Excellent. You guys busy?"

"Steady, but not overwhelming like in the summer."

Matt thought back to the late summer when he had been the trauma chief. "Don't remind me." They walked into the newly refinished snack shop just off the main lobby of the medical center. "Maybe tonight will be quiet."

"We'll know soon enough for me."

Matt approached the empty counter. "I'll have a grilled chicken sandwich on wheat." Matt smiled, thinking that even Linda might approve if she'd have seen his options.

◆ ◆ ◆

Redman drove his B.M.W. west on I-64 towards Fairfax. The interstate system was better than the secondary roads that evening, having been treated with a healthy layer of road salt as the temperature dropped earlier in the afternoon. The light dusting of snow they'd received that morning didn't seem to be affecting the main highways where Redman was traveling. As usual, he was talking on his car-phone as he went. This time it wasn't business.

"I want to show you the new dress I got for the party." The voice was Janice Sizemore's.

"Is it sexy?"

"Layton!" Janice reacted.

"Hey! I was just asking! You know the press will be there. I just don't want you attracting all the attention, that's all."

"I can't help it if they pay attention to me," Janice pouted. "It's very conservative . . . conservative for me, anyway. I think you'll like it."

"If it's wrapped around you, I know I'll like it."

"Layton!" This time she said his name more quietly. "Do you want me to fix something for dinner? Will you be by?"

"Afraid not, honey. I've got some law business to wrap up in Fairfax. I'll eat dinner there," Layton responded, hoping she wouldn't ask any more questions.

She didn't, so he continued, "I'll be back in Louisville by 10:30. Should I stop by then?"

"I'll wait up."

Layton was sure she would.

◆ ◆ ◆

Anne was also on the phone. She was talking to Linda Baldwin, who had answered the phone as if she were expecting Matt to call. Anne explained in as much detail as she could, without using Sam's name, all of her questions about the F.F.P. Clinic.

"Your boyfriend works as a surgeon at the university, doesn't he?" Anne asked.

"He's a surgery *resident* there," Linda corrected. "There's a difference."

"Do you think he'd know anything or be able to find out anything about what Simons is up to?"

"I don't really know. It sounds as though what you're onto here may be more to chew than we really want to get into with our little campus paper."

"I'm not just looking for a story here. Sa— . . . er, this girl's my friend, and I think she may have been deliberately misled by the doctors. I just have this gut feeling that someone else could be hurt in all this."

"We can't write stories on 'gut feelings,'" Linda reminded her.

"I know. That's one reason I want to talk to Dr. Stone. Maybe he could find out something else." She paused. "I don't know . . . Maybe it's all easily explainable and I'm not onto anything, but I'm just not at the point of giving it all up yet."

Linda furrowed her forehead. "Well, it can't hurt to ask. Matt's coming by for supper tomorrow. Why don't you call back tomorrow evening? Maybe the three of us can sit down and make a little more sense of this."

◆ ◆ ◆

Sam rubbed the windshield with her coat sleeve. She strained futilely to reach the far corner of the window and still stay within her shoulder harness. She unbuckled her seatbelt with an audible sigh of frustration. The window was fogging up faster than her defroster could handle. It was cold enough in the noisy car that she could see her breath. That seemed to be part of the problem. Her breath fogged the windshield almost as quickly as she could wipe it off. The sun had set now, and that hadn't helped Sam's ability to see, either. The lights from the oncoming cars temporarily blinded her as the light splayed out on the foggy windshield.

Sam touched the brakes as she approached a turn. The car slid across the yellow line before the tires grabbed enough traction to maneuver back into her lane. *Thank you, God, that no one was coming the other way!* Sam slowed down. An unmistakable feeling of dread surfaced again. Sam shivered and shook her head. *Get a grip, girl! I must just be upset about seeing Layton.* She could barely make out a sign on her right that announced, "Fairfax, 12 miles." She looked at her watch and sighed. *I'm going to be late. I hope Layton will understand.*

◆ ◆ ◆

Leroy Garrison had been driving eighteen-wheelers for seven years. He had a perfect driving record. During a trip to pick up a load of cars in Atlanta, he had stopped to see his sister just west of Fairfax, and then missed his proper interstate connection when he started out again. He had his map on the seat beside him. The weather was cool, the visibility was good, and the road conditions on the interstate system where he had been traveling up until now were excellent. He did not suspect that the secondary roads would be anything less.

◆ ◆ ◆

Sam was driving well under the speed limit but still too fast for the road conditions as they were. As she neared the city, the fear she'd suppressed bubbled to the surface again. Sam began to pray. "Lord, I'm not sure what I'm feeling. I do know I feel scared. Please help me stick to my guns. I know I need to talk to Layton. He has a way of getting to me! I know you want me to let my baby live." Sam paused. She felt an urgency to pray for her baby. "I don't know what to do about the baby, God. I'm just going to place him in your care."

Sam's car hit a patch of ice, startling Sam out of her prayer. Her car again skidded over the double yellow line.

◆ ◆ ◆

Leroy looked up from the map on the seat beside him just in time to see the orange V.W. cross the center line. A head-on impact was unavoidable. Leroy locked up his brakes, causing the tail of his rig to spin to the left. The V.W. slid beneath the body of his cargo shell, and the rear sets of wheels struck the front of the small car on the passenger side. A sickening crunch of metal followed. The eighteen-wheeler skidded to a stop, dragging the V.W. in a reverse direction a full 150 feet. For an instant the truck careened over the small car like a giant hand about to smash an unsuspecting bug. Then, as the vehicles came to a complete stop, the truck rocked back from its position and landed upright on its eighteen wheels.

Sam's injuries were significant but not immediately fatal. Her head and chest took the brunt of the impact. She was thrust forward into the steering column, which collapsed upon impact with her chest. Seven ribs were fractured on the left, driving one rib deeply into the substance of the lung it was designed to protect. As she decelerated suddenly, her heart and her descending aorta were flung forward, creating a small tear in the aortic wall. The aorta was not severed completely; the thin outer layer was still preserved, preventing immediate severe blood loss. The left side of her head was struck as her car passed beneath the truck carriage, severing off her left ear. She never realized any pain. She was unconscious in an instant.

In the cab of the truck Leroy shook violently, and the coffee dripped from the windshield and dashboard. He looked around the cab. Everything was dark. He had pain in his right wrist. He reached into his glove box and retrieved a flashlight. His hands trembled as he slowly undid his seatbelt, opened his door, and hopped to the ground. The smell of hot rubber permeated the cold air. He started towards the rear of the rig, which was hopelessly intertwined with the small, orange car. He stopped after two steps and returned for his emergency supply box behind the driver's seat. The box contained an orange triangle sign, road flares, and a few basic first aid items. He placed the box in the road beside the wreckage. The sound of footfalls approaching caused him to raise his head.

"Is anybody in there?" The voice belonged to Elliot Conley, who had been at his mailbox just three hundred feet away when he heard the crash. Elliot was over seventy years old, but he ran the distance to the vehicles in just a few seconds. He stared in horror at the twisted wreckage.

"I—I guess s-so." Leroy's voice shook as badly as his hands. He walked to the car and put his face against the unbroken driver's side window. Because of the darkness, all he could see was his reflection. He fumbled with the flashlight in his hand and shined it through the exposed window. Elliot positioned his face beside Leroy's. There, pinned against the steering column, they could see Sam's seemingly lifeless body. They stared at her for a few seconds without talking. Both were trying to decide whether she was alive or dead. Leroy centered the light beam on Sam's face. It was then that he noticed the first signs of life. She was breathing, gasping shallow breaths, with bloody bubbles coming from her nose and mouth.

"I saw her breathe!" Elliot hadn't even tried the door until he saw that she was still alive. But the twisted doorframe prevented his entry anyhow. "We've got to help her!"

Leroy didn't need to hear more. He moved swiftly back to the truck cab and grabbed his cellular phone. His hands still trembling, he dialed 911.

Sergeant Scaggs answered the phone. "State police, 911."

"There's been a terrible accident. A girl's been hurt bad—real bad."

The sergeant was used to dealing with frantic calls. He quickly and calmly spoke to Leroy in an assuring manner. "Sir, can you tell me your name and where you are calling from?"

Leroy answered a series of questions as accurately as he could. "We're on Route 68 just south of Fairfax, about ten miles . . . two vehicles . . . one truck and a small car . . . head-on . . . one victim . . . female . . . I think she's breathing . . . No response when we talk to her . . . I don't know; there's blood everywhere . . . Sitting, pinned behind the wheel."

As he gathered information, Kenton Scaggs pulled out a small map and circled their approximate location. The closest ground rescue units were in Grantsburg. He made a call to their fire and rescue units while he kept Leroy on the line. Both units were out on other minor, road-related trauma calls. The next choice was units from Fairfax. He knew the road conditions were not optimal on the secondary roads. From the accident location he determined that the closest level one trauma center would be the Taft University Medical Center.

"Is there a field or large parking lot around there anywhere?" the 911 dispatch officer asked.

Leroy looked around. He squinted at a brick building on his right. "Yes, a small baseball field . . . beside a brick schoolhouse."

"Let's see, that could be the Brown County Elementary School. Can you hold the line, sir?" He immediately put a call into the T.U. flight dispatch. Steve Hampton took the call. He carefully recorded the data given by Sergeant Scaggs, including the location of the school and ballfield. He put the 911 operator on hold and called David Gant, M.D., the trauma surgery attending on call. He would need to approve any trauma flight requests. Dr. Gant picked up the "bat phone" (the name they had affectionately given to the special trauma phone they carried at all times when on call) on the first ring.

"This is Gant." He knew it was dispatch. No one else used that phone.

"Scene flight request for an MVA. Youngish girl unresponsive, with head and chest trauma."

"How about a ground crew to take her to the nearest E.R. for stabilization? Can we pick her up there?"

"Grantsburg rescue squad is the closest, but they are tied up at the moment. The roads aren't that good, anyway."

"Okay. Do what you need to do. Give me more info when you have it."

Steve Hampton returned to talking with Kenton Scaggs. He asked that flares be placed at the four bases of the adjacent ballfield if possible. The sergeant relayed the information to Leroy, who yelled the message to Elliot Conley. Elliot found the flares in the truck's emergency supply box and followed the request, lighting up the baseball diamond with the four flares.

At the T.U. flight dispatch office, Steve finished gathering the brief patient description and buzzed the flight crew. The pilots were given only the location data. All flights were decided as "green" or "red" by an experienced pilot based on flying conditions only. Information about the reasons for a particular flight could interfere with the objectivity of the pilot's decision-making and was therefore excluded. The other known patient data was transferred to the paramedic flight staff.

Within eight minutes of the crash, the T.U. Sikorsky helicopter lifted off the roof of the medical center's critical care wing. In another five minutes the pilots carefully scanned Route 68 south of Fairfax for the crash site. It was senior pilot Captain Jay Randolf who spotted the flares first. They made several slow passes over the area looking for power lines before making their final descent onto the sandy baseball diamond. Dust flew high as the helicopter settled gently onto the ground. Two paramedics and two flight nurses exited the chopper, all carrying supplies. They left the stretcher behind and carried only a backboard. Rapidly they approached the crash scene.

There they found Elliot, Leroy, and now two others busy trying to open the door of the Volkswagen with a crowbar. Dan Stringer, a paramedic, snapped the corner of the driver's window with a small hand tool that had a spring mechanism designed to shatter the window pane. He then reached through the rear window that had been previously broken and folded the front driver's window out. Joel Newsome then reached in and assessed the patient's A.B.C.'s (airway, breathing, circulation). The airway was open but was compromised due to blood loss and decreased consciousness. Breathing was shallow and rapid without good breath sounds over the left chest. Circulation was poor. No radial pulse was palpable. The carotid pulse was present but weak. Joel backed away momentarily, while Dan used the "jaws of life" to remove the post between the front and rear windows. This allowed the door to be pulled free.

◆ ◆ ◆

Matt Stone was startled by the shrill sound of his pager. He had just laid down on a couch in the surgery resident's library. He was drifting off to sleep over a chapter on pancreatic endocrine tumors when his beeper sounded. He looked at the digital message. *Flight dispatch! Just when I thought it was turning out to be a quiet evening.* Reluctantly he got up and went to the phone.

"Flight dispatch here."

"Dr. Stone here. I was paged."

"Hey, Dr. Stone. Early warning here. The crew's on a scene flight. They are on the ground, so I should have an update soon. Sounds like one patient—a young woman with head and chest trauma, involved in an accident with a truck. I just thought you'd like to be aware. They should be off the ground in fifteen minutes, depending on extraction time. It is a short flight—only nine minutes."

"Keep me posted. Thanks."

◆ ◆ ◆

A flight nurse slipped an oxygen mask over Sam's mouth and nose. Paramedic Newsome cut away the coat from Sam's left arm and started a sixteen gauge IV line in a vein near the elbow. He gently placed a cervical collar to preserve the stability of the vertebra. The seat-back was folded out of the way, and Sam was lifted simultaneously by the shoulders, back, hips, and legs by the full flight medical team and gently placed on the backboard.

"Hey, she's pregnant!" Dan was the first to notice as the swelling of her lower abdomen had been shielded by the steering wheel until she was lifted free.

They taped Sam's head to the backboard as an extra precaution to keep her cervical spine immobilized.

While the rest of the team tended to the patient, Susan Crauley talked to Leroy Garrison and obtained all the information he knew about the accident. A few minutes after extricating the patient from the car, Susan assisted by grabbing a corner of the backboard.

"Let's go," Joel instructed as they lifted the backboard together. He was carrying a portable oxygen tank in addition to taking a corner of the board. Steadily they progressed off the road and over the tall grass on the way to the helicopter parked in the middle of the ball diamond. The flares were burning low. Sam was hoisted into the chopper and placed on a stretcher, the backboard still beneath her.

Once they were in the chopper, the paramedics placed warm blankets over Sam's body and assessed her vital signs. The flight crew put on their head communication gear and strapped themselves in for lift-off. Once in the air again, a complete assessment was made and radioed in to the flight dispatch office.

"Flight dispatch, this is T.U. C.A.T.S 1. Do you read me?"

"Roger, C.A.T.S. 1. This is flight dispatch. Do you have an update?"

"Roger, dispatch. We're en route with a young woman approximately twenty years of age who was involved in a head-on motor vehicle accident. She was the unrestrained driver. Vital signs reveal heart rate one hundred twenty two, sinus tachcardia, blood pressure by doppler seventy, respirations thirty and shallow. There are no breath sounds on the left with suspected pneumothorax. Abdomen is protuberant. She is obviously pregnant, fairly far along. Fetal heart tones present by doppler. Extremities remarkable for multiple abrasions but no obvious fractures."

"What is your E.T.A.?"

"Eight minutes."

"Will this be a trauma alert?"

"Absolutely."

"Ten-four."

Steve Hampton called the paging operator, who issued the

trauma alert. The message went out simultaneously on special trauma alert pagers issued to each member of the trauma team, as well as to respiratory therapy and the blood bank, who automatically took O-negative blood to the E.R. in a cooler. Within a few minutes the entire team was in trauma one, a bay equipped with a stretcher, oxygen and suction hook-ups, an overhead X-ray unit, and four trauma carts stocked with supplies. Matt walked over to the dispatch office from trauma one. As the chief resident, he would supervise and coordinate the trauma resuscitation efforts.

Matt pushed open the door to the room in the center of the E.R. where Steve Hampton filled out the flight data record sheets. "Any update?"

"Plenty. Pregnant female, young twenties, head-on collision, hypotensive—"

"How hypotensive?"

"Last B.P. was seventy. They had one IV and were in the process of starting another. They think she has a pneumothorax on the left, as she has some palpable rib fractures but no breath sounds."

"Have they put in a chest tube?"

"No. They haven't been cleared to do that."

"Tell them to put a needle in the left chest to temporize. We can put a chest tube in once she's in the E.R."

While Steve relayed that message to the flight crew, Matt picked up the phone and dialed the paging operator.

"Yes, operator, may I have the beeper number of the senior resident on O.B. call tonight?"

"That's Dr. Williams, beeper 423."

Matt thanked the operator, hung up, then quickly picked up again, and paged the O.B. resident. In two minutes the phone rang.

"Hello."

"Hello. I'm answering a page for Dr. Williams." It was a nurse in labor and delivery. "May I take a message? He is doing a c-section at the moment."

"How far along is he?"

"Just started."

"Tell him Matt Stone from trauma called. We have a pregnant

female coming in from a serious MVA. Have him come to the E.R. as soon as he's free."

"I'll tell him, Dr. Stone."

Matt set the phone down and talked to Steve Hampton again. "What's the E.T.A.?"

"Two minutes to the roof. About seven minutes to the E.R."

"Thanks." Matt headed back to trauma one, where he donned a gown and gloves.

Matt laid out the game plan, giving everyone present an assignment. He first looked at the intern. "Sheila, I want you to open a chest tube tray and make your first priority putting in a left chest tube. The patient has a suspected pneumothorax on the left. As you know, that can cause low blood pressure by pushing against the heart. The flight crew put a needle in the chest to relieve the pressure temporarily." Matt then looked at Charlie Edwards. "I want you to manage the airway. She's been unresponsive, so even if she's breathing we need to protect the airway. I would choose to entubate her nasotracheally unless she has significant facial trauma." Matt then looked at the rest of the team. "She's pregnant—pretty far along, I guess. Have we got a fetal doppler around?"

"I'll get it." The response was from Linda Deaver, who returned carrying a portable doppler in just a few seconds.

"Do we have X-ray here ready for a chest film?" Matt questioned.

"Right here, Dr. Stone," called a short redheaded woman standing in the back of the trauma bay. "Just yell when you need me."

In another minute the helicopter landed on the roof. In another five, the crew was pushing a stretcher through the E.R. doors. Matt met the flight team at the door. "What have you got, guys?"

The patient was wheeled up beside the stretcher in trauma one. As they simultaneously moved the patient onto the table, the flight crew gave the update, and Matt took a quick listen to the chest with his stethoscope for breath sounds.

"Last B.P. ninety over doppler. It improved somewhat when a needle was placed in the left chest." The patient had been totally exposed by the flight crew, who had cut off her clothes and placed warm blankets against her body. Sheila exposed the chest by throwing off the blankets to the level of the lower abdomen. As the update by the crew continued, she painted the chest with a brown betadine solution. A nurse listened and confirmed fetal heart tones with a rate of one hundred sixty. The flight crew added, "We gave a total of two liters of fluid en route. The maternal heart rate came down to one hundred ten after the fluid."

Charlie Edwards quickly passed a plastic tube through the mouth into the trachea, while a nurse held the head with in-line traction to prevent Edwards from moving the patient's neck, which was assumed broken until proven otherwise. After securing the airway, he took a flashlight and shined it into the patient's eyes. "The pupils are fixed and dilated, Matt." Charlie then helped set up the ventilator, which would give mechanical breaths of pure oxygen to the patient through the tube he'd just inserted.

Sheila made a small incision in the left chest and deepened it into the pleural cavity. She then passed a thirty-eight french chest tube into the thorax and secured it with a large Prolene stitch tied to the skin. Two hundred cc's of blood were immediately drained through the tube.

While Charlie and Sheila did their procedures, the nurses secured a third IV and drew blood for multiple blood tests.

"Page Dr. Williams from O.B. and let him know the patient I gave him word about is here," Matt requested of a second nurse. Matt then listened to the chest with the stethoscope again. "The breath sounds are better. How's the blood pressure?"

"Ninety systolic by the doppler," answered a medical student.

"Let's get a chest X-ray now that the chest tube is in. Get some c-spine films after that. Don't forget to shield the baby."

The X-ray tech placed a lead shield over the patient's lower abdomen and yelled, "X-ray!" sending the team scurrying away for a brief moment so they would not be hit by the invisible rays.

Matt then completed a secondary survey of the patient, noting in detail the injuries from head to toe. "The left ear is gone. The pupils are fixed and dilated. Left scalp hematoma . . . left rib fractures and pneumothorax . . . no apparent pelvic injury, rectal heme negative . . . femoral pulses present . . . pedal pulses absent . . . neuro exam shows no response even to painful stimuli . . . What's her temp?"

"Thirty-five degrees," answered one of the nurses. "We measured tympanic membrane temperature."

"Let's make sure all the fluid we are giving is warm. Let's give her two units of O-negative blood through the level one fluid warmer!" Matt was standing at the foot of the bed where he completed his exam.

"Look at this!" Charlie motioned for Matt to look at the patient's chest X-ray, which he had just carried over from the processor.

"Oooh," Matt sighed. "Sheila, you ought to see this." Sheila stepped over. "The mediastinum is too wide. It indicates possible aortic disruption. We need a STAT aortogram to prove it. After that, if she is stable we need a head C.T. scan. If she gets unstable, we just go to the O.R. and do a thoracotomy and let neurosurgery do burr holes in hopes of finding something reversible." Matt delegated out the duties. "Sheila, call the radiology resident on call. Tell them we need an aortogram yesterday! Charlie, call neurosurgery. Get them to see the patient before she goes to the angio suite if possible. I'll call the cardiothoracic surgery fellow on call and let them know we have a patient with a possible thoracic aortic rupture." Matt looked around. "Any word from O.B.?"

"The O.B. residents are all busy in labor and delivery. I just called five minutes ago," replied a sandy-haired male nurse.

Matt paged the cardiothoracic surgery fellow and explained the situation. They needed to be aware of the problem in case the thoracic aorta was shown to be lacerated by the angiogram. The fellow, Jack Wheater, in turn informed his attending, Dr. Michael Simons, telling him only the patient's name and that an aortogram was being done for suspected aortic rupture. Simons acted disinterested and only asked to be called with the results of the angiogram.

◆ ◆ ◆

Michael Simons, M.D. put the phone back in its cradle. *Samantha Stelling! Is that what he said?* Simons walked quickly to his computer and entered his access code on the keyboard. From the start-up screen he opened the data spread sheet listing the names of all the women from Richards' clinic who had made a "donation" to his research. There in the middle of the list was an incomplete entry. At the far left he identified the name he was looking for. He moved the cursor to the box holding Sam's name and clicked "delete." *I don't suppose I'll be needing to save a place for this data anymore.* Simons then executed the moves to exit the program, turned off his Macintosh, and poured himself a drink.

◆ ◆ ◆

Matt walked back to the patient's bedside and was joined soon by Charlie Edwards. "I called neurosurgery," Edwards said. "They are busy, as usual, but will be down soon."

"Thanks, Charlie."

Matt looked on as the blood pressure was taken again by a nurse. The nurse pumped the cuff up and down several times to be sure she was getting an accurate reading.

"The pressure's down," stated the nurse mechanically. "I hear the systolic at sixty."

"Let's open up the fluids all the way." Matt walked over and lifted a unit of packed red cells off of the IV pole above the patient. He sped the flow of blood down the IV line by squeezing the little bag. "Here. Squeeze this in as quickly as you can," Matt said to a medical student standing next to him. The tension in his voice was noticeable. A third, fourth, and fifth unit of packed cells were connected to the three IVs, and pressure bags were inflated around them to push the blood in more rapidly.

The left chest tube, which had drained very little since the initial two hundred cc's, suddenly dumped an additional liter of blood into the collecting system. Matt put his hand on the femoral pulse. "I've got no pulse here. Check the carotids, Charlie."

The senior resident quickly removed the front part of the cervical collar and felt for a pulse just lateral to the patient's trachea. "No pulse!"

"Get the thoracotomy tray open STAT!" Matt sprayed betadine over the chest. "Take a knife, Charlie. We're not going to make it to the O.R. with this one!" A nurse rapidly opened up the thoracotomy tray. Charlie opened the left chest through the fifth and sixth ribs, spilling a large quantity of blood onto the stretcher and floor.

Matt helped Charlie spread the ribs with a chest retractor that forced the ribs apart to expose the underlying heart and lung. A large collection of blood or hematoma surrounded the heart and aorta. Matt took a vascular clamp and occluded the aorta at the arch, above most of the hematoma. "Give her open cardiac massage," Matt instructed the younger resident.

"Her heart is flat! There's no blood left to pump," Charlie yelled as he compressed the heart but got little response.

A nurse inspected the patient's eyes again. "Her pupils remain fixed and dilated, Dr. Stone."

"Let me have the doppler!" Matt nearly tore the small machine from the hands of the medical student. He placed it on the lower abdomen. "Let's have it quiet!" He listened carefully for only a brief moment. "Get me a knife! And get me the infant resuscitation team here STAT! Maybe we can get one live patient out of this! I can still hear a bradycardic fetal heart!"

Matt took the knife and guided it over the lower abdomen in the midline, omitting any kind of sterile prep solution. The parted skin edge did not appear to bleed. He entered the abdomen and made a small incision in the uterus. Overhead the loudspeaker was repeating, "Infant resuscitation team to the emergency room STAT! Infant resuscitation team to the emergency room STAT!" Matt then opened the inside of the uterus, placed both index fingers in, and forced them apart to separate the uterine muscle. He reached his right hand in and pulled the infant's head out of the uterus and onto the abdomen of his mother. Matt carefully suctioned the nose and mouth of the infant and slipped the rest of the baby out into the air above his mother. He then clamped the umbilical cord and handed the limp male infant to a breathless Dr. Ellen Fischer, a neonatologist who had responded to the emergency call.

Matt looked again at the adult patient. Open cardiac massage had been going on for ten minutes. A total of eight units of blood and five liters of crystalloid solution had been given without response. As the patient obviously had suffered a severe brain injury and had been unresponsive to even painful stimuli since her first contact with the paramedics, Matt decided to suspend their resuscitation attempts. "Let's call it."

"I agree. There's nothing we can do," Charlie added. He removed his hands from her chest and pulled off his bloody gloves.

Samantha Stelling was pronounced dead at ten minutes after 7 o'clock on a wintry Saturday in Kentucky.

◆ ◆ ◆

Layton Redman looked at his watch. Sam was late, and Layton was definitely getting irritated. *She failed to follow through with the abortion and refused to answer her phone, and now she's standing me up, refusing to meet me to talk this thing through!* Redman walked around the mall to be sure he had not missed her somewhere. Finally he went into Ruby Tuesday's to have a drink. He ordered a bourbon and water and sat at the bar to stew.

◆ ◆ ◆

The infant resuscitation was ongoing. Dr. Fischer inserted a small endotracheal tube into the baby's windpipe and inflated the lungs gently with oxygen. A second pediatric resident began CPR. A needle was pushed through the bony cortex of the right tibia and hooked to an IV line. A small amount of atropine was given into the bone marrow cavity to speed the heart rate. As the drug kicked in and the baby became better oxygenated, the small heart responded and CPR was discontinued.

The infant was placed in an incubator under warmer lights and taken to the N.I.C.U. (Neonatal Intensive Care Unit) on the fourth floor. The small male infant had again entered a fight for his life. But this time there were others fighting for him too.

◆ ◆ ◆

After an additional forty-five minutes and two drinks, Redman left the restaurant to again stroll through the mall looking for Sam. He finally returned to his car to use the phone. He dialed Sam's number and let it ring twelve times. *Not this game again! Answer the phone, Sam! We have to talk. We definitely have a problem here. How am I going to convince you to put this situation behind us if you won't talk to me?* Layton did not like the lack of control he felt over the situation. *How can I convince you that this baby isn't right for us if you won't see me? How can I keep the public from hearing about this if you have this baby?*

Layton started his car and headed back for Louisville. He fumed for a good forty-five miles before he came up with another plan. If he could get to Janice's place before it was too late, the night wouldn't be a total loss.

CHAPTER
20

SIMONS spoke quietly on the phone with Jack Wheater, his cardiothoracic surgery fellow. Once he had realized that it was Sam Stelling who was critically injured, he knew that this must have been the answer he sensed just a few nights ago. He had been assured that a threat to his work would pass. He just hadn't known the details.

"I'm just calling to give you follow-up on the patient with a wide mediastinum that I called you about," said Jack.

"And?" Simons anticipated the answer. *I know what you're going to say, Jack. I knew this would happen.*

"She coded suddenly before they took her to the angio suite for her aortogram. The general surgeons did a thoracotomy, but she had essentially bled out before their eyes. There was nothing they could do."

"I'm sorry to hear that, Jack," lied Simons. "Such a shame . . . so young . . . and pregnant at that." He hadn't realized that Jack hadn't told him she was pregnant. Jack did not pick up on Simons' slip.

"Yeah, really," echoed Jack. "But you know what? The chief resident did a c-section right there in the E.R. He had evidently called for an O.B. resident, but they were tied up. He had an essentially dead, pregnant patient with a baby who still had heart tones by the doppler. He just slashed her abdomen and took the baby right there! I missed all the excitement by just a few seconds. There was blood everywhere."

"And the baby . . . d-did it die?" Simons showed a slight bit of consternation at this last bit of information.

"No. They resuscitated it and put it up in the N.I.C.U."

"Interesting."

Simons' lack of enthusiasm bothered Jack. He thought he'd have been more excited about such a rare save.

"Anyway, I just thought I'd get back with you, so you didn't wonder what happened all night."

"Oh, there was little chance of that," Simons added with an air of authority. "Thanks, Jack."

"Bye, Dr. Simons."

Simons hung up without an exit word as usual. He sat down at his kitchen table and continued eating the bowl of cereal he'd started before Jack called. Simons liked eating cereal at night. His focus, however, extended far beyond the box of oat bran in front of him.

Interesting twist, with this baby surviving . . . Not that the orphan will live for long . . . His lungs won't be as strong as his little heart is . . . He'll probably live just long enough to be a burden to the taxpayers . . . Too bad I couldn't have used the heart last week . . . At least then the child wouldn't have been wasted . . . Oh well, now the mother's out of the way, and there is no way she can raise any more questions about what I was doing at the F.F.P. Clinic.

Simons finished his cereal and put his bowl in the kitchen sink. He then headed for his bedroom to retire. For now the bothersome paranoia had been quieted, and he could sleep the night without waking.

◆ ◆ ◆

Matt surveyed the scene in trauma one. The patient was lying totally naked and exposed on the stretcher, with thoracotomy and laparotomy wounds gaping. He covered the patient with a sheet and gently closed her eyelids. He did not remove any of the IVs or the endotracheal tube or repair the large wounds created for the open heart massage or the c-section. The county coroner would be involved with an examination of the body to determine the cause of death, and nothing was to be altered except for cleaning the patient up so the body would be somewhat presentable for viewing in case family members arrived. Matt had walked over to the patient's chart to copy down some identifying data for his records when Dr. David Gant walked in.

"Hi, Matt."

"Hey, Dr. Gant," Matt replied. "I'm sorry I didn't get to call you about this one. I knew the dispatch had given you an update. Once she arrived, things just happened so fast . . . By the time we got a chest X-ray and scheduled an aortogram, she became hypotensive again. We had put in a chest tube on arrival because of a pneumothorax, and then all of a sudden she just bled out through the chest tube. I helped Charlie do the thoracotomy."

Gant walked over and pulled the sheet off the patient, exposing the c-section incision. "Tell me about this . . ." Gant's tone of voice was unreadable. It showed neither approval nor disappointment.

"The mother was essentially dead on arrival. She'd been unresponsive to all stimuli ever since the crew picked her up at the scene. When her aorta blew, her blood volume flowed out of the chest tube like nobody's business!" Matt shook his head in disbelief. "We couldn't put it in fast enough. I cross-clamped the aorta above the injury, but by that time the heart was flat and unresponsive. We had given eight units of blood, at least four of which were given after I cross-clamped the aorta. So, with the mom dead, I listened for fetal heart tones. I knew that with the aorta cross-clamped, the baby wasn't getting oxygen either. I heard fetal heart tones, so I just did the section on the spot. I called several times for an O.B. resident, but they were tied up . . . so I just did it myself."

"That's pretty unconventional, Matt."

"It was a pretty unconventional situation, Dr. Gant." Matt paused, studying the face of the trauma attending. "Listen, I don't regret it one bit. The baby lived . . . Well, he is alive so far at least."

"Matt, don't misinterpret me. I think you did the right thing. I just wish I could have gotten here a few minutes earlier."

"Believe me, you'd have been welcome."

Charlie Edwards walked up. He had just gotten off the phone with the dean of students at Appalachian Christian University. He had found a student I.D. in the patient's belongings and had called to see if he could locate the next of kin. "Looks like she had no family, Matt. She's single. There's no way of telling who the father is. As far as the university knows, there are no relatives at all. She was an only child."

Matt looked down at the collection of papers that would be assembled into the patient's chart. He copied her name and medical record number down so he would have it for his operative log. "Samantha Stelling." He smiled. "Dr. Gant, can I list you as my attending for the c-section? You were officially the attending on the case, you know."

"Sure, Matt." Gant smiled too. "Just don't tell the administration. I don't have privileges to do obstetrics in this hospital." Gant turned and started for the door. "Let me know if you two stir up any more trouble."

"Sure, boss," Matt called after him. "I'll let you know."

◆ ◆ ◆

Anne Caudill was having a good day. She had finished writing an English paper for her literature class and spent the afternoon doing layouts for the next edition of *The Weathervane*. She went back to her dorm room and made some hot chocolate, the perfect thing, she thought, for a winter night like they were having—clear and cold. As she sipped her hot drink, her thoughts turned to the mystery surrounding the events of Sam's near-abortion. She hoped that she'd get a chance to find out some more information the following day when she planned on talking with Linda and her friend, Matt Stone. As her mind drifted in and around what she knew and didn't know about Michael Simons and Adam Richards, she remembered that Sam had traveled to Fairfax to meet Layton that night. She and Sam had prayed that things would go according to God's plan.

Anne looked at her watch. 11:00 P.M. *I wonder how things went with Sam. I thought she'd have called me by now.* Anne picked up the phone and dialed Sam's apartment. Eight rings and no answer. She returned the receiver to the cradle. *I hope Sam didn't get caught in his web again. She always got a little starry-eyed when she talked about him.*

Anne shook her head, dispelling the thought. *Sam has her head on straight. She won't let him influence her decision to do the right thing this time.* Just as Anne picked back up her drink, the phone rang. *Sam! It's about time you called!*

"Hellooo." Anne drew the introduction out in a singsong fashion, expecting it to be Sam.

"Hello. Anne?"

Anne was immediately sober, realizing it wasn't Sam after all. "Yes."

"This is Dean Richardson," the man's voice said with a slight tremble.

Anne thought it unusual to get a call from the dean, especially at that hour. She immediately suspected bad news. *My parents?* Her voice cracked as she replied, "What is it, Mr. Richardson?"

"I'm afraid I have some bad news, Anne. Your friend Samantha Stelling was killed in an automobile accident earlier this evening."

"No!" Anne held her hand to her mouth.

The dean paused, listening to pure silence, then continued. "Anne?"

"Yes."

"You knew she was pregnant?"

"Yes." Anne couldn't speak much more than a word.

"Somehow they saved the baby. They knew Sam was dying, so they removed the baby." Mr. Richardson paused again, not really knowing what to say. He finally added, "I thought you'd want to know."

"Thank you," Anne said, her expression blank. Her hand fell to her side, and she hung up the phone, not even thinking to say goodbye.

◆ ◆ ◆

Richards had been asleep for two hours by the time his phone rang. The combination of a restless evening the night before and a heavy meal complete with a six-pack of his favorite Mexican beer had sealed his date with sleep at only 10 o'clock, an early hour for Adam Richards. When he awoke, he thought it must be morning.

But as he looked at his clock and rubbed his eyes, he realized it wasn't his alarm clock nudging him to an alert state. It was the phone. @#$%@! *Who could be calling at this hour?* He reached for the phone, knocking over a small bedside lamp in the process.

"Hello."

"Adam, this is Michael."

"Huh? Oh . . . Michael Simons. What do you need, Michael?" Richards' voice cracked with irritated fatigue.

"I don't need anything, Adam. I just thought you'd want to hear some news. Some good news—depending on your perspective, I suppose."

"What is it, Michael?" Richards wasn't in the mood for little mind games. *Get to the point, Simons!*

"Sam Stelling won't be asking any more questions about our little project, Adam."

"And why is that?" Richards closed his eyes and laid his head on the pillow again.

"She's dead."

Richards sat up in bed suddenly. "She's dead?"

"Assumed room temperature just over an hour ago," replied Simons smugly.

Richards was rubbing his neck and shaking his head. He wasn't sure he was really awake, particularly after the dreams he'd been having. "You killed her?" Adam asked in a raspy voice.

"Don't be a fool!" Simons snapped. "She died in a car accident! Her death was an *accident!*"

"Oh," sighed Richards. He had been a bit frightened when he recalled Simons' promise to see that "she doesn't talk again" if Sam started asking questions. Now it embarrassed him that he'd accused Simons so quickly. Richards offered a weak apology. "I'm sorry, Michael, I didn't mean it like it sounded. I . . . well, I must have been partly asleep."

"Of course."

"Thank you for telling me." Richards sat on the side of the bed.

"There's more."

"Go on."

"They saved the baby. Snatched it from the womb just as the mother died. It's on a ventilator, but it's alive."

"@##$@%!" Adam cursed more out of wonder than of anger. It was his way of saying, "Well, what do you know!"

"It will probably die, Adam. It's under a thousand grams. I just called the N.I.C.U. for an update."

"I can hardly believe it." Richards actually felt awake now. He wasn't sure what to think about this new piece of information. "Thanks for the call, Michael."

"Remember, we have another pump run the day after tomorrow. Call me when you're ready to fly. I'll have Gentry come over and set up beforehand so everything will be ready."

Richards shook his head. He couldn't believe how quickly this man could shift gears and start talking business again, like nothing had happened. "Oh, sure—I'll give you a call."

"Good night, Adam," Simons offered in place of his normal speechless hang-up-the-phone ending.

Click. It was Richards who just hung up the phone this time. He tried to process what he'd been told. *The baby had lived? And it was still young enough to be a legal abortion?* He noticed his hands trembling a bit as he picked up the lamp off the floor. He then headed for the wet bar in his den. Some smooth brandy would hopefully help him sort out his thoughts.

◆ ◆ ◆

Carol tossed restlessly on the bed and sighed. Tony reached over and gently touched her shoulder.

"Can't sleep?"

"I close my eyes, but my mind is just so full. My body is tired, but my mind isn't slowing down much," Carol whispered as she snuggled closer to her husband.

"Is the dream still bothering you?"

"No, not really. I know it was just a stupid dream. It's just . . . well, what if it does take a long, long time, Tony?" Carol paused. "I want a baby *now*." She spoke gently, with a quaver in her voice.

"I know, baby . . . I know." Tony knew he needed only to listen, not to offer an easy answer where none existed.

They spent the next few minutes "dreaming" together of how they thought it would be once they added children to their family—where they would go, what they would do, how they would play, even how they might pose for a family Christmas card portrait like all of their friends did. The dreaming helped. It seemed to fuel their hopeful expectation that someday their dream would be reality.

Tony finally brought them back to the present. He spoke quietly. "Remember 'The Plan'?"

"Which number are you referring to?" Carol prodded her husband playfully in the ribs.

"I'm serious, Carol. I think we need to take your suggestions seriously. You remember—'Pray daily for God's direction,'" recited Tony faithfully. "I know He'd rather we prayed and trusted than to lose sleep over this whole ordeal."

And that's just what they did.

◆ ◆ ◆

Layton Redman made it to his home just after midnight. He'd excused himself at Janice's earlier than they both had anticipated. He just couldn't keep his mind off his problems with Sam. Janice had been put off by his lack of cheerfulness. She had been in a playful mood, but she quickly iced over after experiencing his distant demeanor. She thought he must be preoccupied with the campaign. "Just forget about the campaign for once," she had coaxed, but to no avail. Layton would follow along with her line of conversation for a few minutes, only to slip off into his own world again the next. His fiancée had finally gone off to her bedroom in a huff. Layton had weakly apologized through the locked bedroom door, then excused himself and left. It wasn't exactly what he'd planned for the evening.

Now he stood on his back terrace in the sub-freezing temperature. Sometimes he would come here to think. Tonight he couldn't make any sense of the situation, and the solitude of the terrace didn't help. The cold wasn't doing him any good either. Redman smashed his fist into his hand. *No matter how good I've been at controlling Sam in the past, I feel like I'm losing my influence over her!* He needed a new way to get through to her, but he could come up with no new ideas. Redman sighed. *I'll just have to call her again in the morning. Maybe she'll loosen up and talk to me then. This game can't go on forever. She'll come to her senses if she really thinks she's losing me! I'll try that tactic tomorrow. Then she'll come around. I'll call her in the morning.* She certainly wasn't answering her phone tonight. He'd already tried that a few times in the car on his way home from Janice's.

◆ ◆ ◆

To the uninitiated onlooker, surgical residents appear to be a peculiar brood, thriving on the thrill of a save and yet strangely emotionally untouched by the tragedy of early death. Their senses dulled to the ache that normally accompanies grotesque trauma, it is not uncommon to see a surgery resident leave a room where he or she has just had to pronounce a patient dead and open a pack of crackers for a snack. And so it was, early on that winter morning, that the trauma team, having witnessed far more death than many will in a decade, gathered in the snack shop for some late refreshments.

The team had admitted two more blunt trauma patients since the death of Sam Stelling. These two had lived. One had a cardiac contusion and needed cardiac monitoring for dysrhythmias. The other had a fractured pelvis and a ruptured urinary bladder. The bladder rupture was small and did not cause a leak into the abdomen, and so was merely managed by insertion of a tube into the bladder to keep it from being distended. It was time now for the team to regroup to be sure all the bases had been covered before 5:30 rounds, only two hours away. The team sat around a table eating frozen yogurt.

"Let's see . . . Where do we stand on Mr. Raymonds' workup?" Matt asked the intern.

"I think everything's back. I just need to chase down the results of his latest hemotocrit and his thoracic spine films. Then I'll be done. His orders are all written."

"Where's he going?" Matt wrote the patient's name and his diagnosis down on a new census sheet.

"Room 509."

"Great. How about the last one?" Matt looked at Charlie, who was finishing his paperwork. "Spell that last name for me."

"S-h-i-z-i-n-s-k-i." Charlie paused as he completed the sentence he was writing. "The workup's done. I only need to get approval from cardiology to use their telemetry bed."

"Another great." Matt looked around at the team. They all looked tired. "Thanks a lot for all the help, especially on that first one."

"Man, I didn't know what to think when I saw you listening to that baby and then ask for a knife. I thought you'd completely flipped out on us." Charlie laughed.

"I know I've never seen anything like that before," Sheila added.

"I don't think any of us had," replied Matt. "It's not that common a situation. I haven't done a c-section since I was in Africa." Matt thought the whole thing seemed like a dream at this point. "Say, has anyone heard how the kid's doing?"

Sheila spoke up. "I stopped by the N.I.C.U. on my way down here. He's hanging in there. It looks like he'll be on the vent for a while."

"At least he's alive," Matt added soberly.

"Yeah, at least he's alive," the team echoed.

They quickly dispersed to their call rooms for some sleep, each one thinking about their extraordinarily ordinary trauma call night, and each one hoping for a few quiet hours of sleep before dawn.

CHAPTER
21

Rounds in the N.I.C.U. always attracted a large crowd. The pediatric team, made up of four medical students, three interns, two residents, and a neonatal fellow, followed all of the patients in the forty-five incubator unit. They had just finished morning report and were heading towards the unit. They stepped through the first set of double doors and scrubbed their hands with a bacteriocidal soap solution. They then donned gowns to cover their scrub clothing and walked through the second set of doors. The automatic doors opened whenever someone approached them, allowing easy entry for personnel transporting incubators or other necessary equipment.

Ellen Fischer, M.D., the neonatal fellow, led rounds. They began with a new patient, Baby Boy Stelling, who had been admitted the night before. Dr. Brad Stevens, the intern who had been on call, presented the patient as the remainder of the team listened and made notes.

"This neonate is a twenty-three-week-old male born by emergency c-section last night as the mother expired from blunt chest and head trauma sustained in a motor vehicle accident. He was initially unresponsive but revived with minimal CPR and mechanical ventilation, along with atropine administration. He was transported to the N.I.C.U. where umbilical vein and umbilical artery catheters were placed. He has been sustained on a 10 percent dextrose and electrolyte IV solution, mechanical ventilation, and supplemental oxygen."

The rounds, designed to be instructive for the medical students, were often "Socratic" in format, with the fellow and residents repeatedly questioning the students and interns for information. Dr. Fischer began. "What are the most common problems that we need to look for when dealing with premature infants of very low birth weight?" She looked around. The medical students looked at the floor. Dr. Fischer picked the one standing to her left. "Tom?"

"Uhh, respiratory problems."

"Can you be more specific?"

"Hyaline membrane disease," he stated mechanically.

"What is the underlying pathophysiology?" Ellen Fischer paused. "Jenny?"

"The premature lungs cannot make surfactant, a molecule that lowers the surface tension of the alveoli and prevents their collapse during expiration."

"What happens when there is a lack of surfactant?"

Jenny continued, "The patient has difficulty getting adequate oxygen because of collapsing of the lung."

"Okay. Fair enough. How do we treat it?" She looked at Anthony Gates, the third medical student.

"Supportive care with supplemental oxygen and mechanical ventilation," he stated.

"Any other modes of treatment?"

Anthony was silent. Jenny volunteered, "Surfactant replacement." Anthony rolled his eyes.

The questioning went on for five additional minutes before they settled down to studying the actual data gathered each hour on Baby Boy Stelling. The small infant had a poor prognosis because of his weight and prematurity. He would be started on nutritional supplementation through the IVs for now, until his intestines matured enough to start him on tube feedings. His oxygen would be weaned, and following that, his mechanical ventilation would be slowly withdrawn, if possible. He would be enrolled in a study to see if he showed any improvement by a series of surfactant administrations to assist his lung function. He would be carefully monitored for low blood glucose and calcium and elevation of his bilirubin, which were other common maladies of the premature. After the initiation of feedings he would be observed for necrotizing enterocolitis, a condition where the intestines die. He would be watched carefully for intra-cerebral bleeding, which was also common in this age group.

Once all the team members understood the game plan, Dr. Fischer made final adjustments in the patient's fluid and nutrition orders, and the team went to the next incubator to repeat the process.

◆ ◆ ◆

Isabelle Covey was a practical woman, even if she seemed a bit uncaring. She managed a small apartment complex and rented mostly to students. She had rented to Samantha Stelling. Dean Richardson had informed her of Sam's demise the night before. Now she stood in the middle of Sam's apartment, a stack of empty boxes on her right, a vacuum cleaner on her left, and a clipboard with an apartment application in her hand. She had lost two husbands tragically—one in the Korean war, another in a mining accident. "You've got to get right back on your feet and move on. The past is past . . . shouldn't be relived," she would say to anyone commenting on how she could have managed getting through tough times. So now she carried her practical philosophy over into her apartment managerial skills. Renter dies (it had happened three times to her in the past seventeen years) . . . get a new renter. It's as simple as that. Out with the old . . . in with the new.

She certainly didn't see any reason to let a good apartment sit idle. Sam had paid up to the end of the month, but if Isabelle could get the apartment rented before then, she might even make an extra buck or two in the process.

The practical Mrs. Covey had already called Anne Caudill and asked her to come by to see if she desired to manage Sam's belongings. Mrs. Covey sure didn't want them. There really wasn't much: mostly Sam's clothes and her school things. Mrs. Covey furnished the apartment's furniture.

While she waited for Anne, Mrs. Covey stacked Sam's clothes into boxes. She thought she'd let Anne sort through Sam's desk. When she finished sorting the clothes, she emptied the bathroom supplies. With that done, she scurried to the kitchen. She hoped she would be done by the time Anne arrived. Anne had promised to come by right after Sunday morning chapel.

◆ ◆ ◆

Layton Redman had a routine on Sunday mornings that he followed religiously. Since he filled every Saturday with campaign stops and speech preparation, Sunday remained his only morning to sleep in. He invariably crawled from bed by 9 and fixed pancakes, often eating six or eight of the fluffy plate-fillers while he leisurely read through the papers. Ever since the start of the campaign, he subscribed to four newspapers, all from different parts of the state. He collected and memorized all that the media recorded about him. Almost always, he liked what he read.

Today he couldn't seem to focus on his routine. For one thing the alarm, which he'd forgotten to reset, interrupted his sleep at 7. Then, because he started thinking about his problem with Sam, he remained unable to coax himself back into dreamland again. Finally he decided with some finality that he would go for a jog, something he did two or three times a year to suppress the guilt he felt for ignoring his need for regular exercise. The 15-degree morning air called the finality of his decision into question as soon as he stepped outside, however, so he ended up jogging only as far as the paper box to retrieve the morning's news.

After spending a few hours with the papers, and having consumed his normal Sunday breakfast, he decided to have a go at talking to Sam again. He thought that if she still wouldn't talk to him, he would just have to make another trip east and pay her a surprise visit. He dialed Sam's number. Four rings. *Please answer!* Five rings. *Not this childish thing again!*

◆ ◆ ◆

Isabelle Covey really didn't want to talk on the phone. If someone called for Sam, they probably didn't know about the accident, and that would mean she would have to tell them. *Better to let it ring and let them find out later some other way.* The ringing persisted, however, and finally she picked up after eight rings.

"Hello."

"Sam?"

"No. This is Mrs. Covey."

"I—I'm sorry," stuttered Layton Redman. "I must have the wrong number."

"No, you don't, young man." Mrs. Covey called all men under age fifty "young man." She paused, not knowing exactly how to say what she needed to say. Her practical side pushed her to spill the news rapidly. *Just get it out. It's all history now. Time to go on. No use making him find out some other way. I'll just tell him how it is.* "She's not here. She's dead. She was in a car accident last night. I'm her landlord."

"She's *what?*"

"Dead." Mrs. Covey really wanted to get back to cleaning the oven.

"When?" Layton paused. "How?"

"I told you. Car accident. Last night." *It's best to be brief. Leave the crying, emotional stuff for people without work to do.* She added, "That's all I know."

"I—I can't believe it! I was supposed to see her last night."

"I'm sorry, sir." She didn't know what else to say.

An uncomfortable pause followed. Neither party spoke for several seconds. Redman finally just mumbled, "Thank you" and hung up the phone.

"Humph!" Isabelle grunted, looking at the receiver in response to the *click* she heard on the other end.

She returned the receiver to its cradle and went back to cleaning the oven.

◆ ◆ ◆

When Adam Richards finally awoke, the sun had crept high in the sky. He couldn't recall a better night in the last few weeks. *No dreams! No trouble remembering the night before.* He looked at his watch. 11 o'clock. *Time for some coffee and maybe a trip down to the Fairfax Athletic Center for a swim.* His son planned to come over later in the afternoon, and he wanted to take him to dinner. He might even rent a video if his son was in the mood.

Adam had thought long and hard about what Simons had told him the night before. He had never really worried about what he did to the fetuses in modifying his technique. If allowing the fetus to come out with the cardiac muscle contracting benefited the good of medicine and mankind, well then, so be it. Otherwise the whole procedure would be wasted. He figured that since the outcome for the fetus was the same, regardless of the abortion technique, and since it was the mother's choice to end the pregnancy, not his, he wouldn't be bothered about whether the last heartbeat of the fetus took place inside or outside the womb. He hadn't made that decision. He hadn't changed the outcome by modifying his technique.

The thing that shook him up the most was the risk of being discovered by the medical community. If they perceived that his technique stood out as a dangerous departure from the standard of care, he would perhaps be accused of malpractice. He had always prided himself on doing the very best job he could. That was one reason he'd limited the scope of his practice in the first place. He wanted to do one thing and one thing very well. He truly believed in a woman's right to exert her own rights above that of the rights of the baby within her. *As if the products of conception have any rights anyway!* The medical community would find out about the work he and Simons performed soon enough. He just didn't want that information to get out in a heated, emotional manner by an outraged female, particularly one who felt her rights to a safe, effective abortion were being compromised. Yes, there were risks to doing the abortions in the way the research demanded . . . risks that would seem small, Simons had convinced him, when compared with the good their work would accomplish . . . risks that he hoped the medical community would see in view of the benefit that would be gained by the heart transplant recipients.

He remained confident that the public would not focus on the fact that the success of the whole program depended directly on having a "live" donor. He thought that surely when they looked on the project as a whole, they would see the donor just as Simons had convinced him to see it—as a non-viable donor preparation, incapable of living on its own, only to be wasted if they didn't "rescue" the fetus to be used for a higher good. *Certainly the public shouldn't get focused on the details of the donor as a living, often kicking fetus with a beating heart.*

Richards remembered Simons' exhortation: "We must be objective scientists when we are evaluating the benefits to be gained from this program. We cannot be carried away into an emotional attachment to the donor tissue. We must remain neutral and objective so that we can see the benefit gained from the project as a whole. Sacrifices need to be made in order to recognize otherwise unreachable goals. The surgeon needs to allow his patient to experience the pain of the stainless steel scalpel in order to realize its healing potential. Without sacrifice, there can be no success."

Adam Richards, Sr. sat sipping his coffee while he glanced at the morning paper. His coffee was hot, black, and unsweetened, just as he always drank it. As he smelled the rich aroma of the fresh liquid, he smiled, feeling that a burden he'd carried had been strangely lifted. He felt relief in knowing that Sam Stelling was dead. *Simons is right. A threat to premature discovery has passed.* Now he just needed to be sure something like that wouldn't happen again.

As he glanced at the day's top news stories, he had another reason to smile: Layton Redman stood as a clear front-runner in the governor's race. Layton Redman, who was heartily committed to the preservation of abortion rights and the easing of abortion restrictions, seemed destined for victory. Richards had helped bring him up into his current status, poised for a boring runaway finish. With Redman as the head of the state's government, Richards would have little to worry about in terms of his lucrative business. Abortion would remain and would become even more accessible for all. Redman had promised more state financial support of the "family planning" industry. And Richards had in turn made a significant financial "investment" in Layton Redman. With a careful yet easy "doctoring" of contribution paperwork, Richards had given a one thousand dollar donation to Redman for each of the last one hundred abortion patients in his clinic. On the surface, each of the patients' given names were listed as the contributors. What wasn't so clear was that the money all came from the same place: Adam

Richards. Richards didn't worry about the tax break. He didn't contribute for that reason. *Surely my proper selection and support of governmental servants will more than pay for itself by the return I'll gain in my business!*

As Adam rose to get his third cup of coffee, he noticed the tremor in his hand. He hadn't planned on drinking anything but coffee that morning, particularly because he knew his son would be coming over in a few hours. *Just a small drink won't hurt. I'm celebrating a better mood this morning, anyway. No more dreams! No more threats to premature discovery of my new abortion techniques! No more immediate risks of government interference with my current lifestyle!* He reached for a bottle of Kentucky bourbon. Since he was having only one, he made it a double.

◆ ◆ ◆

For Layton Redman, it had taken a few minutes for the news to sink in. *Sam Stelling was dead!*

He had been shocked at first, not really knowing quite how to react. Then, slowly, he began to piece it together. *She hadn't stood him up after all. She was dead!* His second reaction had been one of disappointment and of sadness. He had found her quite attractive, and he would miss her. Soon, however, his disappointment slowly but surely melted into relief as he realized that with her passing a giant threat to his candidacy had been removed. *Sam Stelling was dead! Sam Stelling was no longer a threat!*

Layton felt no remorse for the child because he assumed that this problem had been taken care of as well. He had no knowledge that the child had survived, no knowledge that he was now a father. He had wanted an abortion; he had not wanted Sam to be killed. But he imagined that this would all work out to his advantage, as there had existed a small possibility that word would get out to the public that she had aborted Redman's child. Of course he would have denied it, but at least this way there would be no way for the accusations to surface. The problem could be at most an improbable, insubstantial rumor now. Ironically, this news precipitated emotions not of mourning but of celebration. Layton was home free! *No more dreams of pregnant women or mothers bringing me an unexpected son for all to see! Sam Stelling and her baby are dead!*

As the news of Sam's death filtered through Redman's thoughts, he remembered the other woman in his life—Janice Sizemore. He had to do something to make up for last night. Flowers wouldn't cut it this time. He had used them with great success in the past, but used too frequently they lost their poignancy. Today he would need something better. Layton picked up the phone.

Ring. Ring. Layton tried to wait patiently but failed. *Come on, Janice, you're always home on Sunday morning!*

"Hello," Janice mumbled sleepily.

"Hello, Janice. I hope I'm not waking you up, darling." Layton looked at his watch. *It was after 12!*

"I had a late night. After you left, I couldn't sleep. I stayed up thinking for a long time." Janice rubbed her eyes.

"Can you share your thoughts with me?" Layton was a bit taken back at finding Janice still in bed.

"I was thinking about us, Layton. What with this campaign and all, I think we need a vacation from each other. We don't even talk anymore. All I hear is campaign updates. I want more than that, Layton. I need more than that from you."

Layton was unprepared for such heavy thinking from his fiancée. They had always been the picture-perfect couple. He well knew that many people would cast their vote for him just because of her and because of her prominent father, a former Senator.

"Honey, it's . . . well, I've been so distracted lately. I know it will be better soon. In fact, I called to invite you to spend the rest of the day with me—maybe out at the lake—just the two of us. No campaign talk allowed . . . just you and me and our future together."

"I don't know, Layton, I—"

"Come on, babe," Layton whimpered softly. "Give me a chance. We've made promises, ones I want to keep. It's not time to back away now. I realize how much I need you, honey."

"Layton," Janice said softly, "I want it to work too." She paused. "I just want you to be with me when you're with me . . . not somewhere else, caught up in this campaign." She had no idea that his thoughts were ever on another woman.

"Does that mean okay?"

"Okay."

"How does 2:30 sound? I'll pick you up at your house."

"I'll be ready for you." Janice's emotions were no match for Layton Redman's persuasive tongue.

◆ ◆ ◆

Anne Caudill looked around Sam's apartment. Everything had already been packed away except for Sam's books and the items in her desk. It didn't appear that Isabelle Covey had wasted any time in readying the apartment for someone else. Anne wanted to cry out, "No, stop! These are Sam's things! You can't just pack them all away the instant she's gone!" But she held her tongue, seeing that Mrs. Covey was well on her way to completing the job. *But it does seem a bit disrespectful to move her things out so rapidly*, Anne thought.

"I've left the desk and a few items on those shelves for you to sort through. If I was you, if I saw anything I liked, I'd just take it," said Mrs. Covey. "She doesn't have any kin, you know."

The statement caught Anne cold. She raised her voice in a quick response. "She's got a son! I bet he would like some of these things to be saved for him." Anne's gaze met with an icy glare from Mrs. Covey.

Isabelle looked away and softened. "I—I hadn't even thought of that. I didn't think the child was old enough to survive."

"He's old enough to be alive," countered Anne, who then sat down in Sam's desk chair and looked at the desktop in front of her.

The landlord didn't respond. She only returned to the more practical duty of removing a small paper calendar from the wall in the kitchen. She looked at Anne, then at the plastic garbage bag in the center of the kitchen floor. She looked at the calendar, which had been marked up with notes by Samantha Stelling. She sighed and took the calendar over to the desk where Anne sat, laying it on top of some mail on the corner of the desk. "Here—I've about finished what I need to do," Isabelle said as she headed for the door. "Just leave the door unlocked when you're done." She exited without another word.

Anne lifted the books from the shelves one by one and placed them into the boxes she'd obtained from the grocery store on her way home from church. She set aside several books on fetal development and pregnancy to return to the library. Anne then turned her attention to the desk. She decided to clean the top off first and began by picking up the calendar Mrs. Covey had taken down from the kitchen wall. On it Sam Stelling had laid out her plans. Her upcoming tests, assignment due dates, and other events had been faithfully recorded. Anne paged through the calendar, which was filled with pictures of horses and Kentucky bluegrass. When she reached August, she stopped. There Sam had circled the seventeenth and had written "Anne's birthday."

Anne began to sob. Her friendship with Sam had been a strong one, as friendships often are when they are plowed out of the ground of adversity. Although she had known her only for a relatively short time, they had shared things with each other that very few were privileged to know. *It isn't fair! Sam was so young, God! Why did you take her home? Why did you take her away from me?* She continued to release her emotions for a few minutes while she held the calendar against her chest. After that, she sat for a long time in silence, just staring at the pages of the calendar.

Anne walked into the bathroom. Fortunately, Mrs. Covey hadn't taken down the toilet paper roll. Anne used a generous portion to wipe her eyes and blow her nose.

When she returned to the desk, she leafed through the mail Sam had placed in a pile on the edge of the desk. On top of the little stack was a postcard with a return address marked "Layton Redman for Governor Campaign Headquarters." Anne picked it up and read the back. Postcard information was basically public domain, she thought. On the back was an acknowledgment for a campaign contribution to the tune of one thousand dollars. *A thousand dollars! Sam didn't have that kind of money!* Anne paused and then remembered what Sam had told her. *Adam Richards! Of course! Sam said that Redman had bragged to her about Richards' support, which he "laundered" through the names of his patients.* This bit of information perked her reporter's instinct. She knew she didn't have much solid evidence to prove what she knew, but this was a start. Somehow she needed to find out more about Richards, Simons, and Redman.

She thought back to the conversation she'd had with Sam just a few days before. Sam didn't want any information she shared with Anne to become public knowledge. "Promise me you'll keep this under your hat until I get this sorted out," she could hear Sam say. She wasn't sure what Sam would want now that she was gone. Anne meditated for a minute on the phrase, "until I get this sorted out." She wasn't sure if that applied now. All she knew was that now in Sam's absence she alone knew the truth about Layton's unfaithfulness, and about his son. She wondered if Redman knew the baby was still alive. She also had some evidence of the under-the-table contributions of Richards to Redman's campaign. Then there was the matter of Simons and his relationship with Richards. *Did that have anything to do with this? How much can I share and still maintain my promise to Sam? How much do I dare hold back if the public is to be informed? If Sam's baby was about to be used in an experiment, how much do I owe to him and to myself to find out just what Simons was up to?*

Anne looked at the piece of mail in her hand. She filed the little postcard in her jacket pocket. She then quickly emptied the rest of the desktop and desk drawers into the boxes at hand and carefully carried them down the stairs and put them into the hatchback of her small Plymouth Arrow.

◆ ◆ ◆

Matt had come home from trauma rounds and passed out on his bed, his clothes still on. His alarm went off at 2 o'clock, interrupting his delayed renewal. Matt showered away his sleepiness and put on some casual clothes. He fed Mike and then drove over to see Linda. It would be his first visit since he'd sent her his "intruder" package.

After Linda let him in, Matt inspected her apartment and gladly found that all of his notes were in place. She had counted on his inspection and put the notes back up the night before. She had even eaten the Twinkie, although she did look at it with a frown before she started. It wasn't as bad as she'd thought, but she wasn't about to tell that to Matt, who would then certainly send her more.

Linda had wanted to fix them dinner but had stayed after church to hear about another anti-abortion protest. Matt suggested they go out for pizza, and Linda agreed as long as the restaurant had a salad bar. Over dinner, she explained more about the meeting she'd attended that afternoon.

"Pastor Paul wants to be careful not to put forward the stereotypical negative protest. The posters are all to be positive, with messages of forgiveness and love. Life, not murder, is to be the theme of the messages. We are going to be marching near the Fairfax Family Planning Clinic, but we are to voluntarily stay off their property, so as not to be accused of obstructing their business. Many of their patients park at the nearby shopping center anyway, so people won't see their cars in the F.F.P. Clinic lot; so a fair number of their patients will walk right by the protest. We were given careful instructions not to yell messages about baby killing, but we will be allowed to urge people to give their babies life, and to ask them about the babies' right to life."

"It will be interesting to see how the media portrays the message. They have such a tendency to highlight the radical, ugly protests. If things are peaceful, they may not cover the event at all," Matt stated.

"I'm coming up to Fairfax in a few nights to confirm where their property begins and ends. Someone got a copy of the adjacent shopping center layout. It seems that the clinic only owns the property within one hundred feet of their back door. They want it measured out so that we know where the marchers can stand so we are staying off the clinic's property. They can't accuse us of obstructing their work if we aren't even on their lot," Linda explained. "I volunteered to come up to do the measurement . . . thinking I might also be able to see you," she added with a smile.

"What night will that be?" questioned Matt.

"What night are you available?" responded Linda with a chuckle.

"Tuesday."

"I was planning to come up on Tuesday," Linda echoed.

After dinner, Matt and Linda headed back to her place. They

were to meet Anne Caudill, student editor of A.C.U.'s school newspaper, who wanted to ask Matt a few questions.

Until Anne arrived, Matt entertained himself with a large photo album of Linda's childhood. While he laughed at the many yellowing photographs, Linda went around and discreetly took down all of Matt's "intruder" notes and placed them gently in her Bible. She wasn't sure she wanted one of her students to see that side of her just yet. Matt's head was so buried in the picture album that he didn't even notice.

CHAPTER
22

ANNE chose her words carefully. Sam's words were fresh in her mind. *Just keep my name out of this, will you?*

"I'm not sure where to start. I had, er, have a friend who went to the Fairfax Family Planning Clinic for an abortion. From what she experienced, it sure seems like something weird is going on up there. Maybe it's nothing, but we thought it might be important. She said I could ask around a bit, but not to use her name."

"Just share what you're comfortable sharing," said Linda. Matt nodded his agreement.

"I shared some of this with Linda already," Anne said as she looked at Matt. "I thought maybe you could shed a little light on this for me."

"I'm not sure I'll be of much help. I guess that depends on what you want to know," Matt stated matter-of-factly.

"I need to start at the beginning. This friend went to have an abortion by Dr. Adam Richards. They called her and asked her to come in early for a suppository that they put in her birth canal. They told her it would help prepare the uterus so they could remove the baby."

"How far along was she?" Matt questioned.

"Approximately twenty-two weeks."

"Oooh, pretty far along." Matt looked at Linda, who was shaking her head.

"They had seen her before and told her she had plenty of time. Anyway, she went back to the clinic in the afternoon to have the abortion. Before they did, they did an ultrasound. They could see enough detail to know that it was a little boy."

Matt and Linda just looked at each other and then at Anne without speaking.

Anne continued, "My friend got really freaked out when they said it was a boy. She knew she couldn't go through with the abortion. Richards put her back up into stirrups to wash out the medicine they had put in her. Remember the suppository I told you about?" Anne looked at her small audience. "I guess that was what he was concerned about retrieving." Anne paused. "Anyway, that's when Dr. Simons busted in—"

"Simons! Michael Simons?" Matt exclaimed. "What was *he* doing there?"

"That's exactly what we hoped you could tell us," Anne replied with the same incredulity.

Matt just shook his head.

Anne went on with her story. "We tried to find out from Richards, but the only thing his office nurse would say was that Richards was working with Simons on some sort of research project." Anne backed up as if remembering something she'd forgotten. "The thing is, when Simons came in he asked Richards, 'Where's my specimen? I've got experiments to run!' Later, looking back, my friend was convinced he was coming after her baby. He had every reason to believe an abortion was going on in there. She had just refused the procedure in the nick of time. That seems logical to me—what other 'specimen' would he be referring to?"

Anne looked at her listeners, who remained sullen and quiet. She went on, "When we asked Dr. Richards about it, he sent word that Simons was just there to pick up specimens for pathology, as they have no pathologists at the clinic."

"No," Matt said, drawing out his word in a quiet, studious fashion. "There's something weird going on all right. Simons doesn't just pick up specimens for pathology. He's one of the highest in command in the surgery department. For him to be there, something pretty important had to be going on. He certainly was not just picking up specimens!"

"Well, Richards' nurse did say they were doing research, so we called and talked to Simons' secretary. She said there was no research going on between Simons and Richards, that they were friends is all," Anne added.

"Somebody's not telling the whole truth here," Matt concluded. They all looked at each other for a few moments. Suddenly Matt got up and began to pace slowly. Matt looked at Anne. "You say she was twenty-two weeks along?"

"Yes." Anne looked at him questioningly.

"Well, I'm no expert on abortion, but as far as I know, abortions done that late take a saline injection right into the uterus, right around the baby. After the baby dies, the mother eventually expels it . . . but that takes hours. Your friend didn't have an injection of any kind, did she? You didn't mention it."

"Not that I know of. She was pretty shaken up by what happened, but her memory was excellent, and she remembered many things in great detail and told them to me. It was almost as if the horror of it all engraved the images into her memory. She could even tell me what color Simons' eyes were. She never said anything about an injection. They were going to sedate her, but she refused before they could do it. The only medicine she got was the suppository, and they told her that would make it easier to extract the baby."

"Something's definitely weird here. It just doesn't add up. The abortion technique, the presence of Simons . . . I don't know. I'm not much help. I can confirm your suspicions that everything might not be aboveboard, but that's about it."

"Can you talk to Simons . . . find out what he's doing?" Anne asked hopefully.

"I don't think so. You don't understand the system. Simons is very powerful. It's not like a resident can just go up and question a surgery attending about his actions or his motives, especially not the vice-chairman of the department," Matt added soberly. "I've come too far to try anything that stupid. That could be my ticket out of surgery training for good."

Linda looked at Matt. "Don't you think you're exaggerating a bit?"

"Don't underestimate Simons' power. Three residents that I know of lost their jobs because of him. If he thinks someone is substandard, he has him removed. Two of the residents performed below his expectations when they were on his service. One was an excellent resident, but his personality clashed with Simons'. The chairman does what Simons wants. I only know of three, but I'm sure there were others before I came." Matt looked at them. "I'm putting it to you as straight as I know. I don't know a resident who has ever been on Simons' hit list and won." Matt sighed and was silent.

Linda broke the silence. "Couldn't you just ask around a little? Maybe not to Simons, but to others who may be involved in research with him?"

Matt shrugged. "I don't know . . ." He looked at the imploring face of Anne Caudill. "Okay . . . okay. I'll keep my ears open, maybe ask a few questions, but I can't make any promises. I'm too close to finishing this five-year program. I can't get on his bad side now."

Linda looked at Anne. "Fair enough?"

"Fair enough," Anne responded. There wasn't much more she could say.

There wasn't much more she could do at this point either. Anne stood up and extended her hand. "Thanks," she added, shaking hands with Matt. "I'll let myself out. I've got some work to do. Editors never sleep, you know!" Anne smiled. And with that, she slipped out the door.

Matt looked at Linda, who was the first to speak. "Quite a story, isn't it? Do you really think something fishy is going on?"

"It's hard to tell. Certain things don't add up, though. Perhaps it won't hurt to keep my eyes open." Matt paused. "Did she say that girl was twenty-two weeks along?"

"I think so. Why?"

"It just seems so blatantly wrong! I mean, when someone gets an abortion at two or three weeks along, it's easier to deny that it's really a baby. But a twenty-two-week-old—that's a different story!"

"I know what you mean," Linda said softly.

"You know, last night when I was on call for trauma, I had a once in a lifetime experience." Matt paused, then added, "I hope." He sat down as he relived the events of that trauma call. "A young pregnant woman came in from an auto accident and died right before my eyes. I opened her abdomen and stole the baby away, just as it was obvious that we were losing the mother."

Linda looked on, not saying a word.

Matt continued, "The spooky thing is, that baby was maybe only a week or two older than the one Anne talked about. And this baby lived! It just confirms to me how blind the public is to what is really going on in the abortion industry! It's so ironic, really. On one hand we have technology that is improving our ability to save younger and younger 'premies,' and we fight like crazy to save them at great expense. On the other hand, and in the same town, you have a woman exercising her right to kill an unborn child of nearly the same age. It just doesn't make sense!"

Linda gently squeezed Matt's hand. "I'm right with you on this one."

Matt shook his head. "I don't know . . . Maybe if we can uncover something under-the-table about Richards' clinic, we can at least slow down the local abortion business a little. That may mean something."

"Just be careful, Matt. If there's really something covert about this, there may be others who won't want anyone to know. You could get in trouble," Linda responded with urgency.

"I'll be okay," said Matt, wishing he was as confident as he sounded.

◆ ◆ ◆

The next morning John Gentry prepared for work at the usual time. He didn't run right in to the hospital, however, as Simons had told him to come in late. He needed him for a pump run over at the F.F.P. Clinic in the afternoon and knew he'd be getting home late. He used the opportunity to see his oldest girl get on the bus bound for the first grade and took his second oldest to preschool. He then drove over to Fairfax General Hospital to pick up an application. He knew switching jobs wouldn't be easy financially, but after discussing the whole situation with Lori, he knew that working with Simons exacted an unfair toll on him and his family. *Maybe the job at Fairfax General will be a way to stay in the area and free myself of Simons' grip at the same time.* He shoved the two-page application into his briefcase, noting the section at the bottom of the second page: "References." *Uh-oh. I'd better think up someone besides Simons for this. I can just see trying to convince him into letting me go without a fight. It's better that I just keep this one quiet until I know something from Fairfax General.*

◆ ◆ ◆

Every Thursday morning at 6:45, rain or shine, holiday or not, the general surgery department gathered for the weekly Morbidity and Mortality (M. and M.) Conference. There, behind doors closed to the public, each surgical case that had a complication or a death the week before was presented by the resident involved. The cases were dissected. The residents were questioned. All present knew whether the resident prepared correctly. The cause of the complication, if it could be determined, was identified and the blame assigned. The residents sulked away humbled but wiser. It was a purging of mistakes made, a confession of technical or surgical judgmental sins, a chance to learn in order to avoid mistakes and to stand up and admit their humanity. It could be a learning experience. It was often torture. It was a stepping-stone, a necessary part of preparation for the oral questioning every surgeon meets in the final oral certification examination before the American Board of Surgery.

Each Monday the chief resident posted the M. and M. list. Each name was followed by a code: IP for Interesting Patient, C for Complication, and D for Death. Each case was assigned to a presenter, the resident or intern involved in the case.

Matt Stone had finished morning rounds on the oncology service and had stopped by the Surgery Education Office to post the list of complications from the week before. He saw that there were already three cases on the list, and three chief residents still needed to add their cases. He liked seeing other cases on the list, as it was less likely that the focus of inspection would rest on him too long.

Matt added two more cases: "4. D. Sanderson, procedure, Hickman catheter, C= pneumothorax, presenter, H. Hunt, M.D. 5. S. Stelling, procedure, E.R. thoracotomy and c-section, D., presenter, M. Stone, M.D."

Matt greeted a fellow chief resident, Stella Long. "Morning, Stella. Quiet night?"

"Not too bad, really . . . an old veteran with an incarcerated hernia about 9 o'clock . . . quiet after that." Stella picked up the M. and M. list and silently read the case list. "Since when do you do c-sections, Matt?"

"Kind of sticks out, doesn't it? I hope you and Bob have a lot to add to the list to decrease the attention paid to my case."

"Sorry, Matt. Can't help you there, buddy. We only had one major case last week, and it went great."

"Thanks a lot," Matt responded.

"See you on Thursday, Matt." Stella laughed as she headed down the hall towards the surgical library. "Maybe you should bone up on complications of c-sections. They're not likely to avoid that one."

Matt failed to see the humor in the comment. The sad thing was, he knew she was right.

◆ ◆ ◆

John Gentry had had a relatively low-key morning. He knew it would definitely be a contrast to his afternoon. He had a few minutes to catch his breath before Simons would be called to come over for a pump run at the Family Planning Clinic. John had arrived early and set up, priming the pump with blood and laying the instruments out in order.

John sat in the corner at a desk, eating his bagged lunch. As he did, he popped open his briefcase and looked over the application for work at Fairfax General Hospital that he'd picked up that morning. Everything seemed pretty straightforward. He would get it typed up tonight, he hoped.

Richards stuck his head in the door. "The patient's ready! This one is well-sedated and ready to dilate. The pitocin is on. Call your boss and let him know to come on over."

"Roger. Thanks, Dr. Richards," replied Gentry. He closed his briefcase and paged Dr. Simons. He entered a prearranged code number onto Simons' beeper display: "54321." Simons told him to enter descending numbers when they were counting down to begin the extraction of the donor P.O.C. Gentry then got up and paced around the lab, checking and rechecking details so Simons wouldn't be disappointed.

◆ ◆ ◆

Several miles to the north, in Simons' plush office suite, Simons received the page. He looked at the display: "54321." *Blastoff! Time for action! No more wasted time for me!* He put down the journal he was reading and picked up his coat and keys. On the way out, he called to Iris, "I'll be out for the evening. Dr. Ulman is on call. Refer my calls to him."

◆ ◆ ◆

Matt Stone took a break between cases. He slipped away to a call room and made what was now a daily, if not more often, call to Linda Baldwin.

"Hello."

"Hi. Working hard?" Matt asked.

"Just finishing up a paper. How are you doing?" Linda responded.

"I'm okay. I'm suffering from Baldwin withdrawal symptoms."

"And just what are the symptoms, doctor?" Linda inquired with a smile.

Matt put on his best serious-doctor bass voice. "Inability of the patient to think about anything except Linda Baldwin . . . heart palpitations whenever the name is mentioned . . ."

"You do sound ill," Linda interrupted with a laugh. She paused, then spoke again. "Be serious, Stone. How are you? That was some heavy stuff Anne laid on us last night."

"Really, I'm okay. I posted my M. and M. case list this morning. It looks like I might take some heat this week."

"Who are you presenting?"

"The pregnant girl I mentioned last night who came in after a car accident and died," Matt responded.

"I wish I could come and see what really goes on. I think—"

"That's all I need. I can see you standing up in the back and yelling, 'Hey, stop picking on him! It's not his fault!'" Matt laughed.

"Very funny!" Linda sulked dramatically. "See if I ever defend you!" Linda laughed now too. When the chuckling subsided, Linda spoke first. "Did you stumble across any leads into what Simons might be up to?"

"Not yet. I'll keep my eyes open. No promises, but I'm listening. Maybe I'll talk to one of the guys in his lab. I'll just pretend I'm interested."

"I want you to be careful . . . especially if Simons is really like you described. That man gave me the willies the way he held my hand and looked at me at the Christmas party last year."

"I remember." Matt nodded again as his beeper sounded. He looked at the display. "Uh-oh, O.R.'s calling . . . Must be starting the next case." He paused again. "I have to go."

"Call me tonight?"

"I should be home by 9."

"Bye, Matt."

"See you." Matt hung up the phone quietly and headed back to the operating rooms.

◆ ◆ ◆

Doris Hatfield was sitting in her studio working on a sculpture entitled "Inward Search" when her son, Adam Richards, Jr., came bounding in after school. She could hear him dropping his books on the kitchen table. She called out, "That's not where they belong! Put them in your room!" She didn't realize that as she yelled, facing away from the door, her son had crept in right behind her.

"Okay!" Adam shot back loudly, causing his mother to clutch at her heart and spin around, nearly falling from her small stool. He grinned sheepishly. "Hi, Mom!"

"Don't do that to me! You're always sneaking up on me like that!"

"I didn't sneak. I just walked in under the cover of your voice."

"Very funny." She turned back to the smooth shape in front of her. "I thought you had band practice."

"We got out early because Mr. Leary had to take his daughter to the dentist. He said she needed a tooth pulled." Adam turned to head back to the kitchen.

"You never did tell me about your visit with your father."

Adam stopped and turned back to face his mother. "It was okay, I guess."

"You guess?" his mother prodded.

"We went out to dinner at Olivia's. Then we went to Fairfax Mall to the movies. That's about it."

"Did you have fun?" Doris thought that pulling the band director's daughter's teeth would have been easier than getting her teenage son to share his feelings with her.

"It was okay. We saw a Stallone movie. Dad snored through the whole thing."

"He was asleep?"

"Yeah. I had to punch him to keep the noise down a few times. He must have been up late working again."

"He was drunk," muttered Doris under her breath.

"What?"

"Stallone's a hunk," she said, covering her comment perceptively.

Adam walked to the kitchen, calling back at his mother, "Got anything to snack on before dinner?"

"We're eating in two hours. You can have some granola. Don't spoil your appetite!" *As if that could be possible!* Doris returned to her work, lightly buffing the smooth surface with a chamois cloth.

◆ ◆ ◆

Gentry carefully adjusted the flow of the silver cardiopulmonary bypass pump. The pump oxygenated blood coming from the venous cannula inserted into the neonate's vena cava. Simons gave the routine pump orders.

"Give me twenty," Simons barked, informing Gentry to pump an additional twenty cc's of fluid back into the baby's circulation.

"Twenty . . . in!" responded Gentry.

Simons then measured the cardiac output with a Swan Ganz catheter that was positioned in the pulmonary artery. "Measure the wedge pressure, and record the cardiac output." Simons paused, watching him record the data, then repeated the process. "Give me twenty!"

"Twenty . . . in!" reverberated Gentry mechanically. Again he recorded the wedge pressure and cardiac output. Once Simons saw that the maximum cardiac output had been reached, he ceased orders for more fluid and began pacing the small heart to see how much more he could make the heart pump in a minute's time. A small wire had been meticulously sutured to the right atria and ventricle. He measured the flow by the volume returning to the pump by the aortic cannula.

"Let's see how much this baby can do." Simons only used the word "baby" in reference to the heart. Simons turned up the atrial rate on the small blue-and-white pacing box. "One hundred fifty . . . record! One hundred seventy . . . record! One hundred ninety . . . record! Two hundred . . . record! Two hundred twenty . . . record!" The output of the tiny heart began to fall, as there was no longer any time for the heart to fill between beats. Simons looked at Gentry. He seemed very pleased. "Okay. Shut her down. I think we've gotten all we can out of this one."

Gentry shut off the pump. Simons pulled the cannulas and the pacing wires. He then snipped the pulmonary arteries, the aorta, and the superior and inferior vena cavas and lifted the small heart from the chest. As he did so, the heart continued beating for a few seconds. He placed it quickly in a formalin container. The surface of the formalin solution was disturbed at first and then became smooth as the little heart slowed to a stop. After the heart had been "fixed" in the solution overnight, it would be ready for slides to be made to examine the cardiac muscle under the microscope.

Beneath a towel placed over the infant's head, the mouth opened and shut several times in a gasping motion as the absence of oxygen stimulated the respiratory centers to send out impulses to breathe faster. In another moment, the motions ceased entirely as irreversible brain anoxia preceded death.

Simons deftly sewed the sternum and overlying skin to prevent the discovery of his work. He then dropped the small female fetus into a hypertonic saline solution to cause the routine skin changes seen in saline injection abortions. Simons quickly gathered his data forms and darted for the door, where he paused. "Thanks," he mumbled and slipped out.

Gentry cleaned up the pump and gathered his paperwork. He carried the container with the small fetus up to a small utility room where Richards stored the rest of his pathology specimens before they were taken to the university pathology department. He left the heart specimen for Simons to examine as he wished. John sighed. It always took an additional hour to clean the room up and to ready it for the next pump run. He looked at his watch. 8 P.M. He wouldn't see his daughters awake tonight either.

CHAPTER
23

ELLEN Fischer, M.D. lifted her stethoscope from the small infant's chest. She was leaning over Baby Boy Stelling's incubator. She spoke to her attending, Dr. Paul Deavers. "I can still hear the typical machinery murmur. I'm confident the patent ductus hasn't closed yet." The ductus arteriosus normally closed soon after birth and prevented blood from shunting from the aorta into the pulmonary artery and overloading the lungs.

"I think it's time to call the surgeons. It's obvious that the indomethacin hasn't worked. I'm concerned that we'll never get this one off the ventilator if we don't get this congestive heart failure under control. To do that, we need to stop the flow through the patent ductus arteriosus," Deavers said.

Fischer nodded her head in approval. "Do you want me to talk to Jack Wheater?" she questioned.

Dr. Deavers shook his head. "No. Just let me talk straight to Dr. Simons. It'll be simpler that way."

Ellen didn't argue. "Suits me," the neonatal fellow responded. Ellen looked at the next incubator. "Do you want to see the new patients?"

"Sure. Let me grab a cup of coffee and call Simons. Get the team together so we can make some rounds."

◆ ◆ ◆

Anne spun around from the desk where she had been doing a layout for the campus paper. She hadn't heard Linda's quiet entry. Linda could see that Anne had been crying. Anne was obviously tottering on the edge of an emotion-releasing sob when Linda's approach startled her.

"O-o-h!" Anne stuttered. "I didn't hear you come in." She turned away and wiped her eyes, then stared out the window of the small *Weathervane* office.

"Anne," Linda said slowly, "is something wrong?"

Anne turned towards Linda and bit her quivering lower lip. She managed only a nod before she began to sob. Linda reached out and put her arms around the trembling student. After a few moments Anne backed up and blew her nose. "I guess you heard about Samantha Stelling."

Linda nodded, adding, "They made an announcement this morning in the campus chapel service."

"I met her through researching this story." Anne picked up a folder and handed it to Linda. "The one about pregnancy on campus and the pressures the girls feel—"

"I know the one," Linda assured her.

"She had become one of my closest friends in only a short time."

"I'm so sorry, Anne. I didn't even know. You didn't say anything about her the other night when you talked to me and Matt."

"I held together pretty well at first. I guess I was in shock. I didn't want to bother you guys with it anyway," Anne said, still staring out the window. She wiped her eyes with the sleeve of the A.C.U. sweatshirt she wore. "I'll be all right."

"Listen, why don't you let one of the other guys do this stuff? You don't have to do it all, you know."

"The work helps me get my mind off things," Anne responded. She paused, biting her lower lip again.

Linda stepped nearer to the trembling editor again, squinting slightly as she tried to read through the anguish on her face. "Are you sure you're all right?"

They were alone in the room. Anne met Linda's gaze. "Can I tell you something in confidence?"

Linda was taken back but quickly responded, "Sure."

"My friend really opened up to me, knowing that I'd keep all of this quiet. Now that she's dead, I'm not sure what I should do. Some of the things she told me may be beneficial to the public. I'm just not sure if I should say anything, and if I should, when."

Linda sat down, taking her cue from Anne who had turned and now sat on the edge of the desk she used. Anne went on, "Sam was carrying Layton Redman's child. From what I understand, the baby somehow lived. They cut the baby out just as Sam died, I hear." She paused, then raised her voice both in pitch and in volume. "Redman's an unfaithful creep in my book! He just used my friend for his own pleasure! Now he's a dad. I'm pretty sure he doesn't even know the baby's alive. I even called the admitting office to see if they knew anything. They list the child's mother as deceased and the father as unknown."

Linda got up and started to pace. "This information . . . you're sure it's accurate?"

"I'm positive. Redman was the only guy Sam ever slept with. She told me that herself. And I believed her. I hadn't known her for very long, but I know she was telling the truth."

"This news could really change the outcome of the governor's race," Linda said.

"I know," Anne shot back.

"Do me a favor. Let's not let this out of the bag just yet. We need to research our story a bit more, maybe even contact Redman." Linda walked to the window and looked out at the snowy lawn. She brightened momentarily as if remembering something. "Do you mind if I tell this to Matt? He's the resident who delivered Sam's baby. He has no idea who that child is."

Anne sat quietly as the news Linda had shared sunk in. Finally she responded, "Matt? Your Matt? He was the doctor who rescued Sam's child?" She paused. "That—that means he was there at the end when Sam died. He would have been the last one to see her . . ." Anne's voice choked with fresh emotion, and she was unable to finish her sentence.

Linda thought about her conversation with Matt. "Matt told me about this the other night. I had no idea that the patient was Samantha." Linda stopped for a moment and handed Anne a tissue.

"He told me that the woman in the accident was never responsive. She never suffered in any way."

Anne brightened. "Thanks for telling me that."

Linda repeated her question quietly. "Would you mind if I told Matt about Sam and her baby?"

"I guess that's okay," Anne replied, then added, "Let's just not allow it to go any farther for now."

"Fair enough." Linda looked down at the spreadsheet that Anne had designed. "Here, let me help you finish this."

"You don't have to do—"

Linda cut off Anne's protests. "I know. I'm your advisor. So I advise you to let me help you."

Anne smiled. She was glad to have the help.

◆ ◆ ◆

John Gentry shifted in his chair where he sat across from Dr. Gerald Martinez, a cardiothoracic surgeon who was the head of the C.T. surgical group at Fairfax General Hospital. The room was richly paneled, and the leather chairs were soft, but John was distinctly aware of an anxiety in the pit of his stomach. Simons thought that Gentry was taking a late lunch. Dr. Martinez paged through Gentry's application and *curriculum vitae*.

"Very, very nice, John," said the C.T. surgeon, looking up from the papers on the teak desk in front of him. "My partners had a chance to look at your folder last evening, and we all agree that you seem to be qualified."

"Th-thank you, sir," John responded nervously.

"What is your main interest in changing jobs? We cannot match what Dr. Simons is paying you. You know that."

John nodded his head. "I know that, sir. I'm not making the change because I'm interested in making more money. I'm more concerned about spending more time with my family. My girls hardly know me anymore." He was inconspicuously quiet about the effect Dr. Simons' new research was having on his mood.

Martinez looked over the form for an additional minute before standing. He extended his hand to John Gentry and grasped his hand firmly. "I'll call your references. If everything looks okay, we should be able to tell you something by the end of next week."

"Thank you, sir." John walked to the door, escorted by Dr. Martinez, then exited quietly by himself. He hoped he had enough time to get back to T.U. before his lunch break was up. Hopefully Simons didn't even know he was gone. Behind him, Martinez looked at the list of references Gentry had given. There were five names listed, all from his former jobs. There was no listing for Dr. Michael Simons.

Martinez punched the intercom. "Val, see if you can reach Dr. Michael Simons for me."

"Yes, sir, Dr. Martinez."

◆ ◆ ◆

Dr. Richards was having a typical day at the office. He was completing an abortion on a thirty-two-year-old woman named Shirley, a faithful patient of his. This was her fourth abortion. She knew the routines well and wasn't about to be talked into waiting until she was farther along. Dr. Richards had started giving all of his patients the option of waiting, citing his inability to fit them into his schedule, or the need for the patient to be adequately prepared. He hoped, in initiating the conversation, that some women would choose to delay long enough that the fetal hearts would be mature enough to be useful to him and his associate, Michael Simons. Shirley, however, always came in early, often right after missing a single menstrual period. This time she had missed at least two. She knew too much to accept a further delay by the clinic.

Richards positioned himself on a stool at the foot of the operating table in procedure unit four in his clinic. A nurse, Frieda Harris, stood at the top of the bed as she and Richards gently talked the patient through the procedure.

"You may feel a little pressure here . . . You shouldn't feel much pain," Richards stated mechanically. He slid a suction rod up through the dilated cervix and began vacuuming out the uterine cavity's contents. Several times there was a lull in the suctioning sound, followed by a snapping release as a larger tissue fragment rocketed through the suction tubing, shaking it rhythmically as it went. Inside the uterus, the placenta and a small female "conceptus" were ripped apart by the vigorous suction device.

Shirley moaned. The nurse gripped her hand. "The doctor's almost done."

Richards pulled out the instrument and looked a second time for bleeding. He put a small pad over the birth canal and looked up at his nurse. "What's next, Frieda?"

"Two more suctions and a Norplant placement. Then you can enjoy your lunch," Frieda replied, smiling compassionately.

Richards didn't return the smile. *If I keep putting in so many Norplant implantable birth control devices, it's going to impact on my abortion business!*

◆ ◆ ◆

Matt was crossing Main Street in front of the T.U. hospital when he saw John Gentry approaching the main entrance to the medical center. Matt knew him from his months on the cardiothoracic surgery service. He hustled to greet him before he got inside the door. "Hey, John!"

John was slightly startled. He was concerned about getting back before he was missed by Simons. "What's up?" he said as he looked up at the approaching resident.

"Do you have a couple of minutes? I just wanted to ask you a question or two."

Gentry looked at his watch. "I have two minutes. What's on your mind?"

Matt looked at him, hoping he would know what he was talking about. "Is Simons doing any research with Dr. Adam Richards?"

Gentry's head snapped up, lifting his gaze from the sidewalk in front of him. "What?" He paused momentarily, then added, "Where did you ever get that idea?"

"From a friend . . . She said she saw him at Richards' clinic." Matt looked at Gentry, whose expression was unchanged and unreadable.

"Must have been a mistake. I think maybe they are friends— that's all. Simons isn't doing any research with him," Gentry lied. He certainly didn't want Simons finding out that he'd told anyone about the research that Simons had silently instructed Gentry to keep "under wraps" until it was time to reveal it.

"I figured as much. Thanks. Say, don't mention this to Simons, would you? He's kind of funny about his own research, you know."

Gentry mumbled, "I know" and slipped through the swinging entrance doors into the hospital.

◆ ◆ ◆

Redman didn't see any problem with the way he represented himself. He had just made an acceptance speech for an endorsement by the Louisville chapter of Women Voters of the Bluegrass. He emphasized a woman's right to choose and the need to keep governmental policy out of the bedrooms of the bluegrass. He received an abundance of applause after that line—so much so that he had to keep restarting his next sentence over and over while the interruptive cheering continued.

Just two hours earlier, Redman had been serving soup to the homeless at a downtown Louisville Catholic church when he was asked about his position on abortion by one of the local sisters. His reply was punctuated by a softening of his expression and a lowering of his voice. "Abortion is an unfortunate tragedy of monumental proportions," he said. "Our goal should be fewer and fewer abortions." He grasped the hand of the nun as he spoke, and she thought she detected tenderness in his deep blue eyes.

Now Redman attempted to eat his own lunch as the Louisville rally wound down to a close. He had barely ten minutes to eat once his speech was over. Janice sat to his right, saying little and smiling a lot. The press sought to ask more questions as he stood to leave, but Redman was pressed for time and needed to move along to his next campaign stop in western Kentucky. Just as he turned to break through a throng of reporters, he saw a small boy about two years of age running towards him. Layton Redman stiffened noticeably as the little boy began yelling, "Daddy! Daddy!" Redman feared he was reliving the nightmare he'd had just a few nights before. When the little boy ran up and hugged the male reporter standing on Redman's left, Layton sighed.

Janice pulled him away from the sea of reporters. "Are you all right? You're white as a sheet!"

Layton nodded his head and sighed again. He didn't speak for several seconds. "I think I just ate too fast," he countered. "I'll be fine." He shot a glance back at the reporter, who threw his giggling son into the air. "It's just a little indigestion, that's all."

Janice looked at her fiancé with concern. "You're working too hard. You've been making too many stops. Maybe we need to get away together more often and let you really forget about this campaign stuff."

Layton didn't reply. The color slowly returned to his cheeks. He crawled onto the passenger's seat of his B.M.W. "Can you drive? I want to rest for a minute."

Janice didn't answer him but just took the keys from his open palm and started the car. She looked over at Layton, trying to see if he was really all right, as he claimed. He almost never suggested that she drive. *I'll be sure he gets to bed early tonight. He needs to get his mind off this campaign!*

◆ ◆ ◆

As usual when Dr. Simons operated in the N.I.C.U., a sizable entourage now encircled him. He and Dr. Jack Wheater were crouched over Baby Boy Stelling in his small incubator. The only visible parts of the baby were the left shoulder and chest. They had covered the remainder of the child with a series of sterile, disposable, paper drapes. The small chest had been prepared with a betadine solution to kill the bacteria on the skin. Simons and Wheater both perspired heavily as they wore surgical scrubs, covered by sterile O.R. gowns, as well as hats, masks, gloves, and shoe-covers. In addition, they stood directly beneath the heat lamps, which were focused on the baby to prevent hypothermia. Simons led Wheater through the procedure.

Wheater glided a stainless steel scalpel blade across the left posterior chest. He paused and applied a needle point cautery to the

points of bleeding, coagulating the small bleeders quickly and efficiently. He then opened a small incision into the chest cavity and
slid his finger inside in order to protect the lung from being injured
as he again applied the cautery unit, this time with a cutting current,
to divide the muscles between the fourth and fifth ribs. He placed a
small rib-spreader retractor in between the ribs and gently turned the
crank, spreading the ribs apart and exposing the lungs beneath. He
pushed the lung tissue aside and began dissection over the small pul-
satile aorta.

"Scissors," Wheater stated, holding his hand out with the palm
open, not taking his eyes off the operative field. His assistant placed
the scissors into his gloved hand in a position ready to use.

"Pick-ups," said Simons.

"Pick-ups," echoed Wheater. Each surgeon picked up on the thin
lining over the aorta, which provided the appropriate traction so the
tissue could be cut.

"What's that structure?" Simons asked as he pointed with the
instrument in his hand.

"The recurrent laryngeal nerve, sir," answered Wheater correctly.

"Very good. Let's leave it alone."

Wheater began gently dissecting out the ductus arteriosus, the
small connection between the pulmonary artery and the aorta.
Simons' comments were supportive. "Good . . . Careful . . . Gently
. . . Good."

"Tie," Wheater said holding out his pick-ups. A silk suture was
placed in his pick-ups, and he passed the tie around the ductus. He
then securely tied the silk suture down, occluding the patent connection and preventing further blood flow. He passed a second tie
around the duct before he divided it carefully between the two ties.
He oversewed each end of the cut ductus a second time to prevent
the chance of the vessel leaking.

"Good job," Simons reported.

They then placed a chest tube into the chest and closed. The ribs
were pulled together with suture, followed by a repair of the muscle
layers and finally closure of the skin.

Simons looked at the small child in front of him and shook his head. *Too bad the medicine failed to cure this one.* He looked around at the small crowd that had gathered to watch. *They gawk as we rescue this child they failed to heal. Oh well, who is better qualified anyway?* His arrogance clouded his ability to see the deeper irony—namely, that he had been asked to help save the very child he would have "sacrificed" just a week before.

◆ ◆ ◆

For the first time in a week, John Gentry arrived home earlier than Michael Simons. His daughters were awake, and although he had missed dinner with his family, he did get to tell them a story and kiss them good night. After he tucked his daughters in bed, he devoured a large plate of spaghetti with mushrooms and meat sauce that his wife had prepared three hours earlier.

As he ate, his mind drifted to the conversation he'd had with Matt Stone earlier in the day. *Matt's a nice guy. I feel bad about what I told him . . . But if Simons found out that I was talking about the research, I'm not sure he'd react with a great deal of sympathy.* He wasn't sure why he felt obligated to lie in order to cover for the man he was growing to hate. His actions surprised even himself.

Now as he had a chance to look back on it all, he wondered if the truth would really be so damaging. He wasn't sure he could keep covering up for Simons in the future. *Hopefully, it won't happen again. Soon I'll be free to say what I want to say.* The job at Fairfax General seemed to be opening up without a hitch—at least without any that he was aware of.

CHAPTER
24

Dr. Stone . . ." The chief of the division of general surgery, Dr. Samuel Fletcher, summoned Matt to the front of the room. Five other residents who had patients on the Morbidity and Mortality list sighed with relief. They were off the hook for the moment. Dr. Fletcher looked at the M. and M. list in front of him. "Present patient Stelling."

"Yes, sir," Matt responded. He stood up and walked to the front of the classroom. Because attendance was required, the conference was well attended by residents and attendings alike. Several others, who worked for the attendings in their labs, sat in the back to view the proceedings. Matt cleared his throat and began. His presentation was orderly and well rehearsed.

"The patient is a twenty-one-year-old white female, an unrestrained driver in a motor vehicle accident. She was involved in a head-on impact and had an extraction time of approximately twenty minutes. She had bent the steering column of the vehicle with her chest and had a head injury. She was unconscious at the scene and completely unresponsive to all stimuli. She was noted to be pregnant, approximately twenty-three weeks. With an initial blood pressure of sixty systolic, the aeromedical transport service flew her to our facility. While in flight, they resuscitated the patient with crystalloid IV fluid, and the paramedic placed a needle in the left chest because of hypotension and a presumed tension pneumothorax.

"On arrival to our E.R. she had a pressure of ninety systolic. Dr. Edwards entubated the patient and placed her on mechanical ventilation. The intern inserted a left chest tube, and initially only two hundred cc's of blood were obtained. The patient did have an air leak through the tube, indicating a lung injury. The physical exam was remarkable for her neuro exam which showed her pupils to be fixed and dilated and a Glasgow coma score of three. Her blood pressure remained approximately ninety, and her heart rate was one hundred and twenty. She had palpable rib fractures on the left. The rest of the physical exam showed her to be obviously pregnant, with her fundal height above the umbilicus. I used a doppler to access fetal heart tones, and they were present. A chest X-ray was obtained."

Matt stepped over to an overhead projector and snapped on the light. He then placed the X-ray film onto the lighted projector tray and projected the image of the chest film onto the screen at the front of the room. He stood back and looked at the film, then spoke as he pointed out the features of the X-ray. "This shows the left first through sixth rib fractures and the widened mediastinum. Also appreciated in this film, if you look close, is a left scapula fracture and a right clavicle fracture." Matt took the film down and returned to the podium.

"Once we saw that film, she was scheduled for an emergency aortogram to rule out a ruptured thoracic aorta. Neurosurgical and obstetrical consultations were called, and C.T. surgery was told about the aortogram. The plan was for an aortogram first, and if this was negative, to proceed with a C.T. scan of the head."

Matt paused and looked at his audience. There had been no interruptions for questions yet. Even with his pause, his audience was silent. Matt continued, "The patient had been given two units of blood after additional crystalloid fluid did not result in a rise in her blood pressure. Then suddenly, before we could get her up to the radiology suite for her aortogram, her blood pressure fell precipitously to a negligible number, and her chest tube began pouring out bright-red blood. We performed an emergency thoracotomy to initiate open heart massage and cross-clamp her aorta above the rupture. She was given six units of additional packed cells, four of which were pushed in after the aorta was cross-clamped. At that point, I listened for fetal heart tones and could hear a bradycardic fetal heart. The mother had remained unresponsive since arrival, so I performed an emergency c-section in the E.R. to try and salvage the baby." Matt stopped speaking.

"And?" prompted Dr. Fletcher.

"And the baby lived. The mother was pronounced dead a minute later," Matt responded solemnly.

"How long was the patient in our E.R. prior to the arrest?" The question came from the vascular surgery attending, Dr. Steve Shepherd.

"Approximately nineteen minutes from arrival until death," Matt replied confidently.

"How long from the time of the accident until arrival in our E.R.?" Shepherd shot back.

"One hour," answered Matt without hesitation.

"What is the pre-hospital mortality from a lacerated thoracic aorta? I assume that is the cause of death here?" The question was forwarded by Dr. Ed Barnes, a trauma attending.

"Yes, that is the presumed cause of death. Pre-hospital mortality is 85 percent." Matt had done his preparation well.

"What is the hospital survival for an E.R. thoracotomy in cases of blunt trauma?" asked Dr. Gant.

"Five percent at the highest. Some series have no survivors," Matt answered.

Fletcher spoke up next. "Do you think a thoracotomy is indicated for a blunt trauma patient when the mortality is so high?"

"Yes, sir, in certain cases when the patient comes in with a measurable pressure and then loses it while in the E.R. It would not be justified if the patient came in without a measurable blood pressure." Matt looked at his questioner directly when giving his answer.

Gant spoke up next. "I think Matt is to be commended at the rapidity of his decision-making when he was under fire. Most of us wouldn't have tried a c-section in the E.R."

Matt stood motionless and didn't smile. Rule number one was never to be too jovial when making a case presentation. It only stimulated more questioning from the audience. If possible, it was advisable to bring up something that the attendings could fight about among themselves, and thus take heat off the presenter. The comments had been fairly benign, as had the questioning. Matt thought he was going to get off easy. He turned and picked up the chest X-ray and slid it into the X-ray jacket. As he turned to walk back to his seat, Michael Simons spoke up from the back of the room.

"Not so fast, Stone. There are a few other issues here. Number one is the speed in which the general surgery team approached this potentially fatal problem. If you have an unstable patient, and you did, you should get the chest X-ray within the first five minutes of arrival, during your resuscitation. Then, if you see the wide mediastinum and the patient continues to have a low blood pressure, you should consider an emergency trans-esophageal echo to make the diagnosis. This can even be done in the O.R. with a team ready to do a thoracotomy."

Simons had stood up so that everyone could see him plainly. He was always intimidating, even to the attending staff. He added, "Your reactions and the handling of this case may be praised by the general surgery staff, but the cardiothoracic surgeon is certainly the expert in cases of thoracic aortic trauma, and I beg to differ!" He paused, then added, "I find your responses slow and inadequate. Your lax approach may well have cost this woman her life!"

Matt didn't defend himself. He knew he had done the best job possible under the circumstances. Talking back would only tend to add fuel to Simons' fire. Rule number two was never to bleed in front of the group. Blood only incites other sharks to attack. Senior residents often advised their junior colleagues, "If there is blood in the water, get out if you can." Matt nodded. "Good point," he said softly. He wanted to sit back down again and made one step to the right side of the podium when Simons spoke up again.

"And another thing! What kind of cowboy, independent surgery resident does c-sections in the E.R. without an attending present or without at least an O.B. staff person?" Simons paused but didn't give Matt a chance to reply before starting in again. "This kind of shoot-from-the-hip, make-it-up-as-you-go style will have you looking for work elsewhere! There's no place for high-risk, low-yield procedures like that without an attending present! That c-section may have well caused the final blood loss that made the patient unresuscitable!"

This time Matt responded sharply. "My attending staff knew about the patient and had gotten updates from the aeromedical staff when the patient arrived. As for O.B., they were paged several times but were tied up doing their own c-section. And as for the c-section, I didn't start that until the mother was clearly gone, with no blood pressure at all. At least we ended up with one live patient this way!" The resident staff was quiet. No one ever challenged Dr. Simons with a difference of opinion. Certainly never a resident!

Simons raised his voice to meet Stone's defense. "Your arrogance is blinding you, doctor! May I remind you that your first priority begins and ends with the mother! Not with the products of conception who will likely never survive without her!"

Matt made no comment. The residents in the room were quiet, their eyes on the M. and M. lists in front of them.

John Gentry, who sat on the back row near Simons, looked at the conference list too. He was certain that this Sam Stelling was the same one they had encountered at the F.F.P. Clinic just a week before her death. He shook his head, trying to make sense of it all. *The baby lived? Her baby survived? Just a week after we were going to use the fetus in a fatal experiment? No wonder Simons is upset. Perhaps he thinks that if people find out about this, they won't think so kindly about his research!* Gentry's thoughts were disturbed by Dr. Fletcher, who called the next resident.

"Dr. Nicely." He paused, reading over the list. "Present Mr. Dellinger."

For the moment, Matt Stone slipped off the hook.

◆ ◆ ◆

Adam Richards, M.D. sat down at his desk and began sifting through the charts in front of him. Most of the work consisted of merely checking the results of lab tests and initialing the papers he'd seen. Three of the charts were on women who'd come in for abortion counseling. Two of them were well into their second trimester and seemed to be good candidates for Simons' study. The third, a fourteen-year-old, had come in with her pregnancy and left after three hours, having had her uterus vacuumed free of the offending child. The child, a boy, had been ten weeks along and had been able to experience painful stimuli for two weeks by the time he was violently and suddenly destroyed.

Richards looked at the charted data before him. One patient, a girl named Vickie, had seemed anxious about the abortion but tremendously relieved when Richards told her that she was not as far along as she thought and that an abortion within the next two weeks would be fine. He explained to her that she would be put in the earliest available slot and then promptly scheduled her for ten days later. He looked over the chart carefully. He carefully whited out the date she'd given for her last menstrual period and substituted a date one month later. The ultrasound would be done to confirm the age of the fetus, but not until the patient was well sedated on the day of the planned abortion. *If the baby is going to be destroyed anyway, it might as well be of some benefit to science.*

Richards felt no remorse in his actions. In some dark way, the experiments provided a justification for the abortions. *This gives my business some real validity! Perhaps one day we can include patients who are having the abortions with knowledge of these experiments, so they will realize that their abortion was actually a positive thing—a beneficial contribution to science and eventually to the well-being of others.*

Richards picked up the last chart before him—a twenty-year-old university student who'd come in for a Norplant and found out she was pregnant. *She will get more than she bargained for from me!*

Just then his secretary's voice came through on the intercom. "Dr. Richards? Iris from Dr. Simons' office just called. She wanted to remind you of your dinner meeting with Dr. Simons at 7 at Georgio's."

"Nice of him to call himself," Richards muttered under his breath. Then, raising his voice, he replied, "Thanks, Arlene. I've got it on my calendar."

◆ ◆ ◆

"You wanted to see me, sir?" John Gentry stood in the doorway to Simons' plush office. Gentry had only been in the office once before in a year and a half.

"Yes, John. Have a seat," Simons replied, motioning to the leather couch along the wall. Above the couch was a large oil painting of Alexis Carrel, a surgeon who had been awarded the Nobel prize in 1912 for work on blood vessel anastomosis.

John looked at the impressive image surrounded by a large golden frame for a moment before sitting on the edge of the couch. Simons observed his employee looking at the artwork. "Do you know who that is?" questioned Simons.

"No, sir," replied Gentry as he shook his head.

"Alexis Carrel, a great pioneer in the field of vascular and transplant surgery, John." Simons paused. "He worked during the first decade of this century to lay a foundation that many have built upon. He was awarded the Nobel prize, John."

"I didn't know that, sir."

"John, you need to have great men to look up to in your life, even men from history, men who provide a model on which to base your life's dreams . . . men like Carrel, John." Simons turned away and looked towards the window beside his smooth mahogany desk. "I visualize goals for us, John. We are capable of no less than Alexis Carrel. He was a pioneer. We are pioneers, too."

John Gentry squirmed uncomfortably each time Simons repeated his name, like they were best friends. Simons continued, emphasizing John's name in nearly every sentence.

"John, I've always known that you were a man with great research talents. I have wanted you by my side for that very reason. Did you know that I felt that way, John?"

"I knew you respected my work, sir. Thank you," Gentry said, looking at the thick mauve carpet.

"I don't want to see you waste your research talents, John. We are on the verge of transforming the treatment of congenital heart disease as we know it. John, I want you to be in on this with me. Do you understand what I am saying?"

"I think so, sir," Gentry lied.

"I could not in good conscience ever allow you to underutilize your talents. John, if the option ever came your way to work outside the area of your expertise, I would be forced out of my goodwill to prevent you from making a critical judgmental error." Simons spun around and looked at John, who raised his eyes to meet Simons'. "I would do this as your friend, certainly," Simons added. "Am I making myself clear, John?"

"Yes, sir," Gentry answered solemnly.

"I have an obligation as your mentor to use whatever means are at my disposal to prevent you from making errors in judgment that will certainly mar your otherwise bright future in research. My intentions are without blemish, I assure you."

Gentry didn't know how to respond. He continued looking at the man in front of him, not knowing how Simons knew of his plans to change jobs. *Mentor! Did he say mentor?* Gentry felt suddenly ill. He stood to his feet and excused himself. "If that is all, sir, I must be going," he said quietly as he headed for the door.

Gentry walked straight to the men's room and splashed some water on his face. *He must have talked with Martinez! Maybe if I call him and explain . . .* He looked at his face in the mirror. His reflection looked sallow, his expression blank. *Lori's not going to like this. She's not going to like this at all!*

◆ ◆ ◆

The rest of Matt's day went a little easier. At least no one else threatened his job in front of a large crowd. He managed to throw off most of what Simons had said. He knew he had done the right thing. He just wished some of his own general surgery attendings would have stood up and agreed with him. He understood that he would need to keep a low profile around Simons for the next few months. He could not give him an excuse to carry out his threat. He definitely couldn't let him find out that he was prying into his business to find out what he was doing at the F.F.P. Clinic! Matt headed home at 8 P.M. He was greeted by Mike, who acted as if he hadn't been fed in a month.

"Hold on, boy!" Matt yelled at the large tan dog. "I'll get you something to eat." Matt looked at the dog dish beside the door. Empty. *That dog eats more than I do!* Matt unlocked the door and went into his small apartment. He pulled the dish inside, poured in a hefty portion of dry dog food, and moistened it with water from the kitchen sink. He put it down in front of Mike, who began noisily devouring the food. "Easy, boy. Don't choke! It's not going anywhere." Matt's words were ignored by the focused animal.

Matt grabbed a Coke from the refrigerator and sat down on the side of his bed. He definitely needed an emotional lift, and he knew just where to get it. He picked up the phone and dialed Linda. *Ring. Ring. Ring.* No answer! *She must be—*

"Hello."

"Hi, Linda."

"Hi, honey," Linda replied. Matt felt better already. "How's your day? I almost thought you'd call me after M. and M." She paused. "How'd it go?"

"Well, the presentation went fine. The general surgeons asked a few benign questions, and I thought I was home free. I was just about to sit down when Simons went ballistic! I felt like a piece of meat in the teeth of a pit bull. He only let go long enough to get a bigger bite."

"What did he say to you, anyway?" asked Linda.

"Basically that I was responsible for the patient's death and that my c-section may have very well killed her."

"That's crazy! What did you say?"

"I made a brief defense and told him that she was already dead before I did the c-section. But because a resident has no place trading words with Dr. Simons, I kept quiet mostly. He will win at any cost. I'm glad I shut up when I did. You should have seen him! He was steaming! I'm not sure why he got so worked up about it. I could be wrong, but he acted like he was mad at me for doing the c-section. It was almost strange, like he had a personal vendetta against me. After I sat down, he didn't say another word. I hadn't heard him speak up in M. and M. conference for months . . . until today."

"That's strange. I wish I could have been there. I'd have told him—"

"Right!" interrupted Matt. "I'm sure you'd have put the little man right in his place. And I'd be looking for another job, too!" Matt laughed. It felt good to just get some of his thoughts off his chest. Linda wasn't laughing. Matt stretched out on his bed. "And how was your day?"

"Pretty fair. I did some work as *The Weathervane* advisor. I had another interesting conversation with Anne Caudill too," Linda remarked. She paused, thinking about how best to tell Matt what she knew.

"Well? Aren't you going to clue me in?"

"Does the name Sam Stelling mean anything to you?" Linda stated in a voice sounding like a prosecution attorney's.

"Sure, but I didn't give her name to you. I never mention names. It's an issue of confidentiality," Matt countered.

"I know. She's the girl that you did the c-section on."

"How did you know that?"

"She attended the school here. She was Anne Caudill's best friend."

"You're joking! I never knew—"

"Neither did I. That's not the end of the story though," Linda said smugly. "Anne knows who the father is."

"That means the baby might not be an orphan after all," Matt responded. "The social worker told me that the baby would be a ward of the state. As long as no one came forward as the father, they had no way of knowing anything—"

"Matt," interrupted Linda, "the baby's father is Layton Redman."

Matt was silent as the words sunk in. "What?" Matt sat upright. "Layton Redman? The candidate for governor?"

"That's the one!" Linda put heavy emphasis on the last word.

"Does anyone else know this?"

"I don't think so. She told me in confidence and asked that it go no further than you," said Linda.

"But the social worker should be told. This changes everything! If what you say can be proven, the baby isn't an orphan after all!" Matt exclaimed.

"Matt, if what I'm saying can be proved in some way, and the media finds out, I don't think we'll have a three-way race for governor any longer."

Matt slapped his thigh. "I hadn't even thought about that."

"Can this sort of thing be proven, Matt?" Linda asked.

"Well, if Redman would consent to testing, it could be proven with a blood test. A blood type would give some idea, but DNA typing would seal it," Matt answered. He paced around his bed, stretching the phone cord as he went.

"Matt, you'll have to promise me you'll keep this quiet until Anne gives us the liberty to share it."

"Oh, man . . . I mean . . . I guess . . . Uh, sure . . . I won't tell anyone until I hear the okay from you." Matt stopped pacing, sighed, and stretched out on the bed again. "Say, I didn't tell you . . . I talked to John Gentry about Simons and whether he is doing research with Richards. Gentry works in Simons' lab. If anyone knows what goes on in Dr. Simons' lab, it's him. He acted kind of weird. He asked me how I ever got such an idea. I told him that I had a friend who saw Simons at Richards' clinic. He said it must have been a mistake and that they are *not* doing research together. It was obvious the guy was uncomfortable and didn't want to talk. Either he was in a hurry, or he just didn't want to tell me anything."

"You don't think this has anything to do with Simons' attack in the conference this morning, do you?"

"No. I specifically asked him not to tell Simons that I'd asked about him. Gentry's a good guy. He wouldn't tell Simons that." Matt hoped he knew Gentry as well as he thought he did.

"I hope you're right. Don't let me make you paranoid," Linda added and then changed the subject. "Say, are you still going to be home Tuesday night?"

"I think so."

"Well, maybe I'll stop in after I visit the abortion clinic."

Matt's silence was noticeable as he wondered whether Linda intended to do some snooping and maybe get herself out on a limb.

Linda added, "I'm confirming where their property line stops, remember? For the pro-life rally. We don't want to step on their property."

"I remember," Matt replied as he wiped his forehead. "I'll wait up for you."

"I'll talk to you before then. I'm going to be pretty late. I don't really want to hang out there during the daytime."

Matt's beeper went off. "Man! This thing always goes off when I'm talking to you!"

"You're so cute when you whine," Linda teased.

"Very funny. I'd better call in. I'll talk to you tomorrow."

"Okay, doctor. Bye, Matt."

"Linda?" Matt spoke quickly, hoping to catch her before she hung up. He did.

"Yes?"

"I love you." He meant it.

"I love you, too." She meant it, too.

◆ ◆ ◆

"A toast . . ." Dr. Simons raised his glass, and Dr. Richards lifted his drink in response. "To the completion of our project." Both men swallowed a healthy portion of the Bordeaux in their glasses. Their mood was upbeat. They were seated at a back booth at Georgio's. They had eaten calamari and linguini, fresh salad, followed by manicotti with a vegetarian sauce, fresh bread, and two slices of Georgio's amaretto cheesecake. They emptied the bottle of Bordeaux, and Richards ordered a second.

Simons speculated about the future. "I can see a day when we will have a whole new approach to all of medicine, not just congenital heart disease. The new administration has lifted all the barriers to our research. Soon we will have fetal organ banks . . . hearts, livers, pancreas tissue for the diabetic, ovaries for the infertile, brain tissue for Parkinson's disease patients. Who knows—maybe we can find cures for other congenital problems! I can see the day where we will prescribe a pregnancy for a woman with a failing kidney or liver or with diabetes, and then use her offspring's tissue to treat the mother's diseases. We are likely to get a closer genetic match that way. We are helping open up a whole new wave of uses for fetal tissue. No longer will we need to waste the one point five million abortions each year. You and I are riding the crest of the wave, Adam. We are front-runners!"

Adam nodded, smiling as much from the buzz he felt from the alcohol as from the speech he heard from Simons. "When will we complete this stage of our work?" he asked.

"We are near an end point. I would like to have forty pump runs in my series before I submit my data for publication. I need to check the final numbers, but I think I only need three or four more."

Adam could hardly believe it. *Have we really done that many?* "I found another two today. I conveniently put them off for a week or two so their 'donation' will be mature."

"Excellent."

"I'll call your office as soon as I have firm dates," Richards reported.

Georgio placed a second bottle of wine on the table after removing the cork. Simons excused himself to find the restroom. He was slightly dizzy upon standing and thought that he'd had enough of the spirited liquid for that night. With Simons gone, Richards drank an additional glass without pausing and then poured another to slowly sip in front of Simons. If he was going to celebrate, he intended to do it with style.

◆ ◆ ◆

Tony slept with his head on the desk in front of him. He'd been writing an essay on why he wanted to be a parent, another requirement laid out by the adoption agency application. Fourteen, count 'em, crumpled-paperwad essay drafts were on the floor and in the circular file. By the time he'd gotten away from his second job, he'd already started yawning. By the time he'd gotten to ten crumpled papers, he shut his eyes for short naps. Now he had three sentences written on his fifteenth attempt and was out cold . . . down for the count.

Carol gently pulled his hand up, encouraging him to stand. "Come on, honey. Let's go to bed. It's after 12."

"Hrrmmmph" was all Tony could manage. He traversed the small apartment holding his wife's hand, with his eyes closed.

In two minutes he was asleep in their bed. Carol managed to pull his pants off but gave up on the rest. *Oh, well,* she sighed, *I guess that's what irons are for.* In a few more minutes Carol was asleep, too.

CHAPTER
25

ELLEN Fischer gently unwrapped the tape securing the small endotracheal tube in Baby Boy Stelling's mouth. The tube had been inserted just moments after his birth and had provided the means to deliver the mechanical breaths from the ventilator into his maturing lungs. For the last few hours, Boy Stelling had gotten no mechanical support from the ventilator. He was doing all the work himself. He would still need oxygen, but at least he appeared strong enough to breathe it in on his own.

Ellen wore gloves, as all caregivers did, in the N.I.C.U. The tape stuck to the neonatologist's gloves, and she shook her hand quickly to dislodge a segment from the tip of her finger. "I'll just have to go home with this baby." she exclaimed. "I'll be stuck to him for life!" She laughed. It was a nice thought anyway. A few weeks before, no one would have thought that Baby Boy Stelling would ever leave the hospital. Now that possibility was one step closer to reality. The tape battle won, Dr. Fischer slipped the tube out of the little infant's trachea. She listened carefully, first with her ears, then with a stethoscope. *No obstruction!* She placed an oxygen hood over the baby's head. It was made of clear plexiglass, so she could still view the infant's face.

"If you do all right with this, little one, we'll give you something to eat tomorrow." Dr. Fischer spoke softly to the infant. "You'd like that, wouldn't you? Yes, you would; you would like that! Look at you!

Breathing on your own like a big boy!" Up until now the baby had been fed through the veins, giving his "gut" a chance to mature. Ellen looked up at the intern who had appeared at her side. She wasn't embarrassed by the baby talk she used to communicate with the patient.

"Dr. Deavers wants us to meet at the X-ray view board to start rounds," the sleepy-looking physician reported.

"Good. I'll be right there," she said. She then looked at the nurse assigned to Baby Boy Stelling. "Get a set of arterial blood gases on him in about thirty minutes. I want to see how well he's breathing off this ventilator."

"Okay," the nurse responded. Baby Boy Stelling was the only one she had responsibility for, as he still required one-to-one care. In the next few days, if he improved, his care would be easier and his category upgraded.

"We'll be around in a few minutes on rounds with Dr. Deavers if you have questions."

"Thanks, Dr. Fischer."

Ellen Fischer picked up a social work consult form on her way to the X-ray view board. *If this baby might really survive, it's time to get someone involved to figure out what to do with him!*

◆ ◆ ◆

Layton Redman set the *Fairfax Herald* on his desktop. Their latest tracking poll placed him solidly in the front of a three-man race, with the support of 54 percent of the eligible voters. That trend had been gradually rising since he'd entered the campaign six months before. Obviously people were sick of party politics as usual. Redman felt that he represented a departure from the established system, but he kept his hand in the party format just enough to swing a few key nominations from within both the Democratic and Republican Parties. Now Redman faced a decision. Should he relax and go off the attack that had boosted him to the front of the pack, shifting into a neutral or defensive mode and sliding into victory?

Rose Drake, one of his regional campaign coordinators, knocked on his already open door. She smiled.

Layton looked up. "Hi, Rose. Come on in. Have you seen the headlines?" he asked, handing her the paper.

"They do seem to like you, Layton," she said as she took his hand warmly and held it for a moment.

He noticed her perfume and stared for a moment into her blue eyes. She seemed particularly striking to him. He broke off his stare and her warm handshake.

"Y-yes, it looks like we might just coast down victory lane this time," Layton responded.

"Perhaps more than you think, Layton. Look at this," Drake said as she handed him a small folder.

Layton had stood to greet her, but he sat back down and began to read the two-page, signed testimonial in front of him. His expression became stern, and he pushed his face closer to the paper. "Where did you get this?" he asked as he finished scanning the short document.

"That doesn't matter, Layton. One of your faithful followers uncovered the story and tracked down the girl just this past weekend."

"Oh man!" Redman sighed and leaned back in his chair. "Have we released this yet?"

"Not yet. We have an aggressive member of the news print media in Louisville who is ready to release the story if we give the okay. The girl said she is willing to be interviewed for TV if that's what they want."

"Careful. I don't want it getting out that we dug this up."

"Don't worry, Layton. I've made sure that the media and the girl won't even know we're in the loop," Rose said with a sultry smile. "Our Louisville contact has been very cooperative up to this point. It will appear that he uncovered the story himself."

"This could potentially knock out one of my opponents and make it a two-man race," Layton said, putting his hands behind his head. "Still, I don't know, Rose, that's pretty private stuff . . . Besides, do we know it's the truth?"

"That may be irrelevant, Layton. It's the public's perception of truth that's important, you know. Besides, no one will know that we found and delivered this girl to the media hounds."

Layton sat silently for a moment, his eyes looking at Rose. She could read his mind.

"Don't worry about it, Layton. You are the man to run this state! The public will stand behind you, even if the opposite camps do yell, 'Foul play!' No one will ever be able to pin this one on you," she hissed. Rose came over and took his hand again. "We're good at this, you know?" Layton kept his seat behind the desk. Rose stepped around and sat in front of him on the desk, carefully retrieving her hot little story before she sat down on his desktop in front of him.

"Let's do it," Layton said, caressing the hand that was already in his.

Rose slowly got up and sauntered towards the door, tightly clutching the small folder. "Better check tomorrow's paper, big boy. I'm sure you won't want to miss it." With that she was out the door.

◆ ◆ ◆

Richards arrived late for his morning office hours. He had to do a D & C (dilation and curettage) on a young patient at St. Christopher's Hospital. Every time he posted a case over there, he felt the eyebrows of the administration rise. They had given him strict instructions when granting him hospital privileges: no non-therapeutic abortions. Only therapeutic abortions were allowed, and then only in select cases. It would seem that Richards would want to seek privileges elsewhere, but surprisingly, he had few conflicts with the Catholic administration. Obviously, they knew nothing about his real work at the F.F.P. Clinic.

The night before, he had been called by a young girl who was in tears. She had a fever of 104 degrees and nausea and vomiting. He had performed a suction curettage abortion forty-eight hours earlier. Apparently he hadn't gotten it all out, and now infection of the remaining tissue had set in. He needed to scrape out the lining of the uterus to remove the missed tissue and relieve the sepsis. He needed a hospital for this one, as the patient needed to stay in the hospital for IV antibiotics. He got around the St. Christopher's Hospital regulations by telling the O.R. that the girl had a "missed abortion," implying that she had spontaneously lost a pregnancy but hadn't passed out all of the tissue. They had no reason to suspect differently and allowed him to do his case at 7 A.M., pushing back other elective cases. He finished rounds and rushed to the office by 9, forty-five minutes late.

Richards picked up the chart in the rack beside the door of his first exam room. *Hmmm. Thirty-eight-year-old female seeking abortion.* He glanced at the reported L.M.P. (Last Menstrual Period). He quickly calculated that she must already be about twenty weeks along. He entered the room. "Hello, Ms. Johnson. I'm Dr. Richards."

The patient had been in a paper gown for forty-five minutes waiting for him. She was cold and not in a very good mood. "Might think of turning up the heat in this place if you're going to make people wait without their clothes on," the patient snapped without saying hello.

"I'm sorry about the wait, ma'am. I had an emergency over at the hospital." Richards turned his attention immediately back to the chart and shifted gears. "I've looked over the information you've given my staff. Any previous abortions?"

"No."

"Any previous anesthetics?"

"No."

"Any health problems during this pregnancy?"

"No," the patient responded curtly, not wanting to offer any information that Richards didn't directly elicit.

"Have you read the information my nurse gave you about the risks of abortion?"

"Yes." The patient looked irritated. "Can we just do this and get it over with?"

Dr. Richards stepped closer to the woman, who appeared older than her stated age. "Please lie down on the table." He carefully examined her abdomen with his hands, noting the fundal height and the position of the baby's head and buttocks. He listened with a doppler and easily located the heart tones up out of the pelvis. *She's farther along than she thinks. She'll make a nice addition to our little experiment.*

"Do you have any questions about the procedure?"

"No."

"Then you may get dressed. Please stop at the desk as you leave to schedule your abortion."

"Wait! Aren't you going to do it today?" the woman responded with some distress.

"No. It is customary to wait for our first available time slot. This way you will have a chance to read the literature we gave you during this visit. The next time, we will do the procedure and answer your questions."

"I don't have any questions. I read everything while I waited. Can't we just get this done?" the woman pleaded. "I'm already showing!"

"My exam shows you to be only eighteen weeks along," Richards lied. "You still have plenty of time to have the procedure without any difficulties." Then, as if to prove his time slots were full, he pulled out a second scheduling book from the pocket of his white coat. "Look, if it will make any difference to you, I'll work you in after our regular hours next Friday," he said with an air of compassion.

"That's almost ten days!" The woman, who had been gesturing wildly with both hands, plopped her hands back onto her lap and sighed. "If that's the best you can do . . . I guess I don't have many options."

"I'll see you next Friday, Ms. Johnson."

Richards exited the room and adjusted the date of the last menstrual period to fit the age he had assigned to the fetus. The ultrasound the next Friday would report a different age for Simons, but Richards would continue to adjust the chart ages in order to stay well within the legal abortion limits.

◆ ◆ ◆

Michael Simons entered his office without saying hello to Iris. But as he breezed by her desk, Iris called out, "I have a new consult for you." Simons took the form from her outstretched hand without talking. He just walked into his office and shut the door.

Simons glanced at the consult request sheet perfunctorily and put the sheet aside. He then turned and picked the sheet up again and reread the request. He was being asked to talk to a mother of a baby with hypoplastic left heart syndrome about treatment options *before the baby was born!* Evidently an ultrasound had been done, and the technician picked up the abnormality and referred the lady on to the pediatric cardiologists, who repeated the ultrasound and confirmed the diagnosis. The baby was due in another ten weeks.

Could this be the one? Could we be ready with an abortion donor transplant to give this little baby a new heart? Simons looked at the timetable and then at his own calendar. Approval for new procedures took time. Even if he presented his data from the F.F.P. Clinic within the next four weeks and it was received with overwhelming approval, he would still face the institution's review board, and that could take weeks. Simons looked at his calendar again. He thought that the least he could do was to press forward at a faster pace. *Perhaps I can swing it after all.* He decided to return to the F.F.P. Clinic that night to examine the heart he'd "received" the day before. If he could get the microscopic comparison done tonight, perhaps he could shave an additional day off the total time until they were ready to do the first transplant.

Dr. Simons got up and left his office as quickly as he'd come. He handed the consult sheet to Iris as he passed her desk. "Get this woman an appointment to talk to me ASAP."

"I already did that, sir," Iris answered mechanically.

Simons hadn't asked for a reply. He scurried out the door and didn't hear her anyway.

◆ ◆ ◆

As the social worker to the N.I.C.U., Debbie Swindol was intimately involved in the progression of the infants from the N.I.C.U. to the floor and beyond. She often helped coordinate special home health care needs for the babies once they were "graduates" from the N.I.C.U. and helped the parents with any special training they might need to care for their special infants. She also helped find appropriate foster homes for orphan children and occasionally helped facilitate an adoption link.

Today she reviewed a new case, that of Baby Boy Stelling, whose mom was dead and whose father was listed as unknown. She needed to find out how easy the father would be to locate. If no father could be found, and no one came forward as the next of kin, the baby would be a ward of the state and handled by the state's adoption agency. Her job was to contact any relative of Stelling's that may be around and to find out if anyone knew the father's identity.

She had pulled the mother's chart and reviewed the data. *Only child . . . Both parents were only children . . . Both parents and grandparents dead . . . So much for any living relatives.*

Now she focused on possible identification of the father. She knew from past experience that unless someone came forward willingly, it was too complex an issue to get everyone accused of being the so-called father appropriately tested in order to determine the truth. The bottom line was that no one could be forced into genetic testing without being willing to do so, or without a court order.

She looked at the mother's chart again to see which physicians had dealt with her. She would begin searching for clues to the father's identity by questioning the doctors and the aeromedical crew who brought the mother in. *Was anybody with the patient in the E.R.? Who was notified of her death? Did anyone call for information about the patient?* She thought that likely the search would be unfruitful, and that the baby would be quickly declared a ward of the state. *Probably better off that way. The father probably doesn't care anyway; otherwise he would have shown some interest in his son by now.*

Debbie checked the signatures on Sam Stelling's admit note. Matt Stone. Charlie Edwards. Sheila Lewis. She scratched a quick note and determined to call them in the morning.

◆ ◆ ◆

Evening came and went without a supper break for Michael Simons. He had never lacked for a love of his work . . . or for himself, for that matter. At 9:30 he ate a candy bar on the way to the Fairfax Family Planning Clinic, a practice he wouldn't let himself do for the first two years he owned his Porsche. Now, although he still worshiped his car, he had relaxed enough to eat a bite or drink a cup of coffee (covered, of course) on his way to and from work.

Now he sat in the small procedure research room at the back of

Richards' clinic, reviewing each pump run that they'd completed to this date. He compiled all of the information on several summary sheets that he'd placed on a stack in front of him. He was nearing an end point. All he needed was several more cases and the data from the microscopic analysis of the donor specimens.

Simons enjoyed being alone in the building. The clean-up crew had even been gone for over an hour. He liked the solitude. No one was around to distract him with compliments.

Simons carefully put a glass slide on the microscope that sat on the desk. On it he had prepared sections of the cardiac muscle from the heart he'd taken so stealthily from the last aborted specimen they'd used. He strained to see the details. He flipped to the high-power lens. There were very few differences between this and the mature baby hearts he'd studied previously. He could see fetal red blood cells within microscopic blood vessels feeding the muscle.

Time escaped quickly. It was soon already past 11 P.M. Although he was on call, he had hoped to get a full night's rest before his open heart cases in the morning. *Just a few more minutes*. Simons placed another slide on the microscope stand.

◆ ◆ ◆

Linda Baldwin waited until she was sure everyone would be away from the F.F.P. Clinic. As she drove towards Fairfax in the dark, she wondered why she had volunteered for this job anyway. She knew why, of course—a chance to see Matt Stone later. As she got out of her car, which she parked in the adjacent shopping center parking lot, she again wondered why she had been so quick to offer her services. *This whole place gives me the creeps! The darkness doesn't help*. She walked to the back of the building, carrying a long measuring tape. *Let's see . . . Gary said that the city plot showed that the property line of the clinic ran only a hundred feet from the back of the building. That would put it right out in the parking lot somewhere*. Richards' building actually sat in the corner of a bigger parking lot for the adjacent shopping center. Linda looked around at the other shops. *How convenient! Stop in and pick up some groceries, get your hair done, and get an abortion, all in one place!* She shuddered at her own sarcasm.

In order to know precisely how close the pro-lifers could come without actually being on Richards' property, Linda planned to put down a few broad chalk marks on the pavement. First she needed to figure out just where the line would fall. She decided to start at the back door and measure it off. She didn't even notice the black Porsche parked in the corner by the building.

◆ ◆ ◆

Simons' digital pager vibrated, indicating a message had come in. "111-34561." Simons looked at the beeper. "@#$%#!" The "111" stood for a STAT emergency call. *Wheater must need me. He never gives me that code unless it's absolutely imperative! I can call from the car.* He hastily picked up the papers in front of him, not bothering to put them into his briefcase. He took his briefcase in one hand and the papers in the other. Once he got to the back door, he had to balance the papers under the same arm he used to carry his briefcase. With the papers grasped precariously, he swung open the door and bolted for his car.

◆ ◆ ◆

Linda knelt beside the back door to begin her measurement. Suddenly the back door flew open, scaring her into eliciting a short, shrill gasp. She surprised the man, who had been carrying an armload of papers and a briefcase, and he tripped with a not-so-comical nosedive over Linda's back and onto the pavement. The man hardly lost a beat; he jumped to his feet and gathered his papers. Other than a look that in the darkness appeared to be embarrassment and fear, the man communicated neither apology nor anger. Within a few seconds, and before Linda had recovered enough to speak, the man disappeared. Other than her own scream, she had also been silent. She had rolled onto her side upon impacting the man, and now as he jumped into his car, she realized she was lying on what must have been one of the papers he carried. She picked up the paper, crawled to her knees, and stood up. She squinted at the car and yelled, "Hey, mister! You forgot something!" As she shouted, she noted the license plate of the black Porsche: "HEARTS." The car sped away, leaving a quickly fading cloud of exhaust.

◆ ◆ ◆

Simons heard the girl yelling behind him as he sped away. He couldn't make out her words, but he was sure she was angry at him for knocking her down like that. Or was she already on the ground? Why would she have been on the ground outside Richards' clinic? *Probably drunk! @#$@ college students!* He wasn't about to stop. He was sure she didn't get a good look at him, and he didn't think she was hurt. *$#@%!* Simons hadn't been that scared in a long time.

Simons picked up his car phone to answer his page. His hands were still shaking a minute later when he put the receiver back in its cradle.

◆ ◆ ◆

Linda stood in the parking lot staring at the receding car. *Simons! That was Michael Simons! . . . At the clinic again!* Linda shook her head. She could hardly believe that she hadn't seen his car earlier. She knew about his car and his license plate from her discussions with Matt. *Wait until he hears about this!* Linda folded the piece of paper and shoved it into her jeans pocket without looking at it.

She quickly stepped off one hundred feet from the back door of the clinic and made a mark on the pavement. She put a loose stone beside the chalk mark in case it rained and washed the mark away. Her estimate was long, if anything. She was too spooked to stick around long enough to make an absolutely precise measurement.

In a few minutes she was on her way to Matt's apartment. Folded neatly in her jeans pocket, unknown to her, was a summary sheet of Simons' latest project at the F.F.P. Clinic.

CHAPTER
26

MATT Stone was in a hurry. He wanted to take part in Life Chain, a portion of the pro-life rally that was to take place Saturday afternoon. First he had made rounds on his own service, then he went to Grand Rounds, the weekly required surgical conference that included all subspecialties. One of the plastic surgeons had given an update on his work with reconstructive maxillofacial surgery. Then, just when Matt thought he was going to escape for the afternoon, he was paged by Debbie Swindol, a social worker for the N.I.C.U. *What could she possibly need?*

"Could I meet with you for a few minutes sometime today?" she had asked sweetly after Matt answered his page.

Matt looked at his watch. The rally had already started. "I guess so. How about right now? I was on my way out the door, but . . ."

"I'm sorry to hold you up. It won't take very long. I just wanted to ask you a few questions. Do you know where my office is?"

"I think so."

"Right outside the double doors leading to the N.I.C.U. on the fourth floor."

"On my way."

A few minutes later Matt stood in her office. He looked at the brightly colored walls. A large bulletin board covered one of them. On it were the photographs of literally hundreds of N.I.C.U. graduates.

"Thank you for coming on such short notice." She looked at him as he gazed at the pictures. "These are all my little friends I've met over the past two years on this job."

"Wow." Matt looked at one photo about halfway down the wall, a boy wearing a cowboy uniform. "Is this Evan Young?" Matt asked. "I remember him from when I rotated through on pediatric surgery. I thought he'd never graduate."

"That's what's so special about my board here. These babies all beat the odds. They inspire me. When I see what they've been through, the nit-picky problems I have are easier to put into perspective."

"Definitely." Matt continued to scan the wall.

"What I'm really after is some information. I'm trying to find out who Baby Boy Stelling's father is."

Matt stopped surveying the pictures and looked straight at the social worker. He was taken back a bit. *What does she know? Does she know that I know?*

"I'm asking you because you were there the night his mother came in. Was there anyone in the car with her? Did anyone come to see her in the E.R.?"

Matt was getting the picture. "She was alone in the car. No one ever came to the E.R. looking for her. The admitting data said she was single."

"Oh . . . That will make this meeting short. You don't have any idea, then?" Debbie asked, closing the folder in front of her.

Matt didn't know what to say. He would not tell an outright lie. He hesitated, then spoke. "I just heard a pretty reliable rumor about the father, but I was told the information in confidence by someone who knows a person who was a good friend of the mother. Evidently the mother, Samantha Stelling, asked that no one be told about this." He stopped and looked at Debbie.

"The father doesn't have to take responsibility for the child. We can arrange an adoption if that's what he'd like. No one is trying to pin a rap on anyone, if that's his beef."

"I—I don't think the father even knows the child exists," Matt said hesitantly.

"Did he know about the pregnancy?" the social worker questioned.

"I think so," Matt responded.

"Does he know that Sam Stelling is dead?"

"I'm pretty sure he knows that," Matt added.

"Dr. Stone, I don't know all of the implications of why the mother didn't want the word about the child getting out, but if the father knew about the pregnancy, then I would think that he should at least be told about his son. It's not like we're letting everyone else in on this and betraying Sam's wishes. This is the father we're talking about here. Doesn't he have some right to know that he's a dad?"

Debbie Swindol's arguments were good ones. Matt hadn't seen it that way before.

"I—I don't know," Matt stumbled. "I told the person who told me that the information would go no farther."

"Dr. Stone, what we're dealing with here is medical confidentiality. The information we get about patients, including all the info about their illnesses and who their family is, is strictly confidential. That would seem to be in the best interest of the involved parties. What I'm asking could benefit the child. Also . . . well, if I were the father, I'd certainly like to know."

Matt sighed. He knew she was right. He looked at her and said, "Look, you've got to promise me that if I tell, you won't spread this any farther than absolutely necessary."

"Of course."

Matt took a deep breath. "The father is Layton Redman."

◆ ◆ ◆

Layton Redman got up early and jogged as far as the paper box. He was anxious to see the headlines. When he got back to the house, he flipped on his coffee maker and took the rubber band off of the newspaper. He bypassed the first page and looked at the state and local news section.

Accusations Rock Nelson's Camp

Tina Richardson, an actress and long-time supporter of Dean Nelson, candidate for governor, has come forward claiming to be Nelson's long-time lover. Nelson denies the charges. Nelson, the married father of two , has been running number two in the polls.

"Ludicrous!" replied Nelson when asked to confirm or deny the accusation. Not so, claims his accuser, who further stated that she'd aborted Nelson's child.

Redman studied the article with interest. He slowly read every word. There was no mention of the Redman campaign, even in a good light. *That's fine with me. Better not to be mentioned at all when dirt like this is being dug up.* It would appear that the accusations came from a source outside Redman's camp. *Just the way we planned it! I think I'll see to it that Rose Drake gets her own private reward from me for this one.*

The candidate plopped the paper down and carried his mug of coffee to the bathroom. He had gotten the paper even before he'd shaved. He filled the sink with hot water and washed his face. Redman stared at himself in the mirror. He began to think about the inevitable questions that would surface in response to the news story. *How will I respond when the accusations of mud-slinging come? And they will come, no doubt about that! I'll deny it! They have no link between us and the story, anyway. The press will believe me. And the public will follow along if I play my cards correctly. Some may think I'm playing dirty politics and won't believe my denial. Oh, well; better to be accused of mud-slinging than infidelity.*

Redman shaved, showered, and dressed. He needed to meet his staff for a luncheon prior to an afternoon radio interview in Louisville. He smiled at himself in the mirror as he prepared to leave the house. It looked like things were definitely going his way.

◆ ◆ ◆

The pro-life demonstration went off beautifully. It had been a coordinated effort of twelve churches from in and around Fairfax, including the fellowship that Linda Baldwin attended. They formed a Life Chain, a human chain that stretched from Richards' clinic on down Centerville Road and all the way down to the Taft University athletic stadium. To say that a thousand people were involved in the chain would have been a conservative estimate. All the signs participants carried were positive. There were no inflammatory statements about murder or killing. The folks from Linda's church were lined up directly adjacent to Richards' clinic as had been planned, with the line of protesters standing just off his property line. Each church had been assigned anywhere from several hundred yards up to a half-mile stretch, depending on the size of the congregation. Along the line of people, each linked to the other with held hands, were families, singles, children, and grandparents.

Linda looked for Matt Stone in vain. She knew he'd be late. She didn't know he'd miss it altogether. The event started at 10 A.M. and ended at 1 P.M. No Matt. *Oh well,* she thought, *at least we have a date for this afternoon.*

◆ ◆ ◆

Matt's visit with the social worker hadn't been his last interruption. His intern had missed rounds that morning because of stomach flu. When Matt saw him, the man looked pale as a sheet. He obviously wasn't feeling well and promptly obeyed Matt's instruction to go to the E.R. to get a few liters of IV fluid. Matt had nearly forgotten about him until he received a page just as he was crossing Main Street. *The E.R.! What do they want? I'm not on for emergencies today!* Matt turned around and walked back to the main lobby, where he called the E.R.

"E.R. Mrs. Robbins here."

"This is Matt Stone. I was paged."

"Yes, Dr. Stone. Eddie Bryan is down here asking to see you. The E.R. physician thinks you should see him too."

"Okay. I'll be there in a minute." Matt hung up the phone and followed the blue line to the E.R.

When he arrived in the E.R., Matt found his intern lying on a stretcher in the back of the area. "What's going on here, doctor?" Matt asked with a smile.

"Belly pain. Started here and ended up here after I came down for my IV," the young physician said as he pointed to his right lower abdomen.

Matt gently touched the young man's abdomen on the left side, avoiding the area that he'd reported the pain in. "This hurt?"

"Not too much."

Matt moved slowly to the other parts of the abdomen, examining the right lower quadrant last. Matt didn't need to ask any further questions to make a diagnosis.

"Ooh! Now you've got the spot." Eddie winced as the chief resident touched his right lower abdomen.

"So, what have you got?" Matt asked.

"Doesn't the questioning stop when you're the patient?" Eddie smiled weakly, then answered, "Appendicitis."

"Correct."

"I was afraid so. You've helped me do at least a half-dozen of these myself in the last two months, so I know what you can do. Will you stay and do the surgery?" The intern didn't look well at all.

"Sure. Did they get any labs?"

"My white count is eighteen thousand. Urinalysis negative."

"Good work, doctor. I'll call the trauma attending on call. Gant's taking general surgery calls too. You'll be fine."

"Thanks. Does this mean I can have a few days off?"

"Don't worry about it." Matt looked at the nurse who'd just arrived. He pointed at the intern. "Some people will do anything to get out of a little call." Matt laughed and pulled back the curtain that surrounded them and then walked off to call Dr. Gant.

Fortunately, the O.R. had a room available right away, so Matt didn't have to wait. The appendectomy took thirty minutes, but by the time he had changed his clothes and dictated a short note, he was thirty minutes late for his afternoon date.

Matt quickened his pace across Main Street, heading for his apartment. In the distance he could see that the small group of animal rights protesters were at it again. When he got to his apartment, Linda was sitting in her car in the driveway.

"What's the matter? Can't you break into my apartment anymore?"

"Lucy's not home," Linda said protruding her lower lip in an exaggerated fashion. "Hi to you, too."

"Sorry. I'll start over." Matt backed up a few steps and said, "Hi!" Linda grabbed his arm, and they went up the back steps to his apartment. "How was the rally?"

"Great! There must have been close to twelve hundred people there!"

"Wow," Matt said slowly as he opened the door. "I had no idea it would be that large."

Linda walked into the apartment in front of Matt. Then she suddenly turned around as if she'd just remembered something and handed him a sheet of paper. "Here. I forgot to give this to you yesterday. I was so excited about telling you I'd seen Simons at the abortion clinic that I forgot all about it."

Matt looked down at the paper, which he placed on the kitchen table in front of him. As he took his coat off, he studied the paper. "Where'd you get this?"

"Simons dropped it when he came out of the clinic. Everything just flew everywhere when he tripped. I landed on this one and didn't realize it until he was driving off. I yelled to him, but he went right on." Linda looked at Matt inquisitively as he stared intently at the columns of printed data. She walked over and looked at the paper with him.

"Have you looked at this?" Matt asked.

"Just briefly. I just thought you could drop it by his office or something." Linda looked at the data. "Why? What is it?"

"I'm not exactly sure. It's a data collection summary of some sort." Matt scanned the column to the far left with a heading of "Donor Mother." Three quarters of the way down the page was the name, "S. Stelling." Beside it was a date that was one week prior to Sam's crash. Matt followed his finger over to the next column, which was titled, "Age of donor heart. 22 wk." The remaining columns were left blank, unlike the others above and below, which were filled with numbers. "Look at this!" Matt pointed at "S. Stelling." "It appears that our friend was about to be in an experiment run by Dr. Simons."

Linda read the paper. "'Donor mother'? What's he mean by that?"

Matt looked again at the column headings. "It looks as if these women who are listed as donor mothers were supplying a 'donation' for a project of some sort. See, this next column says 'donor heart.'"

"You don't suppose that Sam Stelling was Anne's friend who saw

Simons at the clinic, do you?" Linda and Matt stared at each other without speaking.

After a moment it was Matt who spoke first. "If that's true, then she was the one who thought Simons wanted her baby for an experiment!" Matt read the column heading again. His hand went to his mouth as if he were tasting something bitter. "Simons must be using the aborted babies' hearts! Look—the age of the 'donor heart' is listed here as twenty-two weeks beside Stelling's name, just a week before her death! That was the age of her baby!"

"I'm calling Anne. It's time we put some of this together," Linda said forcefully. Linda went straight to the only phone in Matt's apartment, the one on his bedside table. "Where's your phone book?"

"In the drawer under the phone," Matt answered. He then gathered up some clothes and headed for the bathroom. "I'm going to clean up a bit and change my clothes. I've got some Diet Coke in the refrigerator if you want something to drink."

While Matt changed, Linda talked to Anne Caudill. Once she was faced with the new information that Linda had, Anne knew that she needed to be more straightforward about what she knew about the clinic and who had sought treatment there. She had kept Sam's name out of the story, respecting her wishes. It seemed now that Anne, Linda, and Matt all had the same thing in mind: find out exactly what was going on at Richards' clinic before someone else could be misled.

Anne explained all that she knew. She'd already told Linda that Sam was carrying Redman's child, and she'd already told her about a friend who'd almost had an abortion at Richards' clinic. Now she confirmed that the two girls were one and the same, and that Sam had only gone there at the insistence of Layton Redman. She also gave Linda the additional information that Richards was, by Layton's own admission to Sam, making large campaign contributions to benefit Redman's quest for the governor's palace.

By the time they had shared all the details they knew, Linda had caught the detective bug as solidly as Anne. She made plans to show Simons' paper to Anne the next day. Their conversation lasted long enough for Matt to shower, change clothes, and drink a twelve-ounce soda.

Linda hung up the phone. "We were right! Sam had sought an abortion from Richards on the date that's listed on the form. At the last minute she backed out, but not before Simons bounded in and asked for his specimen!"

Matt held the paper up. "He must be doing something with the babies' hearts. All this data—cardiac output, maximum stimulated heart rate, wedge pressure . . ." Matt read from the column headings. ". . . these all indicate how well a heart is doing its job."

"It's obvious he's doing *something* over there. Sam saw him, and I saw him." Linda looked at Matt with a puzzled expression. "Why does everyone, including his secretary and his lab assistant, deny it?"

"Maybe they don't know. Maybe it's a secret. Or maybe they just don't want anyone to know," Matt reflected. "I'm not sure."

"I know one thing," Linda said, changing the subject with a smile.

"What?"

"I'm hungry! I didn't eat anything for lunch because of the rally."

"I didn't eat either. I was operating on Dr. Bryan."

"Don't you mean *with* Dr. Bryan?"

"No, *on* Dr. Bryan." Matt smiled. "Eddie had appendicitis."

Matt and Linda made small talk as they headed for his truck. Although their conversation touched on a number of topics, neither of them could keep their thoughts from returning to the activities at Adam Richards' clinic.

CHAPTER
27

THE morning brought not only new light, but warmer weather as well. It appeared that winter had finally loosened its fervent grip on eastern Kentucky.

Matt Stone started his third cup of black coffee. Mabel Pearson, the bubbly cashier in the cafeteria, let her excitement about the weather forecast splash over onto most of the customers who went through her line that morning. Matt looked up as Mabel gave him his change.

"I saw my daffodils peekin' through the ground!" she said as she counted out his change. "I just know spring's gonna come to Fairfax at last!"

Matt looked at his change, then handed back the extra nickel he'd been given. "Here, I think I owe you this." He smiled at Mabel, who was already telling the next customer about her flowers.

"Thank you, Dr. Stone," she said promptly as she deposited the coin in her cashier's tray.

Matt stopped at a table at the far end of the cafeteria beside the windows. *It is a beautiful morning,* he thought as he gazed at the sunshine. He glanced down at the morning paper, which was spread open on the table in front of him. His eye was caught by a photograph of the Life Chain event. A single photograph of a string of prolifers constituted the only media coverage of an event that brought together over a thousand protesters. What was worse was that their photograph sat next to a second photo of the other protest going on in town that day, that of the animal rights advocates in front of the T.U. hospital. Although their event only drew fifteen protesters, one common caption below two equal-sized photographs told the story: "Protests, protests . . . Anti-abortion protesters and animal rights advocates were busy bringing their issues to the public arena in Fairfax."

This equal coverage of the two events is appalling! The pro-life protest was fifty times as large as this! Matt snapped the photograph of the animal rights protest with his fingers. He noted as well that the language used for the pro-life rally, which had worked so hard at being a positive event, was negative; "anti-abortion," not "pro-life," was the chosen phrase of the media.

Matt sipped his coffee and glanced at the rest of the paper. He hoped Linda's small campus paper did a better job of covering the event. He knew she wouldn't be happy with what he was seeing.

◆ ◆ ◆

Linda Baldwin and Anne Caudill quickened their pace. They'd decided to go for a brisk walk to clear their minds and to help the brainstorming they had been doing about Richards' clinic. The weather had definitely favorably impacted their moods and their decision to accelerate their pace around the track at A.C.U. After a mile they slowed to a stroll, and in a few minutes they were sitting around Linda's kitchen table with a folder open in front of them.

Linda sipped herbal tea while she looked again at a copy of the sheet she'd "intercepted" from Simons. Anne summarized their thoughts.

"It's obvious that these other names must be names of women who received abortions at Richards' clinic, considering that Sam's name is the only one here without all the data filled out. It looks like he was really all ready for her and her 'specimen'!" Anne smashed the sheet with the back of her hand for emphasis. "But how do we prove that? We can't just call these people and ask them if they had abortions!" She sighed and stopped to pour herself some tea from Linda's copper pot on the stove.

Linda stood up and began pacing slowly around the small table as an idea began to formulate behind her green eyes. Suddenly she stopped and set down her mug. "Why *can't* we do that?"

"Do what?" Anne couldn't read the idea that was obviously forming in Linda's mind. "What are you suggesting?"

"Why can't we call the women on Simons' list and just ask them?"

"Oh, right, like they're just going to tell a stranger about something so personal—" Anne's voice trailed off as Linda raised a finger as a silent interruption.

"Do you remember the stack of phone books in *The Weathervane* office?"

"Sure, but—"

"Listen," Linda interrupted again, "I've got an idea that may allow us to tie a few of these loose ends together. We may be able to confirm our suspicions about the campaign contribution fraud and find out for sure if these women have had abortions at Dr. Richards' clinic." Anne just looked at Linda and shook her head. Linda continued, "Look, just give me a few minutes to get my thoughts together. If you could get those phone books while I get us something to eat . . . I think we may need a little extra energy." Linda smiled.

"Now that's a good idea," laughed Anne. "But I'm still not sure about calling these patients—"

"Just get the directories. Try to bring the ones for all the larger cities in the state . . . at least Louisville and Lexington for starters. I'll explain what I'm thinking when you get back."

"Okay," Anne replied as she headed for the door. "Say . . . you're not planning anything too healthy for this energizing snack, are you? I might need some real empty calories to expend here, you know."

Linda laughed. "You sound like Matt Stone."

Anne responded with a curious chuckle and closed the door behind her, still wondering exactly what Linda had in mind.

◆ ◆ ◆

"I'm sorry, ma'am, but Mr. Redman cannot take your call just now. He's in a consultation with a client. Could you leave a message?"

It was the second time that Debbie Swindol had called Redman's Louisville law firm. He hadn't returned her first call. "I really can't leave a message other than to say that he needs to call me about an extremely important issue. Medical confidentiality forbids me from giving out information to anyone except Mr. Redman."

Redman's secretary could see Layton's feet propped up on his desk. He had asked that he not be bothered while he prepared his next campaign speech. "I'll let him know to call you as soon as he is done with his meeting."

"Thank you very much. I'm sure he'll be interested in what I have to say," Debbie added, hoping the secretary understood that this was serious.

The secretary hung up the phone and called back to Layton Redman. It always irritated him when she didn't use the intercom. "Ms. Swindol called again from the T.U. hospital. She says she has an extremely important message for you."

Redman didn't take his feet off of his desk. He strained to reach his intercom button, nearly spilling his coffee in the process. "If she won't leave a message, I'm not calling her back! There are too many lunatics out there to answer the ones that won't even leave messages."

◆ ◆ ◆

John Gentry had been doing a lot of thinking. Slowly he had come to grips with a great many loose ends. He knew he needed to change jobs, both for his own mental health and his family's. He also knew that if he did, it would be an ugly separation from Simons, who threatened to block any move he attempted. John had also begun to have second thoughts about the research. He couldn't believe that Sam Stelling's baby had lived! He thought that perhaps this angered Simons most of all, because if people really understood that babies have a survival chance outside the womb, public opinion would be set against Simons' research. He had winced at the attack Simons had rained upon the unsuspecting Matt Stone. He also grieved at how he had fallen into such a faithful protection of Simons when he himself had been treated so poorly.

That morning he made two decisions. He would tell Matt Stone the truth. He wasn't sure what good that would do, but he knew it was a start. And he would tell Simons that he could no longer participate in the F.F.P. Clinic experiments. He knew that such an announcement just might cost him his job. *At least if Simons fires me, I will be free to look elsewhere for work. Maybe Louisville will take me back if I can't come up with anything in a town where Simons rules.*

The first resolution would be easier than the second.

◆ ◆ ◆

Michael Simons dressed impeccably, as always, for his clinic. Far be it from him to be seen outside the O.R. or the lab in scrub attire. He currently sat across from Rich and Donna Gleason, who had come to him to talk about the treatment of hypoplastic left heart syndrome.

As he talked, Simons continually pointed to several diagrams showing the normal infant heart and blood flow and the abnormalities seen in a baby with a hypoplastic left heart. As he talked at great length about current state-of-the art surgical procedures, Donna alternately squeezed her husband's hand or gently rubbed her lower abdomen.

She was six months pregnant. The baby she carried would be her third, but her first girl. It looked like this child would be born with a congenital heart defect, diagnosed before birth with the aid of a special fetal ultrasound. Because of the defect, they had made this appointment with Dr. Michael Simons. They had traveled 130 miles to talk with him.

The discussion was frank. The Gleasons wanted all the information, including the likelihood of death. Mrs. Gleason had been tearful. Mr. Gleason had been silent.

After Dr. Simons finished with all of the current surgical options, he paused and lowered his voice a notch. "There is one other possibility that I have left out." Simons looked at the couple in front of him, turning from mother to father and then back, making eye contact frequently. "I am currently developing a new surgical treatment for this very illness. This treatment has never been offered before. It could be that if we have enough data by the time your daughter is born, I may be able to offer you more hope than we ever felt possible in the past."

Donna looked at Rich, who looked back at Dr. Simons. The father spoke for the first time. "We don't want you experimenting on our daughter."

"Of course you don't. I understand that entirely. It's just that this procedure has great promise and is quite new. I didn't say that it was experimental."

"If it could save our baby . . . we'd do anything," Donna Gleason stated firmly without consulting her husband.

"I wish I could give you more details, but I cannot explain the treatment fully until it is approved. Once it is, and I'm confident it will be, I'll be in touch with you. Hopefully it will be available by the time your daughter arrives. It definitely will be an option if my research proceeds at an accelerated pace," Simons added sincerely.

"We hope so, doctor. Do whatever it takes to make this treatment available for our little girl," Donna said, again grasping her husband's hand for support.

Michael Simons promised to do just that.

◆ ◆ ◆

Debbie Swindol persisted. This time she said just enough to get Redman's secretary to talk to him while she was on hold.

"Did she leave a message this time? No message, no conversation! It's not hard to understand," Redman replied.

"She asked me to give this message to you: 'Tell him it has to do with Sam Stelling.'"

For a brief moment Layton Redman thought Sam must still be alive. *Maybe the landlady was wrong! Sam must not have died in that accident! She's in the hospital!*

"Is—is she on the phone?" Redman asked, pulling his feet off his desk and sitting up straight in his chair. "Tell her I'll take the call."

"She's on line 3, Mr. Redman," his secretary called over the intercom since Layton had closed his door.

"Hello. Layton Redman here. What can I do for you, Ms. Swindol?"

"Thank you for taking my call. I know how busy you must be."

"My pleasure," Redman lied. He was having a hard time being polite and a harder time being patient. He addressed his primary fear first. He decided on an approach of ignorance. "What do you have to tell me about Sam Stelling? She's not in the hospital, I hope!"

"Mr. Redman, I assumed you'd been informed of Sam Stelling's accident and her death." Debbie was somewhat taken back by Redman's comment. Dr. Stone had indicated that he thought Redman knew about her death.

Redman was so immediately relieved at hearing that Sam was dead that he slipped and stopped playing his little charade. "Oh, of course, the crash . . . She's dead . . . Of course, I knew about that . . . Of course." Layton put his feet back up on his desk and sighed.

The social worker cut right to her central reason for calling. "Were you aware that although Sam died, her baby was removed and is alive?"

Redman's feet dropped to the floor with a thud. "What?" Layton's mouth literally hung open. "The baby is alive?"

Debbie could feel the weight of the surprise she had dropped onto Redman's lap. And she enjoyed it. "Yes, sir, Mr. Redman. It's a baby boy. He appears to be a real survivor, too." She paused long enough for that to sink in. Then she unloaded bomb number two. "I'm calling you because you've been identified as the father."

"What?" exclaimed Redman. He literally did not know what to say.

Debbie let him stew.

Finally he spoke again. "Th-this must be some sort of joke! . . . Slander to injure my reputation! Who told you this? Did Sam tell you this?"

"No, sir. The information came from one of our doctors who took care of Ms. Stelling."

"She must have lied to him!" Redman gasped. "Who knows about this? Who has this information?" he demanded.

"The information I have shared with you is a matter of medical record. It is held in strict confidence, as are other matters of concern only to our patients. We have no medical proof of the fatherhood of the child. If this story were to get out, it would have to come from the source from which our physician obtained it. In any case where there is a child and the parents are unknown, it is our custom to question friends to see if the parents are known. We are not interested in scandal, Mr. Redman. We are only interested in finding out whether we need to consider the child an orphan and therefore a ward of the state. Our interest lies only in the well-being of the baby."

"I just can't believe this!" Redman rubbed the back of his neck.

"Mr. Redman, I can't tell you where the information came from. That I do not know. I can tell you that Sam was not the one who gave the information to us. She came in unresponsive and was never communicative."

"You can't believe this! This may only be an attempt by one of my political opponents to sabotage my campaign!"

"Mr. Redman, if this information ever becomes public knowledge, it won't be because of this hospital's personnel. If it ever does, blood type testing or DNA analysis could be done to clear your name."

"Are you suggesting that I be tested to determine paternity? That cannot be forced legally upon anyone, except by our court system," Layton responded.

"I'm not suggesting anything of the sort. I know we can't force anyone to be tested. I'm only saying that if you are not the father—"

"*I'm not the father!*" Redman interrupted.

Debbie held the phone away from her ear. "Okay, okay, Mr. Redman. I'm only saying that blood testing can show that you are telling the truth."

"Well, as far as I'm concerned the issue is closed! . . . It never existed! This is a cruel political rumor! I'm not planning on defending myself from such groundless gossip. You tell your doctors that it is not possible that I could have fathered that child. I was never in that kind of relationship with that girl!"

"I'm really in no position to debate that with you, Mr. Redman. We only wanted to explore each possibility on behalf of this little baby boy, sir. Thank you for your time." The social worker hung up quickly. She imagined that if she needed Mr. Redman again, he would likely return her calls.

Layton Redman held the phone in his hand as if it were something detestable. After a moment his anger erupted, and he slammed the receiver down on its cradle. @#&%*@! He sighed and buried his head in his hands. He wasn't sure what his next move should be. If the social worker had told the truth, there was no way legally that the hospital would release his name as the father of the child. *But how did they suspect me?* The social worker's words reverberated in his mind. ". . . it is our custom to question friends to see if the parents are known." *Friends? I'm sure Sam had some friends, but I don't even know who she hung out with!* Layton Redman had never been interested in any of Sam's friends. He got up and began to pace around his spacious office.

He stepped to the window and looked at the Louisville skyline. From his office he could look down and see the Ohio River and the bridges linking the southern and northern parts of the city. Redman often quieted his anxieties while staring out of this window. *Let's not overreact here, Layton. The word's not out! No one knows about this. No one will ever find out from the hospital. I could sue them if they let this get to the public!*

Layton stared at a riverboat making its way along the Ohio River. Suddenly he straightened from his position where he leaned against the windowpane. *She said Sam had a boy! A baby boy!* He thought again about the words of the social worker: "It's a baby boy. He appears to be a real survivor, too." *A baby boy! I have a son! I'm a father!* @#$%&*!

◆ ◆ ◆

It was the second time in a week that Simons invited John Gentry to his office. Simons was in a celebratory mood. John sat on the maroon leather couch beneath the oil of Alexis Carrel.

"John, I'm going to push the schedule forward by nearly a month. Last month at F.F.P. we did more pump runs than I thought possible. I have just about enough data to estimate the age of heart I will need to support a small, full-term infant. Richards has been working hard and has several good candidates lined up for our work next week. In fact, after this week I'm going to close out this phase of the work. Then I'll compile the data and take it to the review board to get permission to do our first real transplant. We may in fact already have our eyes on the first recipient. I met the parents only this morning to talk about the treatment of hypoplastic left heart syndrome. It seems the cardiologists made the diagnosis by ultrasound before the baby has even been born. I didn't specifically promise them a transplant, but I did hint at a new treatment I'm developing for their future daughter's cardiac defect. I told them I thought the new surgery might be approved by our review board within two months. That will mean a few extra late nights for me." Simons paused to give his lab assistant time to compliment him for his hard work. Because Gentry was silent, Simons just grunted and continued, "Anyway, I wanted you to know that after next week we will be closing out our work at F.F.P."

"That's great, sir," Gentry responded. "That we're going on to the next stage, I mean," he added hesitantly. *Oh well, I guess I can put up with this for one more week.*

◆ ◆ ◆

Anne Caudill had a busy afternoon on the detective trail. After returning to Linda's apartment with a sixteen-inch stack of Kentucky phone directories, they again reviewed what they knew. They remembered Redman's boast to Sam that Richards had been donating to his campaign in the name of his patients. They knew Sam had received a contribution receipt for money she never sent. If the women on Simons' list were actual patients of Dr. Richards, maybe they had received contribution receipts as well, they reasoned. Together Linda and Anne formulated their plan. They would call as many patients on Simons' list as possible and would simply tell them the truth: they were reporters trying to expose an illegal campaign contribution scandal.

After they first addressed the issue of campaign contributions, they would gently bring up the subject of confirming whether the girls on the list could have also been patients of Dr. Adam Richards.

They reviewed thirty-five names on Simons' list. Anne found actual phone numbers for only seventeen. The others could have been from out of state or perhaps even used false names at the clinic. Of the seventeen, she reached only ten. She was currently on the phone with a Diana Lindsey.

"Ms. Lindsey, I'm a university newspaper reporter searching out a story on campaign contribution fraud. Your name is on a list of people who may have been used in this fraud. We have reason to believe that one person is making large campaign contributions to a political organization in other people's names. We think that maybe your name was used in this scam. Could I ask you a few questions?" Anne was speaking from some notes in front of her.

"I guess so."

"Did you make any campaign contributions to any parties in the governor's race?"

"No. Money's too tight for that," Diana added with a scoff.

"Did you receive any acknowledgment slips indicating that a pledge had been received from you?"

"Come to think of it, I did!" Diana said. "I had a good laugh about it with my boyfriend. I've never voted in my life!"

"Who was the donation given to?"

"The postcard said I'd given a thousand dollars to Layton Redman." Diana paused. "I wish I had a thousand dollars!"

"Thank you very much," Anne replied. "This information has been very helpful."

"Can I get some of that donation back?" Diana laughed.

Anne laughed at that, too. "I'm afraid I can't help you with that," she added. As Diana laughed, Anne prayed a silent prayer for guidance, then continued, "Ms. Lindsey, I'd like to ask you one more question, if I might. If this is too personal, you may feel free not to answer. Let me assure you that the information you give me will be strictly confidential, and I will not use your name in any way." Anne paused.

On the other end of the line, Diana Lindsey stopped laughing and looked curiously at the phone. Anne went on, "We believe that all of the people who had donations made in their names have one common contact person." She paused again, aware that Linda was also listening, and praying. "We believe that the illegal contributions were all made in the names of patients who received abortions by a Dr. Adam Richards. Would you be able to simply confirm my suspicions?"

On the other end of the line, Diana Lindsey was puzzled by her sudden willingness to talk to a stranger about her abortion. She fully intended to simply hang up, but she found herself riveted to the phone. Clearing her throat, she stammered, "Y-yes, y-you are absolutely correct. I am a patient of Dr. Richards. I had an abortion by him only last month." She shook her head, then added, "I don't even know why I've told you this. My boyfriend doesn't even know . . . You won't use my name, you say?"

"Of course not," Anne reassured her. "Thank you so much for this information."

Diana simply stared numbly into the phone. Finally she mumbled, "Uh, sure . . . bye." *Click.*

Linda looked up as Anne counted her responses. Out of the ten women she'd talked to, seven had the same story. Layton Redman had received money in their names to the tune of one thousand big ones each. It wasn't like Redman didn't know what was going on. It was just that his volunteers didn't know any different. Everyone who donated got a contribution receipt. Period. That's how the organization ran. Of the seven who admitted getting the contribution receipts, two openly told of receiving abortions at Richards' clinic, four more admitted to being treated by Dr. Richards, and two just hung up the phone.

◆ ◆ ◆

John Gentry caught up with Matt Stone just outside the clinic building. "Hey, Matt!"

Matt looked around and kept walking toward the hospital as Gentry ran up beside him. "Hi," Matt replied.

"Look, Matt, I've got something to tell you. I don't know any other way to say it other than to just say it." Matt stopped walking and looked at John curiously. John continued, "You asked me if Simons was doing research with Richards. I told you a lie. I've regretted it ever since . . . especially when I heard the presentation in M. and M. the other day . . . and especially when Simons nearly fired you in front of everyone!" The research assistant looked at his feet, paused, then looked at Matt. "Simons and I have been doing some experiments over at Richards' clinic. Richards isn't directly involved, so I told myself I wasn't really lying to you. Anyway, Simons has wanted the research kept very quiet until he has a chance to reveal it in the way he wants." John paused again. "I just thought I needed to tell you." He looked back at his feet.

Matt grabbed his arm. "I know a little about what's going on, John," Matt responded, hoping to draw more out of Gentry. "Simons is using aborted babies, isn't he?"

"How'd you hear about that? You didn't hear that from me!"

"I've even seen some of Simons' data. Something he must have dropped," Matt said slowly. Matt rested his right foot on a bench in front of the clinic building. Then he looked right at Gentry. "It looks like the little premie I delivered in the E.R. barely escaped being a part of Simons' little project, huh?" he said coolly, then waited for a response.

"Yeah," Gentry answered, lowering his eyes to prevent contact with Matt's.

Matt chanced a direct approach. "Just what is Simons working on over there, anyway?"

"New treatment for congenital heart problems . . . transplantation of aborted fetal hearts." Gentry wasn't sure why he was answering Matt's question, although he was very aware that he didn't want to walk away from Stone regretting that he'd lied to him again. This time he opted for the truth. Somehow it felt better to Gentry—and right—to be telling the facts to Stone.

Matt paused to formulate another directed question. "Doesn't he need a live donor for that sort of work?"

Gentry was brief in his response. "Exactly."

Matt didn't know what to say. He was beginning to see the whole picture for the first time. *This explains the way Anne reported Sam's abortion procedure, including the suppository Sam was given. They wanted to abort her child alive!*

Gentry finally spoke up again. "Look, I'm going to get out of this real soon. In fact, Simons is gonna stop the work at F.F.P. Clinic after next week. If he knew you knew about this, he would freak. In fact, if you haven't figured it out, I think the reason he blew up at you in M. and M. is that he was angered by you saving that baby. If people realized that these babies might actually survive, they might not be so quick to accept his new therapy."

"I kind of thought there was something below the surface when he blew up like that. I thought I might be looking for work elsewhere for a while," Matt added soberly.

"He's still upset, Matt. Simons doesn't forget."

Matt just shook his head. Gentry added, "I wouldn't let this get out if I were you. Simons will be more than upset. Having you look for another job might not seem so outrageous to him."

Matt shook his head sharply and blew his breath out between pursed lips. "He liked me when I was on service," Matt responded hopefully.

"He talks to the director of your residency program about you guys all the time." Gentry paused. "The director listens, Matt . . . And Simons always gets his way."

CHAPTER
28

MICHAEL Simons did not totally understand the strong disdain he felt for Matthew Stone. He did, however, recognize the same threatening feeling about Stone that he'd felt about Sam Stelling when she was alive. It was as if the threat that he felt from Stelling had not been totally abolished because it lived on in her offspring— the offspring that, in Simons' mind, had been destined to be a part of Simons' research—the offspring that Matt Stone had stolen from the womb of its dead mother. Simons feared that should the truth about the survival of this one premature infant be known, the validity of his research would be questioned. And Matt Stone was responsible for the life of this little threat. Simons had risen early with these troubling thoughts pushing sleep from his mind. He had tried to comfort himself with the reassurance that the child could never really be a threat. *Nobody knows how close this child came to being part of my work . . . or do they?*

For some reason, he could not be sure that his work was secure. He had risen from bed and slipped to the floor to both empty his mind and to seek the peace of an answer from his "higher self." He sat in the silent darkness. The only light was from the moon that was still in the sky during his meditation. Slowly he comforted himself with an affirmation of his direction: *Speed up the work! Success will convince even the vilest of gainsayers. A successful transplant will be difficult evidence for anyone to refute! A baby with a new chance at a full*

*life, with the donation of tissue that would have otherwise been wasted!
. . . People will see how silly it is just to waste the useful fetal organs if I
just lead the way with a successful model!* But Simons was still aware of
the presence of potential negative criticisms. He again felt renewed
anger towards Stone. *Is he the threat? Is Baby Boy Stelling?* Something
prevented him from coming into a complete resolution of tranquil-
lity within himself.

Simons again attempted to empty his mind, to gain access to the
untapped potential solutions within himself. He concentrated on his
breathing and closed his eyes. Later he again started visualizing success. His eyes were on the goal now. Fifteen minutes later Simons
suddenly opened his eyes and stood up. He had a definite feeling of
success and an answer that would help facilitate it: *Matt Stone must
be dealt with! Matt Stone must be removed from the picture!* With that,
Simons returned to bed. He slept another two hours before his clock
radio rendered its call.

◆ ◆ ◆

Tracy Smith, M.D. stood at the pathology work counter examining the specimens from the Fairfax Family Planning Clinic. She
prided herself in being rapid and efficient. As she dictated, she
paused only long enough to put specimens into and out of their containers. The only way the transcriptionist could figure out what Dr.
Smith said was to play her dictations at half of their original speed.
Fortunately, the dictations were all much the same, so it wasn't too
hard to figure out what she was saying.

Carefully she weighed, measured, and dictated each specimen.
At no time did she wince at the containers that held a larger than
normal number of late second trimester abortions. She completed
the dictations on thirty-five specimens in thirty minutes. It took as
long to pull out and put back most of the specimens as it did to do
her short examinations and rapid dictations.

The specimens were set aside in preparation for their trip to the
incinerator. In six of the containers, the small aborted fetuses contained no hearts. This, of course, went undetected in the rapid documentation of the gross completeness of the abortion process. Once

incinerated, there would remain no obvious physical evidence of the terror these children experienced prior to their untimely sacrifice. The dictation would speak just the opposite message, as Simons had planned: "Complete evacuation of products of conception evaluated and confirmed; gross only."

◆ ◆ ◆

Myron Whithers looked at his daily work roster. *@#%$@! I've got to pick up the pathology specimens again!* He had stopped liking the job the month before. He still had vivid nightmares of the abortion specimens he'd picked up, and he didn't have any desire to freshen his memory. There was enough on his schedule to postpone the worst job until after lunch. *At least I'll be able to enjoy my meatball sub if I put this off until after I eat.* He carried his metal lunch pail over to his locker. When he opened the door, a plastic pathology container fell onto the floor in front of him, nearly landing on his toes. His lunch box clattered to the floor as he made a sudden retreat.

Norm Driver laughed heartily. "What's the matter, Myron? Got specimen pickup jitters?" Norm roared again. He had seen the work assignments before Whithers had and had taken advantage of the opportunity to entertain himself with a little joke.

"#@$%!" Whithers picked up his lunch pail. "This isn't funny!" *I should never have told him about that specimen!*

Norm looked at Whithers, who was obviously both angered and surprised by the little "joke." "Hey, Myron, I didn't mean to scare you." He looked at Whithers again and squinted. "You okay, man?"

"Yeah, I'm just fine . . . Just fine!" Whithers threw his lunch pail into his locker and slammed the door. With that he was off to start his daily work assignments. As he left, he kicked the empty pathology container at Norman, striking his younger coworker in the right knee.

"Lighten up, Whithers! It was a joke!" Norm called after his friend. Whithers, however, walked off to replace a faulty doorknob in the neurology department and didn't turn to respond.

%$#%!*, thought Norm, rubbing his right knee. *That thing bothered him more than I thought!*

◆　◆　◆

Dr. Paul Taylor was dean of the Taft University Medical Center. He was a strong man, and very decisive. He hadn't gotten where he sat today without knowing how to take quick action when he had been clearly shown the options. As the dean, he oversaw the hospital's residents, from psychiatry to cardiothoracic surgery, from radiology to obstetrics. Virtually all of the residents came under his jurisdiction.

Before him sat Dr. Michael Simons, who had come to him with grave concerns over a surgical resident, a resident who, in Simons' estimation, not only showed bad judgment but endangered patients' lives. "Residents like Stone are a risk to patients," he had said. "Furthermore, they are large financial legal risks to the surgery department," Simons reported.

Paul Taylor, M.D. knew well the financial end of his institution's ups and downs. In fact, well-known to him and the rest of the administration was the fact that Simons' department was the most lucrative of all the departments in the hospital. Simons' financial success allowed less prosperous but necessary residency programs to exist. In short, Simons was worth millions to the university. And Michael Simons knew it. When Simons talked money, the administration listened.

"I can't just fire him without some warning, Michael," the dean responded. "We run the risk of a suit that way. What we've learned from past experiences is that we must carefully prepare a case against him and document it meticulously. Then when he calls, 'foul play!' we merely bring out the evidence."

"I really don't think it's safe to have him continue," Simons pressed.

"Have you taken this up with the general surgery section?"

"@#$%, Paul! They're too close to the issue to be objective. They will take it as a matter of pride to let Stone finish his residency. It would reflect badly on their department to fire him in his fifth year! They should have weeded him out a long time ago! Now they feel obligated to keep him for the rest of the program," Simons justified.

"If the incidents are as you have stated, I think a dismissal is in order. But I do feel that the proper way to proceed is with careful documentation of his standard of care. Then we'll be ready from a legal standpoint to dismiss him without backlash."

"From a legal standpoint, he's a liability to us every day he sees patients!" the surgeon shot back. "I'm sure you've heard about the incidents I know of. He practically killed that poor pregnant girl in the E.R. . . . The final nail in her coffin was the butchery he called a 'c-section.' And what about the pneumothorax that occurred on his service just last week? I know he wasn't in the room when it occurred, but where was he? It is his responsibility to be in the O.R. when his junior residents are operating, isn't it?" Simons stood.

"I'll tell you what, Michael. I'll issue a suspension of his hospital privileges. He won't see patients, and he won't be allowed to scrub in the O.R. During the suspension we will run a retrospective analysis of his performance as a resident. If it appears he is a danger as you say, it will be easy to build our case against him. At that point, Stone will be terminated." Taylor stood up and faced Simons. He reached out his hand towards Simons. He knew he had to keep Simons in his corner at any cost. He owed Simons. He knew that. Simons knew it, too. "Deal?"

Simons clasped the dean's outstretched hand. "Deal!"

With that, Simons walked out of the room without another word. He never had been much for good-byes.

◆ ◆ ◆

Matt approached the subject with some caution. He certainly didn't want Simons to find out he was snooping into his research. But he knew he needed to have some hard evidence. He had Gentry's word, but he wanted more. He wasn't sure Gentry would open his mouth to him again, much less to a wider public audience. Simons definitely had Gentry spooked.

Matt had shared the new information with Linda and Anne the evening before. Things were shaping up for quite a news break. They wanted . . . no, they *needed* more evidence. Matt had decided that morning to talk to Scott Tanous, a pathology resident and a friend.

When he found him, Scott was alone, eating his lunch in the pathology residents' office.

"Scott, can I talk to you for a minute?" Matt asked, looking around. He was relieved to see that they were alone.

"Sure," Scott replied and offered Matt some chips. "Here."

"No, thanks," Matt said with a smile, taking some chips anyway. "Listen, I'm looking for some specific information that I think you may be able to help me with. I'm not even sure where to start. Maybe you can help."

The pathology resident looked at Matt curiously. "What's up, Matt?"

"I need to see some of the specimens that come over from the Fairfax Family Planning Clinic. You do their pathology work, don't you?"

"Sure, but—"

"I know it sounds like a weird request, but I really need to look at those specimens."

"Matt, do you know what they do over there?" Scott said, making a disgusting twist of his upper lip. "It would be better for you if you just looked at the pathology reports. We document everything that comes out of there. It's all P.O.C., to use a term they favor. Some of the older abortions will turn your stomach."

"Scott, I know what they send you." Matt paused and looked at a *Far Side* comic on the wall. He then continued, "Have you noticed any evidence that the fetuses have been experimented on in any way?"

"Listen, you obviously haven't seen their work. These specimens are mutilated, shredded even. The smaller ones are vacuumed out a piece at a time. We merely identify as many body parts as we can to be sure something major wasn't left behind. You can't tell much beyond that." Scott looked at Matt for a second, then added, "What are you getting at anyway?"

"Look, I need you to keep this quiet . . ." Matt lowered his voice and looked around again. "If Simons finds out I've been looking into this, I'm in trouble! I may already be on his hit list. Let me just say that I've got a pretty good idea that Michael Simons has been doing experiments on some of the fetuses that were aborted live at the

F.F.P. Clinic. Have you seen any scars such as would be necessary for a heart transplant on the older specimens?"

"Matt, I logged those specimens in myself a couple of weeks ago. I didn't see anything like—" Scott stopped in mid-sentence, striking his hand on the table beside him. Suddenly his conversation with Whithers came back to him. *What was it Whithers had said?* "It *looked like it had been through some kind of operation, with a gash right down the middle of its chest.*" "Wait a minute! One of the environmental service workers asked me about that very thing!" Scott stood up. "What day is it?"

"Tuesday," Matt replied, returning the curious look Scott had given him just a minute before. "Why?"

"Come on!" Scott said, heading for the door. "There should be some specimens that were checked out this morning."

Matt followed Scott down the hall. They took the elevator down to the first floor and walked past the O.R. to the pathology lab. The specimen containers were being loaded by Myron Whithers into large, red, plastic bags. "Hey, Mr. Whithers! Hold on for a moment. We need to look at some of those specimens!" Tanous called out as he entered the lab.

"W-what? These?" Whithers asked, backing away.

"Yes. Could you leave these here for a minute?" Scott said as he picked up one of the larger containers and prepared to unsnap its lid. Whithers nearly fell over backwards as he back-pedaled away from Tanous and the container he was opening.

"O-okay! I—I'll be back later!" Whithers ran out of the door before either of the residents could thank him.

Matt looked at Scott. "What's with him? He acted like you were about to set off a bomb or something."

"He took off in a hurry, that's for sure!" Scott replied. He put on a pair of rubber gloves and lifted a small fetus out of the formalin. The skin was blistered and red, as were most of the babies killed with the searing action of the hypertonic saline. Gently he pried apart the stiff arms that were folded over the chest. The child had been dead so long that it was not very pliable. There, on the chest, the two doctors could barely detect a fine incision. Anyone who wouldn't have known it was there would have missed it. Scott looked up at Matt. "Looks like you might be right about this, my friend."

Matt picked up a scissors from off the pathology worktable behind him. "Here," he said as he handed the instrument to Tanous, "you're wearing the gloves."

Tanous slit open the incision, which had been closed neatly and tightly with a series of tiny sutures beneath the skin. He then clipped a larger suture that reapproximated the sternum. The chest gaped open. He gently pulled the chest cavity open wider for a closer inspection. Both residents looked into the small central cavity of the infant's chest. *NO HEART!*

Matt Stone and Scott Tanous just looked at each other, and then around the room. Everyone else was out eating lunch. Finally Scott spoke up. "What do we do now?"

"You've got to let me keep this as evidence—"

"It's supposed to be incinerated, Matt. There are regulations about this sort of thing!"

"Quick—let's look at the rest of these big containers!" Matt was obviously undaunted by Scott's protest. "No one will have to know you helped me!"

Within three minutes, they had found four other infants with sternal scars. Matt took each container and put them in a large, brown grocery bag.

Matt carried the bag to his O.R. locker. His plan to oversee the junior residents in clinic, then return for the specimens was interrupted when he was paged to the dean's office. Matt quickly and quietly put the bag into his locker. *What could Dr. Taylor want with me?*

◆ ◆ ◆

Layton Redman reclined at his desk again, back from a short campaign speech and dinner at the Louisville Rotary Club. He was decidedly calm. Since no one had come forward and accused him of any infidelities yet, what with Sam Stelling dead for weeks now, he was confident that no one would. *Perhaps it was good that I decided to release that controversial Nelson story. Now if a story ever does come out about me, it will be an easy assumption that his camp is just making up mud to sling.*

Redman had been quite upset last night and had even canceled a date with Janice, citing his need to work on a speech. That wasn't true, of course, as he'd given the same speech at least three dozen times before. He just couldn't face her. Whenever he was the least bit distracted and inattentive to her needs, she became almost unbearable.

Layton sat and looked at his daily planner. He still had an interview to tape for Channel 6 news and a debate to organize. His secretary buzzed the intercom. His door was shut, preventing her usual yell. "Mr. Redman?"

"Yes?"

"There's a reporter on line 2. She wants to ask you about a paternity matter. She said you'd want to talk to her. I told her you were busy, but she insists you'd want to hear her out."

"@@$#%$&*!" Redman picked up the phone and punched line 2 with his index finger. He tried to sound pleasant. "This is Layton Redman. How may I help you?"

Anne Caudill smiled. She figured the word "paternity" would get her in. She had called twice before with other messages but had never gotten past Redman's reception "wall." "Mr. Redman, thank you for taking my call. I know you must be busy. I'm Anne Caudill, a reporter for the Appalachia Christian University campus newspaper. I wonder if you'd mind answering a few questions?"

"I may." Redman was brief and very guarded.

Anne decided to start with the least inflammatory subject. "I have been informed that Dr. Adam Richards has made contributions in excess of one hundred thousand dollars to your campaign by sending in money in the names of his patients. Are you aware of this?"

Redman was actually relieved that the question was about this. He knew about the money, but he also knew that on his end all the contributions were from separate people, so he could plead ignorance. *So that's what this is about! Some people will say anything to gain my ear!* Redman formulated his answer carefully. "I know nothing of contributions that violate the current state limits. If you have evidence of this, my staff would be glad to participate in an investigation to terminate such activity." Layton smiled and sighed. He was a smooth liar, and he knew it.

"Thank you, Mr. Redman. I have one more question," Anne added before Redman had a chance to interrupt. "I have been made aware that you fathered a baby boy who was born to one of your volunteer staff at our school. Would you care to comment on this?"

Redman coughed. @@$#%$&*! *Sam must have talked!* "Sure, I have a comment! There is no truth in your statement!" Layton was actually lost for words, a rare event for a politician.

Anne pounced again and continued her verbal inquisition. "Would you be willing to undergo DNA testing to prove that you are telling the truth?"

"No! There is no reason to submit to testing," Redman said with clenched teeth.

"I'll record that as a denial, sir," Anne replied matter-of-factly.

Redman was in a corner. He wanted to stop the interview quickly. "I'm not taking any more questions, ma'am. This interview is over!" He pushed the phone across his desk as he forced the receiver back into its cradle.

Redman put his head on his desk. *The word is out!* "@@$#%$&*!" he said so loudly his receptionist could hear him. He didn't even care.

◆ ◆ ◆

Forty-five minutes after his meeting with the dean, Matt Stone walked home instead of to the clinic. With his privileges suspended, he was refused the right of any clinical patient contact, even under the observance of others. With the current situation, his long-held dream was on the verge of caving in. A job loss here, due to the reasons put forth, would effectively ban him from a surgical residency anywhere. He would have to give up his surgical dream entirely!

As Matt walked, a continuous stream of thoughts and emotions poured through his mind. He had asked where the accusations came from. The dean had only answered, "Concerned faculty observation, Matt." *It had to be Simons! He was the only one to question my actions in the way I handled Stelling's case! And that was the only case that the dean pointed to as evidence of my negligence and dangerous clinical judgment!* Matt pondered the source and slowed his pace. He didn't really have anywhere to go by any certain time. That was a feeling he wasn't used to. He knew that if Simons had initiated his suspension, it was unlikely to ever be revoked. The same thing had happened three other times that Matt knew of. All those residents had been forced to look for work elsewhere, and none had become general surgeons.

Matt slowly climbed the back stairs. Mike slept on the steps. Matt looked at his dog curiously. *So that's what he does when I'm at work.* It had been too long since Matt had been home in the middle of the day.

Matt's first move was to call Linda. Fortunately, she was home. He explained the situation as well as he understood it. Linda offered a slightly different evaluation.

"It's a spiritual attack, Matt, pure and simple! Sure, Simons may be mad because you saved Sam's baby. That's what Gentry thought, right? But Simons isn't acting just on anger. There's something dark motivating him, Matt." Matt listened carefully without talking. "You've said yourself that Simons is the only one who criticized your actions in M. and M. and that all of your general surgery evaluations have been top-notch! It doesn't make sense to me any other way." Linda was beginning to pick up some righteous anger of her own.

"I—I think you're on to something. I know the accusations are groundless. And I know most of my attendings would agree. The problem lies in the amount of influence Simons' money has bought him with the administration. If he wants something, it happens, and usually without much delay," Matt said with a sigh.

Linda sighed, too. Then she brightened with a new thought. "Since you are unexpectedly free, how about coming down for the evening? I'm going to be helping Anne with tomorrow's *Weathervane.* I think you'll be interested in our main story."

"Is she going to expose Redman?"

"She's planning to run a story on the campaign contribution fraud. She's got enough evidence from all the people she contacted from Simons' list to raise some serious questions about his fund-raising."

"What about Simons and Richards? Any mention of their research?" Matt asked anxiously.

"I'm not sure we have enough to go on with just Simons' summary paper and Gentry's comments. We might have to wait until we have more hard data on that story."

Suddenly Matt remembered his meeting with Tanous and the "hard data" he'd confiscated. He'd totally forgotten about it in the wake of his suspension. The fetuses were in his O.R. locker! Matt chuckled nervously under his breath. "Wait a minute before you decide on your final story selection! I think I have something that might add a little weight to your story line."

◆ ◆ ◆

Adam Richards sat clearing off his desk, a duty that required daily diligence or he would never see the fine teak wood grain again. He looked at his phone messages. Three notes from an Anne Caudill, identified as a reporter. He looked at the first message: "She has questions about your choice for governor. Please return call." *No need to answer that!* He glanced at the second: "Ms. Caudill called again. She is asking about your contributions to Redman's campaign." *No need to answer that. The contributions are so spread out, no one will ever know I made them all.* Message number three made him reach for the flask in his top drawer: "Anne Caudill asks whether you are doing research on aborted babies." *@#$@%!* Richards sipped from the brown flask. He then dialed the number listed on the first note from Anne Caudill. He had to get a feel for what she really knew.

"Hello . . . Anne speaking."

"Ms. Caudill, this is Dr. Richards. I'm returning your calls."

"Oh, thank you, Dr. Richards. I know you're a busy man. I won't take much of your time. I'm a reporter for the school newspaper at A.C.U. I wondered if I might ask you a few questions."

"Sure."

"Are you willing to give me your choice for the governor's race?"

"Layton Redman."

"Have you ever made a campaign contribution to him?"

"Yes."

"How large?"

"That is my own private business."

"Dr. Richards, we have compiled a list of people, all of whom have been your patients and all of whom have received receipts for campaign contributions to Redman's campaign that they did not make. We also have on record a personal testimony from a friend of Redman's that points to you as the source for these multiple contributions. Would you have a comment on this?"

"No comment," Richards replied flatly.

"Have you ever made contributions to Redman's campaign in someone else's name?"

"I said I have no comment!" *How does she know this? Was Redman giving out this information?*

"I would like to ask you another question, sir," Anne added quickly without giving Richards a chance to respond. "Is it true that you have modified your abortion techniques so that you are actually receiving live abortions that can be experimented on in your clinic?"

Richards froze. *How does she know this? Has Simons been talking? No one else could have told her! The patients are all too anesthetized to know one technique from another. Wait! . . . Stelling! Could she have mentioned her experience to the media?* Richards stuttered into the phone. "L-look, Ms.—Ms.—"

"Ms. Caudill," Anne prompted.

"Ms. Caudill, I don't know where you are getting your information, but you are totally misinformed! My practice is very routine. Everything is done according to the highest standards of medical care. I do not deviate from acceptable medical practice, I assure you!"

"Thank you for your time, Dr. Richards." Anne hung up the phone.

Adam Richards laid the receiver down on his desk, leaving it off the hook. He then finished the liquid in the flask and went home in search of some more. *The media knows I'm aborting live babies for research! @#$%@!*

◆ ◆ ◆

"There's little we can do about this, Matt. I'm afraid the dean is convinced that a suspension is necessary," Dr. Samuel Fletcher answered soberly. "The problem is that our hands in the general surgery department are tied over this thing. I know you are our resident, and we hired you, but we've been left out of the loop on this one. The dean notified me of the suspension only this afternoon. He advised me to adjust the call schedule and service coverage to do without you indefinitely."

Matt just stared at the receiver of the phone he was using as he listened to the somber words of one of his mentors. Finally when Dr. Fletcher was silent, Matt asked, "Isn't there anything I can do?"

"I wouldn't do anything for now. Your salary will continue to come for thirty days. Hopefully it will have all blown over by then. If it looks like it hasn't, or isn't likely to resolve within a couple of weeks, I would advise you to find an attorney to represent you before the University Hospital Review Board."

"Isn't Dr. Simons on that committee?"

"I believe he is. Why?"

"I have a suspicion that he's behind all of this. I w-won't stand a chance w-with him on the review committee," Matt said haltingly.

"Let's just give it some time first, Matt. You still have the support of the general surgery staff. I'm sure we'll discuss it at our departmental meeting."

"Thanks, Dr. Fletcher."

"Sure, Matt. Try and take it easy," he added kindly. "Good-bye."

"Bye." Matt hung up the phone. Now he was even more convinced of the origin of his problems. *If the general surgery staff wasn't even aware of the problem until this afternoon, it has to have come from Simons!* Matt was also becoming convinced that Linda was right. *This is a spiritual war!*

He went to his tattered, spiral personal phone directory. He looked up the number for his uncle, Tom Downs, on the Eastern Shore. It was time to initiate a prayer chain. It was time to fight back!

◆ ◆ ◆

Later in the afternoon, when Anne and Linda were putting the finishing touches on the *Weathervane* story on campaign contribution fraud, Matt arrived to report on the events of his day. He also brought one sample of the results of Simons' work.

"I'm not sure you really want to see this," Matt cautioned. "It's pretty gross." He slowly opened the plastic container. The formaldehyde fumes provided a pungent warning not to get too close. Anne and Linda were both anxious to see, feeling sure they were strong enough to take what Matt was about to show them. Linda sat down after only a quick peek.

Anne gasped and put her hand to her mouth. "He's so small, but so perfect," she said as she looked wide-eyed at the tiny fingers and toes and eyelids. "What happened to his skin?"

"It's a result of the hypertonic saline. We know that the abortions Simons uses are born alive, so he puts them in saltwater after they die to make them look like all the other specimens, so no one will suspect they have been treated any differently." Matt then rolled the baby over and revealed the small empty chest cavity. It was then that Anne ran quickly to the bathroom and emptied her lunch into the commode.

Matt looked at Linda, whose head was buried in her lap. He sheepishly put the fetus back into the container and snapped the lid. "I'm sorry," he said when Anne walked in slowly from the other room. "I guess I thought—"

"Don't worry about it, Matt," Linda and Anne said simultaneously. Anne added, "I'm glad you brought it. I can't believe people buy the abortionists' argument that abortion products are just tissue! Even someone like me, with no medical training, can see they're wrong!"

Matt carried the container back to his truck, then locked his truck. *It wouldn't do for someone to accidentally stumble across this!*

After Matt returned, the trio regrouped. They reviewed all of the evidence they had—from Sam's experience and Gentry's testimony to Simons' paper and now the evidence of the tampered-with fetuses. They also considered what good a story would be if they waited a few weeks to find out more. Gentry had said that Simons was planning to close out the F.F.P. Clinic work after next week. A story at that time might have no influence on what Simons did from then on. On the other hand, a story now might raise enough public outcry to hinder any further experiments on live aborted babies. They also thought soberly about what the consequences of an inaccurate story might be. They reviewed the evidence again. Everything seemed to be in place.

Matt suggested that they pray before making their decision. Linda and Anne, both of whom had been discussing the spiritual battle they felt was raging, quickly agreed. And so the three stopped discussing the situation with each other and began an earnest discussion with their Heavenly Father. They prayed for guidance, discernment, and safety. After several minutes of waiting, they were filled with a sense of God's peace and his presence with them. It was several more minutes before anyone opened their eyes or spoke.

None of them needed to ask what the others thought. Matt, Linda, and Anne had all received the same answer: *Expose the truth!*

◆   ◆   ◆

Adam Richards had seven drinks before he got home at 5:30 P.M.—two in the office, three at Sammy's Tavern, and two more in his car as he drove around the city on Circle 6. He had missed his turnoff and just decided to go around the city again. He really wasn't in a hurry. He didn't need to go anywhere else to get a drink. He had a bottle in the car.

Later he wouldn't remember parking his car in the garage. Actually, to call it "parking" was being polite. He squeezed the car in beside a recycling bin so tightly that he scraped the driver's side door, again forcing him to get out on the passenger's side.

Once inside, Richards continued to drink, first beer and then a bottle of very expensive 1983 champagne that he'd been saving for a special occasion. At 10 P.M. he was still awake, and he began to fear a recurrence of his nightmares. If news like he'd gotten today didn't bring them on, he wasn't sure what would. Slowly he took six five-milligram Valium tablets. He didn't really remember taking so many and hadn't really intended on it. He just couldn't remember from moment to moment whether he'd taken any or not.

By 11 P.M. Richards was unconscious, asleep in the middle of his kitchen floor.

◆ ◆ ◆

By 11:30 P.M. the printing was done, and Anne held a copy of the next day's *Weathervane* in her hand. The headlines screamed out about the scandals detailed within. "T.U. Professor Teams With Local Abortionist To Perform Experiments On Live Aborted Babies" stood above a subtitle, "Layton Redman's Son Narrowly Escapes Research Activities." Lower on the first page was a second heading: "Redman Faces Charges Of Campaign Contribution Fraud."

Anne yawned. When she held up a copy of the newspaper to Linda and Matt, she dropped it quickly and shook her hand. "Ouch!" she shouted, as if the paper were physically hot.

"Tell me about it!" Linda responded.

Their work was almost complete. The *Weathervane's* top stories would be in the offices of the editors of Kentucky's largest newspapers by 1 A.M., thanks to a fax machine. The newspaper would be in the display racks across campus by 5 A.M. It would also be waiting in the fax machine at the office of Kentucky's State Medical Board and in the office of Dr. Paul Taylor. Faxing top stories to the general public newspapers had become routine; Anne had recommended it. Linda had suggested adding the State Medical Board to the list. Matt had suggested Dr. Taylor. It certainly wouldn't hurt to pass the stories around.

CHAPTER
29

THE editors of the larger city newspapers rarely got their tips from the small-town reportings of school papers. They had enough of their own news to report. The editing staff of the large city newspapers reviewed the small town and college newspapers, however, to be sure that their smaller competitors weren't breaking fresh ground they should also plow. Even rarer, a story first carried in the smallest papers sometimes developed into material used by the major wire services.

When the stories from *The Weathervane* chirped through the fax machines in the newsrooms across Kentucky, most of them were filed in a stack for review later that morning. In a handful of TV stations and newspaper offices, senior editors dispatched reporters to Redman's camp, Adam Richards' clinic, and Dr. Michael Simons' office for their response to the stories. By late morning a swarm of reporters would be quizzing both Anne Caudill, asking her for her sources, and also the men she had exposed.

This small-town university newspaper story wouldn't end with *The Weathervane* presses. A landslide of interested reporters would soon print versions of their own.

◆　◆　◆

Adam Richards arrived at his office late, after seven reporters had been there for an hour. They represented two local TV stations, as well as the *Fairfax Daily*. The Louisville reporters arrived after Richards. The reporters chatted patiently with the office staff, who were clueless as to the reason for all the attention. The receptionist even served them coffee, smiled, and spelled her name for the paper. "That's Sally Dinguss with one g and two s's."

Richards had been up since 5 A.M., if you consider being on the kitchen floor going to sleep at all. Since 5 he had downed two cups of black coffee, and when that was no help in removing the pounding in his cranium, he started on a brand-new fifth of Maker's Mark Kentucky bourbon. He didn't even bother to pour it into a glass.

By 9 o'clock he was thoroughly intoxicated but decided he'd better get to work. He looked at himself in the front hall mirror. He was still in his clothes from the night before. He smiled unevenly at his reflection. He had red wax from the bourbon bottle on his front incisor. "It's good I looked in the mirror!" he slurred as he wiped the wax on the sleeve of his sport coat. With that, he stumbled to the garage. His car was lodged against the recycling bin so tightly that even if he'd been sober he would have had trouble moving it. Richards cursed and found his way back to the kitchen to call a cab. While he waited for his ride, he finished the bottle of bourbon.

It took the yellow cab only ten minutes to drive him to his office. It took another five for the cab driver to find Richards' wallet, pay himself, and deposit the doctor in the front waiting room of his own clinic. Richards normally parked in the back and used a private entrance, but today he wouldn't have known the difference.

"Dr. Richards!" The young receptionist and another office assistant came running to his side. "Are you all right?" Richards stumbled across the waiting area with the help of his two human crutches. Sally, his receptionist, saw the cameraman from Channel 4 pointing his instrument in their direction. "Turn that off!" she yelled.

"Who are you?" Richards demanded.

"Mike Roberts, Channel 4, 'News at Noon,' sir," shot back the man wearing a blue blazer. "Can we ask you a few questions, Dr. Richards?"

Sally cut in before he answered. "Can't you see he's ill?" She looked at Richards. "Come on, let's get you in the back!"

"Is it true what they said in *The Weathervane*, sir? Are you doing live abortions for research?" a female reporter from the *Fairfax Daily* shouted as Richards was about to disappear into the hall.

With that, Richards reeled around and stood on his own feet without Sally's support. Richards squinted his eyes at them and raised a fist in the air. He slammed it into his opposite hand and shouted hoarsely, "It's all true!" Then he slumped again on Sally's shoulder. He looked as if he might cry right there. The alcohol that had been his comfort had betrayed him and was forcing his emotions to the surface. He looked at the female reporter in the front. "I did it for science—for humanity! I did it to help infants with heart disease! We are working for great advances!" He turned and limped to his office. "Let them follow," he said to his receptionist, waving his hand. The liquid that had loosened his emotions had also demolished his defenses.

At the door of his office he brightened. "Come this way." He led them to the laboratory at the back of the building. Most of the women working in the front had never even been in the room, Sally included. He opened the door and turned on the lights to the modern surgical research laboratory. The latest in cardiac monitoring equipment stood awkwardly out of place in the office meant for gynecology. The large silver cardiopulmonary bypass pump sat idle beside the nearly new operating table. "This is where it happens," he said. "We wanted to change the way congenital heart disease is treated forever."

Richards sat on the operating table in the center of the room, seemingly exhausted.

"Dr. Richards, will you take questions?"

Richards slumped. "@#$%!"

"Is it true that the fetuses are aborted live so their beating hearts can be studied?" The question came from a man from Channel 16.

"The aborted tissue was just that—an abortion. What we did was to use otherwise wasted tissue and do something useful with it." Richards' thinking was amazingly clear for the amount of alcohol he had consumed. Ethanol tolerance, for him, was an asset.

"Is that a yes?" the reporter persisted.

"What does it matter if it was alive or not? @#$%! The mothers who decide to end their pregnancies determine if their babies will live or die! It's a woman's right! @$#&%! It's my right to do the procedure however I see fit!"

"Does the lifting of federal restrictions to allow research on fetal tissue from elective abortions extend to research on *live* abortions?"

"@#$%! I'm free under the law to do abortions as I see fit!" Richards echoed again.

"Have the modifications you are using been shown to be safe?" The question was from a tall, slender reporter from the *Fairfax Daily*.

The question struck a definite nerve with Richards, who had always had the greatest fear of accusations concerning the safety of deviating from standard medical practice.

"I've had no problems!" the doctor shouted back.

"Do the infants feel pain?"

"@#%$! I've told you! It is just immature tissue! Tissue that would otherwise have been wasted!"

The man with the video camera winced. With Richards' language, the tape would need to be edited to use as a daytime news story.

"What exactly is done to the aborted tissue?"

"Ask Michael Simons that! This is his brainchild, not mine!" Richards snapped back.

With that, Richards walked slowly and unassisted back to his office and closed the door. As he walked, he held up his hand to indicate he was taking no more questions.

He slumped into his chair and looked at his desk. On the top of the stack was a phone message from a Dr. William Troyer from the Kentucky State Board of Medicine. Richards held the paper with two fingers by the very corner, as if it were some kind of vile insect. He dropped the message into the trash. "@$#%&!"

◆ ◆ ◆

All six phone lines into Layton Redman's office were blinking. Eventually they were all put on hold. In fact, every line into the Redman volunteer office in downtown Louisville was busy. Layton Redman came to work early and canceled his campaign stops for the day. He literally couldn't get out of his office without facing a mob of reporters, much less give a campaign address. Finally, at 2 P.M. Redman scheduled a press conference in which he agreed to take questions from reporters in a controlled setting. He knew it would be on TV.

Redman hung up the phone and immediately put it on hold. He had been on the phone with Janice. He had wanted her to be at his side at the press conference to send a message to his constituency, but she had flatly refused. *If she won't believe in my innocence, how will I ever convince the voters?*

He planned a short statement. He would claim foul play and cast a suspicious suggestion in the direction of his opponents. Redman looked down at his nearly empty notepad in front of him. He had written only a few sketchy ideas. He seemed to flow better in front of the cameras when he wasn't reading. He had written, "The front-runner is always a favorite target." Redman paused and underlined "always." He looked at his watch. *Show time in five minutes!* He sighed and put on his coat. He walked down the hall slowly and waited at the side entrance to a large conference room. He could hear his campaign manager issuing a statement he had written earlier in the afternoon. After he heard his introduction, he stepped through the door to the brightly lit podium and began his defense.

"I looked with interest at the story printed in the small campus newspaper that was faxed to me only this morning. I read it with interest, as it was all news to me. I suppose I suspected that mudslinging would begin as I pulled away in the polls, but I had hoped we could avoid that and run an 'issues only' campaign. Concerning the accusations, I shall address them one at a time, as Rose Drake did with you earlier. Number one, the contribution fraud: I can assure you that we have checked on Dr. Adam Richards' financial support of this campaign, and we find his personal contributions well below the state limit. As to whether contributions were made by him under false names, of this we have no record. Our camp will perform a full investigation of this. I can assure you that we had no prior knowledge of wrongdoing if any wrong was done in the first place," Layton lied with a smirk.

"Concerning allegation number two, that I have fathered a child by a woman who is now deceased, I find this charge totally reprehensible. Samantha Stelling worked hard for our campaign, and to suggest that she and I had an affair of this nature is a hostile attack of the worst kind. This fine woman recently passed away! A campaign to smear her reputation postmortem is an accusation so low, it doesn't even warrant a response. Have the decency to have respect for the work she did while she was alive. May our memory of her remain unspoiled!"

Layton Redman looked at the crowd of thirty-some reporters sitting and standing in the conference room. He purposefully made eye contact with as many of the reporters as he could. He knew many of them. A blonde woman in the back had been invited and brought over for this very event, courtesy of a Louisville TV station, just that afternoon. Redman didn't recognize her. Anne Caudill preferred it that way.

Redman paused, looking at his notes. "I think that about sums it up. I'll now take a few questions."

The questions came rapidly, many spoken at once, hindering Redman from hearing any individual clearly. He did notice that the attractive blonde in the rear of the crowded room stayed politely quiet. Redman pointed to a friend from Channel 4. "Jeff?"

"Yes, Mr. Redman. Could you tell us what steps you will be taking to investigate the contribution fraud?"

"We are asking anyone who has received a receipt from us who didn't make a contribution to please contact us. If we can compile a list and make some connections within the group, we may be able to pinpoint the problem." Redman pointed to a local newspaper reporter. "Tim?"

The well-dressed reporter stood, glad to be recognized in the middle of the shouting throng. "It is somewhat interesting that these allegations surfaced only now, when Mr. Nelson has fallen in the polls after the controversial story of his alleged affair became public knowledge. Do you suspect that the reporter who broke the story about you acted as a puppet of one of the other candidates?"

Anne Caudill stirred uncomfortably in the back row but remained silent.

"We certainly have our suspicions, Tim. The timing of this falsehood would make that possibility more likely. The front-runner is often a favorite target of mud-slingers. We've seen that before, time and again," Redman added with a note of sadness in his voice. "I just wish we could raise the campaign above all the vicious rumors and stick to the issues that are important to the voters of the Bluegrass State."

Another dozen hands went up. The young woman in the back remained motionless. Redman pointed to a woman in the front row, whom he recognized as being from Channel 27.

"The article mentioned that you had been contacted and asked if you would undergo DNA analysis to clear up the allegation, but that you had refused. Is that accurate?"

"That is accurate. I find the suggestion that I participate in bloodletting preposterous! Not only is it unnecessary, but it can only lead the public to believe that I think that my fatherhood is a possibility, which it is not!" Layton looked at his questioner's eyes for a moment longer, then moved to another question. He pointed to a man in a tan sport coat.

"Do you acknowledge that you knew Samantha Stelling? If so, what was your relationship with her?"

"We are getting redundant. This information was all covered by Rose in the briefing. Yes, I did know her. She worked as a volunteer on my staff at the campus of Appalachia Christian University. Really, we've been over this before," Redman stated with obvious irritation in his voice. "I'll take one more question."

Redman saw the hand of the attractive blonde go up in the back of the room. He pointed to her. "Miss?"

"Anne Caudill, *Weathervane* reporter, Appalachia Christian University." The crowd murmured, and Redman cursed under his breath.

Who let you in here? I thought my staff screened this crowd! They had, but Anne had been listed as arriving with the local Channel 5 evening news.

When the crowd quieted, Anne spoke up strongly. "Samantha Stelling was a friend of mine. I resent the inference that my report of your affair was an attempt to harm her reputation after her death!" Two video cameras were now focused closely on Anne's face. "I was not prompted into action by any of your political opponents! I reported the truth on my own as I received it from Sam Stelling, not from your competition! My motivation is not to mud-sling but to report the truth as it relates to your character, which should be a central factor in the voters' minds! My friend had no reason to lie! She was heartbroken over the situation! She loved you and did not want to damage your reputation! It was only after her death that I decided that it was permissible to bring the truth to the people of Kentucky. They deserve the truth. I believe there is reason to question your motivation to refuse DNA testing! If you are telling the truth, why won't you be tested?" Anne was nearly shouting. She had talked so rapidly that Redman had not been able to shut her up. The talking in the room had swelled to a roar as Anne concluded.

"This is obviously a political assassination attempt on the part of one of my competitors!" Redman shouted. "I have given you my statement, and I will stand by it. These allegations are groundless mud-slinging!" he added, pounding his fist on the podium. "No further questions!"

Redman quickly exited through a side door, flanked by his personal staff. The media mob, however, did not follow him. They collapsed around Anne Caudill.

◆ ◆ ◆

The reporter scene was no different in Michael Simons' office. Simons, however, refused to talk to anyone and tactfully issued a series of "No comments" as he headed from his office to the clinic and again when he passed the press on his way from the clinic to the O.R. To all appearances he was cool. Inside he was boiling. His schedule was too busy for him to sit down and figure out just where the leak had come. *I must have underestimated Samantha Stelling*, he thought as he trudged back to his office after he finished in the O.R. Fortunately, by then the media force had left to edit their work and had left his office empty except for Iris. *But I had felt so confident that the threat from Stelling had passed!* He thought uneasily about the situation. *Stone? Could it be that he has something to do with this? He couldn't possibly know about this!* The thought crept over Simons with a gradually increasing discomfort. *If it was Stone, I'll certainly be fin-*

ished with him soon anyway! Then in time, when this blows over, I'll continue my work!

Simons passed Iris without speaking. Iris gave her routine greeting. "Evening, Dr. Simons. Busy day?" Iris finished the note she was making, then rose and followed Simons into his office. "The dean's office just called again. He wants to see you. Says it's urgent."

Simons only grunted. *Let the @#%@# wait!* On his desk was a copy of *The Weathervane* that had been given to Iris by one of the reporters. Simons read the article, pausing every few seconds to vent his frustration. "$@#%!"

Simons didn't return the dean's call. Instead, he quietly left his office and headed for his car. He had experienced enough today without talking to Dr. Taylor.

From his car phone Simons called John Gentry. "Go and retrieve all of our equipment from Richards' clinic. You can use a maintenance department truck. Just check it out in my name. We are concluding this phase of our experiments. I want you to do it today! I don't want the media combing through his clinic and seeing what we were doing before I have a chance to explain everything myself. If we take it out tonight, they won't have a shred of evidence that the allegations are true."

"But, sir, I saw—"

"No buts! Do it STAT!" *Click.* He didn't give Gentry much of a choice, or a chance to respond. After his instructions, he just hung up the phone.

All Gentry wanted to say was that he'd seen the whole clinic laboratory on the "News at Noon" on Channel 4.

◆ ◆ ◆

Matt Stone was enjoying the day as much as he could under the circumstances. Even though he was suspended from patient care activities, he was still allowed to go to conferences. And because he had more time, he had been asked to give a talk on thyroid nodules to the family practice residents. He had spent the morning making slides on the computer in the surgery residents' library. By mid-afternoon, word was out about some controversial research that Dr.

Simons was involved in. Matt didn't participate in the discussions that he heard going on in numerous places along the general surgery office corridor. Instead, he just quietly slipped by and went home to catch what news he could find himself.

When he arrived home, he opened an airmail letter from Kenya. It had taken two weeks to arrive. The letter was from Tenwek hospital, where he had served ten months before. An urgent need existed. The surgeon was leaving in July. They had known Matt would be done with his training by then. "Would you consider coming back and helping out for a year?"

Matt stared at the letter and sighed. *Why does this have to come now? I'm not even sure at this point that I'll be able to complete my training at all!* Matt shook his head, chasing out an unwanted thought: *All these years of training wasted!*

◆ ◆ ◆

Adam Richards drowned the memory of his conversation with the State Medical Board in Mexican beer. He still had a case left over from a party he had given the year before. "We will be conducting a full investigation of the activities surrounding your clinical practice . . . . A formality . . . Of course, you understand our obligations to respond to the public outcry . . . It shouldn't take more than a few months to clear up . . . ." Dr. William Troyer had assured him it was all routine. It didn't seem routine to Adam Richards.

When the news came on, Richards squinted to see himself on camera. His image was followed by Redman's and then by a tight-lipped Simons who said, "No comment!" quite plainly into the camera as he strode by. The final segment in the story was an interview with Anne Caudill. Richards shouted at the image of the young woman being questioned on the tape. Anger ulcerated within him. Standing up, Richards continued his verbal barrage at the young reporter's face. "@#$! You #@%$@!" he yelled as he propelled his Corona bottle toward the TV screen. The set imploded with a sharp crack, the image blackening after a flicker of light seemed to rip through Anne's face. Adam Richards continued shouting obscenely at the darkened screen for several seconds before opening another beer and collapsing again onto his overstuffed couch.

◆ ◆ ◆

A new Ford Bronco was parked in the visitors lot at the far end of the T.U. medical center parking deck, where no one was likely to scratch it with a car door. The owner, a tall man with a tailored suit, walked in at a brisk pace, unrecognized by the other visitors arriving or leaving at the same time. The man had stopped in the lobby's coffee shop for a cup of black coffee and some cheese crackers. He sat alone with his face toward the wall in the corner booth, slowly sipping his coffee and appearing to be deep in his thoughts. He didn't want to eat a meal, though he was hungry because he had skipped his dinner. The crackers tasted surprisingly good to him, and he returned to the counter and bought another pack. He didn't appear to be in a hurry. He hadn't really intended on coming to the hospital today at all, but his day hadn't gone as he would have expected, so he had decided at the last minute to make this trip. He sat back in the corner booth until he finished his small makeshift supper and his coffee. He then stood up, carefully placed his suit coat across his arm, and set off to find the Neonatal Intensive Care Unit.

Seven minutes later he approached the receptionist at the desk outside of the unit.

"I'm here to see Baby Stelling," he said timidly.

"I'm sorry, sir," the unit secretary for the N.I.C.U. stated impersonally. "There will not be general visiting hours again until tomorrow." The well-dressed man looked again at the visiting hours posted beside the double doors. The secretary pointed at the sign. "See? Only immediate family members can visit at this late hour."

The man turned to go, then slowly turned around and returned to the window.

Before he could speak, the secretary repeated her warning. "Look, sir, there are no exceptions! The unit is no place for visitors most of the time anyway," she added. The man strained to see the babies in the incubators behind the glass window on the other side of the receptionist. The secretary looked at him suspiciously and renewed her impenetrable stance. "You're with the press or something, aren't you? I should have known," she continued without letting the gentleman speak. "Baby Boy Stelling's mother was mentioned on the news tonight. I saw the story myself!"

The man looked at her soberly and repeated his request to see the baby. Before she could refuse again, he added softly, "You see, I'm the boy's father."

The secretary's eyes widened. She had seen the accusations about Layton Redman on the evening news. Everyone in the unit had been talking about it. "You're—"

Redman held up his hand. "Please. You said family members could visit," he said quietly but firmly.

The girl's eyes remained fixed on Redman as she backed away. "I'll get his nurse."

CHAPTER
30

THE N.I.C.U. secretary wasn't the only one surprised by Layton Redman's visit. He had surprised himself as well. Now as he headed back to Louisville, he reflected on the past twenty-four hours.

Badly beaten in his media clash with Anne Caudill, he had retreated to the solitude of his plush office and locked the door behind him. His phone lines still on hold, he had stared out of his window and onto the Ohio River below. Just a day before, he had heard for the first time that he was a father. He had originally dismissed the thought and denied it. His defense mechanisms solidly in place, he had assured himself that the child belonged to someone else. As he stared out of the window, however, a growing dissatisfaction with his life and the frustration over his campaign forced him to look again at the lie he was trying so desperately to believe. Sam's baby really was his, and he knew it!

He had not known what to do. He only knew that he sensed a longing to see the child he had fathered. He was not ready to admit any wrongdoing to the public. He was too tied in to his spotless image that he had fostered so well up to that time. He did feel that seeing his son would somehow initiate a healing of the emptiness he felt within himself.

He acted abruptly. He had ripped his own campaign poster from the wall of his office, throwing it as a loose, crumpled ball onto the hardwood floor. He then exited his office in a half-jog, avoiding the media and shouting to his receptionist to cancel all events for the following day. With that, he disappeared. Several hours later he arrived inconspicuously at the T.U. medical center in Fairfax.

This morning, after spending the night at the Fairfax Oasis Hotel, Redman had visited his son for the second time. Seeing the small yet seemingly perfect little baby stimulated a strong, visceral reaction within him. The child looked helpless in his position in the center of his monitoring and feeding devices. Redman felt helpless, too, in the nearly alien surroundings of the modern N.I.C.U. facility.

Now Redman looked ahead as a steady stream of motorists easily passed his Ford Bronco on I-64, heading west to Louisville. He was doing 55, ten mph under the limit. He wasn't in a hurry. His campaign luncheon had been canceled.

Layton Redman was at ease with himself for the first time in days. It certainly wasn't because his problems had been solved. He still had more than his share, brought on by his own immature self-love. He had stopped running, however, and had gingerly taken the first step in assuming responsibility for his own actions.

That first step had been painfully hard: facing the son whose life he had fought so hard to terminate. The second step would be even more difficult.

◆ ◆ ◆

Evidently Adam Richards wasn't the only one who had talked to Dr. William Troyer at the Kentucky State Board of Medicine. It was all over the front page of Fairfax's morning paper: "Probe Initiated. Richards' And Simons' Controversial Research Investigated. Live Aborted Fetal Hearts Used For Transplant Project."

"#@$%@!" muttered Richards as he threw down the paper. He was near exhaustion. He had stayed up well into the morning and had then only napped in his easy chair. He sank lower and lower into a self-absorbed pity. He had lost his wife and his son, and now he saw his job status being ripped away. He tried to think about something else—*anything* else, but he couldn't. Even the alcohol that had freed his tongue with the reporters couldn't free his mind of the oppression that he found unbearable. He had tried, of course, but his alcohol tolerance had grown enormous.

It wasn't until he had finished a case of Corona that he decided upon a plan. He saw only one escape, but by then he was too inebriated to carry it out. He had turned from the beer to his favorite bourbon and from there had managed the short nap in his chair. When he awoke, he was urinating in his pants. He was still too drunk to care. He stayed there for an additional hour and then decided to look at the morning paper, which had already been deposited on his front steps. The headlines reminded him of the resolution he'd made only hours before. He had stopped drinking after consuming most of a fifth of bourbon. He knew he would need a steady hand to carry out his plan.

◆ ◆ ◆

"You will regret this, Paul!" shouted Michael Simons, who had just been informed of a suspension of his privileges by the dean, Dr. Paul Taylor.

"I am telling you that I have no choice in the matter, Michael! Until the state board is through with their investigation and you have been cleared, your presence can only be interpreted as a legal risk!"

"I've known William Troyer for years, Paul! He assured me that he is under pressure from the public to appease them with an inquiry from the board. It's nothing serious! I cannot accept a loss of my privileges over such a formality." Simons paused and walked to the window. "I have attorneys who will be quick to make your life miserable, Paul. You can't afford to have me take my business elsewhere!" Simons paced as he talked, pointing vehemently at Dr. Taylor's chest each time he yelled his name.

"You seem to forget your violations of the university policies as well. There is to be no research that hasn't gone through acceptable review committees . . . no private work at other facilities that may benefit organizations other than the one who employs you . . . no using university instruments in a private research venture! And I haven't even mentioned the questionable ethical nature of your work."

Simons stood and faced the dean. "I can get a faculty appointment anywhere I desire!" he said with barely controlled rage.

"No state will grant you a license while you are under formal investigation, Michael." The dean smiled sweetly.

"@#$%@!"

The dean pressed his intercom. "Show Dr. Simons to the door, would you, Jan?"

Simons didn't need to be shown the way. He slammed the door violently, sending the window glass showering onto the carpeted entrance hall.

◆ ◆ ◆

Layton Redman cleared his throat. For the second time in as many days he had called an urgent press conference. Normally spontaneous, Redman read mechanically from an index card in his hand.

"In light of recent events that have surfaced in the campaign, I have been involved in serious soul searching. I regret deeply the hurt I have caused my supporters, my family, and my fiancée, Janice Sizemore. I can only say that I know that the pain I have caused is far-reaching. My volunteer staff has worked hard for the goals they believed in. I have let them down." Redman paused and looked briefly at the cameras before returning his eyes to the small card in his hand. "I am hereby announcing my withdrawal from the governor's race. Current circumstances prevent me from adequately running a campaign, much less our great state." Redman looked up again. "Thank you very much."

Hands shot up all over the crowded conference room. Several reporters shouted their questions.

Redman quieted them with an outstretched arm, then added, "I am unable to take your questions at this time." With that, he exited the room, flanked by his campaign coordinators.

◆ ◆ ◆

The hour was getting late, but Paul Taylor, M.D. worked diligently at his desk. It seemed that the need for mending the university's public relations problems were going to demand more than one or two late nights at the office for him. His receptionist was long gone, so he was only mildly surprised when he looked up and saw the tall gentleman standing at his door without a warning from his secretary. "May I help you?"

"Yes, sir," John Gentry said politely. "I thought you might be interested in some information I have, sir."

"Come in, uuh—"

"John Gentry, sir," the man said with outstretched hand. "I work with Dr. Michael Simons as a research assistant, and—"

"If you've come here on his behalf, you might as well save your breath. I've got an obligation to the public to—"

"I've come on behalf of Matt Stone," John interrupted. "I thought you might be interested in another opinion. Matt didn't ask me to come. I heard about his suspension," he said hesitantly. "I think I know the reason for Simons' push to have Matt fired."

The dean looked at John questioningly. "Please sit down," he said. "Maybe I need to hear this after all."

◆   ◆   ◆

Adam Richards, Jr. had seen the news. He knew his dad was in trouble. He knew his dad needed some extra support. He also knew that it wouldn't come from his mother. She had hardly spoken to his father in months, except through their attorneys, who were mostly concerned about how to split up the profits from Richards' lucrative abortion business. He was surprised when his mom said she'd take him over for a visit. Normally she only let him visit on the weekends. Perhaps she, too, understood that Adam, Jr. wanted to provide at least some sort of family support for his father.

The sun had already set when Doris Hatfield pulled into her former husband's driveway. Apparently Adam Richards was home, as evidenced by the lights on in the house. Adam, Jr. jumped out of the car and headed for the front steps. His mother watched and waited as he rang the doorbell. When she saw him try the doorknob and open the door, she backed out of the driveway and turned right to return home.

Inside, Adam called for his father. "Dad!" he shouted as he went into the living room. He saw the empty beer bottles and an empty bottle of Maker's Mark bourbon. *He's probably drunk! And here I thought maybe he'd talk to me!* Adam headed up the stairs to his father's bedroom. The bed was made. There was no sign of his father anywhere. "Dad!" He looked in the bathroom. Two more empty bottles of Corona but no dad. He looked in the guest room. Same story. *Maybe he's out drowning his troubles. I'll check the garage for his car.* Adam went back down the stairs and went through the living room to the kitchen on the way to the garage.

It was then that Adam saw his father lying on the kitchen floor in front of the refrigerator. The body really didn't look much like his father at all. His color was a pasty, pale blue. He was lying in what seemed to be more blood than Adam thought should be in a whole body. His eyes were open, his mouth gaping open in a stiff O.

Adam ran to him and began to scream obscenities, hardly knowing what he was saying. He wanted to embrace his father, but he was repulsed when he cradled his dad's head in his hands and encountered the cold, clotted blood that was matted in his hair. It was then that Adam saw the revolver for the first time. "#@$%!" He was shaking. Slowly he stood and walked to the phone. He didn't know whom to call. He finally dialed 911.

"State police . . . 911," the male voice responded authoritatively.

"I'm calling to report a shooting," Adam said, suddenly aware of the blood on his hands and the phone. "I think it's my father!" was all he managed to get out before collapsing to the floor.

◆ ◆ ◆

The remainder of the night was a blur. The 911 dispatch quickly traced the call and sent city police and an emergency paramedic crew to the location. Adam Richards, Sr. was pronounced dead at the scene. The police questioned his family and placed his body in a plastic bag to be taken to the morgue for later examination by the Brown County coroner.

The E.M.T. crew found Adam, Jr. lying beside his father, incoherent. They turned their attention to him when they saw that the patient they had been called to see was already beyond resuscitation.

After a positive I.D. by Doris Hatfield, Richards' former wife, the police released his name to the press with the notation "dead due to apparent suicide."

◆ ◆ ◆

The morning, which came slowly for those related or formerly related to Adam Richards, came quickly for Michael Simons. He had spent the night at his computer, rearranging his data from his work at the F.F.P. Clinic and storing it under different headings to make the information nearly impossible for the uninitiated to retrieve. Now as he sat at his breakfast table sipping a fresh cup of Colombian coffee, a new battle plan unfolded in his mind. He had just seen the headline from the *Fairfax Daily*: "Adam Richards, Local M.D., Dead From Apparent Suicide."

Simons began to scheme. *My research has nearly been spoiled by falling uncontrollably into public knowledge! The work will likely never be accepted if the public is allowed to hear of it in this fashion. I must change their perception of our project—and change it immediately! Then later I can present my data at a highly specialized research conference with my peers, away from this place where the closed-minded conservatives are making such a fuss—a place where I can highlight my research in the manner in which I desire. For now, the most important priority is to divert the eyes of the press, and the public they hold at bay, off of me and onto—* Simons' thought was interrupted abruptly as he looked back at the paper's headlines and smiled. He was getting yet another idea of how to deal with his present problems.

He quickly scribbled a note to himself on his daily planner. *Since press conferences are becoming so popular, maybe I'll just hold one myself.* Simons smiled again and finished his cup of coffee.

◆ ◆ ◆

Matt sat nervously in a leather chair across the desk from Dr. Paul Taylor. He was surprised when he'd been called back into the dean's office this morning, and he hoped faintly that the dean planned to tell him that he was being reinstated in good standing in his residency spot.

The greetings were out of the way, and Dr. Taylor reclined comfortably in his chair. "I wanted to tell you that I think I was a bit unfair in not telling you where the accusations about your judgment came from," he stated in a fatherly tone.

"I think I know that, sir," Matt responded. "I don't think it's any secret that Dr. Simons made these threats only last week in our M. and M. conference, Dr. Taylor."

"So it's a known fact, then. Well, I also wanted you to know that I have been informed about a possible conflict of interest on Simons' part in his making accusations about you. It seems that if this story in the press is to be believed, your actions in saving the Stelling baby may have threatened the foundation of Simons' research. I was informed of his bias against you in regards to the threat to his research only yesterday," Taylor added.

"Who told you—"

"That's not important. Certain people around here still don't like to cross Michael Simons, and information like that may not be received too favorably by him," the dean added.

"That's for sure!" Matt smiled. "Does this mean that I'm back in?"

"Not by a long shot, Matt," the dean said with a frown. "It only means that when the data collection is all in, I'll consider Simons' bias and perhaps give more weight to your own department in evaluating you."

"I would like that, sir," Matt said with a half-smile.

"I still haven't figured out exactly what was going on at Simons' clinic, Matt. If you haven't heard about it yet, I'm sure you will soon. We have been forced to suspend Simons too, and to investigate his research activities. The sheer volume of calls from the local community expressing disdain for what they think Simons was doing has forced the university into a full probe into the matter, if for no other reason than to satisfy the public."

"Did Simons' have an explanation for what he did?" Matt asked, hoping to prod the dean into saying more.

"Simons won't tell the media or me anything! He only swore

that I was making a grave mistake in beginning the investigation. In fact, he notified my office only this morning that he is going to finally answer the media's questions in a conference this afternoon. I'm going to be there to see what he has to say about all of this."

"His side of the story, huh?" Matt paused. "That ought to be interesting." Matt rubbed his chin.

"All he said was that he was going to present the definitive records to clear up what he is calling a big misunderstanding. He said that in light of Richards' death, he is now free to share some of the details of the evidence to contradict the one-sided story that has circulated in the media."

"Evidence?"

"That's what he said." The dean looked at Matt questioningly.

Matt only returned the look and kept his thoughts to himself. *I'll show you some evidence!* Matt broke off his train of thought. "Say, is this open to the public?"

"As far as I know, but the media are the only ones who have been formally invited. 3 P.M., sixth floor, general conference room."

For once Matt was glad he didn't have clinical responsibilities that would prevent him from attending the conference. *This might be the only good thing to come out of being suspended!*

◆ ◆ ◆

Doris Hatfield looked with compassion at her son, Adam, Jr., who stood at the kitchen sink washing his hands *again*. This time he scrubbed his fingernails vigorously, as if removal of every molecule of blood that had been caked beneath them might also remove the memory of last night's trauma, which stained his mind as well. Doris had her own mixed emotions. Her first thought was that now she could get her share of Richards' money that she had been battling to receive for so long. *Maybe you will finally get something of benefit from your father*, she thought as she stared at her son standing at the sink. She was sad too, however, as she had hoped a helpful relationship would eventually develop between her son and her former husband.

Her current spouse, Lamar Hatfield, had made it only too obvious that he wasn't interested in the boy.

"Come on, Adam. I've fixed you a sandwich," Doris said gently.

"I'm not hungry," Adam responded mechanically.

"You haven't eaten anything all day. At least drink some milk."

Adam dried his hands and looked at his mother, who seemed relatively unaffected by the events of the day. Adam just shook his head and began to walk towards the stairs.

"Here! You can take it to your room," his mom said, holding out the sandwich and the glass of milk."

Adam paused and took the milk, ignoring the sandwich. He then continued to plod toward the stairs, his steps slow and heavy.

Doris sat back down at the kitchen table. Although she'd already eaten, she slowly began consuming her son's sandwich too. Eating was certainly better than thinking, and it seemed to take her mind off of her problems for a moment anyway.

◆ ◆ ◆

Matt Stone had arrived at the conference early. He talked to a few reporters who had gathered to question Michael Simons. As the conference began, Matt slipped quietly into a seat on the back row, unseen by Simons who faced the bright lights of the video cameras.

Simons spoke in low tones. His demeanor was one of compassion and perhaps that of someone who prided himself on having knowledge of a subject not known to all. He talked without hostility, and his manner seemed uncharacteristically open, in contrast to the hostility and defensiveness that might be expected from a cornered animal. Simons, in fact, didn't feel cornered at all. Inconvenienced, yes . . . cornered, no. He realized that he would have to change his plans, but he believed in his own superior ability to rise above this petty challenge and to secretly go on with his research.

"I have known Dr. Adam Richards for a long time, first professionally and then as a personal friend. He was a perfectionist—and an innovator. He cared for his patients with compassion, and he provided an important service for his patients, as well as for the state of Kentucky." Simons paused and squinted towards his audience. The people appeared as dim silhouettes against the bright camera lights. "I'm sure you are all aware of the recent passing of Dr. Richards." Simons paused again. "There were certain things that I couldn't share with you when Adam was alive because I couldn't compromise our friendship, which was quite close."

He looked at the people on the front row, who were busily taking notes. "Adam and I had both been through broken marriages. We found solace in our relationship with each other. I was eventually able to deal with my own pain by pouring myself deeply into research projects in addition to my clinical duties. Adam Richards did not have that outlet. He was a good clinician, but he was no researcher. Adam began to have problems with depression. Realizing my own limitations to help him, I urged him to get professional help. But he sank deeper into a pit of despair, eventually drowning himself and his problems in alcohol. I began to notice hints of psychosis only recently. I believe his desire to find purpose in his work, combined with the mind-altering effect of a continuous flow of alcohol, precipitated the story you have been told. The story of research on aborted babies told to you by Richards is nothing but a product of a serious psychotic depression."

Several hands shot up, and the lights were adjusted to allow filming of the audience and to allow Simons to see his questioners. But instead of answering questions, he continued, "Adam Richards desired to make a mark on the field of medicine through research. We had talked many times of his fantasy to break out of the monotony of his day-to-day practice. I truly believe he was secretly jealous of my accomplishments in research and wanted to mimic my success. Eventually his fantasies about cutting-edge research became inseparable from the realities he dealt with on a daily basis. His chemical addiction further blurred the lines between truth and non-truth, and finally his ethanol-induced fantasies were as real as the monotony of daily clinical practice.

"Since we were close friends, it was only natural for me to be a part of Richards' fantasy world. Weaving a famous researcher into his psychosis merely lended more credibility to his already twisted notions of rising to fame as a medical research scientist. His sincere belief in this make-believe world entangled gullible reporters into believing in his fantasy as well. In turn, this has snowballed into the present situation with state board investigations and my current suspension from medical practice. It was these allegations that have led me to share these details with you. I'm sure the true Dr. Adam Richards would agree and understand. What we saw of him in the last few days was a mere distortion of what my friend really was and represented. Alcohol has robbed us of a great man."

Again Simons paused for effect, looking at the floor in front of him, his air still that of someone who was experiencing great pain over the necessity of revealing the dark secrets of a former friend. "Before I take your questions, let me show you the written proof I have gathered." Simons slowly opened a maroon leather briefcase. He took out a stack of yellow typed reports and slapped them down on the podium with a thud, the sound resonating through the P.A. system, as if somehow emphasizing the weight and conclusiveness of his case. He looked at his audience, which was visible to him now. He did not recognize Dr. Matt Stone, who sat in the back row beneath one of the video cameras

"These are the pathology reports that are the official legal record of all the specimens from the Fairfax Family Planning Clinic for the last six months, the time that the majority of our supposed research took place. Here you will find detailed descriptions by our own university pathologists of each abortion specimen from the clinic. I have personally gone over these records so that I could be sure I am giving you accurate information. I am driven to do so to clear the good name of my friend and associate, Dr. Adam Richards. Here in these documents you will find no mention of any evidence of any specimens being tampered with in any way. There is no evidence of any modification of Dr. Richards' technique to allow the live abortion of any fetus. All of Richards' late abortions were accomplished by saline injection, which results in a stillborn conceptus. Each of these reports documents the typical appearance of an abortion done in this manner."

Simons reached into his open briefcase again, pulling out another thick stack of paper. "Dr. Richards' office provided me with copies of his office procedure note dictations, indicating no deviation from standard abortion procedures that would allow the kind of experimentation that has been alleged." Simons paused. "In short, this whole story is a horrible misunderstanding precipitated out of the psychosis of a deeply depressed man. There is no—I repeat, *no*— evidence that any of his confessed wrongdoings are accurate in any way!"

He again looked at the press, making serious attempts at eye contact. "I hope that this matter can be brushed aside quickly by the press, this institution, and our state medical board. This should serve to quiet my accusers and allow me to be reinstated quickly and without unnecessary delays. I will now be glad to answer your questions."

Matt Stone looked across the aisle from where he sat. He caught the eye of Scott Tanous, who had come to the conference at Matt's urging. Scott rolled his eyes as if to say, "Can you believe this?" and then turned his attention to the reporters as they fired their questions at Simons.

The first man to be recognized was from Channel 6. "What are we to believe about the equipment we viewed at Richards' clinic? Are we to believe that was only fantasy, too?"

"The monitoring equipment that you saw was typical for any modern operating facility, including one like Richards' and exists for performing safely monitored abortions." Simons wanted to keep his answers brief, if possible.

"What about the cardiopulmonary bypass pump? That is a highly specialized piece of equipment with no place in an abortion clinic," shot back a second reporter near the back.

"I'm not sure that Adam Richards in his psychotic state would be able to tell the difference between a complex system of suction cannisters used in his business and a cardiopulmonary bypass pump. He didn't have one. He is incapable of running one. What we have here is just another example of how one man's fantasy is portrayed as truth by an unsuspecting media. How would you know Richards was telling a lie? He himself was unable to recognize what he said as such."

A radio reporter in the audience spoke in a murmur. "I thought there was a good explanation for all of this. It certainly sounded too bizarre for the truth."

Several more questions were handled in a similar fashion by

Simons. The media seemed satisfied. After all, Richards had committed suicide, giving even more plausibility to Simons' words. Just when it appeared that the conference was about to break up, two young men stood at the back of the conference room.

Simons assumed the men were standing to signal the end of the brief conference. "If there are no further questions, I'd like to thank you for attending." Simons stepped away from the podium.

Matt Stone raised his voice above the murmuring of the crowd as the meeting started to break up. "Since the questioning is over, I'd like your attention for a moment please." The crowd turned, and for a moment the reporters were silenced. "I'd like to introduce Dr. Scott Tanous from the Department of Pathology. He has some comments about the specimens that came from Dr. Richards' clinic that I think you will find beneficial in your search for the truth in this matter. The truth that, I might add, is seeming more elusive all the time!" Before anyone could issue an objection, Dr. Tanous spoke up with his volume well above the whispers in the room. The cameras were now focused on Dr. Tanous.

"I have performed a recent review of the actual specimens from Dr. Richards' clinic, not just the reports of the specimens that Dr. Simons has copies of there," Tanous said, pointing to the stack of papers on the podium. "It is apparent to me that certain things that are not normally a part of the examination were overlooked. We are not accustomed to seeing the types of changes that are present after the type of surgery these babies underwent. For this reason, we had no reason to examine the specimens for these changes, and the evidence of any experimentation has gone unreported by the pathology department until now. I have personally reexamined a large number of abortion specimens from the clinic and found quite a few older specimens with sternal scars and some without hearts altogether—clear evidence for post-abortion activity!" The crowd noise swelled as Simons reapproached the podium.

"This is ludicrous! This resident is as deluded as my psychotic friend, God rest his soul!" Simons stared at Tanous, who remained unmoving. Then Simons looked at Matt Stone and raised his voice several notches. "This resident is feeding our pathology department nothing but vengeful lies! His job is in jeopardy because I brought

his incompetence to the attention of the administration. He is motivated purely by a desire to avenge his accuser and to take the attention away from his own pitiful performance as a resident!" The crowd
fell silent.

Simons continued, raising his voice even further in spite of the
quiet in the room. "I have personally checked into the availability
of the actual abortion specimens so I could have Richards' and my
name cleared from all of this confusion!" Simons focused back on the
pathology resident and pointed at him. "I was told by your very own
department, Dr. Tanous, that these specimens had all been incinerated, and so I know for a fact that the specimens are not available
for the type of reexamination that you describe! An examination, I
might add, that would clear my name from these accusations indefinitely!" Simons added with a shout.

Matthew Stone approached the side of the pathology resident.
He had gotten Tanous into this exchange. Now he knew he had to
stand beside him. "True enough! The specimens are routinely incinerated! But we were able to save several that bear the marks of cruel
experimentation before the evidence was destroyed!" Stone lifted a
plastic container from a large brown bag he held. "Just where is this
baby's *heart*, Dr. Simons?"

There was a simultaneous gasp from the crowd as those near
Matt Stone stepped away from the closed container and those in the
front close to Simons strained to get closer for a better view.

At that point Michael Simons knew he needed to close the conference and close it fast. Simons grabbed the microphone from its
perch on the podium. "Ignore these vengeful conspirators! I will
leave copies of the evidences I have pointed to on the podium for
the media's full review! Please recognize the truth I have presented
this afternoon!" Simons was nearly screaming, but the crowd had
closed in around Stone and Tanous, who were now joined by John
Gentry, whom Matt had also urged to attend.

Simons left through a side exit to avoid the throng. The reporters
didn't even see him go. They were too interested in what was going
on in the ever-tightening circle around Matt Stone. They listened
attentively as Matt introduced John Gentry as Simons' research
technician.

◆ ◆ ◆

"Carol?"

"Speaking," Carol Jennings replied, searching her brain to identify the voice on the other end of the phone line.

"Layton Redman here. I'm calling to see if you and Tony are still interested in adopting a baby." There was silence on the other end, as Carol was just beginning to process what he'd said. "Maybe I can help you out after all."

CHAPTER
31

DR. Paul Taylor looked at the application in front of him and sighed. It had been two of the busiest weeks of his life. Since Simons' news conference, all of the evidence, including Gentry's testimony, had been reviewed, and Simons' loss of privileges was changed to a permanent dismissal. Simons' state license was suspended and would be permanently withdrawn after a full investigation by the State Board of Medicine. The cardiothoracic surgery department had been thrown into an instant upheaval that had quieted now to a dull roar, allowing the initial steps to be taken to find a replacement for Simons.

Finding a surgeon of the caliber of Michael Simons would be difficult and had made the dean reluctant to act without the full support of the surgery staff. They had all agreed. Even discounting the questionable ethical nature of Simons' work, the infractions of the truth in the attempted cover-up sealed Simons' fate with the review committee.

Today Dr. Taylor would be meeting with the first of many candidates for Simons' job. As he paged through the list of publications from the candidate, he noticed a conspicuous absence of any research interests in cardiac transplantation. *Maybe this guy will fit in here—*

His thoughts were interrupted by Jan, his receptionist. "Dr. Taylor? Dr. Edward Seale is here to see you."

"Send him in," Taylor responded, closing the candidate's application folder.

Work for Paul Taylor would not return to normal again for a long time.

◆ ◆ ◆

Linda looked over Anne Caudill's shoulder. She was proud of the work Anne had done. Anne had worked hard and had been rewarded by seeing the changes her work had accomplished.

Anne was studiously editing a follow-up story to close out her exposé on Redman, Richards, and Simons. She accentuated the story with a photograph of Richards' clinic, complete with the "Closed" sign clearly displayed in the front.

"You've worked hard, Anne," Linda said to the student, who had also become her friend. Anne spun around. She hadn't heard Linda's quiet approach.

"You scared me!" Anne laughed, clutching her sweater. "I didn't hear you come in!"

"You just concentrate so efficiently . . . I think I could have driven my Volkswagen in here without you knowing it," Linda added, joining Anne in a hearty laugh.

"Here," Anne said holding up the layout. "What do you think?"

Linda studied the layout. "It's good . . . very good."

"You know I couldn't have done it without you," Anne said, pointing at the picture of Richards' clinic. "I owe a whole lot to you and Matt," she said slowly. "To think I almost got him fired."

"You did nothing of the sort. Matt acted on his own accord when he saved Sam's baby . . . and when he decided to challenge the authority of Michael Simons." Linda paused, wanting to change the subject. "Anyway, that's not what I came up here to tell you."

Anne just looked at her, waiting to hear what Linda had to say. "Well? What is it, then?"

"I just wanted you to be the first to hear that I've finished counting the votes from everyone on the staff, and you've been picked as senior editor-in-chief for next year. The job's yours, Anne."

Anne's mouth fell open. "That is, if you want it," Linda added with a smile.

"Want the job? Are you kidding?" Anne looked at her suspiciously.

"I'm serious, Anne. You're their first pick." She paused. "I think you'd be great." Anne continued to stare. "Do you want the job?"

"Of course I want it." She stopped suddenly. "What about Dean Franklin? I thought he was a shoo-in."

"He felt so strongly that the job should be offered to you first that he refused to be considered." Linda held out her hand, offering to seal Anne's decision.

Anne ignored her hand and hugged her instead.

◆　◆　◆

"Venous line's to you," Gerald Martinez, M.D. stated as he unclamped the line leading from the venous cannula in the patient's chest heading towards the cardiopulmonary bypass pump. "We're on bypass."

"On bypass, full," John Gentry echoed as he neatly recorded the time on his pump flow sheet. "Pressures are good."

Gentry couldn't help but smile. Everything had worked out better than he could have imagined. Dr. Taylor had gone to bat in support of him after he agreed to cooperate fully with the investigation into Simons' research. And after only a week Gerald Martinez had offered John the job at Fairfax General Hospital. Martinez had quickly recognized what was really going on. So the information he'd sought from Simons wouldn't be used to prevent Gentry from getting the job after all. Initially John had been angry that Dr. Martinez had contacted Dr. Simons, but his frustration melted into understanding as he realized that he should never have expected Dr. Martinez not to talk to his then present employer, especially when all of the cardiothoracic surgeons around knew of Dr. Simons.

Gentry wasn't the only one who felt like smiling. Now, after only a week, Martinez and his partners were all smiling about their new pump technician.

More importantly, John's wife, Lori, and their three daughters were smiling too.

◆ ◆ ◆

Matt Stone delicately dissected the superior mesenteric vein from the overlying pancreas. A careless move here could cause life-threatening hemorrhage. He worked carefully and meticulously towards the rock-hard cancer located in the head of the pancreas. The cancer had squeezed off the common bile duct and was shutting off the bile flow from the liver, resulting in the jaundice the patient had presented with. Slowly Matt moved up along the superior mesenteric vein to the portal vein. At that point the tumor apparently invaded the vein, rendering the patient unresectable for cure. As Matt worked, his attending could be heard quietly encouraging his technique. "Nice . . . Nice . . . Gently . . ."

Matt looked up at the masked attending standing across from him on the other side of the patient. "I think he's unresectable. The tumor seems to invade the portal vein."

"Here . . . let me feel this one more time." Dr. Mike Stanley slipped his fingers around the portal vein, gently palpating the vein above the pancreas. "You're right. Now what do you do, doctor?"

"Let's bypass the common bile duct to relieve the obstruction."

"How?"

"Roux-en-Y loop of jejunum."

"Good option. Do you want to do a gastric bypass, too?"

"Sure do . . . Up to 20 percent will obstruct without it," Matt added.

"Okay. Let's do it." The attending smiled behind his mask. The two men were thinking the same thing: it was good to have Matthew Stone back in the O.R. again.

◆ ◆ ◆

Even the surgical mask she wore couldn't contain Carol Jennings' smile. She sat in a rocking chair beside an incubator in the Neonatal Intensive Care Unit. The name on the incubator still read

"Baby Boy Stelling," but that would change in another two weeks. Tony smiled, too, as he watched Carol give a bottle of formula to the small infant in her arms.

Layton Redman had taken the initiative to arrange a private adoption. First he needed to prove his paternity. He submitted to DNA analysis in order to be recognized as the boy's biological father. He then had one of his partners petition the state court to declare him the legal father. He then quietly had a private adoption arranged in order to give the child to Tony and Carol. The last move he had arranged with the greatest of secrecy. He had no intentions of letting the media get in on any of this. He was through doing things just because of the way they looked to the media. As a favor to the Jennings, Redman's firm handled the whole thing at no charge. Layton knew that was the right thing to do.

After Carol finished feeding the baby, she burped her soon-to-be son and then watched excitedly as his nurse gently weighed him. He was steadily gaining weight, but it would still be twelve more weeks until the baby would be heavy enough for "graduation" from the N.I.C.U.

In the next twelve weeks, Carol would make the trip to hold and feed her son every day.

◆ ◆ ◆

Matt and Linda were sitting at a corner table at Philipo's restaurant in Fairfax. Matt looked at Linda tenderly. He had never felt so strongly towards a woman before.

"I've been doing a lot of thinking . . . and a lot of praying," Matt began. "I just can't seem to get any peace about taking a job in the States right now. I've been thinking a lot about returning to Africa. Tenwek Hospital will be without a surgeon starting in July." Matt paused, trying to read Linda's face. "They want an answer by the end of this month." Matt's eyes met Linda's. "How do you feel about that?"

Linda looked down, then reached out and grasped his hands. "Matt, you know that I've never felt for anyone else the way I feel for you." Linda paused, then looked up. "I don't want you to go away," she said, a tear welling up in the corner of each eye. "But that's just the selfish me talking," she added. "I want what the Lord wants . . . what's best for you . . . and for us." She squeezed his hand tightly when she said, "us."

"I—I want to return there, Linda," Matt said slowly, gazing softly into her green eyes. "I think that's what the Lord wants for me too." He returned the squeeze she had given him. ". . . but it doesn't end there." Matt took a deep breath. "I want you to go with me." Linda looked at Matt questioningly. "I love you too much to want to be away from you for a year." Matt broke away his right hand and slipped it into his coat pocket. He retrieved a small, black, felt-covered box and handed it to Linda. Her gaze went from the box, then returned to meet Matt's. Linda didn't speak. She slowly opened the jewel box and gasped.

"Matt! It's beautiful!" She took the diamond out and slid it onto the ring finger of her left hand. It was a perfect fit!

Her gaze met Matt's again.

"Well?" Matt said quietly.

"Yes," Linda responded.

Matt leaned forward as Linda lifted her lips to meet his. A full minute later they realized that their waiter had served their food.

CHAPTER
32

THE next eight months passed quickly. Summer had drifted away, yielding to yet another crisp, colorful Kentucky autumn. Tony Jennings worked only one job again. Carol worked weekends when Tony stayed at home. Tony, Jr. grew like a little weed. He had been back in the hospital only once since his discharge, to be treated for pneumonia, which cleared with antibiotics.

Now, as Tony "created" dinner, Tony, Jr. played in his high chair. Carol sang as she set the table.

Tony sautéed mushrooms, green peppers, and onions for a pizza. He turned his attention to his son, who seemed preoccupied with a small, stuffed puppy.

"What'll it be for dinner tonight, son?" Tony asked, leaning towards Tony, Jr. "Pizza? Cheeseburger?"

"Tony!" Carol snapped with a laugh.

"Oooh, okay! Mommy says you have to have this . . ." Tony said, holding up a small jar of creamed spinach. "Yum! Yum!" he added sarcastically.

Tony, Jr. turned away from his puppy. "Dada!" he squealed as he saw his daddy's face.

Carol responded by trying to get him to say, "Mama." She repeated the word several times for him, only to be rewarded with another "Dada!"

Tony laughed. "Let's face it, Carol. The boy knows who does the best cooking around here. He must be hungry, that's all."

Carol put the jar of baby food in the microwave for a few seconds. "See, son," she said, "Mommy can cook too!"

She brought the jar over to little Tony, who seemed to be more interested in the spoon than in the food. Carol's mouth opened and shut with every bite she fed to her son. Every time he swallowed, she applauded. Every other bite ended up on his chin.

Eventually he did manage to eat most of the spinach, in spite of the "yucky" faces his father made in the background.

◆ ◆ ◆

At the same time, in the mountain highlands of western Kenya, Matt Stone stepped out of the operating theatre into the cool African night. He had just finished an operation to relieve a bowel obstruction on a forty-year-old Massai warrior. The man had been brought up from the south and had traveled for two days before his midnight arrival. His abdomen had been greatly distended, his abdominal tenderness generalized, and Dr. Stone had recommended surgery after his brief examination showed evidence of peritonitis. They had started IV fluids and had given nearly four liters of fluid before the man's heart rate dipped under one hundred. By 2:30 A.M. the patient and the surgeon were ready for the O.R. There Matt had found the small intestine filled to capacity with large Ascaris worms, many approaching ten inches in length. After evacuating what seemed to be a gallon of the worms and repairing a tiny tear in the small bowel, Matt had irrigated out the abdomen and closed.

Innumerable stars dotted the African sky. Matt looked up but continued walking. The chill in the air made Matt quicken his steps. He passed the labor and delivery hall next to the O.R., and the gentle, rhythmic moaning of several Kipsigis women could be heard above the quiet of the night. He paused and talked to two of the travelers who had come with the patient from Massai Mari. Their friend would get better, but he would need to stay for a week or two before going back. He would need to be on some medicine, Matt explained through a nursing student interpreter. They thanked him, and Matt continued down the hill.

Matt lived in a small cinderblock house vacated by the surgeon who was on furlough. Quietly he unlocked the door and stepped into the main living area. There was no heat except that provided by a large central fireplace. Matt stirred the coals and added another piece of wood. He then quietly prepared for bed, placing his white coat on the the right corner bedpost. He slid into bed and cuddled up next to the sleeping form beneath a well-worn comforter.

Linda Stone awoke and pulled her husband closer. Matt Stone smiled through a yawn, closed his eyes, and went to sleep.